M000114075

Christmas

Under

Construction

Dear Friends,

Welcome to Mistletoe Lodge.

The second book in the McKenna sister's series, Christmas Under Construction welcomes my readers to a rustic lodge renovation. As Molly's dream of a Christmas Village is about to become a reality, Megan takes the reins on the renovation of Mistletoe Lodge with the help of a handsome new contractor, Stone Reynolds. With Christmas Village opening Thanksgiving weekend, Mistletoe Lodge opening at the beginning of December and Molly's wedding set for Christmas Eve, the usual McKenna chaos is in full swing. Spend this Christmas with Megan, Maxie and Molly for a sleigh ride filled with family, love and holiday joy.

I love to hear feedback from my readers. Please stop by www.ryleeridolfi.com. Send me your thoughts at contact@ryleeromance.com.

Merry Christmas,

Rylee

Paisley Cottage Books

The McKenna Sister Series

Mistletoe, Mayhem & Mr. Right

Christmas Under Construction

Rylee Ridolfi

Christmas Under Construction

Paisley Cottage Books

Paisley Cottage Books, New Jersey
Christmas Under Construction
Copyright @ 2020 Rylee Ridolfi
Cover Art: Dimple Asha

This is a work of fiction. Names, characters, businesses, places, events and incidents are either the products of the author's imagination or used in a fictitious manner. Any resemblance to actual persons, living or dead, or actual events is purely coincidental.

All rights reserved.

Printed in the United States. Not part of this book may be reproduced, scanned or distributed in any printed or electronic form without permission.

For information regarding permission, contact the Rights and Permissions Department,
Paisley Cottage Books
paisleycottagebooks@gmail.com
Library of Congress Cataloging-in-Publication Data
Ridolfi, Rylee
Christmas Under Construction
Paperback ISBN: ISBN: 978-1-7341418-1-8
Ebook
1.Novel: Romance 2. Christmas
I. Ridolfi, Rylee

This book is dedicated to my sweet mother Lee Duffy, an avid reader of romance. I am the woman I am today because of her. She taught me to love with my whole heart and cherish the people I'm lucky enough to call my own.

A special thank you to my editors, Ashley Russo and Debbie Shumaker.

Chapter One

Megan McKenna knew that dating when you're young and starry-eyed is like having a blank credit card at a Versace sample sale; the number of potential treasures endless, the hunt exhilarating. Conversely, she also knew, dating when you're older, divorced, with children, two meddling sisters, and an impossible mother is the equivalent of teaching a t-rex to apply lipstick. Megan had decided to avoid the whole unpleasant ritual of dating.

However, tonight, to appease her nagging sisters, Molly and Maxie, she reluctantly agreed to a blind date. Megan, a little older, a bit curvier and a lot more apprehensive, also knew the odds of finding Mr. Right on a blind date shared the same odds as losing weight during the Christmas season. Nevertheless, it's been a year since Megan's marriage ended and according to her mother, two sisters, two daughters, and apparently her hairdresser, it was time to get back in the dating game.

She surveyed the cramped bedroom in the rundown lodge she now called home. The old lodge, located at the foot of Mistletoe Mountain, was a far cry from the stately, white stucco estate she once called home. The lodge, by most people's standards, would be considered quaint. The small two-bedroom suite she shared with her two daughters, Sophie and Olivia, however, felt more like a temporary holding cell. She wondered how in one year she had managed to go from a mansion in the suburbs to a shoe box in a barely habitable ski lodge. Tonight, however, she needed to concentrate on her date.

The cramped bedroom resembled a crime scene; drawers dangling half open, clothes strewn across the floor with piles of "no's" rapidly growing. She decided on a simple classic look, a black Versace, straight, knee-length dress. The mirror told her yes, however, she felt the awkward uneasiness of a preteen slipping on a padded bra for the first time. Nothing about dating felt natural. For Megan, confidence used to come as easily as breathing, however in the year following her divorce, she had lost a bit of her self-assurance.

Tonight's date, David Meyers, met the standards of her dating coaches, Molly and Maxie. David, one of Connecticut's most eligible bachelors, according to her hair stylist's sources, is the CEO of MCAP, with a sizable net worth. Money fell into the "must have" side of Megan's new suitor ledger. Having become accustomed to the country club lifestyle she and her ex-husband shared, going backward was not an option.

"It's only a drink," she reminded herself.

Megan had one last fashion issue to conquer- shoes. Some say money can't buy happiness, but Megan knew a closet full of designer shoes could certainly bring a girl a sizable bit of delight. She made her way over the piles of clothes, then opened her closet, not much larger than a hamster cage. Her mind momentarily drifted to the walk-in closet she adored, with its color coordinated shelves, vanity in the center and an eight foot by nine-foot wall dedicated solely to her prized shoe collection. Now those shoes were crammed along with her clothes, the kids summer clothes, and a few boxes of Christmas decorations in the storage area in the basement of the lodge. Inhaling deeply, she shook her head and reminded herself her situation was temporary. One day her shoes would once again know the joy of having their own space. After all, shoes were important. Shoes suggested the ever-changing mood of a woman; playful, practical, sporty, easy, confident. Black strappy heels said, "Look at me," pointy toed stilettos said, "Hey there big fellow, check this out" and low pumps said, "Proper business attire." She studied herself in the mirror, then decided on a medium heel, Kate Spade black pump; a subtly sexy, midway choice which said, "Here I am, but eyes up here." As she slipped on the left heel, she noticed the right one appeared to have gone missing, which could only mean one thing. "Sophie!"

Stone Reynolds stood outside the rustic lodge admiring the warmth and character the old structure oozed. He thought for a minute about what his good buddy and doctor ordered - three months, no work and strict rest. The Doc's orders were a sentence worse than prison to a man like Stone. The concept of rest remained a foreign concept to him. This lodge is exactly what he needed to help him recover; a small job, one he could work on without his crew. A hands-on contractor job, one he could sink his teeth into like the old days, before his only role was to order people around. He promised himself he'd keep normal hours and keep this professional, not personal. Doc surely couldn't begrudge him this one small joy. He would do his job, then go home promptly at five o'clock, with the exception of tonight, when he agreed to meet his client about the renovations at six o'clock. He entered the ski lodge and heard the sound of a small voice greet him.

"Hello," said the little girl with glasses so large they threatened to swallow her face. She sat on the opposite side of the old oak hospitality desk, barely able to see over the counter.

"Hello, you working the desk tonight?" Stone asked peering over the counter looking for the rest of her.

"Uh huh," she said, pushing up the heavy frames on her freckled button nose.

"Is there maybe someone a bit, well, taller I can talk to?" asked Stone, rubbing the shadowy scruff that covered his chin.

"Yep, my mommy," she said pausing, her eyes slowly roaming from his feet to his head. She hopped down from her stool and made her way around the counter next to him. She was much shorter than he first imagined. At six foot four, most people seemed small to him, but this one's ponytail didn't even clear his mid-thigh. A small black pug wearing a set of pearls stood by her feet.

After eyeing him up and down, she put a tiny hand on her waist and said, "I know why you're here."

"You do?"

"Yes, but before I get my mommy, I have a few questions for you."

"Shoot."

"Are you nice?" she asked with one eyebrow raised.

"I think so."

"Do you have any pets?"

"Yes, I do, a dog and he's quite large," said Stone wondering where this line of questioning was going.

"I want a pig, but mommy says they smell. I said, 'Kids smell and you have two of them.'"

"Good point. Are you a lawyer?" he asked.

Shaking her head, no, she continued with her interrogation, "Are they your real teeth?"

"Um yes," he said, running his tongue across his top teeth.

"Do you have any old wives?"

Cocking his head to the side he answered, "No."

"Do you like cartoons?"

"I do."

"What shoe size are you? My aunt Maxie says a big shoe means a big skipper. I think that's a boat."

He raised his eyebrows, "She does, does she?"

The two were interrupted by a flustered woman who hobbled into the room. The woman barely looked up her eyes scouring the floor. She shouted, "Sophie, are you wearing my other black heel? Why is Gloria wearing my pearls? Olivia, where is Sophie?"

Stone couldn't help but stare at the woman who appeared oblivious to his presence. He found his eyes fixed on her long black hair tossed over to the side in a Veronica Lake, old Hollywood style resting casually on her ample chest.

"Oh gosh, I'm so sorry. I didn't realize you were here already," said Megan, flustered at the sight of him.

"Mommy, you look pretty, but why are your lulu's showing?" said Olivia whispering loudly through her cupped hands.

Stone raised his eyebrows allowing a slight smile to sneak across his face.

"Olivia, not now," Megan said, widening her eyes and tugging up her neckline.

"They're all squished up, they look like a butt," giggled Olivia.

"Please excuse her. I'm new at this. I may have overdressed, but I'm actually unsure of how to dress for this type of thing. I can't seem to find my other shoe. You dressed casually," she said, eyeing his worn Levi's that hung perfectly on his tall frame. Her eyes followed his flannel shirt down to his work boots. His dark loose wavy hair fell just below his collar. His rugged unshaven face somehow made the flannel attractive. "Should I change?" she stammered. She realized she was rambling, but couldn't put her finger on the expression he wore smugly across his tanned face.

"I don't think that'll be necessary. You look very nice. And don't worry about being new at this, I do this all the time. It doesn't take long. We can get right to it and if it is good for both of us, we'll get down to business."

Megan, taken aback, stared blankly at his frankness, until Sophie, another small child wandered in. "Here it is," she said carrying the missing shoe.

"How many times have I told you not to wear mommy's things or to put my jewelry on Gloria?" said Megan, snapping the shoe from Sophie's hand.

"I had a royal ball to attend," proclaimed the little girl, a spitting image of her mother.

The small red haired one whispered, "He has a big dog. I think he's nice."

"Okay Olivia, thank you for greeting our guest. Sophie please take your sister and start your bath water. Be good for Aunt Maxie," said Megan, before kissing the two girls and sending them on their way. "David, I'm sorry about all this," she said.

"Not a problem, but the name is Stone."

"I thought you said your name was David."

"Nope, Olivia and I covered many important things, such as whether I have a dog, if these are my real teeth, any old wives, oh and the size of my skipper. We never got around to names."

"Maxie! I'll kill her," Megan mumbled under her breath.

"We had an appointment at six to discuss the business of the lodge renovations. Did you forget?" he said clearly amused with her awkwardness.

"That's tonight?" said a flustered Megan.

"Yes, it is tonight. Who's David?" asked Stone.

"Not relevant," said Megan.

The front door of the lodge opened and a short version of Mr. Clean walked in wearing thick black glasses, carrying a dozen multicolored roses still in plastic wrap.

"I'm guessing that would be David," Stone said, squinting one eye.

David made his way across to Megan, puffed out his chest, and handed her the roses. "You must be Megan, taller than I like, but we'll work with it. You might want to deep-six the heels."

Immediately regretting having caved on her no dating rule, Megan politely said, "Nice to meet you."

The bald man stretched his eyes wide as he surveyed the old lodge, "Heard someone was attempting to bring back this old lodge. Tough nut to crack. I mean some things are better off left as a memory, right?" he said.

Stone's eyebrows arched, he cocked his head and answered, "Nonsense, this old girl has a lot of life in her."

"And this is?" asked David pointing to Stone.

Fidgeting, Megan needed to escape the awkwardness and quickly responded, "Um, he's just the contractor, let's just go."

"Okay Meggie, maybe we could be Megid. See how I did that, Megan and David; I crack myself up sometimes."

"Nice one," said Stone shooting Megan a sarcastic wink.

"Excuse me, David. I'll be out in a minute. I just need to clear something up," said Megan.

David walked backward to the door and shot both hands like pistols toward her.

"Wow, looks like a funster," said Stone with a devilish grin.

Megan dug both fists into her waist, she furrowed her brow and said, "My personal life is none of your business. We can meet here tomorrow, same time."

"Sounds good, you can dress up or down whichever," he said before whispering in her ear, "And Meggie, your lulu's most definitely don't look like a butt."

"Off limits," she said as she stormed out.

Chapter Two

T he next morning Megan pulled into Starbucks, feeling slightly triumphant over surviving her first date. A horrendous first date indeed, however, it still counted as a foot back in the game. She ordered a large pumpkin latte doused with whipped cream and cinnamon, then inhaled it as if it was the oxygen she needed to exist. A grin danced across her face at the thought of fall in New England. Autumn in Connecticut never disappointed. Megan loved watching the reddish brown, burnt orange and golden leaves swirl slowly to the ground, descending from newly barren branches. Autumn is Megan's favorite season; the bridge from summer to winter. She loved the smell of wood-burning bonfires and the delicious scent of cinnamon apple pies permeating the air. Fall meant letting go of summer. Yet, the notion of letting go had a particular sting to it these days.

Megan's world at the moment felt a bit like those swirling leaves, aimlessly floating about, unsure of where they might land. Megan sipped her latte, cherishing the notes of cinnamon and nutmeg. She thought about her new role in the old rundown lodge her youngest sister had purchased as a final piece to her Christmas Village.

Molly's dream of a destination, Christmas-themed village seated at the foot of Mistletoe Mountain was nearing completion, with a soft opening set for Black Friday. As if that wasn't enough, Molly and Hunter would be married on Christmas Eve in the chapel at the foot of the mountain.

Molly and her fiancé Hunter worked feverishly round the clock on every aspect of the design for the village. For Molly, this was the culmination of a lifelong dream. Molly is the definition of a Christmaholic. The idea of being a kid again, even if only once a year, is the gift she hoped to bring to anyone who visited the village.

Molly, who had earned a degree at Wharton, was the sister the family banked on for success in a career. Maxie, the middle sister, was tough, strong-willed, and recently finished her Bachelor's degree in Accounting. She had stepped right into the financial aspects of the business. She and her grade school sweetheart, Anthony got engaged a year ago. Anthony's catering business had done so well he opened an Italian restaurant called, Tony's on Main. Christmas Village had brought the three sisters together. Everyone's lives were settling in, except for a very unsure Megan.

Megan's talents were more visual than definable. She was the beautiful sister for whom life simply came easy. Never without a boyfriend, able to skate through high school with a bat of her long black lashes, and until now, had never even attempted to work outside the home. It wasn't until the love of her life, Chase Barrington proclaimed he had fallen in love with the razor smart young intern at his firm, that Megan's life took a downward spiral. Now as a single mother of two young girls, she needed to figure out what she was good at besides making grown men drool. Megan desperately wanted to be a part of the new family business, however without many identifiable skills, other than the ability to put together a killer outfit and identify when every major boutique in town was receiving the latest merchandise, she floundered when it came to finding her role in Christmas Village. Molly suggested she take the reins of interior design for the lodge; the last loose end would be the restoration of the new Mistletoe Lodge. The old lodge had great bones, with ample windows facing the picturesque slopes. However, the hardwood floors desperately needed refinishing along with the paint and furniture, which were sorely outdated.

Molly knew with Megan's work as society club social chair she had done her share of decorating for various events. She used that same sense of impeccable taste when decorating the mansion she shared with Chase. Megan agreed to try her hand at design. Megan felt intimidated by such a lofty job. Molly, however, insisted she trusted Megan's judgment. Molly's only request was to simply keep with the theme of the Christmas Village.

As the last dollop of whipped cream melted into her cup, Megan thought about the arrogant contractor who had the audacity to judge her date. Molly hired a local handyman, Stone Reynolds to do the work. Stone Reynolds was the kind of man Megan had put at the top of her '*do not disturb me*' list. Megan preferred to spend time with more cultured, intelligent, and of course, wealthier men. She would simply give him a list of odd jobs to do and avoid him. After all, how much of her time would be required to spend with the handyman? She hoped their meeting would be brief. After replaying the awful date in her head, she needed a distraction from last night's fiasco. She returned to the lodge unsure of what she had gotten herself into, yet somehow, she felt it might just be exactly what she needed. She headed straight to the lodge's main room. Megan surveyed the old space and began jotting down a list of ideas.

She went about the day with her usual chores; getting the girls through school, homework, and dinner. She could do this. The whole working mother thing suited her. Later, she revisited her list. Her list was abruptly disrupted by the piercing sound of Sophie's scream. Megan rushed to the little girl.

Sophie her head to toe pink outfit complete with a boa, and Gloria standing next to her in a small pink tutu stomped her heeled foot, and said, "Mommy, Olivia brought a smelly sea creature into the lodge."

"It is not a sea creature," said Olivia wearing her overalls and yellow knee-high rubber boots.

"Is so," Sophie persisted. "Make her take it out."

"He needs me," begged Olivia, clutching a jar in which the helpless creature flailed.

Megan ran toward the two in the main lobby entrance. The girls were deep in a tug of war with a plastic jar filled with cloudy water and some type of creature bobbing inside. Gloria barked. Megan attempted to break up the fight.

"Stop," she said, wedging herself in the middle reaching to grab the jar.

Olivia, who was small for her size, was unable to hold on to the jar, her tiny hands slipped off the side. The jar sailed into the air emptying its contents onto Megan's head. As seawater dripped down her face, she felt a fluttering in the center of her bra. The creature had slipped into her shirt and rested squarely between her lulu's.

Slipping and sliding, she struggled to get her footing. Unbuttoning her blouse and digging, she fished around deep into her bra and pulled the slimy creature out. Catching the critter, she quickly released it and threw it right into the face of Stone Reynolds, who had slipped in unnoticed during the entire fiasco. While not alarmed, he seemed deeply amused by the whole dance.

"What are you doing here?" Megan screamed, wiping her wet tendrils off her face.

"Meeting, same time as last night, ring any bells?" he said, pulling the slimy little critter off his face.

Crying hysterically, Olivia said, "Please save his life. He needs water. Give him mouth to mouth."

Stone casually walked past the soggy, half-dressed Megan and grabbed a coffee mug off the desk, filled it with water, gently dropped the creature in, then bent down and handed it to the little girl whose large glasses fogged with tears.

"I think he'll make it, kid," he said.

She threw her tiny arms around his neck and hugged him tightly, a gesture that seemed to make him mildly uncomfortable.

"Crisis solved. I'm ready when you are," he said, barely acknowledging her ample breasts in a gray lace bra, now visible from her half-unbuttoned soggy blouse.

"You're early. Three minutes early. What is it with you and bad timing? Three minutes later and I would have had this whole situation handled. Now, if you'll excuse me, I need to change."

"Again, no dress code required by me," Stone said, smirking.

Maxie, her younger sister walked in and headed straight to Stone. "Hi, you must be the hot handyman, I'm Maxie," she said, extending her hand out toward him.

"Stone Reynolds, and you must be the Maxie I've heard about."

"All good I'm sure," she winked before taking the two little ones' hands.

Maxie gave Megan a devilish smile, "Molly says I'm on duty for Sophie and Olivia while you have some sort of meeting with a contractor. Come on Gloria, your boa is soggy. He's hot."

Stone, raising an eyebrow, gave Megan a sly grin.

"Excuse us," said Megan, pulling Maxie by the sleeve. They headed down the hall out of earshot of the handsome contractor. She ushered the little ones off to their room "Maxie, he is impossible. A Neanderthal. I can't work with him. I won't work with him."

Maxie turned back and stretched her neck, down the hall and spotted him standing by the fireplace taking measurements. "That, really, that's your Neanderthal? That's one sexy Neanderthal."

"What do you mean sexy? He's a jerk."

"A jerk with a great bum," Maxie said, following the two little girls down the hallway.

"You're impossible." Megan, ignoring Maxie's obvious poor taste in men turned her attention to the little ones, "And you two, I'll deal with you when I'm done." She left the girls with Maxie and headed to her room. She grabbed a towel and wiped off the remains of the creature. Peeling the swampy shirt from her damp body, she washed up then threw on a black button-down blouse, pulled her hair back in a low ponytail and went back to the Neanderthal.

"Hey, welcome back. You're late; five minutes late. Time's money, you're paying me, but I guess I'll let you slide this time."

"Clearly this is awkward, so, let's make this quick so we don't need to be in the same room."

"I'm hurt."

"You're impossible. Here is a list of my desires."

"I didn't think we were there yet, but I can do desires," Stone said, eyeing the list.

Feeling the blood begin to bubble up inside she attempted to keep her tone even, "You know what I mean. This is what I need done to this lodge, and the quicker the better."

Reading the list, he ran one hand through his wavy brown hair and rested it on his five o'clock shadow, then shook his head side to side. "No can do."

With arms firmly on her hips she squared her shoulders and stated, "Excuse me? You're the handyman. I'm the client. You'll do what I tell you."

Stone pursed his lips together and shook his head. "I see, you're one of those bosses who order people around, sort of a power dominance thing. Kind of intriguing, but still no can do."

Her tone now elevating into a growl, she planted a foot down hard and said, "Fine, I don't need you. I'll find another handyman."

"Okay," he said, handing her the list and walking toward the front door.

"Wait, where are you going?" Megan said, just as the door closed behind him. She grabbed her cell and dialed Molly.

"Molly, I need another handyman."

"Slow down, Meggie. What seems to be the problem?"

"Egotistical pig just walked out. Get me another one."

"Meg it doesn't work that way. He's the best contractor in the area. Not to mention his bid is very reasonable. I really think he's the right person for this job."

"I'm sure we can find another one."

"Not we Meggie, you. You wanted this job, now you need to fix this. His number is on the computer. Beg, plead, offer him your first born, use your charm, whatever it takes. Get him back," said Molly before hanging up.

Why, why, of all the contractors in the area does he have to be the best, more like the cheapest? She would consider calling him, but tonight she had two little girls and a salamander to deal with.

Chapter Three

S tone Reynolds didn't come cheap. His work had been reviewed in magazines internationally. He studied design at the prestigious School of Architecture in Prague under the world's most famous architect, Pierre Warden. Stone's career took off when he was asked to work as an apprentice under Pierre on a village in a small town off the coast of France. The village's homes were commissioned by a local person who partnered with Pierre. The job was simple, with a wide-open slate. Every detail was meticulous, down to the landscape all of which was designed by Stone. Ivy climbing the stone walls with bright colorful flowers representing the countryside. To date, the village in France remained Stone's favorite project. Next was a series of mansions in Dubai, with state-of-the-art conveniences. Here, the two created a visual masterpiece, a billionaire playground with twenty units, each selling for over ten million. At twenty-five, Stone Reynolds had established himself as a world class architect. He could write his own ticket. His work took him to the most exotic locations, where he began designing luxury hotels, each with precise detail to fit the motif. Work became his passion; money became his drug.

That was a different life; one he left behind per doctors' orders. He returned to Connecticut, to the small, quiet town where he spent most of his childhood. He could rest and recuperate there. Despite the work he was doing on the small rundown house he purchased for a song, he had pretty much settled into a relatively unhurried lifestyle, at least for a few months. That all changed one sunny day when his neighbors, Joe and Tilly, brought him to Bennie's Bagels on Highland, in the center of the town. The three were munching on warm onion bagels with what Joe called the best darn brew in fifty states when a spunky redhead walked in.

The woman's enthusiasm was contagious. Her green eyes twinkled as she spoke of the project that she referred to as her lifelong dream. A village, not just any village, but a Christmas themed village. As she described the destination location, her attention to detail was remarkable. Every fiber in her was alive with excitement as she delved into the unknown. Bennie smiled at the young woman's ambitious goals; half at her naivety, maybe mixed with a little doubt, but Stone knew this feeling all too well. He remembered the feeling when he and Pierre began the village in France. It was an open slate; the land like clay in Michelangelo's hands. His eyes brightened when he heard her say she needed a contractor to take on the old ski lodge on the side of Mistletoe Mountain. She needed the best. That's when Joe piped up and caught the redhead's attention.

"You want the best, he's right here," said Joe, pointing to Stone.

"Is that so?" said the redhead, "How did he earn that title?"

"Well, he bought a rundown house that was barely standing on one leg. In a month, he has begun to bring it back to life. The man is pure genius. He's your boy."

The redhead extended her tiny hand. "Molly McKenna, and you are?"

"Stone Reynolds."

"Mr. Reynolds, does this sound like something you might be interested in?"

"I'd like to hear more about it."

Not five minutes into Molly's description he was sold. His mind was revving with ideas. He loved the idea of being a part of something with such deep passion.

"I can't afford to pay you all that much, but I promise I'll come as close to your asking price as I can."

Money didn't matter to Stone anymore. Getting back to doing what he loved was enough for him. Before he knew it, he had set up a meeting at the Mistletoe Lodge. He knew he was sliding a bit into the "Work" category that Doc Anderson forbade him from, but he would not overdo it.

Quiet finally set into the lodge at nine o'clock that evening. Megan had quelled the fighting of her two daughters, which was no small task. Peace talks between foreign nations, paled in comparison. Megan never dreamed she would be parenting alone. She and Chase were a team. They made a promise, they built a life, and he threw it away like an old bubble gum wrapper. Since the divorce, Chase and his new fiancé had moved to the East side of town. At first, he saw the girls every three weeks, but as his wedding day approached, his time with them dwindled. Now once a month for a few hours was the best they could hope for.

Divorce felt much like the black plague. Its toll reached far and wide, dragging her into a vortex of uncertainty. Megan knew the day she heard the words tumbling out of his mouth that life as she knew it was over. Nothing would ever be the same in the family they had created. Her devastation consumed her, yet she hadn't realized the impact it would have on her two young girls. After all, Olivia was just four and Sophie six. They would adjust to a new normal, kids did that, they would adapt to their environment. What she hadn't taken into account was that although they had adapted, they also changed in response to the new situation.

Sophie, the spitting image of her mother, with long black hair and big dark eyes wrapped in spider-like lashes might as well have been born with a tiara on. Her wardrobe consisted of a closet full of pink tutus, frilly dresses, and as many of Megan's heels that she could smuggle. She had taken the divorce worse than her sister. Her attitude rivaled that of a thirteen-year-old. By six, she had perfected the foot stomp, arm crossed 'whatever' face. Every day was a constant barrage of "where's daddy" questions. Worse came when the move from their only home left Sophie feeling unsettled. Suddenly, she needed to control everything; what she wore, ate, watched, played, and bedtimes. The list was endless, the struggle exhausting.

Olivia, four going on forty, was small for her age. With a head of red ringlets and a spray of freckles across the bridge of her nose, she resembled her aunt Molly, not only in physical features, but also with her demeanor. Her green eyes hid under oversized glasses, which were more like goggles. Olivia was, as Sophie put it, an odd duck. She wore a uniform of sorts; overalls, and a favorite pair of yellow rubber boots. Olivia lived by a "save the whales, turtles, fish, dog, cat, ant" initiative. She loved nature and cared for every creature she came across. Since moving up to the lodge, she spent much of her free time wading in the pond, collecting and studying the outdoors. She was a shy, introverted child. Megan wasn't sure if this was in response to the divorce or just her nature. Either way, Olivia was the polar opposite of her sister, and this made the new normal anything but peaceful.

After putting the girls to bed, Megan fixed herself a cup of tea, extra cream, no sugar and snuggled up with Gloria in front of the massive fireplace. What did the Neanderthal mean, "No can do?" This is her project. She envisioned the lodge as luxe, with fluffy white fur chairs, silver studded modern sofas with steel legs, and crystal chandeliers flanking the main sitting area. White walls with dark wood floors; yes, it was her vision, not his. He just needed to execute her visions. For some reason unbeknownst to her, Molly had her heart set on this particular contractor. Normally, Megan would have just flipped open her computer, pulled up a dozen names and picked one, but this was Molly's baby. With the stress Molly was under with the upcoming wedding and the timeline of the opening of Christmas Village, Megan knew what she had to do; call the Neanderthal.

She rustled through the lobby desk and found the number. Stone Reynolds, just a number, no business card. "Really? Ugh," she moaned before picking up the phone.

Three rings then a husky voice answered, "I thought you'd call."

"Really? That is how you start our conversation? You make it impossible to talk to you."

"Sorry, hello, changed your mind? Better?"

"Not really, but it's a start. Let me make this simple for you, dumb it down if you will. I have impeccable taste in design. Now I understand for a man like you, it may be a bit out of your element, but not to worry. I'll make all the decisions. I assure you that your ideas, as small and insignificant as they are, will only waste both of our time. However, if you must explain why you cannot do what I've asked, I'll give you five minutes tomorrow night, say around eight."

"Well I appreciate you dumbing it down, and with an invitation like that, I'd be hard pressed to turn you down."

"So, you'll come?"

"It's a date," Stone said in a devilish tone.

"It most definitely is not."

"I'm wearing jeans and a tee shirt. Does that work for you?" he said smugly.

"Goodbye," she said before slamming the phone down. What ideas could he possibly have; camo themed walls, microfiber couches? She shivered at the thought of it. She would give him five minutes to stroke his oversized ego, then she'd proceed with luxury.

Chapter Four

T he next day, with the girls at school, Megan fixed herself a salad of baby spinach and tuna and sat down at the table with her laptop. Upon Maxie and Molly's insistence, she had unwillingly created an online dating profile after her nightmare date with Mr. Clean. She trolled through pages of available men in the Connecticut area. Then she began reading her messages.

So, you're a fisher eh? It's your lucky day. This catch will satisfy your appetite; no bait required. You'll be hooked.

"What does that even mean? Next," she sighed.

Hello, a little about me. I can read backward, a trait you won't find in many men. I eat only orange colored food. Also, I enjoy long hikes in the buff. If you're feeling my vibe, hit me up, babe. Llac em. (Can you read it?)

"Why am I even entertaining this? This is insane. I could find more quality men in prison. I knew this was a bad idea," she said before shutting the lid of her laptop. It was easy with Chase. They met in high school. Chase was one year older, the captain of the football team, and she the captain of the cheer squad. Crowned prom king and queen. They were beautiful, ambitious, and both enjoyed the finer things in life. Things progressed and before you knew it, a ring on her finger led to a one-million-dollar white stucco home on three acres with two kids. Easy. Now, nothing was easy; not children, not dating, not even her contractor.

Angry that she let him creep into her mind, she returned to the pros and cons of entering the dating world. First, everyone was a freak. Con. Second, she had two little girls she was bringing into the fold, not to mention a body that wasn't quite as perky as it once was. Con. Still, the warnings of her mother, Silvia, bellowed in her head. *You don't want to be an old spinster like Aunt Lidia, alone with cats, eating Ramen in front of reruns of The Golden Girls.* No, that would not be her life. She was Megan McKenna, Ms. Winter Queen two years in a row. She would persevere, just not today.

Stone sat down at the tall drawing table he had built in school, with its metal legs and worn pine surface. He pulled out his drawing pencils and began to draw a few sketches of his rendition of the perfect rustic ski lodge. His most valuable skill lied in his ability to listen to his clients and create the exactly the feeling they desired. He missed this more than he realized. As his company grew, he became involved in every aspect of the project, from hiring crews to the financial end of the business. Slowly, the thing he loved most about architecture, design, became a smaller part of the big picture. Growing a multimillion-dollar business became a near twenty-four hour a day job. Long nights with little sleep are what landed him in the hospital. He would not make that mistake again. Yet with the pencil in his hand, the blood ran through his veins like lightning as his fingers sketched images. He felt alive, filled with purpose. The money he had agreed to was chump change, but the chance to bring life to someone's vision? Priceless.

Stone was so caught up in his work, he let time get away from him. Seven thirty, showtime. He collected his drawings and tucked them neatly into a large brown leather folder that King Henry of Denmark had given him in appreciation for the town center he had built. He stopped at the pewter mirror that hung just to the left of the hall. He ran his fingers through his thick brown waves and studied his five o'clock shadow. Wondering if it was a tad too scruffy, it struck him odd that he even cared what he looked like. "Don't do it man," he instructed himself. "Ignore any attraction to a girl like Megan." He knew her type; conceited, snobby and demanding, not to mention a bit scatterbrained, with a hot mess of a life. This was work, a little distraction from the deafening silence in the tiny house he was restoring. That was all.

Tonight, Megan would give Stone a few moments of her time then get back to the designing of the lodge. But first, she had two little girls to get to bed. Megan found Sophie playing in her room. "Sophie, where did you put my pearls?" asked Megan.

"Gloria's wearing them tonight," said the little girl with two fistfuls of Barbies.

"Sophie, how many times have we been over this? Gloria is a seven-year-old bulldog. Dogs do not wear jewelry."

"She looks good in them."

"Where is Olivia?"

"Reading in her room. What else would she be doing?" said Sophie.

"You need to go to get ready for bed. Mommy has a meeting."

Sophie dropped the dolls in protest. "I'm six years old. I don't need to go to bed at eight o'clock."

"I have a meeting. It won't take long. I should be done in no time. Just get in your PJs and play in your room. I'll be in to kiss you girls goodnight, probably by eight fifteen."

The little girl stomped off, dragging her Barbies by the hair.

Megan would give Stone a few minutes to trip over his words. She would make every effort not to laugh at his ideas. After all, Molly liked him for some reason. She slipped on a crisp white button-down with navy skinny jeans and black riding boots. Why she cared what she wore was a mystery to her. He would have on his uniform of faded Levi's and a button down. But not her. Megan would look the part of a professional. She pulled out the small cards with Silver stardom paint chips on them, along with swatches of grey satin fabric for the tufted chairs. What would an uncultured redneck like him know about luxury design anyway? They didn't need to agree. She was sure she could out-think the tool, then convince him to see it her way. Maybe she'd even let him think it was his idea. A man like this was not hard to manipulate. Seven fifty-five, let the games begin.

Like clockwork, Stone Reynolds entered the Mistletoe Lodge at seven fifty-six. She greeted him, proud that she had everything under control this time; no wardrobe malfunctions, no fighting children, no random weirdo dates lingering in the background.

"You're here. I'm impressed," he said, eyeing his watch.

"Of course, I am. Now as to not waste either of our time, let's get right to it. You mentioned you had a thought or something?"

"Yes, it is a thought. So, I took the liberty of sketching my 'thought' for you so you could understand it," Stone said, using his fingers to air quote.

Oh no, he did not air quote me. He acted like he needed to dumb it down for her. *Pace yourself Megan,* she reminded herself.

"Perfect. Why don't you bring your little drawing over here to the table and let me have a look?"

He took off his jacket and carried the leather portfolio over to the table. Megan pulled out a chair on the right side of the table for him, then headed over to the opposite side. Stone smiled then passed the chair on the right side heading straight to her side of the table. He pulled out the one directly next to her and dropped the portfolio on the table. She felt her back stiffen with the closeness of his body. She couldn't help but get a waft of his musky cologne; a sensual scent, rugged, strong with hints of leather and suede. He smelled good. It had been a long time since she felt the breath of a man on her shoulder. Focus. A leather-bound portfolio was a bit more than she had anticipated, but a fluffy exterior wouldn't snow her.

"While I realize you have given a great deal of thought to this project, I think I bring a different perspective. While including elements of a rustic ski lodge and family-themed entertainment destination spot, I believe you'll find these a bit closer to Molly's vision."

Who did he think he was using words like perspective, elements, destination as if some redneck had a clue about what Molly wanted? Without as much as an acknowledgment of his words, she flipped open the portfolio and pulled a set of blueprints out. Her breath caught in her throat. The sketch, done to scale with colored pencils to give exact color themes was breathtaking, utterly the most amazing thing she'd ever laid eyes on. The upstairs walls were removed, giving sight lines to the rooms on the second floor. The staircase widened, making it feel grand with thick rustic rails. Oh my God, Megan, don't cave, don't give him credit. Think, think, this is your project, you are in control.

"Well, any thoughts about my 'thought'?"

"I, it's…" she was fumbling. Then without warning, Olivia appeared, one ponytail higher than the other, her glasses on sideways, and Suppy, her favorite stuffed sloth, swinging from her tiny hand.

"Mommy, my belly doesn't feel so good."

Perfect timing! She would escape the debate table and grab a few white crackers for the pale little one.

"Excuse me," she said, working her way to Olivia. She picked the little girl up. "Okay sweetie, let's get you some crackers and…" before Megan could finish, Olivia hurled all over Megan and Suppy along with her new salamander PJs.

"Ahh," screamed Megan, she didn't do well with vomit. Throw up was the only thing Chase handled. The smell made her own stomach churn. "Oh my gosh, I think I'm going to, to…" rushing to the trash can she pulled hunks of regurgitated pretzel from her hair, before she began hurling into the can.

Sophie strolled in with her pink PJs and pink slippers. "Mommy, Maxie says the hottie from Plenty of Sharks thinks you're an animal, a, a, hippo, no, a moose, yeah, a moose, no maybe it was a 'cougar'. Yeah, that's it," she said.

"Sophie, get your sister a towel."

"Ewwwww," she screamed before slipping on the wet throw up laden floor. Then, in true Sophie style, she let out a scream so shrill the windows shook. "I have throw up on my new pink slippers!"

Calmly, Stone made his way to Sophie and helped her up. He handed her a towel then took her slippers to the sink. He wiped Olivia's pale freckled face and poured her a glass of water. He tossed Suppy into the sink with the soiled slippers. Then he handed Megan a towel and a glass of water.

Megan wiped her face. Still nauseous from the smell of her own hair, she managed to choke out, "Thank you, I don't do well with vomit."

"Clearly. Why don't you go clean up? I'll get Olivia some crackers."

"Really? Okay, thanks. I'll see if Maxie can help. Can you wait until I get back?"

He handed Olivia some saltines he grabbed from the jar on the counter, then nodded. "I've got all night."

The sting of humiliation once again in front of this man sent a nagging reminder that she wasn't handling her new working mommy duties very well. She carried Olivia to the bathroom and instructed Sophie to change her PJs and climb into bed. After a quick rinse in the tub, she put Olivia in bed.

"Is Suppy going to be okay?" asked a very pale Olivia.

"Who cares about that old worn out thing, what about my new slippers?" snapped Sophie.

"Everything will be fine. Now mommy needs to shower and to finish my meeting." She kissed their heads and headed straight to Maxie's room. She'd kill her. A hippo? Could she feel any more embarrassed? Doubtful. Megan knocked lightly on Maxie's door. "Do not ask. Please just sit with the girls for a few."

Maxie headed to their suite and Megan stepped in the shower and wiped her face clean. Rubbing her thick black hair with a towel, barely brushing it, she threw on some leggings and an oversized wool sweater that hung off her shoulder. Given the extra time to think, her mind struggled to wrap itself around the pure talent in every sketch. Maybe she should hear him out. She owed him that, at least, for his heroic throw-up rescue. She headed back to the main lodge to find Stone sitting by the fireplace.

"Feel any better?"

"Yes, thank you. I just want to toss the smelly things in the washer."

"Already done. Molly gave me a floor plan, so I knew where the washroom is. Suppy, I believe it was, is going to make it."

"Wow, you didn't have to do that."

"I kind of did, given that you might have had a repeat performance if you had touched those wet things. With the meeting and all, I figured it was in the best interest for both of us."

"Sorry, I don't know why every time you're around I seem to be in crisis."

"Crisis and kids go hand in hand, right?"

"I guess they do," she moved over to the worn sofa in front of the fireplace. "Can I get you a drink? Coffee, hot cocoa, vodka?"

He chuckled, "Would you consider a beer unprofessional?"

"After what you just witnessed, I'd consider it a requirement to finish this meeting." She made her way to the kitchen and grabbed two beers and returned, this time taking a seat directly next to him on the couch.

She handed him one of the beers, then said, "Shoot, give me your pitch."

"Alright, Molly said she wants this place to feel like home. She wants guests to relax and mingle. This small area here will serve as the check in, and this huge space will be a homey, comfy area akin to sitting in your own living room. I was thinking we would knock out this wall, and expose the upstairs rooms with a thick wood railing overlooking this space, with a grand sort of open woodsy staircase. What this place is missing is the warmth of a vintage ski lodge. We panel the two-story ceilings in a honey pine and flank it with thick worn log beams. The fireplace is the focal point of the room, but the brick is outdated. I'm thinking we stone the whole wall, all twenty foot by forty foot high. Am I rambling?"

Megan could barely keep pace with the brilliance of his mind. He was good, very good. Molly was right to hire him. However, she didn't want to seem too excited. *Play it cool,* she reminded herself.

"It's just a lot to take in. I'm digesting it all."

"Okay, how about we take a break and drink our beer?"

"Deal," she said, clinking her beer to his.

"So, hippo, huh?"

"Maxie is going to be the death of me. It's nothing really."

"Plenty of Sharks nothing?"

"My love life, off limits. Remember the rule?"

"It's just so darn tempting to go there with all this great material."

"Funny, really. I'm laughing on the inside."

A loud squealing sound pierced the air. "That's the washer. We're going to need new ones." She jumped up and headed to the laundry room. She tossed Suppy and the slippers in the dryer and returned with two more beers.

"This one's for saving Suppy."

"Suppy seemed worth saving. Getting back to the design. I've found a way to incorporate your elements into Molly's vision, but first, we need to talk about the actual structure. If it's okay with you, I'll leave my sketches and notes and you can look at them on a little less stressful night. You do have a few less stressful nights, don't you?"

"Yes, but lately things have been a bit off."

"Understatement, but we'll go with it," he said before collecting the four bottles from the table and heading to the kitchen.

"You don't need to do that. You've already done enough."

"Something tells me your crazy night isn't over," his head nodding toward the doorway. Megan turned to see Sophie standing with her hand on her tummy. "Mommy, my tummy is rumbly."

"Oh no, not you too. Thanks, Stone. I'll look over the notes and sketches, then get back to you, but for now, I have a sick princess to deal with."

Chapter Five

It had been three days since Stone met with Megan. He wondered when or if she'd call. She was complicated and definitely in over her head with this project. It would be easy to just walk away. After all, he was on strict orders to rest, yet he connected to Molly's passion. For some reason even thinking about the word passion brought Megan rushing to his mind. Work helped keep his mind off her; those eyes, mind-altering, that smile, intoxicating, and that body made stringing together coherent thoughts near impossible. He pulled out a drill and some screws and started rebuilding the front railings of the modest house he purchased. He needed to stay clear headed. A woman was the last thing he wanted right now.

Stone had come close to love once, or so he thought, with a beautiful woman who was the daughter of one of the hotel chain moguls. He met Claire during his meeting with her father to sign the five-million-dollar contract to build a series of luxury hotels in Dubai. She was not unlike what one would imagine the daughter of a billionaire to be; spoiled, demanding and shallow, but her thirst for adventure appealed to Stone, who had until now spent all his time making a name for himself. They traveled the world, played in the most exotic of playgrounds, and partied with young Hollywood. Stone, so taken by Claire, planned to propose. What he didn't realize was he was just one in a long line of men that she met through daddy, and his time would end as soon as a richer suitor entered the scene. Claire nonchalantly explained he could never accommodate her lifestyle with his current means, however, if that were to change, give her a call. The words stung so deeply; Stone vowed to do just that. This began the era of Stone Reynolds, workaholic. Stone Reynolds would stop at nothing to be one of the richest men Claire ever met. He would give her everything she desired, and in return, he hoped for her heart. It marked the beginning of the end.

The cold November winds howled, banging mercilessly against the old lodge's drafty windows. Megan knew she needed to call Stone and give him the go ahead. There would be more meetings and long nights. He was impossible, overconfident and dangerously sexy. Megan liked money, lots of money. She liked educated, cultured men. Stone, with his strong jawline and dimpled chin, his weather-tanned face with crystal blue eyes which twinkled when he smiled, was the kind of guy Maxie brought home; the wild, bad boy type. She wouldn't let him get in her head.

The next day, the door of the old lodge swung open bringing with it blasts of the chilly evening air.

"Hey, where're my girls?" said Chase.

"How many times have I told you to call before coming over? You don't have the right to just pop in because we're staying at the lodge. This is our home for now."

"Relax, Meggie. You were always so uptight. I need to talk to them about the wedding. You are coming, right? No RSVP? I know it's awkward not having a plus one and all, but swallow your pride and be there for your girls," he said smugly.

"Daddy!" yelled Sophie, running into his arms.

"Princess!" he said, picking her up.

Megan hated how he disappeared for weeks on end, then blew in like daddy of the year. She didn't begrudge her daughters the chance to know their father, but hated his hero status after all the disappointments. Where was he when she was getting hurled on? When Sophie didn't get the part as head princess in dance class? When Olivia lost her front tooth?

"Bree needs you two for princess gown fittings," he said.

The little girl jumped up and down wildly, "Yes, yes, I can't wait to be a real princess."

His phone rang once. With lightning speed, he swiped to answer. Megan remembered the endless calls she had made to him when they were together that went straight to voicemail.

"Babe, I'm with my angels. When do you need them?"

Then silence, and a few minutes later, "Okay babe, calm down. I'll call Richard. I'm sure it's a mistake. I'll be there in ten."

He hung up his phone, shrugged his shoulders toward Megan. "You know how stressful weddings can be. I have to go. I'll call you, princess when I'm going to pick you up."

"You have two daughters. You know that, right?"

"Right, tell Olivia to get excited, for the big day."

"Daddy, don't go," cried Sophie. "You just got here. I want to show you my dance for the recital. You're coming, right?"

"Wouldn't miss it," he said as he kissed her on the forehead.

"Sophie, I need to talk to daddy alone for a minute."

"Great, here we go. Now, what did I do wrong?"

"Really? Do you have to ask? You march in here unannounced, get Sophie all excited, then, as usual, disappear, not to mention you forgot all about Olivia."

"Oh, come on Megan, you know the kid is a little invisible sometimes."

"Nice, real nice."

"You just can't get over it, can you? I found someone and no one will even look at you. I get it, you're going to be thirty-five next week. Yeah, I remembered, but don't take it out on me."

"You are so ..." she started shaking hands.

"I'll call about the fittings and don't wait too long to RSVP. Pete Snogg is coming alone. You remember him, a big boy with a lisp. You can sit with him."

There was no way she would let him see her squirm. He knew her well, her Achilles' heel. Age would not be something Megan would accept gracefully. Sunday was 'her' day. That's what the McKenna's called your birthday, 'Your Day.' Now staring down the barrel of thirty-five, she quivered to even hear the word "birthday" out loud.

Thirty-five meant elastic waists, soccer mom haircuts, and sensible shoes. This felt like a spell in purgatory before she would settle into Sunday Night Bingo and orthopedic shoes.

She was the pretty one, Maxie the rebellious one, and Molly the brains. With pretty slipping away right in front of her, she feared there might be nothing left. Megan's "the most beautiful woman in the room" title had been relinquished. She would quietly fade into the background until one day she just disappeared into the sea of average, middle-aged women.

"Megs, what do you think of Jay?" asked Maxie, coming down the stairs, chomping on a chocolate-covered donut.

Megan stared at the dark chocolate icing hugging the fluffy pillow of carbs. Transfixed by the sinful snack, she barely heard Maxie's question.

"You know you can eat one, Megan. They aren't poison."

"Easy for you to say, you're not going to be thirty-five, where the mere mention of carbs spreads your behind three inches."

"Oh stop, I know twenty-year-old's who would kill for your body."

"Maxie, what happens when my looks fade? I mean, who am I without them?"

"Are you kidding me, Megan? You are a great mom, sister, daughter, friend."

"That's like what you say to the fat kid. You're really nice."

"You didn't let me finish. Your looks will never fade. You're a classic beauty; like Audrey Hepburn, Raquel Welch, all legends in their old age. I know what you need. A little uh, uh," she said while thrusting her hips front to back.

"Maxie, you're unbelievable."

"No, I'm practical. When is the last time you had sex?"

Moving a smidge closer to the donut she said, "Chase."

Maxie gasped, "Surely there must be a second Chase."

Molly walked in and said, "What did I miss?"

Maxie placed her donut on a buffalo check plate. She waved both hands up and down in front of Megan as if she was a Price is Right showcase. "Our girl here hasn't had sex since her scumbag ex-husband."

Molly, their straight-laced sister's eyes widened. She picked up the donut and stuffed the remainder of the pastry in her mouth to silence her opinion.

"Meggie, this is for your own good. Here goes -- Get off the pity party train and get out there and get some action. You don't need to marry the guy, for God's sake. Just see if it still works," said Maxie.

"I'm fairly certain it still works; the body doesn't lose the ability to..." said Molly beginning her logical description of how science works.

"Stop, both of you. I'm fine."

"No, you're not. You're freaking out about your birthday. Now let's get back to my original question; what do you think about Jay?"

"Who's Jay?"

"I sent you an email. Do you ever check your email? He's from Plenty of Fish."

Molly's eyes again widened before she began frantically searching for more carbs.

"Speaking of Plenty of Fish, the other night when Stone was here, a guy called me. How did he get my number?"

"About that, you're not exactly utilizing the site to its capacity and by that, I mean you haven't done a thing."

"Not true, I talked to a couple of guys."

"Stone was here?" asked Molly.

"Yes, I called him back."

"Heck yeah, you called him back. Why don't you give him a tumble?" said Maxie swaying her hips.

"Maxie, he's our contractor. It wouldn't be appropriate," said Molly.

"For the love of Pete, he's our contractor, not our second cousin. He's freaking hot."

"No, now back to the conversation. Who is Jay? Do I even want to know?"

"He's blonde, tall, smart, rich and handsome. But the best part, wait for it," Maxie said drum rolling two pencils on the counter. "You have a date with him tonight."

"What? I can't, it's a school night."

"Got you covered. I'm taking the girls to mom's for dinner so you can get ready in peace. You're meeting at Le Ruge at seven."

Molly nervously rummaged through the cabinets, found a bag of chips and started jamming them into her mouth.

"Molly, did you hear that? Now she's making dates for me. Tell her how absurd that sounds."

Both sisters' eyes were peering into Molly like a burning ray of sun.

"Well Molly, tell her."

Molly lowered her head and in a barely audible voice mumbled, "I just think maybe it's time to give someone a chance. You know when I asked you to take on this renovation and you were hesitant? Dating after divorce is sort of like doing some construction work on yourself. You know, change the scenery, give your love life a makeover."

"Ha!" said Maxie, slapping her hands together.

Megan grabbed the bag of chips from Molly's hand and poured them into her mouth. "You're right, both of you. Chase just reminded me of how the pool shrinks for women of my age," she said, between chips.

"Screw him," said Maxie.

"Divorce is hard. Everyone tells you how to fix your broken heart, but no one tells you how you're supposed to fix your broken self-esteem. He didn't want me anymore. He wanted younger, perkier, blonde," she said as an uncontrollable faucet of tears opened down her face.

Molly started crying with her. Maxie, the toughest of the three sisters, threw her shoulders back and jumped into fixer mode. "Molly, pull yourself together. Megan, that's enough. The skank fixed her sights on him then went hard like a bull rider holding on until she tamed him. Chase doesn't even know what he wants. Right now, he wants what the witch tells him he does. You're not eighty. Get out there. What could it hurt?"

"You're right. Okay, Jay; He's normal, right?"

"Absolutely."

"Seven o'clock?"

"Yep."

The three girls hugged. Maxie swayed her hips and sang, "Go Meggie, go Meggie, get your groove on."

Chapter Six

Megan packed up the girls, kissed them goodbye, then headed straight to her closet and began the arduous task of picking an outfit for the date. She had more clothes than Molly and Maxie combined, but again she was swimming in new territory. She eyed a red short dress, a bit too much for a first date. Next, a white blouse and black straight skirt, too business like. Classy, smart and confident; yes, she knew just the one, a knee-length, winter white long sleeve knit dress with a straight neck and gold chained belt to cinch her tiny waist. It hugged her curves yet showed no skin except her shapely legs. She straightened her long, silky black hair and dusted on a light smokey eye and a bold red lip. Now to find her off white classic pumps. That and a gold bag, and she was ready.

She looked once in the mirror and smiled, "What do you think Gloria, maybe I've still got it?" She asked the pug curled up on a pile of discarded outfits.

Pulling on her luggage colored wool coat, she grabbed her keys and headed out to her minivan. Somehow, that practical decision to turn in her leased white Lexus for a family sized van now felt like the last knife Chase had dug in her side. Now she truly fit the soccer mom cookie cutter mold, not to mention the darn thing had starter issues. The bitter air stung her face as she trotted to the van. Slipping the key in, she crossed her fingers and prayed the motor would purr. Megan turned the key a half turn to hear the motor hum. Oh, thank God, she thought. Now to find Le Ruge. Her nerves twisted her stomach at first now were knotted into a ball. She wasn't entirely sure what this guy even looked like. The picture was a bit blurry, but Maxie was right, he seemed smart and classy. How much worse could he be than Mr. Clean? Open mind, Megan. Her directions landed her there a few minutes early. Since she hadn't had the heat fixed in the van, she decided to head in and wait. Who cares about fashionably late and all those stupid antiquated notions?

A tall waiter with a very noticeable toupee greeted her. "Welcome Mademoiselle, are you alone or meeting someone?"

It was a simple question, not one meant to pour salt in the wound. The answer to both, yes. Yes, she is alone and tonight she would try and change that, even if just for one night. Suddenly painfully self-aware of her aloneness, she prayed this stranger would appear within the next second before she lost her nerve. So caught up in her own neurosis, she hadn't noticed a short bald waiter in a bow tie had appeared next to her.

"Excuse me, Mademoiselle. I believe a friend of yours has asked me to retrieve you."

A sudden sigh of relief breezed over her. A friend, that sounded nice. Meeting a friend for dinner doesn't make you a lonely cat woman. Dating lesson number one noted; it's all in the perception. She followed him through the restaurant. Although she had never been there, she had heard great things about the trendy new upscale restaurant.

The room dimly lit, glowed from single candles on each table. A piano bar sat just to the left of the entrance; beautiful soft piano music played lightly in the background. She had a good feeling. Then, they turned the corner and saw him, sitting there.

"Stone, what are you doing here?" she asked with annoyance dominating her tone.

"Great to see you too Megan. You clean up nice. I'm dining, odd as it sounds, contractors eat too."

"Here? At this restaurant? Really?"

The waiter, now clearly uncomfortable, pulled out her chair.

"Oh no, this isn't my date," she said dismissing Stone.

"Date? As in 'Plenty of Sharks' date?"

"Why do you keep popping up at the worst times?"

"Megan," waved a man heading their way. He was handsome, about six feet, thinly built and nicely dressed.

"Jay," she said as she felt Stone's eyes shift toward the man.

"You're even more beautiful in person. I can't imagine how that is even possible," said the gentleman.

"I like this one," whispered Stone in her ear as he stood to shake Jay's hand. "Stone Reynolds, a friend of the beautiful Megan."

"Nice to meet you," said Jay, extending his hand. "Waiter, this table right here next to my date's friend would be lovely. Is that possible?"

"That's not really necessary," said Megan.

The waiter biting his lower lip said, "Yes sir, here, allow me," as he pulled out the chair at the table adjacent to Stone.

"Nonsense, it would be lovely," said Jay.

"Agreed," said Stone.

Jay sat down in the seat directly next to Stone's. Megan, opposite of him, would have an eye to eye seat across from Stone.

"My name is Frank. I'll be your server this evening. Please take a moment to look over the menu. If you have any questions, feel free to ask," he said, placing two black and cream menus dressed in black padded jackets in front of them.

"So how do you two know each other? Should I be worried? He's quite handsome," said Jay.

Stone raised an eyebrow. "He's just my contractor."

"Oh, those hard hat guys. I know them well," said Jay.

Again, Stone raised his eyebrow then chimed in. "Megan and I are working on a very big remodel. As a matter of fact, I've been dying to hear what she thinks of my ideas."

"That's exciting Meg. Tell me all about it," said Jay.

The waiter appeared with two wine glasses and a bottle of Château Latour. "Is this satisfactory sir?" he asked as he poured Jay a sample. With a swirl of the glass, a whiff and a sip of the wine, Jay gave a nod to the waiter who poured them both a glass.

She hated the name Meg, but he was scoring big on the handpicked wine. Clearly, he had taste, class, and sophistication, unlike Neanderthal. Trying to avoid conversation with said Neanderthal, she flipped open her menu. A smile formed on the inside. Yes, this is the life she is meant to live. This is how she and Chase lived. Why would a guy like Neanderthal be at a place like this? Probably won some type of raffle. Either way, the date was going better than she expected.

"So, Meg back to your project. Are you an interior designer?"

The question, again, was innocent, but the answer *was* no. *No, I'm actually nothing at the moment, ugh. Not true, I'm a housewife that my two successful sisters took pity on. No, I have no talents other than looking pretty, if I do, I just haven't discovered them yet.* Oh my gosh, what do I say? She felt her face turning a shade of scarlet. At first, she fumbled over her words, "I, no, well not exactly, I…"

"She has impeccable taste. The lodge is lucky to have an eye like hers on the job," said Stone winking at her.

Why did he do that? I was perfectly capable of answering. No, you weren't, she reminded herself, but still, she wouldn't give him credit for saving her.

"That's fabulous. I have an eye for design myself," said Jay just as Stone's food came.

Thank goodness. Stone moved his seat closer to the table and seemed to step aside from their conversation as the waiter approached to take their order.

"We'll start with an order of Les Huitres, and if Fondue Bourguignonne works for you, two orders along with a side of Gratin Dauphinois."

Megan nodded, unsure of what any of that was outside of gratin, which she deduced was a potato. Her phone buzzed. She looked into her purse to see a text from Stone. She swiped and read, *Oysters, good choice. You know they are an aphrodisiac.*

Eat and leave, she texted back under the table. Which part of that was an oyster and more importantly, how did he know? Lucky guess, she imagined. Smiling at Jay she asked, "So tell me about yourself."

"Did I mention how beautiful you are? That lipstick is perfect with your complexion. It's Hibiscus Luxe from Mac, right?"

"Umm, yes, it is. That's incredible that you knew that."

Another text- *Incredible... more like freakish.* She pecked back *Or a man that clearly knows women, unlike you.*

Yeah, that's it, Stone texted back.

"As my profile said, I'm a successful businessman. My partner and I opened The Pip in 2012. It's a poetry slam club. It's all about free expression, self-acceptance, and appreciating all types of lifestyles."

Stone smirked and pecked the keys of his phone. She glanced down to read 'He's *'special'*.

You're jealous, she pecked back.

"How about the lovely Meg? Tell me about yourself."

Again, the name Meg was like nails on a chalkboard to her. It reminded her of the old lady two doors down where she grew up. Poor old, fat, lonely Meg. Ugh, focus. "I have two lovely daughters and ..." Panic rushed to her lips, what now? *I'm divorced, bitter, lost, sad.*

"Yes, two girls. And how old are they?"

He was a perfect date. Handsome, cultured, sensitive and very invested in the conversation. Frank appeared with two plates of Les Huitres.

"Sophie is six and Olivia is four. Sophie is my little princess. She loves ballet and playing dress up. She enjoys the finer things in life like her mother," she offered with a coy flirty smile.

"The finer things in life, ay? My kind of lady," he said as he lifted his glass in a toast. Things couldn't be going better. She gave Stone a "look at me" stare. Dinner arrived and the conversation flowed easier than she could have imagined. Everything seemed easy, comfortable.

"This is nice," said Jay. "I read people quickly and I think you are quite lovely. I've had dates with some real crazies."

"I'm sort of a novice in this arena. If I'm being honest, I really wasn't sure about the whole dating site thing."

"Honesty is so important. I'm thirty-seven, have a brother in Wisconsin, own my own home, and enjoy your company very much. Tell me what you enjoy."

A breezy smile relaxed across her face, "I enjoy fashion, getting dressed up, just like Sophie, I guess. I ski and enjoy music and golf."

"Dress up, huh? I have a question for you."

"Shoot," she said with a newfound confidence at how well this was going.

"Hypothetically speaking, if you came home from work and found your man wearing your clothes, heels, etcetera, would you be okay with that?"

Stone choked on his drink bringing tears to his eyes.

"I, well, that's something I…" she was stumbling. Where was the great Stone now to cut the tension, help a girl out? No, instead he sat holding back laughter, watching her squirm.

"In the spirit of full disclosure…" Jay began.

Oh, please don't do it. No full disclosure.

"I dabble, well if I'm being completely honest, I like to dress up in women's clothing some days. When dating I usually size up the woman's body type first to see if we could share, ya know?"

No words, she had no words. One last text from Stone. *I must leave before I bust a gut. You're right Megan, he does know women. LOL.* He stood and approached the table. She held her breath.

"It was nice meeting you Jay. You two kids have fun. And might I say, you look good together."

Jay stood and extended his hand. "Pleasure, Stone. We do, right? Same build and all."

"Exactly what I was thinking," said Stone winking at Megan behind Jay. "Megan, let me know when you make a decision." He disappeared and headed toward the coat room.

She could feel the blood rushing from her toes.

"Excuse me, will you Jay? I need to talk business with Stone, just for a second."

"Certainly."

She stomped her way to the coatroom, opened the door and ran straight into Stone's arms. She closed the door behind her. His cologne teased her senses. He made no attempt to widen the space between them. For a second, they were silent. He looked handsome in the light of the coat closet. *Wine! She had two glasses at this point, that must be why*, she thought. The door opened and a gentleman and his wife entered, stopping abruptly as they saw the two standing an inch away from each other.

"Aw, um as I was saying," Megan started.

"I don't believe you were speaking," said Stone.

"Love life off limits. I'm struggling to see how we can work together if you can't follow simple commands."

"So, you like issuing commands?"

"You're impossible. While it pains me to say that your work actually, okay, if it were up to me, I would design everything much better. However, for some reason, Molly insists on you. Her judgement is a bit flighty at the moment with the wedding and all. As to not upset her, the job is yours."

"Well with that kind of begging, I can't resist the offer."

"You'll report tomorrow. We'll speak only as needed. You **will** stay out of my love life. Scratch that, out of my life period. To be clear, I don't like you at all. Got it? Don't like you."

Stone moved in a bit tighter, stealing all the air from her and whispered in her ear. "Got it. I like it when you boss me around."

"Why are you still here?" she said inhaling deeply, her breath a mix of arousal and fury.

"See you in the morning. Have fun with twinkle toes in there. Don't do anything I wouldn't do," he said, his chest grazing hers as he attempted to move around her. "Oh wait, I doubt he does anything that I do."

"Don't like you, Stone," she said as she managed to move toward the door and head back to Jay. There sat Jay anxiously waiting for an answer to the world's most awkward question. *What do I say to him?* Quick thinking, she texted Molly. I need a Hail Mary.

"There you are, sweetheart. I thought you may have bailed on the date. It has happened a time or three."

"No, I just needed to talk to Stone." Then her phone rang. She answered, "Molly, you know I'm on my date, is everything okay? Oh no, when? I'll be right there. Just tell her to wait. Mommy is coming."

"Is it the little ones?" he asked.

She felt a wave of guilt like Sister Peter was standing over her in the Catholic elementary school lunchroom, but this was a white lie that needed to be told. "Jay I'm so sorry, my little one needs me. I hate to cut this short; you understand right?"

"Surely I do. I'll call you. Maybe we can get together and bring some heels and skirts for fun."

"Yes, that would be lovely. Okay bye," she said scampering out of the restaurant as if her feet were running on hot coals. This was a disaster. She would deal with it in the morning. She hurried to her car. The November air brought a not so gentle reminder that winter was knocking on the door. She unlocked her car door and hopped in. A sigh of relief overwhelmed her as she felt the comfort and safety of her van. Slipping the key into the ignition she turned it a half turn to hear the sound of silence. "Come on, not tonight please," she pleaded with her van. Patience, she reminded herself, then she tried turning the engine over again. Nothing. Banging her head against the steering wheel she asked, "Really could this night get any worse?" Then came a knock on the door. *Now what?* She rolled down the window.

"Meg, I thought that was you," said a slender brunette.

"Caroline." Caroline Bisset, her rival in high school, stood inches from her minivan crisis. In school, both girls vying for the title of Cheer Captain, both fighting for Chase, both fighting for the right to be remembered as the most beautiful girl in Cherrywood High.

"Meg darling, is this 'van' dare I say, yours?"

"Technically yes."

"Dreadful. Is it dead? Do you need Charles and I to call you a cab or something? He's pulling the car around. You remember Charles, right? Sure, you do, he and Chase were best friends. Oh, I'm sorry about Chase leaving you for that stunning tart. You must have been so humiliated. Wait, are you here alone?"

Swallow me van please make this stop.

Then he appeared. Stone stood next to Caroline. *Yes, this could get worse.* Caroline took one look at Stone and smiled. Her demeanor changed instantly as she eyed the stranger up and down. "Hello there," she paused for his name. Without thought Megan jumped out of the car and grabbed Stone, kissing him hard on the lips. It was hot and impulsive. Her mind kept telling her to move away but her lips refused to obey. Stone was in no rush to end the kiss either.

Caroline coughed, Megan jumped back and said, "There you are. Sorry, how rude of me. Caroline, this is Stone."

Stone put his arm around Megan's waist and pulled her in close. "Nice to meet you, Caroline. Megan, we need to get going, hun."

"Right. It was so great to see you again Caroline." Then she and Stone walked to his car. He opened the door, allowing Megan to disappear into the car. When inside, she didn't allow him to speak. "I still hate you, are we clear?"

"Perfectly."

"Also, I'm needing a ride. No words."

"Got it." They drove in silence. They turned down the winding road to the lodge. He pulled up to the lodge's main entrance. She barely waited for the truck to come to a stop.

"Report in the morning," she said.

"Yes boss. And Megan, you can hate me anytime you'd like." The truck door slammed hard behind her.

She barreled through the lodge door and quickly slammed it behind her.

"Meggie is that you?" asked Molly.

"Yes."

"Was that Stone's truck in the driveway?"

"Don't ask."

She pulled off her coat while heading over to the sofa where she plopped, one-foot dangling.

"That bad, huh?"

"If my date being more interested in wearing my heels than me, or the fact that my car died, or, oh yes, the icing on the cake, Caroline Bisset offering to help me in my broken down, mommy-is-dateless van bad, then yes."

"Wine?"

"Lots of wine."

Molly headed over to the kitchen, grabbed two bottles of red and two tall stemmed glasses and returned. She popped the lid off the first one and Megan grabbed it from her, swigging from the bottle.

"So, Caroline Bisset."

"Yes, she must be in town visiting her mother. She was dripping in diamonds, looking like a million bucks. I swear time hasn't touched her."

"About that," Molly started, "She and Charlie just bought the Hampton Mansion on Kuser. Charlie just signed a twenty-four-million-dollar contract with the Jets and Caroline, well she is, I guess, a bit famous."

Megan sat up, chugged a huge gulp and stared dead at Molly.

"She wrote a self-help book, 'From Beauty Queen to Timeless Beauty,' filled with tricks to stay young. Apparently, it's a bestseller."

"Tricks? The only trick she used is a date with a plastic surgeon's skilled little hands."

"Did she mention Chase?"

"Of course, she did, along with the fact that he left me for a hot young thing. Oh, and she felt the need to call attention to the fact that I was sitting alone in a dead van as well."

"What did you say?"

"Nothing, actually. I saw Stone standing outside the van. He had been dining at the same restaurant, so I sort of kissed him. I mean, what choice did I have, right?"

Molly pressed the glass to her lips and gulped down half the glass.

"Wait, you kissed Stone the contractor with the hot bum? I need all the details," said Maxie as she came into the room in her pjs. "I was going to get a cup of tea to help me sleep, but I'll grab a glass instead." She reached for a wine goblet then plopped on the sofa. "Go girl, spill," said Maxie.

"There is nothing to spill. He was there. I grabbed him and kissed him. End of story."

"It sort of sounds like the beginning of a story," said Molly. "I'm glad you two are getting along now."

"Getting along? Never. I can't stand him. He's arrogant and rude and intruded on my date."

"Right, yes, clearly hate, yes," said Molly, trying to stay with the script.

"How'd your date go?" asked Maxie.

Molly shook her head and whispered, "Crossdresser."

"Don't do me any favors trying to fix me up again, Maxie."

"So, crossdresser huh? That's a hoot, but the whole 'kiss the hot contractor thing' is what I want to hear more about," Maxie said, nudging her.

"It was nothing. Caroline Bisset showed up at the most inconvenient time asking about Chase and I impulsively kissed him to shut her up."

"Heck yeah! That would shut up that over botoxed face witch," said Maxie, "but more importantly, I bet the kiss was hot."

Megan swigged a few more large gulps and thought for a second of the hot passion that welled up inside her during that brief erotic meeting of their lips. "No, it wasn't hot. It was anger that just sort of morphed into a confused chain reaction of events that resulted in a two second kiss." She tipped the empty bottle, then requested another one.

"Meggie, maybe you want to head to bed, you seem a bit tipsy. And remember, that mom is coming tomorrow morning. You may want to save some wine for that," said Molly.

Chapter Seven

T he sound of awful country music blasted in Megan's dream. She opened one eye, then attempted to pry them both of them both wide. Sadly, it wasn't a dream, she thought as she pressed a pillow over her face, remembering her overindulgence in wine the night before. She heard voices above her.

"Do you think she's dead?" asked Hunter.

"Definitely the color of dead," said Stone. Extending his hand, he said, "Stone Reynolds, general contractor."

"Yes, I've heard good things about you. I'm Hunter, Molly's fiancé."

"If you heard good things you were misinformed," said Megan, opening one eye to see a set of worn Levi's and a toolbelt swinging around his hips. Attempting to stand, she stumbled. Stone reached a hand out to catch her.

"I'm perfectly fine," she said, banging her knee into the old mahogany coffee table.

"Yes, so it appears," Stone said.

"Rough night, Megs?" asked Hunter.

"You have no idea. And who is playing that ridiculous music?"

"Kenny Chesney has never been referred to as ridiculous," answered Stone.

"Of course, it's you. There is one redneck in all of Connecticut and he has to be in my living room."

"Well you might want to get used to it. I love country music, and this is how I work," said Stone heading back to his drawings.

"Is Silvia here yet?" asked Maxie. "Morning, hot contractor guy."

"Who is Silvia?" asked Stone.

"Uh oh, you haven't been prepped. Let's talk," said Hunter, pulling him aside.

As if the wind heard them, the door of the lodge swung open and ushered in none-other than Silvia.

Silvia, dressed in a classic black turtleneck and high waisted black pants with her hair impeccably set, wasted no time snapping at the group. "Hunter, have you even spoken to Tom from the band? And the color for the bow ties is most definitely off. You need to go now and fix that. Do you even know how many people I've invited to this wedding? Very influential guests will be here, everything must be perfect."

"The bow tie is red. Can that be off?"

"There are twenty-two shades of red at Holman's. Get the right one. Good heavens what happened to you, Megan Marie? You look worse than Aunt Josie after she did that awful colon cleanse," said Silvia, eyeing up Megan's gray colored skin and unkempt hair.

"Thank you for that mother," she said.

"You're not getting any younger. You need to start taking better care of yourself. How do you ever expect to attract a man if you look like a homeless cat woman?"

"Here we go with the cat woman again. Now I'm homeless, too? Nice."

"I'm serious, the big three five is breathing down your neck and you act like you can just lie around like a slob. Your Ms. Winter status won't carry you forever. I heard you had a date with a man of means last night, how'd that go?"

"It didn't go, if you must know. He was not my type."

"Megan, when are you going to realize that you are in no position to have a type."

"For God's sake mother, I'm not ninety on an oxygen tank. And if you must know, he was a man of means who wears women's panties by night."

"That sounds odd, but you know in this new-fangled world anything goes. Was he a doctor?"

"Really? That's the question that comes to mind after I tell you he's a crossdresser? I'm not doing this now, mother," she said, marching past Stone. "Lose the country music."

"Frankie Finklestein still works at the bank with his father and word has it he's still single."

"Frankie Finklestein isn't interested in women, mother," Megan shouted as she walked out of sight.

"Megan, don't you walk away from me. I know what I'm talking about. This is for your own good."

Just then, Silvia noticed Stone as though he had been completely invisible until that moment. "Handyman, listen. This place can't have all these tools and dust stretched out all over the floor on Friday night. We're having a birthday party for Megan. It's a surprise. The lodge must look perfect. She would never expect it to be here. Nor would I. For the life of me, I can't figure out why the girls chose this dump. Are we clear?"

"The name is Stone. You must be Silvia," he said, extending a hand.

She ignored the gesture and said, "Yes, I am. Now this will be clean, correct?"

"Yes, mam."

She marched out, leaving winter's chill in her wake.

"Wow, you weren't kidding about her, man," said Stone to Hunter.

"Her bark is worse than her bite. She grows on you."

"Hope I'm not around here long enough for her to have a chance."

"I'm off to see a man about a red bow tie. Nice meeting you, Stone."

"You too, Hunter," said Stone before turning up Luke Bryan.

Chapter Eight

Friday came with the familiar sounds of two young McKenna's yelling at the top of their lungs. Megan rushed down the hallway to quell the storm.

"You can't wear that to mommy's birthday," stomped Sophie.

"Mommy doesn't care what I wear," answered Olivia, pulling on her yellow boots.

Megan found the two in a tug of war with a yellow boot. "What's all the racket about?"

"Sophie says I can't wear my yellow boots to your party."

"Olivia, now you ruined everything. It's a surprise. You always ruin everything."

Olivia's big green eyes filled with water, fogging her glasses. "I'm sorry, mommy."

"Don't cry sweetie. It's fine. You didn't ruin anything. Now spill, Sophie, when is this party?"

"Tonight, but we'll get in trouble if you know. Aunt Maxie said you would be mad," said Sophie looking down at her tiny feet in Megan's beige heels.

"No one's getting in trouble. It'll be fun. I was just going to sit in my pajamas lopping the icing off Timothy's famous bonbons. Why would I be mad if I get to be with my two favorite girls at a party? Now let's keep this between us, okay? Mommy is going to forget I heard anything about a party. Now go play."

A party? What were they thinking? Let's paint a scarlet letter across my chest, old lady coming through. Maybe I should cut to the chase and look into cat breeds. The truth was, the idea of spending the night in her pjs and eating delicious balls of calorie laden bonbons seemed wildly appealing. A dark room with no makeup, no worrying about which dress shows the few extra pounds she was carrying in the hips, no push up bras to hoist her chest into an unnatural butt-like state. Just a safe place where she could celebrate the beginning of the end. She headed out to the main lodge only to be greeted by Blake Shelton singing about drinking to forget being dumped. This is exactly why she hated this hick music; a string of sad songs about love gone wrong.

"Hey there," said Stone. "You look more miserable than usual. Not an easy feat to pull off, but kudos to you for nailing it."

"Not in the mood."

"I'm almost done with the stone work on the fireplace. I'll be heading out early today, so I'll be out of your way."

"Why, why are you knocking off? Do you know something? Is something happening that would make you leave, say, like here?"

"More crazy than usual to boot, but I like it. Keeps you interesting. Not sure what you're asking, but the rant is kind of cute."

"Why do I talk to you at all?"

"Because you enjoy bossing me around, remember?"

"Right, that's it."

"Listen I've put up a bunch of tape and barriers along with a sign warning to stay away from the bookshelves because they are fragile. I need to rip them out but I only removed about half the nails, I'm trying to preserve some of the wood for another project. I don't want it to tumble. Okay?"

"Whatever," she said heading toward the kitchen.

"Okay then, bye. I'll see you tomorrow, bright and early."

"Saturday? You'll be here on the weekend too?" she said whipping back around to the main room.

"Knocking off early is setting me back a bit. I'm a very punctual person. Got to catch up."

"Ugh, whatever." Her phone dinged. Maxie with a text, *Hey, we're all meeting at O'Doul's Pour House for drinks around seven. Mom said she'll take the girls. Molly is in a bit of a wedding bells crisis. Need back up.*

Nice one Maxie, guilt me into my surprise party. How could she say no to her baby sister in crisis? She loathed birthdays. Okay, here we go. I better start now if I need to try and look good for this debacle, then wondered, since when did she need three hours to look decent?

Megan kissed Sophie and Olivia goodbye as they left with Silvia. The lodge was quiet. She surveyed the work Stone had begun. He knew what he was doing. Self-taught she assumed, good nonetheless. Why was Molly so darn intent on him? Her blood boiled as she thought about his smirk while intruding on her date. Then her mind quickly revisited the kiss. Why, why did she kiss him? Yes, because Caroline was breathing down her neck with 'you're a loser' stares. That's it, perfectly understandable. She would have kissed anyone right about then. Then she thought about the dress-wearing Jay and decided she'd never have kissed him. Stop Megan, it was a foolish one-time knee-jerk reaction, move on. That's exactly what she did. Her mind promptly revisited the notion of a cat.

She showered and dressed for O'Doul's Pour House. The reason why her sisters would have chosen a dive bar to have a party for her escaped her. Sticky floors and dimly lit bars hardly said Megan Marie McKenna. The only silver lining was Caroline Bisset would never step foot in such a dive.

"You ready," said Maxie from the main lodge area.

Megan came out eyeing Maxie for any signs of weakness. She would break her before they even arrived at O'Doul's.

"Mom said Sophie and Olivia are making s'mores in the oven."

Megan stopped for a minute. The girls had said the party was tonight and they were going. No way would they be at O'Doul's. Maybe they weren't really going to O'Doul's. Of course, they would stop at moms on the way and that's where everyone would jump out yelling those words more obscene than any four-letter word -- *Happy Birthday! Welcome to the downward side of thirty.* Honestly, why anyone had birthday parties after twenty-five was a mystery to Megan.

"So, what's the big Molly crisis?" asked Megan, deciding to make this difficult for Maxie.

"There is a problem with the electrical system at the foot of the massive tree in the center of the village. The quote she got was out of this world. I told her we can't afford it. It calls for rewiring all the circuits connected to Santa's cottage. Being the tree is the backdrop for wedding pictures, things quickly got very messy."

"Can't she get cheaper quotes?"

"Yes, but with a little longer than a month before Christmas, time is of the essence and the cheaper ones won't start until January. What's all this?" said Maxie pointing to the tape around the bookshelves.

"This is Neanderthal's work. He didn't finish. He's a real gem, that one."

"You're the one that kissed him; just saying."

"Well don't just say."

Megan thought this was a pretty elaborate story for a birthday party. The two girls headed to Maxie's car and turned left out the driveway. They were taking the route to O'Doul's. She wondered if the girls misunderstood and thought they were invited. They turned into the gravel lot and Megan spotted Hunter's car. Here goes, show time. *Act surprised when they announce your slow decline to lonely feline status to a room full of strangers.*

"Hey Meggie, don't look so gloom and doom. We're cheering her up, right? Some positive brainstorming, happy faces."

"Of course," Megan said with a forced smile as she headed toward the mahogany wood trimmed doors, each with a drunk leprechaun centered on the glass pane greeting guests at the entry of the Irish pub. She pushed open the doors to the dimly lit room flanked with bar stools and pool tables. Off to the left, a makeshift stage that offered local bands a chance to show their talent, or lack thereof. The dance floor empty, with the exception of one drunk man dancing with a blow-up doll, no doubt the remains of a bachelor party. She braced herself when she saw Molly, Hunter and Tony wave from across the room. *Whew, no shout out just yet.*

Molly ran over and grabbed Megan's hands. "What am I going to do? My wedding is in a little over a month and my venue just went dark? Not to mention it's the focal point of Christmas Village. No holiday themed village can have an unlit tree," Molly said scratching at hives brewing on her neck.

"Molly we'll think of something. There has to be one electrician in the area who has a soft spot for romance."

With puppy dog eyes Molly took Megan to the table, sat down and said, "I think sappy electricians are extinct."

Hunter and Tony gave Megan a hello hug, yet still no mention of her birthday. Maybe this was not about her at all. The girls were dead wrong. She felt a modicum of relief wash over her. Waving her hand toward the perky young waitress, she ordered a Margarita and settled in. "Okay first, what electric is affected?" Megan asked, noticing Maxie waving someone over to the table.

Maxie's eyes lit up and with a sheepish smile she said, "Wow, look who's here."

Rylee Ridolfi

Megan turned to see Peter Wence, a former classmate from high school heading toward them.

"Meggie, Peter has just moved back from LA and is also just recently divorced. Isn't that great?" said Maxie pulling over a chair from the adjoining table.

Megan's eyes seared straight through Maxie's soul. A set up, that's what this whole awful night was about. "So much joy in reveling in the fact that both our marriages ended, leaving our life's plan afloat," said Megan swigging her frosty Margarita.

"Still a bit raw I see," said Pete, "Well the good news is you'll survive. And do you know how I know this?" he asked before getting up and heading to the stage. "Hello there, can I borrow that mic for a minute?" He whispered something to the band then took the stage.

Megan rolled her eyes not caring for a minute how he knew anything.

"Hey there O'Doul's friends. My name is Doc Pete and I have a special prescription to share with a friend of mine who is still painfully reeling from her divorce."

"Oh my God, no he did not just say that into the mic?" Megan said, her face flaming red, her eyes squinting like barrels of sunshine that just broke through a cloud. Maxie squinted one eye and Molly raked her neck and sunk deeper into her seat.

"We've all been dumped, cheated on, tossed aside for a newer shinier model, right? Well tonight we rally around our girl, Megs. I'm going to need your help on this song. On the count of three, one, two, three." The first three notes of Gloria Gainer's, *I Will Survive,* rang out. Megan's mouth dropped open wide open in disbelief as the crowd

~ 70 ~

switched up the lyrics to "*You* Will Survive." Pete stepped off the stage and moved toward her just in time to hold the mic in front of her open jawed face and went silent when the words, "I Will Survive " played. Dead silence from Megan. "Come on now, Megs." The crowd began chanting, "Megs!"

Shooting a death stare in Maxie's direction. Maxie threw up a few hand gestures urging her to sing the lyrics. Feeling the entire crowds' eyes glued to her she whispered, "I Will Survive," so quiet she could barely hear her own words.

"I think you can do better than that Megs. Like you mean it now. Let it out," said Pete into the mic.

"I will survive," she sang miserably off key, but decidedly louder that time praying it would make this awful humiliation end.

"That's a girl," Pete said, finishing up the song with a twirl on the dance floor ending in a split.

"He was so shy in high school. How was I supposed to know?" said Maxie shrugging her shoulders.

"I don't need to be set up. I'm perfectly fine being alone," said Megan jumping off her stool and running right into Pete with a handful of drinks, two down her shirt and one which splashed all over her face. She turned to Maxie, "Can we go now, please?"

Maxie's eyes turned to Molly, who nodded to Maxie with a "get her out of here before she goes postal" stare.

Pete grabbed a bunch of towels and went in for her chest. "I got this. You've done enough," Megan said.

"Leaving so soon? We haven't even caught up."

Megan and Maxie headed to the car. "What were you thinking? Let's publicly humiliate Megan? That sounds like fun."

"Megan, it wasn't like that. I ran into Pete in the bank. He looked good, said he was a doctor in Beverly Hills, and my radar went up. When he said he recently went through a divorce I thought bingo, fate."

"Do us both a favor and don't think," she said as she slammed the door. The car ride home was pretty quiet. They pulled into the lodge and Maxie bit her lip. "Sorry Megs."

Catching a glimpse of her silk blouse stained orange, her hair standing up on the left side made her long for elastic waist pants. Maybe they weren't so bad after all. They were like a badge of honor, earned after so many rounds with life. Something to be embraced like a banner that read *I give up*. This is what freedom from caring looks like.

She stormed out of Maxie's car. Maxie tried to keep up with her as she opened the door and a sea full of faces yelled, "Surprise!"

Maxie whispered in Megan's ear, "That's what the sorry was about."

"Here mommy, we made this for you," said Sophie carrying a Ms. America sash that read *I'm Thirty-Five Today*. "Wow, thanks girls," she managed to get out. Perfect, a sash as her scarlet letter.

"Do you want a hat, mommy?" asked Olivia holding a pink fur trimmed birthday hat. "Well sure," Megan said, at this point it wasn't going to make a difference.

"Okay guests, if everyone will please head down the hall to the main dining room, we'll get this party started," said Maxie. "Go change," she said in Megan's ear.

As the crowd moved toward the dining hall, she saw him standing there with that all too familiar smirk on. "Rough night? I'm beginning to think you have some kind of bad karma voodoo around you."

"Thank you for pointing that out. Why are you here?"

"Some party going fool clearly can't read the yellow tape. Silvia called me with some pretty strong words suggesting in short if I wanted to live to see tomorrow, I'd stop what I was doing and get over here."

"I guess you were in the middle of something, right?"

"Certainly nothing as fun as you," he said before humming the tune to "I Will Survive."

"I despise you."

"At least you're consistent. Oh, and Megan, Happy Birthday."

"Ugh," she moaned, before marching toward her room. After slipping into a new shirt and brushing out hardened fruit from her hair, she sprayed a few rounds of dry shampoo and meandered back to the main lodge. He was gone. That was something to celebrate.

Molly rounded the corner rushing toward her. "Are you okay? I'm so sorry. We were just trying to get a drink or two in you before your party. Max and I tried to talk mom out of it but she insisted, and well, you know mom."

"So, the whole electrical thing was a lie?"

"No, unfortunately that part is true. But this is your party. So, no wedding talk tonight."

As they entered the main dining room, Megan couldn't help but note the extremely outdated lunchroom style tables, plastic chairs, peeling walls, and a gray and white linoleum floor. It was a far cry from her last birthday at the Country Club.

Sophie ran toward Megan. "Come on mommy, we have presents!"

Megan sat with Sophie and Olivia on either side of her. The girls handed her brightly colored wrapped gifts.

"Open mine first," said Sophie. Before Megan had a chance, Sophie ripped off the pink and white paper to reveal a picture frame with Sophie in her dance costume.

"It's beautiful. Olivia, do you have one?"

"Yes," she said, quietly pulling one from behind her back. She pushed back her heavy glasses and said, "I hope you like it."

"I'm sure I will, sweetie," Megan unwrapped the tiny box and opened the lid. Inside was a small rock with a painted heart with two stick figures holding hands.

"That's you and me, mommy."

"It's perfect."

"It's a stupid rock, she picked it from the lake that she lives in."

"Sophie, that's enough. I love it."

Molly jumped in and handed her the next gift.

She peeled the ribbon off Molly and Hunter's gift; a wool cream-colored sweater hat with a puffy ball on top along with matching gloves. Next was Maxie's gift, a new pair of ski boots in black and taupe. Last, her mom and dad's gift, a set of new skis.

She continued opening until Sophie said, "It's time for cake."

"Alright then, who can argue with that?" said Megan. The guests ate, chatted and toured the old lodge. Megan spotted Stone and Olivia in the corner. She made her way over. "Olivia, mom mom has some ice cream for you."

"Okay," she said before scampering off.

"Why are you still here?"

"Just having a chat with my favorite tiny human. Great kid you got there."

"Olivia?"

"Yes, you sound surprised."

"No, of course she is, I guess I'm just used to everyone telling me how great Sophie is with her dancing, her obsessive desire to be dressed in pink, and her outgoing personality."

"She's great too, but Olivia is smart and dedicated to her passion. I like that in a kid."

"It's sort of strange that she talks to you. I mean besides the fact that you're an overconfident jerk and all. She's usually very shy."

"What can I say, we bonded. She's an interesting conversationalist. For example, she mentioned how you can't wait for everyone to leave so you can lick Timothy's buns. Best conversation I had all night."

"It's not Timothy's buns, it's bon bons."

"Whatever turns you on. Molly invited me, given that I was dragged here on a Friday night and all."

"Well I'm uninviting you. It's my party and I can do that."

"That's fine. I have to be at work early tomorrow; boss is a real piece of work."

"Go."

The crowd thinned, and Megan thanked her family for making this otherwise miserable day tolerable. After tucking the girls in, she returned to the kitchen to pour herself a cup of tea. She boiled the water and dropped a mint tea leaf bag into her new thirty-five and fabulous mug, then she spotted something on the counter. A gift. A small box, with no card. How did she miss this one? She opened the foiled wrapped box and looked inside; A pair of nose plugs and a note.

My mom wasn't good with the smell of throw up either. She discovered nose plugs to be highly effective. Thought they may come in handy in the future. Happy Birthday, Stone.

Megan sat down on the worn sofa licking the thick decadent chocolate from her box of bonbons. Nothing made sense to her anymore, not her failed marriage, her dueling daughters or her complex contractor that for some reason, she wanted to kiss again.

Chapter Nine

T he next morning, the downslide to thirty-five roared in like a lion. Sitting up in bed, she twisted her back and found herself barely able to get out of bed, making the girls woefully late for their Craft Day. Sophie, in hot pursuit of a missing pink UGG, refused to go until she found the boot to complete the perfect outfit. Megan had completely forgotten to help Olivia glue down the letters on her poster, which rained onto the floor when the little girl picked up her project. After ripping the girl's room apart, the pink UGG was found. Letters glued, not all of them straight, but secure enough. She piled them into the minivan, only to find that the engine was once again, in quiet protest. Moments before a complete breakdown ensued, she spotted Maxie backing her car out behind her. She flagged her down then piled the girls into her Toyota Camry. Sophie and Olivia, bickering the entire ride.

"Johnny Wicker said Olivia is a nerd. I'm not sure what it means, but I'm sure she is one," said Sophie.

"I am not," said Olivia pushing her thick glasses up over the tiny freckled nose that barely supported them.

"Sophie, that is not nice. We don't call each other names. Apologize right now," said Megan shaking a finger into the back seat. The girls' banter elevated over Maxie's radio belting, *Frosty the Snowman.* Thankfully, they turned into Meadows Elementary parking lot a few minutes later. Maxie pulled into the fire lane against Megan's orders and shouted to the girls to make a break for it.

"We'll talk about this later," Megan shouted as they each slammed a door. "My back is killing me, my children hate each other, even my car won't cooperate. Is this my life?"

"You look like you could use a coffee. Did you eat?"

"No and I need to take a billion ibuprofens for this back."

"Okay here's the deal, I'll drop you at Bennie's. You get yourself a large caramel latte and your favorite French toast bagel. Enjoy the peace and tranquility for a bit, and I'll be back in about a half an hour. I have a few errands to run."

Megan's tension filled face melted, "That sounds like paradise."

Maxie pulled into Bennie's parking lot. "Paradise delivered."

"Take your time, Max. I think this is exactly what I need." Megan leaned over to release the door handle and moaned.

"Maybe you ought to have that looked at."

"And I'll get some orthopedic shoes while I'm at it."

Megan made her way slowly to the door, swung it open and inhaled the sweet aroma of freshly brewed coffee and too many flavors of bagels for her senses to distinguish. Megan had spent the last twenty years of her life denying herself the pleasure of carbs as often as humanly possible.

Today however, she decided in honor of elastic band pants, to indulge. Bennie himself welcomed her and asked what he could get her. "Hmm, I'll take a large English Toffee Caramel latte with whipped cream and cinnamon sprinkles, and to go with that, a raspberry white chocolate donut. That's all," she said smiling as she sighed at finding paradise.

"Really, that's all? I mean, third world countries eat less sugar in a year," said the voice behind her. She turned to glare daggers at Stone.

"How is it possible that you are in my paradise?"

"Freud would best be able to answer that."

"No, why are you here?"

"Here at Bennie's? Mostly for coffee, but occasionally I'll have a bagel and sometimes I mix it up with an egg, bacon and cheese."

"Stop speaking. You're everywhere. I'm going to start having night terrors that you're in my toothpaste."

"I would strongly suggest having that dream analyzed."

"You see, that's it. That right there. You grate my nerves, confuse my brain, and annoy my every fiber."

"So, you like me now?"

"No, I can't stand you. If possible, I dislike you even more than five minutes ago. You show up at all the wrong times, you even ruined my date."

"I ruined your date, really, because things would have been so different with Tina Turner if I had been in another restaurant. Might I remind you; I was eating peacefully; no one told you to sit next to me."

"I would not have sat next to you if you hadn't summoned me over."

"I summoned you?"

"Yes, and you threw me off my game."

"And if I hadn't summoned you, you and twinkle toes would be planning your coordinating outfits for your next date."

"Hate you. Are we clear?"

"Well if by hate you mean you're softening, then yes."

"Impossible," she groaned.

"Megan, one large English Toffee Caramel latte with whipped cream and cinnamon sprinkles and a raspberry white chocolate donut," said a pimple faced, extremely perky teenage boy.

"Yes, yes that would be me, and thank you for announcing that order to the WORLD," she said, grabbing her order then turning around to catch Chase and his bimbo making their way into Bennie's.

"Really, not today," she moaned.

Stone, not bothering to turn around said, "Not even going to ask what you are referring to, but if it's not too much trouble, can you step aside so I might place my order?"

"Shut up, just kiss me," she said puckering up.

"Wait, I get it, this is Regan, your other personality. Boy, is she going to be mad when she finds out what you're up to!"

"Just do it," she said, leaning into his chest.

"Okay and for the record, I like Regan much better." He pulled her in close and gently took his hand and tilted her face up towards his. His lips were soft and warm, his scruff abrasive but in a good, painful kind of way. That darn cologne permeated her senses as she closed her eyes and gave into the kiss. The kiss lasted much longer than either intended, only to be cut short when she felt Chase's hand on her shoulder.

"Megan, what are you doing?" barked Chase, eyes blazing.

"Hmm?" she asked, still a bit unsteady.

Still wrapped in Stone's embrace she nonchalantly took a sip of her Caramel Latte and managed to say, "OH, Chase, hi."

"Who's this?" he said puffing his chest out and pointing a gloved finger at Stone.

"This is Stone, my boyfriend," Megan answered, snuggling in a bit closer to Stone.

"Boyfriend, really? That's funny, because your plus one card is still void."

"Stoney here is going to be away that weekend. But that's okay, I'll just have to live without him for one little weekend, right pookie?"

Stone smiled then stretched out his hand. "Chase, nice to finally meet you."

Chase pulled his hand away quickly. "Finally? How long have you two been together?"

The bimbo, eyeing Megan's four-inch-high pile of whip cream snapped, "Megan, you better have those girls to the final fitting tonight at five. And tell, umm the little one. Whatever her name is, Ollie…"

Before she could finish, Stone chimed in, "It's Olivia."

"Yeah that one, no stupid mucking boots at my wedding."

"You know Olivia? You introduced him to my daughters? Are you freaking kidding me?" said Chase. "Look, I know you're not handling my leaving you, and you're suffering from some kind of midlife crisis, but for God's sake, don't act so desperate."

Stone took one step closer to Chase. The extra four inches he had over Chase made his words just a bit clearer. "You might want to rethink your words, that's no way to speak to a lady. Come on, Megan. I think we're done here," said Stone, taking her hand and walking to the door.

As they headed out of Bennie's, Megan whispered, "Put your arm around my waist."

"How about a bit lower?"

"NO."

"I was talking to Regan."

"Waist."

"I'll walk you to your car."

"That won't be necessary. I don't have a car."

"Okay then, if you're alright, I think I'm going to go find some coffee elsewhere."

"I'm fine," she said, wincing in pain as she stepped off the front step at Bennie's.

"What was that?"

She drew a deep breath and shook her head. "Nothing, I'm fine. Maxie will be back," she paused to check the time on her phone and noticed a text from Maxie. *Running about forty or so minutes late. Enjoy paradise,* with a palm tree emoji.

"Why?" she said, dropping the weight of her head back, her eyes rolled upward towards the clouds.

"Don't ask, Stone. Walk away, Stone," he mumbled to himself.

"I can hear you."

"Fine, what's the problem?"

"Maxie is my ride and she is going to be another forty-five minutes."

"It just so happens I'm heading your way, actually all the way your way. I'm going to the lodge. Do you need a lift, Regan?"

"I'd rather freeze here on the steps of Bennie's."

"Well since you asked so nicely, I'll get the car. And you owe me a coffee."

No man had ever gotten under her skin like this one. He was so infuriating, but smelled so darn good. He disappeared into the alley and returned in a few minutes. He pulled up next to her and put the truck in park. Making his way around, he opened the door and took the latte from her hand. She bent her left knee to climb into the car. Stopping suddenly with a jolt of pain, she grabbed the door of the truck. Stone put the latte on the hood of the truck and said, "Okay, lean on my shoulder to take the weight off that left leg. I'll lift you in."

Silently she followed his instructions. After he secured her into the seat, he grabbed the latte and jumped in the driver's seat.

"Thank you," she managed to say quietly.

"Which hurts more, saying thank you or your back?" he said smiling with those beautiful white teeth. "How did you hurt it anyway?"

First, she had no idea how he knew it was her back, and second, she wouldn't dare tell him the truth. "Getting out of bed with my thirty-five-year-old rapidly deteriorating body, I wrenched my back. Old field hockey injury."

"Field hockey, really? I pegged you for more of a cheerleader."

"I did both." She texted Maxie, *no hurry, I got a ride.*

"I hope he's hot."

"He's not," she answered looking over at him. Megan despised flannel shirts. They screamed 'lumberjack.' Although beneath that lumberjack shirt and worn Levi's was a rock-hard body. She hadn't seen it, but she couldn't help but notice when he carried in wood or stone for the mantle. His biceps were as if an Italian sculptor had chiseled them to perfection. He was tall, but not too tall. His backside was, as Maxie pointed out, *fine*, but she would never admit it. His lips were full, but not too full, with a perfect Cupid's bow, as if Cupid and Lisa Rinna gave birth to them. Perhaps the sexiest thing about him was his eyes; crystal clear blue seas of water, outlined by the blackest of lashes and thick strong brows. They seemed to look right through her. *Snap out of it*, she reminded herself, he was a jerk and this was a temporary working relationship at best.

Her fatal attraction quickly ended when he flipped on that ridiculous country music.

Stone turned to her and said, "So that's your ex, huh?"

"Unfortunately, yes, and the bimbo he left me for."

"She's a real gem. He'll regret that one day, mark my words."

"Regret picking her?"

"That, and losing you."

She felt a small gasp expel from her lungs. That was the nicest thing any man had said to her. She did hope Chase would regret it, and a small part wished he would come to his senses and run back to her. The logical part of her brain told her he was a lying, cheating scum, however the sentimental part of her wondered if they could have saved their family. They pulled into the long driveway and saw both Molly and Hunter's cars parked out front.

"That can't be good," said Megan.

Stone parked and came around to help Megan climb out. "Two ibuprofen and ice; twenty minutes on, twenty minutes off."

Molly came running out of the lodge. Her wild red curls out of control, mimicking her body language. "Stone, please oh please tell me everything's going as planned in the lodge. The rehearsal dinner is in the main dining room and well, it looks like you haven't touched it."

"Tomorrow I'm going to need everyone to use the back entrance. We are doing demo on the upstairs walls, opening it for an open concept welcoming staircase. I have honey colored oak floors being installed on Tuesday.

Megan and I are going out to look at the furniture next week, and the windows have all been replaced. The shiplap covered walls are being painted a milky white today. I'm finishing up the main area and pulling the décor together, then I'll do some work on the guest suites."

"Oh my gosh, I love you. Megan, isn't he the best?"

Stone turned to Megan, raised one eyebrow and said, "Go on, tell her how great I am."

"He's okay. And since when are we going furniture hunting next week?"

"I hired a crew to finish the floors so I could free up some time to go with you."

"Crew? Is that more money?" asked a frantic Molly.

"I gave you my word on the price. I'm a man of my word." What she didn't know was he went against doctor's orders and took on this job, which was getting bigger by the minute, and hiring a crew was coming out of his pocket. Work wasn't about making money anymore.

"Stone, how can I ever thank you?" Molly said.

"Right now, the look on your face is thanks enough."

Molly kissed Megan and hurried out the door. Megan turned to Stone, "Should I be involved tomorrow? It sounds like a lot of changes are happening."

"Not unless you're interested in busting down some walls. It's very therapeutic."

"Fine, I'm in."

"Really? Okay then, if your back is up to it. You'll need to wear a hard hat and I suggest something like jeans, you know causal."

She shook her head then walked toward her suite. Since when did she wear a hard hat or want to demolish property?

Chapter Ten

The next day, Megan slipped on some faded low-rise jeans, a navy Ralph Lauren tee shirt and her pink suede lace up booties. She sent the girls out the back door to play with Maxie, then headed toward the sound of loud power tools.

"Hey there, back feeling better?" Stone said, wearing plastic glasses and his yellow hard hat. He knelt down and handing her a hat and pair of glasses.

"Yes, thank you. I'm ready to bust some walls as you so eloquently put it."

They headed up to the second floor. "Now this wall is coming down. We'll build some rustic wood railings in its place. We're going to frame out the supporting beam with barnwood, so this is all coming down." He picked up a heavy sledge hammer and handed it to her. "Go on then, take some of your anger out on that wall."

Megan was surprised at the weight of the hammer. She slung it back and dug deep into the wall, sending cracking dry wall crushing to the ground. A smile quickly covered her face. "That was fun."

"I'm glad you think so, because this wall spans across five guest rooms in each direction."

Stone stood next to her as they beat on the drywall until a piece opened up to the second-floor ceiling in the main room. Megan's eyes widened. "Look, you can see everything, the glass wall, the fireplace, the entry. This view is going to be amazing."

Stone, with his eyes focused on her, "It sure is," he said with a coy smile.

Megan worked until lunch then gathered the girls to eat. Even though the workers had taken a break, Stone gave Sophie and Olivia hard hats to wear at lunch. Olivia loved that it matched her boots. Sophie asked if she could put rhinestones on hers.

Stone spent the remainder of the day putting up drywall in the newly opened main lodge area. With the walls knocked down, the second-floor rooms were on full display. The open floor plan gave a wide-open view from upstairs, allowing the guests to look over a wooden banister to the exposed beamed ceiling, a full glass wall with views of the lit mountains, and a roaring two-story tall fireplace. Their vision had begun to take shape. As the project unfolded, his pride elevated. For the first time in a very long time, he felt a sense of joy back in his work. After a long day, he packed up his tools and prepared to leave, until he turned to see little Olivia trudging in the front door in her yellow boots, struggling with the weight of a red bucket she was teetering between both hands. With splashes of water christening the front foyer, the little girl barely noticed him.

"Whatcha got there, little Red?"

"I think it's a goldfish. Do you think I can keep him?" she said, her big green eyes filled with hope.

"Hmm let me have a look in the bucket." He studied the small fish that by now had nearly swam himself into a heart attack with fear. "Do you have a fish tank?" he asked, taking the heavy bucket from her and setting it down carefully along the fireplace.

"No, not really. I have a glass bowl that mommy let me keep from my real house," she said, her voice trailing a bit.

"Your real house?"

"That's the one I used to live in with mommy, daddy, and Sophie."

"I see."

"Daddy left us. I don't know why." She put the bucket down and sat down on the stone slab seat in front of the massive fireplace. "Can I ask you a question, Mr. Stone?"

"Sure can, and you can just call me Stone."

Her eyes filled with water beneath fogged glasses, looked up at him with a sadness that tugged hard at his heart. In a small voice she said, "Am I a nerd?"

"Why would you ask that?"

"Maybe that's why daddy left us," she said, her eyes turned down to the floor and a tiny finger catching a tear as it rolled down her freckled cheek.

Stone got down on one knee and took her tiny hand in his. "Do you know what a nerd is?"

"No," she said, pushing her oversized glasses up on her button nose and sniffling.

"It's a really cool kid that embraces being different. Do you know they used to call me a nerd?"

"No way," she said looking up at him with wide eyes magnified by the large glass they hid behind.

"Yes way, scout's honor. You see, I was different when I was little. I liked to build things and then take them apart, and then build them a different way."

"You did?"

"Yep. While other kids were out playing tag, I was building, and guess what?"

"What?"

"It made me a very successful adult. Do you know what that means?"

"No."

"It means I can buy as much ice cream as I want. I can have as many pets as I want, and I love what I do every day. And you know what Little Red? I have a feeling if you keep being a little different, you will be very successful, too."

"You really think so?" she said with a smile so broad it met up with the edges of her glasses.

"I do. One more thing, Olivia. You are definitely not the reason your daddy left you. You're an amazing little girl who I just happen to like to hang out with." What Stone didn't know was Megan had walked in behind them just in time to hear the last part. The sight of Stone's large frame wearing his yellow hard hat, work boots, plaid shirt and tool belt around his waist, down on one knee in front of Olivia made her heart swell.

Megan cleared her throat, "Hey little bug, what's in the bucket?"

"It's my friend," she said, trying to hold the bucket up for Megan to see.

"Olivia, how many times have we discussed no bringing home friends."

"But mommy, I can't put him back, he'll freeze."

Megan's patience was rail thin. "I don't have time for this tonight."

"How about I hold onto your buddy until you two work this out?"

"Would you? I don't think he eats much," said Olivia with grateful eyes.

"Got it."

"Thanks Stone, I have to get these two to bed."

"Ok I have a few things to finish up, then I'll be on my way. Night Little Red."

Olivia blew a kiss in the bucket then rushed to Stone's side and threw her tiny arms around his thighs. "Thank you."

Megan's heart felt like the remnants of chocolate on a summer's day. She headed back to her suite to bathe the two girls. She read them, *Santa and the Train*, then settled them into bed. Startled by a loud bang she headed back out to the main room, surprised to find Stone gathering up some wood that had fallen from the mantle.

"Sorry about that. I'm a bit of a perfectionist when it comes to details. The smallest thing will catch my eye and I just can't leave until it's right. I'll be heading out, but we do need to talk about the decor."

"Nothing to talk about. I think the modern luxe, with crystal chandeliers and clean lines will be perfect. I just need some inspiration for the actual Christmas décor."

"Really, I'm thinking more rustic, weathered wood, vintage lodge feel."

Megan shrugged her shoulders then fell onto the sofa. "If I'm being honest, I can't seem to get the feel of Christmas this year. I'm blank."

Stone sat next to her and said, "When I take on a renovation, I've learned I need to stay open to possibilities. Sometimes a blank slate is exactly what you need. What you need is some Christmas inspiration."

Megan popped up. "That's it! Get your coat. I know exactly what we need."

"We?" he winked.

Megan texted Maxie to keep an eye on the girls then said, "Don't make me regret this." She zipped up her white fur trimmed parka, pulled on her boots, then tucked her long black mane into a white furry hat. She led him out the door and down the long walk toward Christmas Village. The twinkling lights could be seen quarter mile down the walk.

"Where are all those lights coming from?" Stone said, eyeing the brightly lit sky.

"That is Molly's baby! It's basically the North Pole coming to Connecticut."

"How have I never seen this before?"

"You usually go out the south exit from the lodge. It's sort of hidden by Mistletoe Mountain but when the guests walk just North of the slopes, a winter wonderland appears.

"It's late so you won't find any of the workers in there, but I can give you the grand tour."

"I would like that."

Two massive gates monogrammed with the letters NP greeted them. Just inside the gates a banner read, "Welcome to Christmas Village."

"Ok so where to first? We have a Bavarian village, Santa's Workshop, a Gingerbread Bakery, Naughty and Nice Stop, Candy Cane Shop, Vintage Christmas Shop, and of course Molly's coveted Mistletoe Lane; a walkway with twinkling white lights and mistletoe clusters strung that leads to the Holly House Restaurant."

"Are you kidding me? This is the most fantastic thing I've ever seen. I feel like I'm in a Burles and Ives print. It's magical."

"It is, isn't it? I've been so caught up in my drama I haven't looked at the village through fresh eyes in a long time. I bring the kids up to help with small things, but it's usually daytime and the lights aren't the same. It's quiet tonight and there's something about it, I can't put my finger on it," she said looking up at the night sky and realizing they were standing on the walkway of Mistletoe Lane. Molly's mistletoe with tiny crystals hung just about their heads. Stone gazed up and then his eyes met hers. He leaned in just inches from her mouth when a loud power bang signaled and the lights started to close down on the back half of the village.

Megan jumped, "Timers," she said stepping back. "Come on, the front half stays on longer. They strolled past the windows and peered into the vintage themed stores. "It won't be long now until Santa makes his grand appearance." Her face softened. "This is exactly what I needed to reboot my Christmas décor ideas."

"Well this and maybe a little Christmas spirit," he said winking.

"It's November, I'm not Molly. That girl starts the Christmas season in September."

"I think we need to borrow a little of Molly's holiday enthusiasm to come up with a spectacular lodge design."

"Maybe you're right, we need to get a little festive to bring this thing to life."

Cupping one hand over his ear he said, "I'm sorry, can you repeat that? It sounded like you said I'm right."

"I believe I prefaced it with 'maybe;' the verdict is still out."

"Only a matter of time until Reagan and I win you over."

Megan shook her head. They walked back to the lodge, and as the evening temperatures began to drop, they quickened the pace. He leaned in a little to block the sharp winter chill. She smiled quietly, nestling into his arm.

"Megan, I know you're going through a lot with Chase and all, but don't let him steal your holiday."

"I'm sorry about the whole bagel nightmare," she said, feeling broken by the way Chase made her feel.

"No need to apologize, fake boyfriend has its perks. From where I sit the guy's a real jerk, don't let him talk to you that way," he said before disappearing into his truck.

Chapter Eleven

Megan tossed and turned all night remembering Stone's words. He was right. Chase had long talked down to her. Even in their marriage, he made her feel she needed to be on her 'A' game at all times; hair, makeup, the whole nine yards. If she wasn't feeling well, she felt the need to apologize for her appearance. If she gained a few pounds, he was quick to point it out. Long gone were the days of Chase and Megan, Cherrywood High's most fabulous couple. From the outside, their marriage was picture perfect because that's what Megan wanted everyone to think. Even Megan's family was stunned to learn that their relationship was in trouble when Chase's affair came to light.

She swung her long legs off the bed and summoned the courage to face his new bride today. Her babies would be fitted for their flower girl dresses. She drew a deep breath and reminded herself the quicker she got there, the sooner it would be over. Revenge dressing seemed to have a role in today's outfit choice. She needed to look good, no great. Settling on skinny jeans with heeled booties and a cream-colored angora sweater that clung in all the right places, she moved onto her makeup when she heard a voice at the door.

"Mommy, can I wear heels in daddy's wedding?" asked Sophie.

The words stung all over again, 'Daddy's wedding.' "No Sophie, Bree has pretty ballet shoes for you to wear. Where is Olivia?"

"She's filling up the tub," said Sophie nonchalantly.

"The tub, whatever for?"

"Some dumb pet she found."

"Oh no," said Megan before running down the hallway. She opened the door and found Olivia kneeling, pouring her bucket into a filled tub. "What are you doing?"

"I'm saving another friend."

"How many times do I have to tell you; you can't collect fish or whatever that is from the pond and dump them in our tub. We bathe here."

"But mommy, I can't find the bowl from our house."

"Olivia Grace, get your shoes on. And no boots," Megan said.

"Stone likes my boots," she said.

"Don't argue with me. We'll talk about this when we get home. We can't be late."

Megan cleaned up Olivia, tossed the friend into a bucket, then the three made their way to Bella's Bridal. Inside, Bree stood in the window pacing. Megan took a deep breath and unbuckled her belt. "Let's get this over with."

Sophie jumped up and down. "Look at all the princess ball gowns in the window. Can I go in mommy?"

"Go ahead, I'll get Olivia out. We'll meet you in there." Megan moved around to the rear of the car, opened the door and began unbuckling Olivia from her car seat. "Come on Olivia, what is taking you so long?" Megan said, stretching her back muscles before pulling the small girl out.

"I don't want to be in the wedding," Olivia said in a small broken voice.

"Olivia, it's one day. Is this about your boots."

"It's not my boots," the little girl said now with a full face of tears rushing down her freckled cheeks. Her chest rose and fell with each heavy breath.

"Sweetie, what are these tears about?" Megan said, collecting her in her arms. "I want daddy to marry you. Bree isn't nice. I want us to be a family again," she wailed, red spots sprinkling her pale face.

Megan fought the desire to join in the wailing, but knew she needed to put on a strong face. "My sweet little freckles, look here. We're a family. The best family ever. Daddy and Bree getting married isn't going to change you and me. You'll see baby, I promise. Now come on, I'll be with you every step of the way." She took Olivia's tiny hand and clasped it with both of her hands and squeezed tight. Megan wiped her tears, and the two headed in, hand in hand. Bree, waiting at the door, snapped at the two immediately.

"Glad you two could make it. Now go Ollie, and get in your dress."

Megan rolled her eyes at the witch and made her way to the dressing rooms, where she found Sophie in a rhinestone tiara and diamond encrusted heels. Bree's equally awful maid of honor was supposed to be helping Sophie, but sat glued to her phone.

"Sophie Marie, get those shoes off right now. Do you know how much they cost?"

"Can I get them?"

"NO, Sophie you may not."

Megan took Olivia into the dressing room and removed the dress from its wrapping. She slipped it over Olivia's head, the mounds of tulle nearly swallowed her whole. "Ridiculous," Megan mumbled as she opened the door, fully prepared to ream out the bride to be, when she saw Bree standing there in her wedding gown. The contoured shape hugged her narrow hips, accented her young perky chest and tight, high butt. She was beautiful, she was young, she was Megan's replacement. The finality of her marriage shook Megan to the core. The door opened with wedding bells jingling, behind it stood Chase his eyes fixed on Bree.

"You Bree, are the most beautiful bride that has ever walked down any aisle."

Before Bree could blast him for seeing her in her gown, Megan rushed back into the dressing room. "Are you okay, mommy?" said Olivia, still looking like a paler, sweeter version of a witch slowly melting underneath the weight of the dress. Megan wiped her eyes. "Yes baby, let's get you out of this. We're going."

Megan and Olivia stormed out of the dressing room to find Sophie and Chase practicing the daddy daughter dance, Sophie on his toes singing as they waltzed around the room. Olivia ran to the front door, Megan in high pursuit, followed by Chase.

"Where's she going? She didn't get fitted," said Bree, both hands on her teenage boy hips.

"We're leaving. I'll have my seamstress fix this atrocity. Come on, Sophie, now."

Chase grabbed Megan's arm, sending a volt of electricity to her heart. "Wait, let me bring the girls home."

"I want to go with mommy," Olivia said, both tiny hands clamped around Megan's arm.

"I want to stay with daddy and Bree in the princess shop," said Sophie.

"I'll bring her home after dinner. Please Megan, it's so important for Bree and Sophie to bond."

"Okay, but have her home by eight. I'm serious, Chase."

"Great, and thanks Meggie."

Megan hurried the little girl to the car. Her hands trembled as she attempted to stuff the key into the ignition. She prayed it would start and her get away would at least be dignified. "How about we get some dinner, Pumpkin?"

"Can we get Bobbie's?"

Bobbie's, an old-fashioned burger joint, was a favorite of the girls. "That sounds perfect."

Megan and Olivia headed to the little burger joint. They sat in a booth with a jukebox, and ordered vanilla milkshakes and cheeseburgers with an order of golden fries, served in a 1950's Chevy cardboard car. Olivia pushed a quarter into the jukebox, pushing the button for

Build Me Up Buttercup. Her and Megan sang together, swaying in their booth.

Megan took the sweet little girl in her arms, "It's going to be alright bug, you'll see."

Olivia nestled in close to Megan's embrace.

Feeling better, they headed home. She pulled into the lodge and parked. A very quiet Olivia had fallen fast asleep. Megan opened the door and saw her little freckle faced baby's eyes closed behind her thick glasses dangling sideways on her button nose. Megan unbuckled her and lifted her out. The twisting action sent a twinge of pain down her left leg. Frozen, unable to move from pain, she canvassed the lot to see if Maxie was home. On Friday's, Maxie usually helped out at the restaurant, then spent the night in the apartment above the eatery. Panic quickly overcame her. She tried to lean in and put the little girl back down, but excruciating pain shot straight down her leg. Car lights pierced the chilly night as they made their way down the long road toward the lodge. *Maxie, oh please be Maxie*, she prayed. As the lights got closer, she realized it was a truck. Not just any truck, but his truck. For the first time, she was happy to see Stone.

He pulled in and spotted Megan with Olivia in her arms leaning against the van door. "Megan," he called out.

"Stone, I need help," she said, hating the needy voice that just squeaked out of her. He came quickly, taking the little girl from her arms.

"I got her. Here, lean on me. I'll get you in the house."

"What are you doing here?"

"I left my phone. I took it out to make a note of some measurements for a little surprise I have in mind, and forgot to put it back in my pocket. I didn't think you would mind if I swung by and picked it up."

"No, I'm actually grateful to see you, for once."

"Thanks Regan," he said as he put his arm around her waist and helped her into the lodge. "Now where do you want Olivia?"

"Can you put her in her bedroom? I know it's a lot to ask, but I just can't."

"Okay, which one?"

"Down the hall, make a right, room 115 is our suite."

****

He carried the girl down the hallway to the suite marked 115. He opened the door to a charming, brightly colored room. Megan had decorated the living area in teal and cream with a few touches of pink, feminine and cheerful. He opened the first door on the right and found what was obviously Sophie's room, a mix of hot and light pinks, tiaras, boas and ballet slippers. He closed that door and moved to the one immediately next door. He opened the door and found a queen size bed wrapped in white with an array of white fur pillows tossed across the headboard. A large modern silver dresser sat directly across from the bed. A sash hanging from the mirror read 'Ms. Winter Princess.' He quickly closed the door and moved to the one across the hall. Inside, a bright sunny yellow room, filled with fish drawings and four pairs of yellow boots. "Bingo." He laid the little girl in her bed and removed her thick glasses. She looked smaller than usual in the big bed.

Pulling the covers up, he closed the light and headed toward the door. He made his way toward the main room of the lodge where he found Megan lying on the sofa.

"Do you have ice on that?" he asked.

"No, I barely made it here."

He went into the kitchen and wrapped a bag of frozen peas in a towel and brought it back. "Frozen peas are a contractor's best friend." She smiled. "Here, may I?" he asked sitting next to her.

"As long as you don't try anything funny."

He gently rolled her to her left side, then began rubbing her low back on the right side. As much as she wanted to protest, she couldn't. It was the first real relief she felt since this awful day began. The door to the suite opened. Chase and a sleeping Sophie walked in. Megan jumped up, then moaned.

"What's he doing here?"

"He, you mean Stone, my boyfriend."

"He can't be here. The girls live here. You need to clean up your act. This midlife crisis has gotten out of control, and it stops now."

Sophie picked her head up and asked, "Daddy, why are you yelling?"

"Sorry baby, mommy has me a little wound up." He placed her down. She rubbed her eyes and looked at Megan.

"Mommy be nice to daddy."

"Sophie Marie, go to bed. This is grown up talk. I'll be in to tuck you in a minute." The little girl kissed Chase on the cheek. Then she headed to bed, but not before giving Megan the evil eye. Again, he had managed to swoop in and become Mr. Wonderful, all while making her into the bad guy.

"I think it's time for you to leave, too," said Stone.

"I'll leave when my wife and I are finished."

"I'm not your wife. Now, I think you should leave."

Chase fixed his gaze on Stone, "You'll tire of her. I don't know what took me so long."

Megan picked up the throw pillow from the sofa and hurled it at him, hitting him squarely in the face. "Get out."

Chase turned and marched toward the door, then slammed it hard behind him, sending a picture of the girls crashing to the floor.

"Are you sure it was field hockey and not football?" said Stone, picking up the picture and laying it on the table.

"My aim is pretty good, isn't it? I have to tuck Sophie in bed."

"Do you want me to check her? Chances are she's asleep."

"You're probably right." She tried to stand back up and let out a moan before dropping back to the sofa.

"You are benched from practice and games until this thing subsides. Do you need help to your room?"

"Can you be trusted?"

"After I saw your arm, I think I can be," he said, giving her a wink.

Rylee Ridolfi

Stone gently picked her up effortlessly. His strong arms securely held her close to him as he made his way down the hallway. He put her down just outside the door.

"Thank you. And Stone, you just might not be the worst contractor a girl could have."

"You like me," he winked before heading down the hallway.

Chapter Twelve

The sound of drilling jarred Megan awake. Her first thought was at eight o'clock on a Saturday morning, anyone using loud hand tools should be shot. Megan crawled out of bed and made her way to the center of the suite to find Sophie and Olivia in a full-on tug of war. Now, instead of killing Stone, she wanted to kiss him, for the peaceful sound of metal grinding. *Kiss him,* what was wrong with her? Why did her mind keep circling around to his lips? *Stop, focus, hired help,* she reminded herself. *He's like a pool boy, of course that's it. Everyone lusted after their pool boy.* Distracted by the girls' high-pitched rant, she regrouped. "What's going on?"

"Sophie took Suppy," said Olivia still tugging mercilessly on the poor, beat up stuffed animal.

"She got salamander juice on one of Barbie's shoes," said Sophie, pulling hard.

"Enough," Megan said, "Both of you to the couch." She took the tired looking sloth and shook it at both girls. "What has gotten into you two? This is not how families act."

"We aren't a family anymore. We're broken," said Sophie.

"Not true. We're just a new version of us. We all have to work together. You two are different. Molly and I were very different. When we were young, we didn't always get along, but as you get older, you'll see, sisters are everything."

Sophie sat with her arms crossed, nose in the air, not unlike what Megan would have done at that age. Olivia sat hands folded, little feet swinging off the couch with her eyes fixed on the limp sloth.

"Here Olivia, you take Suppy. Sophie, let's see if we can get whatever it is off Barbie's shoe." Before they could make it to the sink, there was a knock on the door.

"Hey sis, it's Maxie."

Megan opened the door and said, "Thank goodness, I'm in the middle of unsuccessful peace talks."

"Don't sweat it, it'll pass. Do you remember you and Molly? You freaked when she used one of your good skirts to make a welcome flag for her little toy holiday village. It was seriously World War III."

"They're so different, but the thing that makes it worse is Chase ripping us apart. They feel divided. I'm trying, but I don't know, Max. They seem like they are always at odds."

"Look," Maxie said pointing to the two sitting on the floor playing a board game. "It passed. Now onto important issues, like Mark."

"I'm not even asking," Megan said working her way to the kitchen grabbing three bowls and spoons. "Did you eat? We have Cheerios, Fruity Pebbles and Lucky Charms."

"For the record, none of that counts as food, and don't change the subject."

Megan pulled the coffee from the cabinet and filled the pot with water. "I know you'll never say no to coffee," she said, placing two mugs along with cream and sugar on the table. "Girls, come get breakfast."

"Eat away, I can talk, you chew and listen. Mark is forty-one, never married and a business man that travels to exotic places."

The girls grabbed their bowls and asked if they could eat in front of the TV. Megan had relaxed her rules since the divorce. After handing them both a juice and bowls of cereal, she sent them packing then filled the mugs with coffee. She sat down next to Maxie and asked, "And I should care, why?"

"Because you two have been getting along really well," Maxie said, dumping a mound of sugar into her mug.

"MAXIE!"

"No biggie, I just responded to a few messages he sent us."

"Us, Maxie, *we* are not dating. *I* am, if I even decide to. And I'm not feeling it."

"Okay, well since we got that out of our system, you two are meeting tonight just for a quick drink at Sammie's. Seven o'clock. Come on Meggie, give him a chance."

"Why?"

"Because he's hot," Maxie said, bobbing her shoulders up and down.

"You said Stone was hot."

Maxie raised her eyebrows and lowered her head, "He is. Don't even tell me those eyes haven't made you wonder about what's under that shirt?"

"Maxie, eyes do not make you wonder what is under a shirt."

"Hmm, must just be me."

"Alright, let me see him," Megan said, swirling her spoon around the cloudy brew.

Maxie smiled, pulling her phone out with the picture already loaded.

Megan's eyes widened with surprise, "Wow, he is hot. I mean look at those abs and that smile. You know I love wavy hair. Okay, maybe."

"Here's his number if you change your mind. But trust me, you won't."

"You're impossible. Have you made this your one-woman crusade?"

"Things are slow in the romance department for me, so I'm living vicariously through you."

Megan's face turned serious, "Is everything okay with you and Tony?"

"Yeah, Tony just works so much. He gets home late and is always tired. We don't spend much time together."

Megan's spine straightened. Her face washed with worry.

"Don't, I know what you're thinking. Tony isn't Chase. Not all men cheat Meggie. Try not to be so quick to judge."

"I'm sorry Max, it's just that I didn't see it coming. Looking back, I wonder how I missed it. Maybe because I didn't want to see it."

"You're better off Meggie. The right guy won't hurt you."

Another knock at the door. "Meggie, it's dad," said Edward through the door.

The girls ran to the door. "Pop Pop!" they cheered. Edward McKenna made his way through the door and picked up both girls, one in each arm. After the divorce, Chase disappeared and Edward stepped in. He made sure to take the girls every Saturday for a few hours. Both girls adored him.

"Silvia made some cookies for them. We have big plans for the day. First, we are going to the zoo."

"Isn't it cold for the zoo?" asked Megan.

"They have several exciting events planned in the inside arena."

Olivia jumped up and down. Sophie crossed her arms.

"I thought you might react that way Princess Sophie, but what you don't know is the zoo is having a special, 'Play with Snow White and all her animal friends' today," said Edward kneeling down in front of Sophie.

"Really?" she said. "Can I wear my tiara?"

"Not only can you wear your tiara, but I hear they have sparkly wands there, too."

"Mommy hurry, let's get dressed. I want to wear my pink skirt, with my pink furry jacket."

"Hey dad, did I ever tell you you're the best?" Megan said.

"Not nearly enough," he said, kissing her on the forehead.

Megan helped the girls get ready and made sure to bundle them up. "I hear the temperature is going to drop throughout the weekend."

"Then it's hot cocoa back at Pop Pop's place after the zoo. Kiss your mommy. Let's get this show on the road."

"Wait, I need my zoology book to identify the animals."

"Nerd," said Sophie.

"Sophie, apologize to your sister."

Olivia had already rushed back to her room. She returned a few minutes later with a hardback book, she slipped into her yellow backpack, alongside Suppy.

"Have a good time. Be good for Pop Pop and no fighting."

After the three had left, Megan cleaned up the half-eaten bowls of cereal and sat down to finish her lukewarm coffee. Maxie now on her second cup wasted no time in picking up the hot contractor talks.

"I hear you and Stone are going furniture shopping today."

Megan grimaced, "Yes, we sort of disagree about the décor. I want modern; he wants more rustic. Our plan is to blend the two."

"Sounds sexy."

"It's not."

"Come on, a little flirty fun never hurt anyone," Maxie said, raising her shoulders up and down.

"What is it with you, you have me dating Mark and now I'm flirting with Stone?"

"Are you? Flirting with Stone?"

"Heavens no. Maxie you know I would never go for a guy like him."

"Right. Gorgeous, talented, funny. Hell no, what was I thinking?"

"That's not what I mean. He's," she paused, "You know, blue collar. I like men with class and money. I'm sorry, it's who I am. Blame Silvia, she taught me to like the finer things in life and I won't settle."

"I didn't say marry him, just have a romp."

"A romp? Do I look like the kind of girl that romps with construction workers? You like the bad boys, not me."

"Just saying, that booty seems like it's pretty good for romping."

"Maxie Ann, I need to get dressed, you need to take a cold shower."

"Okay I'm leaving. Wear something sexy. You never know. Slumming can be fun."

"GO."

Megan looked through her closet with angst. She definitely wasn't going for sexy. She chose a pair of black leggings, a long black turtleneck sweater, and boots that came just above the knee. She pulled her long black hair into a sleek, low ponytail and dusted taupe and brown shadows over her large, dark eyes, a few coats of mascara made them undeniably the sexiest thing about her. She grabbed her gray and black snakeskin Dolce and Gabbana bag and headed out to the door. What was Maxie thinking suggesting that she finds that man desirable? Never. She found designer suits hand tailored to a man's body desirable. Shiny black dress shoes, crisp white button downs with brightly colored ties, now *that* was desirable. She smiled at how different she and Maxie were when it came to men.

As she headed down the hall, she heard that awful country music blaring from his radio, yet in a strange way she felt a twinge of excitement knowing he would be right around the corner. *Oh no*, she stopped immediately, conjuring up images of Rigby Jones, the chubby boy who lived down the street from her growing up. When those first few notes of the annoying ice cream truck song rang out, his plump little body froze, his eyes filled with desire, his lips smacked with anticipation knowing the sugary calorie laden frozen treats would follow. Country music had become her ice cream truck. As soon as she heard the first notes of those grating love sick, beer drinking lyrics, her cheeks flushed, her pulse rose, her mind spun, her eyes filled with desire, her lips smacked drunk with sweet anticipation knowing he'd be there. Fanning herself, she felt instant guilt having judged poor Rigby all those years. *It's not our fault,* she thought. *We are conditioned like Pavlov's dogs. The tempting vice that seduces us unhinges a person appealing to senses beyond our control. Snap out of it, Megan.* Odd, she thought, who knew a man could evoke such emotion. Manolo Blahniks, yes, the savory mix of sweet and salty the week before your period, yes, but a man? No; It was mind blowing. Mind blowing in a bad way, of course. *He is the enemy*, she reminded herself. Play it cool, nonchalant. That was the plan, until she saw him standing behind the counter in the kitchen, naked.

Quick, she instructed herself, *think of something that would kill the stirrings of excitement, an unexpected rise in the number on the scale, the cancellation of Sex and the City, the return of clogs*. It was no use. Those abs like ripples in the ocean led down to the very spot where the counter met his well-defined hip bones. His chest, broad and muscular. Dreamily, she allowed herself to ponder, "Why is his skin the warm golden color of summer, Italian maybe?" she said, not realizing that her thoughts had slipped out of her mouth.

"Yes, I am Italian, it comes from my mother's side," he said with a delicious smile.

"Oh my gosh, can you read my mind?"

"Sometimes, but it's definitely easier when you are speaking out loud."

"More importantly, why are you naked in my kitchen?"

"I've never had a complaint about being naked in anyone's kitchen before, except I'm not actually naked." He stepped out from behind the counter wearing his faded Levi's a few inches below his navel. She felt a flush of heat rise from within her as her eyes traveled down to the top of his jeans.

"I was painting a few sample swatches on a board to give you options when Gloria marched right through them. I tried to pick her up, but she kicked the can of paint, which I caught. I managed to save the floor, but not my shirt. I thought maybe if I put some water on it right away, it may help."

Still looking at the waist, she summoned up the words to offer to throw it in the washer for him. "I, do you, we have a washer down the hall. You know that right. I'm trying to say…"

With a smoldering half smile he stopped her from her verbal roller coaster and said, "That's not necessary. I have an extra flannel in the truck. It's a hazard of the job."

Regaining her head, she said, "Yes, it sounds very dangerous you know with beasts like Gloria threatening your attire." Megan turned her glance away from the tanned canvas of his torso, toward the fat pug sleeping by the fireplace.

"You have no idea the hazards I've endured."

"Fortunately, you seem relatively unscathed by this one. Where are those paint swatches?" she managed to say somewhat breathlessly.

He walked toward her, and her heart pounded. She wondered if he could tell. His body brushed hers as he pulled a board up and placed it on the counter. His skin glistened from little sprays of water that were left behind from his washing episode. His bicep rippled as he held the board up and named each color. Truth be told, she hadn't heard a word he said. Her mind was racing with thoughts of 'romping'. What was happening to her? She wasn't the kind of girl who had thoughts like this, especially not with his type. It was Maxie getting in her head. *Pull it together Megan,* it doesn't matter if he has a great body, not your type, as a few notes of Luke Bryan's Strip It Down belted out from the stereo rendering her speechless, drawing her tongue to her lips, feeling a bead of sweat burrowing under her turtleneck.

"It's highly uncharacteristic of you not to have an opinion."

"You look hot. I mean, I'm hot. I mean, that color is just too hot. You know, too warm of a color."

He raised one eyebrow and studied her. "Are you feeling okay?"

"Yes, long day."

"It's barely ten o'clock."

"Are we going to analyze my mood or pick a darn paint color?"

"Mood is rarely something that needs analyzing with you. Just a color will do."

"I like the washed red along with the creamy white color. How about we paint one wall behind the desk red and keep the rest neutral to really pick up all the natural colored pine? The widened staircase should be a shade darker, maybe we use Special Walnut," she said, grateful he hadn't picked up on the 'I want you so bad I can't breathe' mood she currently fell victim to.

"And she's back. I like it. Now the furniture, I was thinking we'd stick with the warmth theme."

"I think we can come to some agreement on that. Now you should put a shirt on so we can romp, I mean shop."

"Okay I'll grab it in the truck and pull around to grab you."

Megan rushed to the mirror and patted some pressed powder on her flushed cheeks. *This is going to be fine, really. Just furniture shopping, two professional adults who don't even like each other. Absolutely no flirting. What could happen?*

A honk told her it was time to go. She headed out and tried to avoid eye contact with those baby blues. Slipping into the passenger seat, she felt her pulse elevate when that cursed country music permeated the air. Almost immediately, the darn music had her mind conjuring up an order for one set of luscious lips, one hard set of abs. Her order was interrupted when he reached over and pushed on her buckle. His breath brushed her neck.

"What are you doing?" she said faintly.

"I've been meaning to get that darn buckle fixed, but it's usually just me. I don't want you straining your back."

"Right yes, buckles are important for saving lives." *That was so lame what am I saying?*

"So, I was thinking of Chelsea's Furniture Barn. You okay with starting there?"

"Wow, are you serious? I love Chelsea's. It's upscale, and the quality is unmatched. You surprise me."

"Why, because I know good furniture?"

"I don't know it's just so swanky in there. It doesn't seem like your style."

"And what is *my style*?"

"I don't know, more down home, I guess."

"Yes, I carve my furniture out of recycled trees I tear down with my bare hands."

"I didn't mean that."

"What you did mean is that I'm not as good as the uptight, white-collar snobs whose company you prefer."

"No, I," she stumbled a bit as she tried to reword what he just said, yet in essence he was spot on with what she meant. "You are just more, you know, cabin in the woods, and I'm more Chalet on the mountain. Anyway, I'm glad we're going."

He looked at her with a half-smile. "Almost killed you didn't it, to choke that out?"

She tried to tune out the music until they turned onto Mulberry Drive. The streets were lined in brightly colored orange, yellow and red mums. Pumpkins large and small filled wheelbarrows, crates, and store windows. Pilgrims and cornucopias aplenty. Autumn was in full bloom.

"Look how beautifully the town is decorated."

"Do you like fall?"

"Yes, it reminds me of family, Thanksgiving and all. Do you have any family around?"

"No, my mom passed," he paused, "My dad was heartbroken, his world had ended. Our relationship just crumbled after."

"I'm so sorry. That's amazing that a man can feel that kind of love so deeply."

"Not all men are incapable of loving someone with their whole being. Chase is a poor excuse for a man. Don't give up on the whole male population."

"I can't imagine being loved that way."

He looked at her and smiled, "You deserve to be."

She could feel her face blushing as they turned into Chelsea's parking lot.

He pulled the truck in and parked. He grabbed the keys and hopped out. As he headed around to the passenger side to open the door, he could see her struggling with the buckle. "Here, let me help," he said as he leaned in, pressing his body slightly across hers. He fumbled a bit then the buckle broke loose. Pulling back, he realized her ponytail had tangled in his suede puffer vest button.

"Oh sorry, here let me try and untangle it." She moved closer, "Ouch it's pulling. He moved closer; their lips were inches apart. She swore her breath had stopped as her mind raced with thoughts of kissing him. She could see in his eyes that he was feeling the same thing. He tilted his head a bit, their eyes locked. The sound of a car horn honking startled them both. An angry patron trying to open the door in the spot next to them rolled down the window and shouted, "Get a stinking room." Stone pulled his truck door in closer to let the jerk get out.

"Thank goodness, it's all untangled," Megan said a bit winded.

"Great," he said as she stepped out of the car, neither acknowledging the clear physical attraction or the rude stranger's suggestion. They calmly walked in the double wide barn doors that led to one of the city's finest showrooms. A tall, thin man with pronounced hip swing strolled up and introduced himself as Chartreuse. Stone raised an eyebrow, Megan stretched out her hand. Chartreuse took it with both hands and said, "Darling, the adventure begins. I'm your furniture fairy godfather for the next few hours. Together we will make beautiful rooms, yes?"

"Sounds delightful," she said.

"Sounds like we are in a musical," said Stone.

"Don't pay any attention to him. We need to start with comfy sofas. And Chartreuse, this is going to be a big order."

"Sweet peach, that's my favorite kind. This way loves," he said sauntering down the aisle.

"I'm more of a loner when it comes to picking out my furniture. How about we give you a shout when we're close," said Stone trying to avert his eyes from the awkward swing of Chartreuses' hips.

"Nonsense, love, Chartreuse knows all. Trust in me."

They walked down a row and turned left, which was right before a staircase that led to the aisles of sofas, chaises and loveseats. "Here we are, in sofa heaven. What is the palette we're searching for?"

"We're searching for something dark, welcoming, comfy, yet durable. It says 'you're home'," said Stone.

"Actually, we are looking for something white, chic that says you've arrived," Megan said.

"Yummy, we have conflicting styles but fear not, I have the answer," Chartreuse said, his arms both stretched out toward a warm luggage color, rustic yet rich, in a soft leather.

Stone saw the buttery caramel luggage colored sectional and rushed toward it, Megan following close behind. The two plopped onto the sofa, Megan on the chaise, Stone next to her.

"This is so wide. I believe two could fit on this chaise," she said, stretching out.

"Is that an invitation?" said Stone. She tossed a throw pillow at him.

"You two are in perfect sync, like Bonnie and Clyde, Sonny and Cher, Fred and Ginger. Love is written all over your pretty faces, mwah," he said tossing air kisses to them.

"Oh, heavens no, no, no. Sonny and Cher? No, we are just working together. I would never, I mean, I don't find him the least bit attractive, whatsoever. No attraction, nothing," she said,

In a similar protest Stone joined in, "No way, not if she were the last woman on the planet. There are trolls I find more appealing."

Chartreuse listened with one eyebrow raised and both arms tightly crossed.

Out of the corner of her eye, Megan spotted Chase and Bree coming down the elegant staircase, heading right toward them. Without thinking she reached across the chaise, took the back of Stone's neck and pulled him close, then pressed her lips against his. The two locked lips until they heard Chase's voice in the background.

Chartreuse' eyes widened, Stone's eyes closed, Chase's eyes filled with fire.

"Megan, what the heck?" Chase said loudly.

"Chase. Are you following me?"

"Why would I do that?"

"I don't know, every time I look up, you're there, like a bad penny," Megan said, releasing her firm grip from Stone's neck.

"Funny because every time I look up, you're making out with him," he said his eyes furrowing.

Chartreuse cocked his head and sent a raised eyebrow toward Megan.

"We're buying a bed for our love nest, right babe?" Bree chimed in.

"Great, we are buying a sofa, so how about you move on," Megan said.

"We aren't done here, Megan. We need to talk," Chase said his shoulders squared. Bree took his hand as if she had missed the entire interaction and drug him away.

As the two marched off, Chase's face fuming, Chartreuse placed his right hand across his chin and his left hand on his hip, "No attraction, last woman on earth, eh?"

"Oh that, it was nothing. I mean, Chase is my ex. He left me for that witch. Now can we carry on?"

"If you say so love."

"We love the color. Does it come with matching chairs? I think we are going to need two sectionals and one…" Stone said before he leaned over and smacked his lips on Megan's. She opened her eyes wide to see Caroline Bisset and her football star approaching. Megan wrapped one leg around his and giggled before resuming the kiss.

"Megan?" Caroline said in her annoying high-pitched voice.

Rylee Ridolfi

"Hey Caroline. Wow, twice in one week. What a coincidence."

"Megan, is that you?" asked Charles. "Holy field goals girl, you look hot," said the jock, moving closer. "How the heck are you?"

"Charles, good to see you," she said, untangling her leg and sitting up straight.

"Nah, it's Chuck now. Come here girl, let me give you a hug. Wow, Chase is a real idiot if you want my opinion."

"She doesn't want your opinion," said Caroline. "Stone, right?" she said, extending a hand.

"Yes, good to see you again," Stone answered.

"We recently moved back to town. Maybe we could all get together for a drink," said Charles.

"Charles, I'm sure they're way too busy to have drinks with us, since every time we see them, they seem to be in some type of cocoon."

Chartreuse again raised an eyebrow and shot a curious look at Megan.

"We're just busy with the lodge and all. I'll give you a call when things slow down," Megan said.

"Come Charles," said Caroline, ushering him away.

Both Megan and Stone leaned back on the couch. Chartreuse folded his arms, one eyebrow raised, a foot tapping and said, "Ok 'not attracted to each other couple', is there anyone else that may invoke a smooch session? Oh look, there's the UPS guy, or maybe Ethel from delivery. Anything? No?" He waited, "We good to proceed then?"

"We'll take it," they both answered at the same time.

"Mm hmm, you two have more heat than two chinchillas in hell, just saying."

Stone ignored him and said, "Chartreuse, I need a specific piece. Hard to find, but I believe this is the shop that could locate it for us."

"I'm all tingly, don't keep me in suspense. I live for these challenges."

"It's a coffee table that has rustic logs as the feet. I'm going to replace the top with snowshoes."

"Oh, bless my heart, that gives me the image of being in a cabin on a snowy mountain top."

"Exactly what we hope to evoke," said Stone.

"We?" Megan said both hands on her hips. "Chic, luxurious, remember? Crawl out of your redneck mountain man mode and focus."

"Crawl out of your Ms. Moneybags mode and look at the project for what it is, a snowy mountain retreat. We aren't decorating the Ritz."

"We aren't decorating at all. I am. So Chartreuse, there is no need for you to look."

"If I may interject?" Chartreuse said with one finger up.

"You may not," said Megan abruptly. "Now, can we please place this order."

"This way," he said, as he headed toward the register.

Stone and Megan said nothing as she paid for the pieces. Chartreuse wrote the order and processed it, thanked them, and handed them his card.

"Now things are a bit testy, but you two are definitely in sync. Listen to Chartreuse. I not only have the ability to decorate like an HGTV star, but I'm an expert in love. Some people have intuition, I've been gifted with sextuition, the ability to see undeniable chemistry. And my meter is ringing off the hook kids. Don't fight it, give it a go. You know, take it for a test drive, it may stall out like an old, hollowed out fifty Chevy, or rev with endless delight like a Maserati. Only one way to find out," he winked.

"Maserati's are overrated," said Stone. "Keep a lookout for my table."

Megan stormed off toward the car. Stone followed.

The car ride home was icy. Stone blared his country music and Megan plugged her ears. When they pulled into the lodge, Megan opened her door and jumped out, slamming it behind her. Stone drove off before the door even met the metal frame.

Megan, in all the fighting, had completely forgotten she had agreed to a date tonight. She needed to shift gears. Edward had called saying the girls wanted to sleep over so she could get ready in peace. Edward and Silvia had been godsends since Chase left. He had agreed to every other weekend visitation, but never followed through. She had picked up the pieces and filled in the voids for them, and loved them enough for two parents, but still the occasional overnight at her parents allowed her to be an adult. Tonight, she would be an adult. Perhaps Mark was a man she could be an adult with, unlike Stone Reynolds. Impossible Neanderthal, thinking he had some say in the décor.

Memo to self, talk to Molly about him overstepping his boundaries.

Molly would straighten him out then everything in the design universe would be as it should. She opened up the Plenty of Fish site and screeched when she saw the men who were trying to talk with her. At least Mark was hot. She was hot, or at least she used to be. *No*, she reminded herself she still was. She enjoyed handsome men by her side. It wasn't a sin, just a preference. She pecked away at the site until she brought up her conversation with Mark, which Maxie had orchestrated.

She thought about Maxie going on about how hot Stone is; Stone Reynolds was unpolished in his worn Levi's and work boots. She doubted he even owned a tie. His scruff just short enough to reveal those dimples didn't make him hot. Certainly not, it made him unkempt. An image of him shirtless in the kitchen brought a flush to her cheeks again. So what, he had nice abs, but so did Mark. No, Mark's abs were exceptional. She read the messages. He seemed smart, funny, and had thick, wavy hair. Yes, he was far more interesting than Stone.

She slipped on a pair of black skinny jeans and a gray wide-neck sweater. It was loose, yet the way the left sleeve dangled closely to falling off her shoulder, teasing just a hint of skin was just enough. Tall black suede boots and she was out the door. Sammy's, the local bar was known for the best wings in the area. Maybe if the drink went well, they would share a plate of honey barbeque wings, her favorite. She smiled with hope that a great date might offer.

Parking was always a problem at the beloved bar. She didn't mind the two-block walk. The November air was perfect- crisp, and cool with the smell of wood burning stoves filling the air. Pumpkins and jack-o-lanterns lined porches. The night sky was quiet and still. She turned the corner to see the black door of Sammy's adorned with an orange and gold wreath. Her stomach fluttered with possibility. Inside, the dark bar offered a bleak chance of identifying anyone quickly. She hung her coat and headed to the main bar to have a look. Across the bar, she spotted the wavy brown hair. She couldn't really see his face, but she was sure it was him. He didn't disappoint. She smiled and gave a little wave. He responded with a smile and raised his glass. He pushed his chair back and started toward her. She kept her eyes fixed on him with a sly smile until she felt a tap on her shoulder.

"Megan POF?" said a voice from behind her.

Startled, she turned around, "Um, yes."

"Hi, I'm Mark," said the man who extended a short chubby hand.

What was happening? Mark was coming toward her. Who was this man behind her claiming to be Mark? The wavy-haired man finally made his way through the thick crowd carrying two drinks.

"Hi pretty lady. I'm Kent, and you are?"

"Kent, your name is Kent? That's, not right?"

"Hmm, I'll bring your complaint to my parents when I see them next."

"No, I mean aren't you Mark from POF?"

"Oh, no sorry, wrong guy, but I could be. I don't hate the name Mark. We could talk it over with my folks, name change and all."

"Mark right here," said the man behind her waving the pudgy hand like a school boy.

Kent looked over her shoulder and said, "Mark, ah you're the lucky guy from POF. Well high five brother, she's a winner. And you, if you change your mind about the name Kent, give me a call," he said sliding his card across the bar.

"Who was that?" asked Mark.

She studied him. His long waves seen in the picture were replaced with a few thin thread-like straps of hair drawn across the top of an oddly shaped skull. His body looked more like a helium inflated version of the man in the picture. She was certain that if there were any abs under that shirt, one might first need to remove bulldozers of fat cells to reach the sad little pancaked muscles begging for mercy. This wasn't good. Megan would never be seen in public with a man like this. "Umm, you don't look like the man in your profile pictures."

"Nah, few guys do. We don't take selfies like you ladies, so we just slap up the best one we got."

"And when exactly did you get that one?"

"I'd say, and don't quote me, somewhere between eight and ten years ago."

"Don't you think that's a bit misleading?"

"Why? I'm still a smart, funny guy, just a little more to love." He summoned the bartender with a wave and said, "So two orders of wings for the lady and I, and the first round of drinks on me." He climbed up to the bar stool and patted the one next to him.

Megan found herself trolling for familiar faces, praying Chase and Bree weren't there or worse Caroline. A perky waitress promptly served a plate full of wings to the bar and Mark dove in as though the bell to a wing contest just chimed. This was a nightmare, Mark, the once handsome, ripped ab Adonis, now sat before her dribbling wing juice down his face onto the large landing pad of his protruding stomach. He threw back beers like water to a desert bound survivor. In between occasional burps, he managed to ask a few questions, mainly about her looks. She found herself drifting between thoughts of what the girls were doing, the number of ways she could kill Maxie, and for some reason, the blazing hot kisses she had shared with Stone at Chelsea's. Why was he so stinking hot? *No*, she reminded herself he wasn't hot, not in a handsome, sophisticated way, but in a rugged, sexy, strong, manly way. The latter would never appeal to a woman of Megan's social status. However, the insane suggestion Chartreuse had made about a test spin dangerously whirled around in her mind. Whether she took him for a ride per his suggestion, or a romp per Maxie's suggestion, either surely would spell disaster. She and Stone are from very different worlds and outside of the sheets, the two could never find anything in common.

"Do you dance?" Mark said, rolling his rounded shoulders while raising his eyebrows up and down.

A brief image of his wing stained belly jiggling to the hip-hop music made her feel a tad bit nauseous.

"No, not so much?"

"Come on, let's give it a spin. I think you'll like my moves," he said, as he gyrated his small hips that tittered under that massive belly, threatening to snap any second. As his hips rolled around and finished with a big forward thrust not once, or twice but a third time, the tiny button on his Hawaiian shirt broke free revealing a stretched out faded tattoo of a whale. "Hey look who wanted to say hi, Megan, this is Moby Dick," he said, opening the shirt further, preceding to make the rolls of blubber under Moby wave.

"Oh, excuse me, that's my phone," she said, quickly grateful for any call, even a sales pitch would be welcomed.

"Hello," she said anxiously.

"Megan, it's Stone. Can you hear me? Where are you?"

"I'm," she paused watching the Moby rise and fall. "It doesn't matter, just talk."

"I wanted to apologize. I'm sorry I sprung the idea of the table on you without any warning. It was wrong of me. I get kind of excited when I'm all in a project. Can we maybe talk this out sometime?"

"Yep how's now? I can meet you at the lodge in fifteen."

"Umm is that okay, with the girls and all? I know you need to get them to bed."

"Nope, perfect. They aren't there. See you in fifteen then. Bye now."

"Yeah okay," Stone said with surprise in his tone.

Rylee Ridolfi

She hung up the phone. Mark had only been half listening as his eyes were fixed on a girl in a short white dress twerking on the dance floor.

"I'm so sorry, I have to go. It's a work thing, kind of a time emergency. It was nice meeting you," she said, extending her hand.

Ignoring the handshake, he went in for a bear hug. She could feel the whale squishing against her, leaving behind a smudge of little wing sauce on her gray sweater. "You're one fine woman Megan, and there's a whole lot of Mark that would like to make a little motion in the ocean with you, if you know what I mean," he said, thrusting Moby toward her out of the screaming buttons.

"That's very nice of you Mark," she said through clenched teeth. "Sorry to rush out, but got to go." Her brain felt it may explode frantically trying to erase any images of intimacy between her and Moby Dick. Why was the sound of Stone's voice on the other end of the phone music to her ears? Why was she running to him? In a strongly worded dialogue, she began with herself she said, *Megan, this is simply about getting as far away from Mark and Moby as quickly as possible.* Convincing herself that a hedgehog could have called and she would have sent her running made her feel somewhat better. She pushed her way through the hordes of couples entangled on the dance floor, only making her need to escape that much more pressing. She made great time to the lodge. The ride was a blur in her mind, but as the lodge came into view a sigh of relief washed over her that she was done with that awful date. She turned off the engine and pulled down the mirror on the dash. She fluffed her hair and smeared a layer of lipstick over her lips. Why did it matter this was business, she reminded herself as she opened the lodge door? Pulling off her jacket she flung it on the hook and made her way to the couch.

Megan heard a glass clank in the kitchen. Startled, she jumped only to find Stone standing in the kitchen.

"Rough night?" he asked, noticing the smudge of wing sauce down her shirt.

"Oh my gosh you scared me? How did you get in here?"

"Besides having a key, Maxie let me in."

"Where is she? I need to kill that girl."

"Another bad date?"

"You wouldn't believe me if I told you."

"That bad huh? Plenty of Fish gone wrong?"

"Yes, but I think discussing the lodge is exactly what I need. Truce?" she said, extending a hand.

His eyes narrowed with uncertainty. He extended his hand, "Regan is that you?"

"Very funny. Now, we need to somehow find a way to blend these themes. I was thinking the lodge naturally gives off the scent of piney, resinous wood, an agarwood scent mixed with a hint of burning embers from the fireplace. I'd like to infuse some notes of Balsam fir, fresh pine needles to give it the smell of Christmas even without the tree. And maybe mix in a bit of cinnamon and winterberry. I've found a few wall mounted scent diffusers I'd like you to install. Also, I know you're not about fur, but accents in fur are a must for a cozy ski lodge."

"I agree."

"You do?" she said with a distinct uptick in her voice.

"Yes Megan, you're good at this. You have a vision that is spot on."

"Don't do that. I know you're just placating me."

"Look at me Megan. I don't placate. I tell it like I see it. At first, I dismissed your ideas for being too upscale, but after seeing the old girl start to come to life as the walls opened up, so did my mind. There's room for both of our ideas here," he said moving a bit closer.

The air seemed thicker as she tried to think clearly. Gazing into his eyes she heard the front door of the lodge barrel open, blowing Chase and Bree in behind it.

"Chase you can't just walk in here. How many times do I have to say we aren't open for business yet? For now, the lodge is my home."

"Oh, but the trucker can be here?"

"Great to see you again Chase," said Stone, unfazed by his comment.

"What do you want? "Megan said, feeling her nerves starting to unravel.

"Bree decided since we're getting married soon, we feel we should start overnights with our girls."

"OUR girls, they are not *her* girls. She has never given a minute's thought about those girls. For that matter, she doesn't even know their names," Megan said, her face the color of a radish.

"Oh nonsense, Sophie and Allie," replied the bubble headed blonde pecking at her cell.

"It's Olivia," both Megan and Stone said at the same time.

Chase arched his back, partially at Stone but also with the uncanny way the two were perfectly in sync. "Well it doesn't matter, I have court papers that say I get them every other week, so if you have a problem with that then I'll see you in court."

Megan, visibly shaken lunged toward him, until she felt Stone's strong arms around her waist. "This is unbelievable. You don't look at them, then suddenly you want to be the Brady's."

"I'll be here next Friday at six. Have them ready. Oh, and Megan, you have a little schmutz on you," Chase said, about to graze her breast where the wing sauce smudge laid.

Stone grabbed his hand and politely twisted it down and slightly off to the left leaving Chase's face grimacing with pain. "I think you might want to rethink that action buddy. I think you're leaving now."

Bree was so busy on her phone she hadn't even noticed the altercation. Stone ushered Chase to the door. Bree scampered behind working her long red nails on the keys.

Stone slammed the door and said, "Well that was unpleasant."

Megan ran to the kitchen and grabbed a towel, doused it in water and scrubbed her shirt until the fibers nearly tore off.

Stone placed a strong grip on her hand then gently removed the towel from it. "I don't think the shirt should pay for the crimes of your ex."

Megan began babbling. "Stupid fat whale got wing sauce all over my good sweater. Who falsifies selfies? Who does he think he is taking my babies? He can't take my babies," she said before her eyes burst into tears.

"I'm not exactly sure what we are talking about fully, but no tears. They're still your girls. It'll be okay."

"How do you know; you don't have kids?" she snapped.

Stone paused for a minute, rather than taking the sharp comment as an insult he calmly said, "You're right, but I wish I did. I'll tell you this, if I did, I'd protect them with my life, just like you. You're a great mom, Megan. It won't change anything. They love you." He wiped the tears from her eyes and pulled her in close. She rested her head on his sturdy chest and wept. He held her tight and allowed her to let it out. "Do you know what you need?"

"Jesus, carbs, a mob contact?" she said, sniffing.

"Wrong on all accounts, although some do have merit. What you need is pumpkin pie."

"Pumpkin pie?" she said wide eyed.

"Yep, get your coat."

"Look at my shirt."

"Believe me, it's hard not to, but where we're going, there is no dress code."

"Where are we going? Should I be scared?"

"Maybe, they say the pumpkin pie addiction is real. Come on," he grabbed her coat and held the door open. The air had turned decidedly cooler. The autumn leaves swirled around them as they headed to the truck. They headed down Route 29 to the other side of town. As they made their way into the older blue-collar neighborhoods, Megan stared out the window. "What are we doing here?"

"Pumpkin pie was the promise and I always deliver. Here we are, Aunt Charlotte's hometown cooking," he said as the big tires pulled into the little gravel lot. Aunt Charlotte's little pink diner with candles in the window, welcomed customers like you were going to grandmas. A tear filled her eye.

"You're upset right, because it isn't up to your culinary standards?"

"No on the contrary, I haven't been here since I was a kid."

"You, really? I didn't figure you for this side of town."

"There's a lot you don't know about me."

"I like intrigue," he said as he jumped out of the truck and came to her side. The two headed in and were greeted by a little white-haired woman with hot pink glasses. She stood about four foot eight with the spunk of a giant.

"Stone my boy, get over here," she said, reaching up to kiss him on her tippy toes. "And who's the pretty little girl you've brought with you?"

"Megan, this is my Aunt Charlotte, literally my aunt. Aunt Charlotte, this is Megan."

"Good gracious, let me adjust my glasses. There, yes of course, Megan McKenna. Oh, my heavens, it's been years," she leaned in and squeezed Megan hard.

"You remember Megan, do you? Any stories you can share, especially the embarrassing ones?" said Stone nudging Megan.

"Little Megan and her family came every Sunday for pancake breakfast until the big move. How's the family dear?"

"They're great. Stone here tells me you serve the best pumpkin pie in all of Connecticut."

"Darn straight I do, now sit right down here and let me have your jackets."

Stone took his off and extended a hand to Megan. "Um I think I'll just keep mine on."

"Are you cold, sweetie?" Charlotte said with worry lines etched deep beneath her glasses.

Stone shook his head, "No, she has a silly smudge on her shirt. Tell her we're informal here."

"Stone you big lug, girls care about things like that. I wonder what he was doing when my sister, rest in peace, was teaching him about the girlies. Now you come with me. Stone, you take these jackets. You know where they go."

Megan followed her to the back of the restaurant. The room was filled with antique vases, roller skates, a jukebox, some recipe books, and a desk with pastel colored picture frames filled with black and white pictures. Charlotte made her way through the mess to a box in the corner. She opened it up and pulled out a pink and white hoodie that read 'Aunt Charlotte's Home Cooking since 1955.' "Here dear, I think this should fit."

Megan held a picture in a pale blue frame with a little boy and his parents. The woman looked very similar to Charlotte. The little boy had a head full of wavy hair and big blue eyes. His little arms outstretched around both parents. "Is this Stone?"

"Oh, bless him, yes that's him with Anna Lynn and Colter. Gosh, they were so happy back then."

"Back then?" Megan asked.

"They were thick as a fresh jar of honey, until Stone went off to chase his dream and his momma got sick. His daddy blamed him for breaking her heart. Truth be told there nothing Stone could have done to save her. The two haven't talked since the funeral."

"That's awful. He must feel so bad."

"Stone has tried, but that darn Colter is a stubborn man. Stone's a good boy. He hasn't missed Sunday breakfast with me since he returned, Early, six o'clock before we open. Just him and me. It's special. Let's see this on you," she said, holding the pink sweatshirt up to Megan.

Megan slipped it over her head. Her shiny black hair fell in dark contrast to the baby pink shirt. "It's lovely, thank you." The two headed back to the diner.

"Now wait a minute. How long have I been coming here and I never got one of those?" said Stone.

"I didn't think pink was your color," said the little woman.

"Now that is being sexist. Let's have some of that pie I promised the girl."

"Extra whipped cream? It's homemade," Charlotte asked, rubbing her tummy.

"Then yes, please," Megan said.

"And two hot cocoas with those mini marshmallows and chocolate chips please," said Stone.

Megan looked around at the diner and smiled, "Not much has changed and I love that. Keeping tradition is important. I want that for the lodge. I want to do it right so when guests come back year after year, they smile and feel at home. Nostalgia is everything to me. I like things you can count on."

"Like?"

"M&Ms, the warm crackle of a fire on a cold night, and especially, snowmen."

"Snowmen? You can count on a snowman?"

"Yes, people come and go. Some come back, some don't. Some leave without notice, without any promise they'll return, but a snowman, well you know when you build him, he'll make you smile. You know when he's going to leave because he'll melt when the temperature rises, but you also know he'll come back every year as promised when the air gets a chill and the dew point drops. He's a constant. I can count on snowmen."

"Snowmen, huh? Well that's a new one to me."

"Here you go, two slices of fresh pumpkin pie. Grew the pumpkins out back. Extra whipped cream and some cocoa. And for you, one extra-large, extra pink hoodie," Aunt Charlotte said before dropping a hoodie on Stone.

"Perfect," he said, slipping the pink hoodie over his flannel.

"Are you seriously going to wear that?" Megan said, laughing out loud at how foolish he looked.

"Yep."

"What if someone comes in?"

"Who cares, I don't need to impress anyone."

Megan froze in awe of that statement, then quickly realized that what others thought of her had always been her problem. She did need to impress, not just anyone, but everyone. The pressure to be perfect nearly killed her. It consumed her through her high school years, and then into her marriage. She couldn't fathom not caring what other people thought. She envied him. He was his own man. No airs, audience to appease, no competition, just himself.

She ran her fork through the fluffy whipped topping down through the flakey crust. The pie stood five inches high. She put the fork to her mouth and closed her eyes as she let it saunter in her mouth. She inhaled and let out a slow moan.

"That good, huh?"

"I don't usually eat pie."

"Seems to me anything that can bring that emotion out you ought to introduce back into your life."

"Are we still talking about pie?"

A sly smile broadened across his face.

The two ate pie, drank the warm chocolate and laughed about visits to the diner. Megan stayed away from the topic of his parents, but enjoyed the stories about his crazy aunt intervening on his behalf when prom dates were going awry. Charlotte was full of energy and couldn't help but beam when she looked at Stone. She had never married nor had children. Stone was like a son to her.

A gray-haired gentleman put a quarter in the jukebox and pulled his lovely wife to the center of the diner. "If I could have your attention," said the gentleman. "Sixty years ago, this beautiful woman agreed to be my wife. Tonight, I want to ask her to marry me all over." He got on one knee and pulled a small box from his pants pocket. "Eleanor, you have given me the best years of my life. You're my sun, moon, and pumpkin pie. Will you do me the honor of marrying me all over again and sharing the rest of time by my side?" The tall slender silver haired woman pulled him to his feet, grabbed his cheeks and kissed his face. "It would be my honor, Herbert."

The whole restaurant cheered. The jukebox played Nat King Cole's "Unforgettable." Couples joined in and Aunt Charlotte made no bones about pulling Megan and Stone to the floor. The two laughed realizing they had little chance at saying no to the headstrong woman. Stone pulled her in close and sang the words in her ear.

"You, my friend, are unforgettable in that pink hoodie," Megan whispered in his ear.

He twirled her out then pulled her in close, "As are you with a dollop of whip cream on your lip."

Her fingers quickly rushed to her mouth before realizing he was teasing.

The floor had thinned out without either of them noticing. As the song ended, the two started into each other's eyes. Megan pulled away. She made her way to the counter and thanked Aunt Charlotte, and promised she wouldn't wait so long to come back. Barely looking at him she asked if they could leave. Her feet carried her to the truck like a bow off an arrow. Stone ran after her. He grabbed her and turned her around. Her eyes were red. "Hey what's wrong? Is it my shirt?"

She punched his shoulder, "No. Thank you. I know that wasn't a date or anything, but it was probably the most fun I've had with a guy in forever."

"Let me get this straight, you kiss me at random intervals when you hate me, you're punching me to thank me, and you moan while eating pumpkin pie? I think I got you figured out."

"If you know me so well, what am I thinking right now?"

"Man, that guy can rock a pink hoodie, pumpkin pie rivals intimacy, and right now is one of those times when we should kiss."

"Right on two of those," she smiled coyly.

"Well I know I'm pretty freaking irresistible in pink, so the second one must be you want to kiss me. You know you do, Megan McKenna."

He leaned in and kissed her. "Should we be doing this?" she asked. Their lips wet and curious.

"Probably not," he said as he held her closer. He pushed her up against the truck and let his hand trail to her thin waist. "Not the best idea," he said again as he pressed his body up against hers.

"I mean it's not proper for business and pleasure to mix," she sighed heavily as she felt his scruff rub gently against her neck.

"You're right," he said, still holding onto her.

"I mean things could get messy," she signed breathlessly.

"I said you're right," he said this time pulling away.

"I am?" she said as her eyes popped open.

"Yes, this is a bad idea. You're my boss. Let's keep it professional."

"Right," she said, fixing her hair.

"Then we should probably go," he said.

He walked back to the restaurant and stuck his head inside, "Aunt Charlotte, we have to get going."

"Sweetie how long will you be in town? Where to next?" she said, following him out to the truck.

"Not sure."

"Don't you disappear without saying goodbye, you hear. I'll see you in the morning for our breakfast," she said, grabbing him and kissing his cheek. "And Megan McKenna, don't you be a stranger dear," the little woman said, giving her a big squeeze.

He opened the truck door to let her in.

An awkward silence filled the cab of the truck. They pulled into the lodge and Stone undid his seatbelt.

"That won't be necessary," said Megan opening her own door. She undid her seatbelt and disappeared into the lodge.

****

Stone felt a stab in his heart. He wanted her badly. The attraction was real, and not just physically. They connected on many levels, but business and pleasure are what got him into trouble before. He loved Claire, or so he thought. He wound up in a hospital for three months, and it cost him both the chance to say goodbye to his mother and the love of his father. History would not repeat itself no matter how appealing he found Megan McKenna.

Chapter Thirteen

Megan pulled the pillow over her head to muffle the sound of drilling, sanding and loud pounding, wishing she could sleep in just one day a week. Afterall, today was a Sunday morning and the girls were not home. She reluctantly made her way to the shower, dressed and poured a black coffee and a bowl of Rice Krispies. She knew she needed to go out there and face him, but last night left her feeling utterly confused. His actions said he was attracted to her, but his words said differently. Megan had never been turned down, so to speak. She realized it was her suggestion the two of them getting involved might not be a good idea, but she had hoped he would disagree, and convince her it would be fine. She swirled her spoon around until her soggy Krispies puffed up and floated around the top of the bowl. She took a gulp of coffee then decided it was time to face him. She would hold her head up high as though nothing happened. He was probably banging around just trying to get her out there. NO country music, odd. She made her way down the hall and into the main lodge to find two older gentlemen wearing masks and goggles sanding the floors of the main lodge. The one closest to her removed his mask and said, "Sorry if we woke you Miss, I know it's Sunday morning and all. Mr. Reynolds hired us to get this all done while the little ones were away. He figured the noise might scare them, and the dust is not good for them either."

"Where is Mr. Reynolds?" she asked, her arms on her hips.

"He's off today; had some work to do around his house. We'll be here most of the day, hopefully we can refinish them all today."

"Fine," she said, marching off to the kitchen. Even when he was being a jerk he was thinking of her girls, which is more than she could say for Chase. This wasn't done. He didn't get the last word. She went over to the check-in desk and rummaged around in the drawer. Molly had left his contact information on it. She vaguely remembered seeing an address scribbled on the back. She fumbled through the drawer, pushing aside two drawing pads, and three of Sophie's sketches before she saw it; Stone Reynolds, 223 Lexington Lane. She would pay him a visit and let him know it was her idea that they don't carry it any further. Megan made her way back to her suite, grabbed her keys and purse, fluffed her hair, then set out for Lexington Lane.

The skies were dark and the wind was so strong the few remaining leaves blew inside out. The storm they had been calling for couldn't have been more than a few minutes away. She punched the address in her GPS and headed for the opposite side of town. Twenty minutes later, she sat in front of the rundown shack. *Could this be right,* she wondered. The porch rotted out on the entire left side barely clinging to the steps. The once blue shaker style shingles were bleached pale gray from the sun. The mailbox appeared to have been run over by a car at least once, but she was able to gleam the number 223 dangling from the edge.

She was right all along; Stone Reynolds was a wanna-be contractor down on his luck. Poor Molly with a heart of gold gave him a chance. He suckered her for way too much money. Where did he get those drawings? It didn't matter, she was certain now that he was not the type of man she could ever consider. Fate had sent her here to remind her of that. A loud crack of thunder pierced the sky. Perfect timing. As she opened her door, the skies opened wide releasing a drenching downpour. The mere twenty feet to the door was enough to soak her completely. Her hair dangled in wet tendrils as she made her way to the porch. The wood planks nearly buckled beneath her. She pounded on the door. The sound of that awful country music blared through the windows. She banged again, louder this time.

The door opened, and behind it was Stone, shirtless with low hung gym shorts and sweat beading on his chest. She hadn't noticed the dumb bell in his right hand.

"Chest," she blurted out as though her hormones had just spoken for her. "I mean, let me in?"

"Megan what are you doing here?"

"WE aren't finished. I mean, about last night. Are you going to invite me in or let me drown or worse fall through your dilapidated porch?"

"Sorry, yeah come on in. I usually use the side door. Here do you need a towel or something?"

Her eyes wanted so badly to look away yet they couldn't. His rippling abs dripping with little bubbles of sweat. His pants hung dangerously low. Those darn twangy notes of country had her cheeks flushing, her pulse rising, her mind spinning. The country anthem messed with her head. She wondered if Rigby had overcome his weakness for the ice cream song. In a blink her mind was back to his abs. *Why did he look so hot when she came to shut him down?*

In her haste to remind him that she was the one that was not interested in taking it further, she had forgotten to grab a coat. A decision she now regretted immensely, as the rain had soaked clear through her shirt. He headed down the hall to the bathroom to grab a towel. She watched as he walked. His back rivaled the front for the most attractive body part of the year.

He handed her a towel, then offered a flannel. "Can I get you something to drink?"

"Water will be fine," she said wishing for ice cold water to dunk her head in. "And yes, a flannel would be fine since you took so long to answer the door, leaving me waterlogged."

He smiled then left to retrieve the shirt. He returned with a navy and red flannel and directed her to the bathroom. The room could have fit in her purse, small, cramped and dark. Awful to live in squalor, she thought. No wonder he jumped at this job.

She followed the sound of his voice singing to Blake Shelton. She tracked him down to a small kitchen swaying his hips slightly in front of the fridge. The romp gods were simply not making this easy. The walls, covered in dark wood paneling from the seventies, were accented with lime green metal cabinets. A tv tray doubled as a kitchen table. Two metal chairs he salvaged from recycling, no doubt, sat on one side of the table. He was a fraud, and poor sweet Molly had bought into his big talk, but Megan wouldn't be so naïve.

He poured her a glass of water filled with ice and pulled out a metal chair. She sat down and took a gulp, then blurted out in a not so eloquent way, "You don't get to tell me that it isn't going to work."

"Megan please, I owe you an explanation."

"This is my decision, not yours."

"Listen, I don't have a good track record with mixing business and pleasure."

She pictured the trailer trash he must have mixed with and again felt reassured about her decision to be clear.

"I was involved with one of my client's daughters. Things got serious quickly, and well," he paused. "I lost focus. She became the fire behind my work. I got so caught up in pleasing her, I lost everything."

"Everything?"

"Yes, everything that matters. I can't go there again. It's not you."

"Oh my gosh, did you just 'it's not you' me? It's most definitely not me. I do not want a relationship with you. As a matter of fact, you are the last person I would ever want a relationship with."

"Okay then we agree we keep this professional."

Flames of fury burned inside her. Megan McKenna was not the type of girl that men dismissed. "Yes, from now on you'll answer to me as my hired help. Are we clear?"

He nodded. "Very clear, boss. So, we can still talk?"

"We'll talk about work and nothing else. Just like I said the day I met you, my business is none of yours." She stood to walk out and slipped on a wet puddle in the middle of the floor. She sailed halfway across the room inches from the cabinet before she felt the warmth of his skin. His strong arms wrapped around her waist. He pulled her to her feet, the distance between them centimeters. Neither one moved. Then the sound of pounding came crashing around the corner.

"Mack stop!" yelled Stone, as an oversized golden retriever jumped up on Megan's back and pushed the two to the kitchen floor. Laying on top of Stone, she could feel his heartbeat beneath his bulging pecs. He sat up, pulling her with him.

"What was that?" Megan said her eyes wide, her breath shaky.

"Sorry, that is Mack. I'm afraid the puddle was Mack as well. He has a bit of a drooling problem."

"Oh my gosh I slipped in drool," she said, wiping her boot on the kitchen rug. "Get that beast away from me."

"He's harmless."

"Tackling me is hardly harmless."

Stone made his way to the hall and grabbed her a hoodie. "Here, this will keep you dry." She ripped the gray tired hoodie from his hands and marched toward the door. Slipping the hoodie over her head she turned to him. "We'll never have this conversation again. Clear?"

"Yes boss," he said, opening the door for her. She ran through the pouring rain and jumped into her car. One last look as he stood shirtless in the door. What the heck was wrong with her? This guy probably hooked up with every low budget client that came along. He was near penniless. She needed to find a man of substance. She would head back to the lodge and check her dating profile and remind herself what type of man she wanted.

Chapter Fourteen

The next week Megan and Stone avoided each other as much as possible. The floors were finished and the main room began to take shape. Megan had agreed to go on a date with a doctor from Mercy General. He was new in town and the distraction was exactly what she needed to get the bottom feeder off her mind. The girls were staying in with Maxie. Megan dared to allow herself to be a little optimistic about finding an educated, well to do prospect. He had moved to town a little over a month ago and just joined the site. She wore a green sweater dress that sat a few inches above her knee. The material hugged her curves and complimented her hourglass figure. Classy, but sure to get his attention. She straightened her hair and decided to go with a cat eye and red lips. A pair of high heeled boots completed the look. Megan stopped at Maxie's suite and found the girls in a sea of pillows in front of a Disney movie. Maxie hurried around in her kitchen filling bowls with popcorn.

"Woah mama, you look hot," she said, putting the bowls on a serving tray.

"You think? He seems nice. A little shy. Doesn't say a whole lot, but he's cute, smart and rich. I can't for the life of me figure out why he would need this site."

"The dating trifecta. I'm excited for you, although the tension between you and Mr. Hottie Pants isn't getting any lighter."

"Stone, no he's so not in my league. If I wanted to shop at the Discount Mart and live in a rusted-out trailer home, we'd be perfect, but I think you know me a little better than that."

"Yes, I do, but I also know that sometimes the heart doesn't see dollar signs."

"My heart and Stone Reynolds are two things that should never share one sentence."

"He who protests the loudest…"

"Goodbye Maxie," Megan said as she headed into the living room. "Where are my kisses?" she said opening her arms to the little ones.

The girls jumped up and hugged her, she gave them both a kiss and warned them to not make Aunt Maxie nuts.

"I'll text you if I'm going to be late." She winked at her and headed out the door. She walked out to the lodge and found Stone sitting on the couch with a sketch pad on his lap. She made sure not to put her coat on so he could see her form fitting dress. He definitely noticed. He looked up and the pad fell to the floor.

"Big date?"

"None of your business, but if it were your business, yes, with a Cardiothoracic Surgeon. He's rich and educated," she said putting her coat on slowly, making sure he was watching.

"That'll make all the difference in the world."

"What's that supposed to mean?"

Christmas Under Construction

"It means you have no idea what to look for in a partner, and until you learn that, you're going to be on that site for many years to come."

"Says the love expert," she stormed out the door and slammed it hard. No low-budget carpenter was going to analyze her. She drove to the new restaurant on Main and parked across the street. Inside she saw well-dressed couples dining in the elegant room. A smile snuck across her face as she saw Ray through the window. He was strikingly handsome, strong jaw, dark black hair and broad shoulders. He still looked every bit as good as his picture. His suit, impeccably tailored, turned the eyes of several women waiting in the lobby. Megan was greeted by a young waiter who held the door for her. "Welcome."

Ray turned to see her in the doorway. "Megan."

"Ray," she said, smiling. He took her coat and handed it to the coat check boy. The host took two menus and escorted them to a table by the window.

"And I was worried about dating sites," he said with a smile. "I thought you might not be real."

"I'm a bit skeptical about them too. I've met my share of crazies."

"Would you like to share a bottle of wine? I took the liberty of ordering one to the table before you got here."

"That would be perfect." Things couldn't have been going better. They ate and talked about what they are looking for in a partner.

"This is going so well. I've got to be honest; I'm a little off my game," he said, reaching into his suit jacket pocket.

"Why?"

"Well I usually bring Minerva along with me, but since I moved, I'm winging it alone."

"Is she a phone app, like Siri?"

"No, excuse me one second," he dialed the phone then said, "Hey she's wonderful. I think you're going to like her." He set the phone on the table and turned it toward Megan and said, "Mom, this is Megan. Megan, this is my mom, Minerva."

The woman on the phone's nasally voice barked, "Raymond she wears a bit much makeup, kind of trampy if you ask me, and obviously you're asking me."

"Is she talking about me?" said Megan.

"She's mouthy too. You can do better."

"Oh my gosh, are you seriously interviewing me with your mother on facetime? Good luck, Raymond."

"Megan, don't go. It's not you. She doesn't like anyone."

Those words again, *It's not you.* She felt the blow, like a right hook to her self-esteem. This couldn't be happening. First rejected by the hired help, now she wasn't good enough to bring home to mom. *What am I saying, he is a wacko, Megan? It really isn't you,* she repeated as she hightailed it to her car. She couldn't drive away fast enough. This whole dating thing was a disaster. Her car lights turned into the lodge. She sighed a bushel of relief to find that Stone's car was gone. She would avoid the whole ugly dating rejection saga. Inside, she threw her coat on the couch and sat down. The refurbished floors now warmed the interior with a mix of honey and a worn blackened finish. She marveled at how amazing they looked. The full wall of windows Stone opened up provided a view of the entire mountain. She didn't want to admit it, but he had done a remarkable job so far. How did he have money to pay those extra workers on a Sunday? More importantly, why was he always on her mind. Sleep, that would help this awful date disappear. Maxie had the girls for the night. As Megan put the key into the door, she heard something inside her place.

"Megs is that you?"

"Maxie what are you doing here?"

"Suppy," she said, holding up the weathered stuffed animal. "Olivia is asleep but I promised to bring him back. You're here kind of early. Dare I ask?"

"No, other than the fact that he brought his mother along via phone chat. It was special, let me just say. I'm done."

"Meg okay I'll admit he sounds a bit off, but what about Phil? Oh, that's right, Phil had a top tooth that crossed over the bottom tooth. And there was Todd, who you couldn't stop staring at his hair because you were convinced it was a toupee. And Mike, oh yes, he had squinty eyes, right? Meggie, I think it might be you."

"IT'S NOT ME!" she barked. "They just aren't right. I need chemistry and none of them have it."

"Maybe if you looked past the snaggle tooth or the squinty eyes, you could get to date number two and see if there was chemistry."

"Maxie, Todd's hair was sliding toward his soup. I can't be with a man that has fake hair."

"Megan, listen to me. No one is perfect, but sooner or later you need to give someone a chance."

"I need to get some sleep; I have an early day. After I drop the girls to school, Molly asked me to meet with the electrician up at the village," Megan said, clearly ending the dating conversation.

"Molly found a reasonable electrician?" Maxie said.

"Supposedly he's really cheap. She has to meet with Father Rick about the wedding."

"Okay, but we aren't done with this conversation. We're not giving up," Maxie said before letting herself out.

Megan was thankful for the peace. She curled up in her bed and tried to make the images of sliding toupees, waving stomach tattoos, and snaggle teeth disappear. The next morning, she drove the girls to school and headed straight to the village. Megan smiled when she saw the massive gates with NP written on them. She allowed her troubles to disappear as she passed the gates into the magical winter wonderland.

She hadn't even noticed a handsome young man standing by the thirty-foot Christmas tree.

"Hey Megan, it's me Walker," said the young man.

"Hi, you're the electrician, right?"

"Yeah, don't you remember me?"

"Should I?"

"Yes, I helped my dad do the wiring at the Ms. Winter Princess Pageant."

"That was a long time ago. How old were you?"

"Sixteen. I remember all our conversations."

"Really, we had conversations?"

"Oh yeah, you told me the pageant title was everything you ever wanted, you know to be the prettiest girl in the town, and land the richest boy and have a mansion."

His words pierced with shallow spikes. Did she really say those things? She did want those things back then, but in her heart, she had no idea of what she truly wanted. Now years later, she was no closer to having that answer. "Well a lot has changed since then."

"Yeah, now I own my dad's company."

"Good for you. So, you can handle this? There's something that keeps cutting the power. I don't have to tell you how important the lighting is to Christmas Village, not to mention my sister's wedding."

"I had a chance to look at it. You don't have enough power. I just need to add more amps."

"Okay what time frame are we looking at? Our opening day is Thanksgiving weekend, which as you know doesn't give you much time."

"Not a problem, should be done by this weekend."

"Great, here's my number if you need anything. Or, feel free to stop up at the lodge anytime."

"Thanks Megan. I'll talk to you soon."

Megan returned to the lodge to find Stone's truck out front. He's the builder, why did seeing his truck make her stomach twist up like a butterfly convention? She would go about her business and ignore him. The bedding she had ordered for all the rooms had arrived and she needed to inventory it and separate each according to room. Inside, she found Stone pounding something into the wall on one side of the massive window.

"What the heck is that?" she said, angry she hadn't been involved in this decision, whatever it was.

"Vintage toboggans I'm repurposing for bookshelves. I found nine-foot ones so they will flank the windows nicely. I wanted to surprise you. Do you like?"

Megan wanted to lay into him for going over her head, but she couldn't believe how simply amazing they looked. It was unique, creative, and gave the large room character. "I thought we discussed all decisions go through me. I didn't approve the purchase. How much were they?"

"They are on me, my treat to the lodge. Now it's on you to fill them with fabulous pieces, which I know you'll do perfectly."

She hated his level headed cool demeanor. "Okay I can do that. I'd like to fill it with the classics as well as Christmas stories. I also saw some great pieces at Vera's on Main. A deer head in chrome, a woodland set of battery-operated candles, you know rustic charm with a bit of elegance. I'll check them out later this week."

"I have a few more surprises, but if it's okay with you, I'd like to show them when they're finished. I promise you won't be disappointed, and if you are, I'll get rid of them."

"Fine. I have a ton of packages to open for the rooms. I believe they left them in the dining room. I'll be in there, if you need me," she said, tossing her jacket on the coat rack and heading down the hall. Megan opened the door and saw boxes piled to the ceiling. She had ordered several types of comforters all with complimentary colors to mix and match the rooms. There were red with black moose, black and red plaid, black with white snowflakes, and cream with red and black vintage skis, toboggans and snowshoes. The sheets are all solid colored red, black and cream. The rooms needed a bit of rehab themselves, but with new bedding and a few wooden plaques, pictures, and knick knacks, Megan was sure she could spruce them up.

Several hours later Stone called out to her and said, "Hey, there is some kid here with flowers. Won't leave until he gives them to you personally. I guess you and Doctor Love hit it off after all."

Megan rushed past him in the doorway. She turned the corner to see Walker standing there behind a ton of flowers.

"Hey Walker," she said, her eyes wide with surprise.

"He's a thoracic surgeon?" Stone said with one hand under his chin with a pensive expression. "Gosh, I must be getting old. He looks like a baby."

"Quiet," Megan said, taking the flowers from him.

"Meg I'm so sorry for not accepting your invitation to go out. I mean in my defense, you're Ms. Winter Princess."

"I get it," said Stone.

"I mean you're hot and you know, a cougar. I guess I choked. But it would be a dream come true."

"No, no that isn't why I gave you my number, Walker."

"Don't second guess this thing. It's cool, Demi Moore opened the door for women your age to try the younger guy," said Walker.

Rylee Ridolfi

"Kid's got a point," said Stone.

"Why are you still here?" Megan said, thrusting the flowers into his face. Please get a vase for these in the kitchen, all the way over there."

"It's just getting good. Hang in there kid, she's not an easy nut to crack."

"Megan, think about it, you and me. It makes perfect sense."

"In what universe? Listen, I don't want to be cold, but there is nothing between us and there never will be."

"Cold. That rests in arctic territory, brrrrr," said Stone from afar.

"I've always liked you Megan."

"Liked me or thought I was hot?"

"Same thing, right?"

"Not right. Thanks for the flowers Walker; now we are done here. Finish the work on the electric and send me the bill."

"If you change your mind, here's my number. We could chill," he said, handing her a card.

"I won't."

Walker left with his head burrowed.

"Did you have to be such a dream crusher?"

"Why are you still talking to me?"

"Aw come on, you let the kid down pretty hard. After all, you did lead him on."

"I did not lead him on. I gave him my number to call if he had trouble with the work he's doing on the village."

The door swung open and Molly walked in looking as if she just learned Santa's not real.

"Oh no, now what's wrong?" Megan asked.

"Everything. The opening is in a week and a half and I haven't even had a chance to train all the staff. I mean some of the kids yes, cashiers and food staff, yes, but not all of them. And Friday, Hunter and I were supposed to taste delectable cakes and choose one for our wedding, but now we have to go to Hunter's family in New Jersey for a 'Surprise shower,'" she said before pacing in quick steps from one side of the room to the other. Shaking her hands and puffing her breath in short and quick bursts, she began to take on a bluish tint. Her hands found their way to her neck and raked at the trail of hives that had begun to form.

"Molly, calm down. We'll sort this out," said Megan, getting a wet washcloth for Molly's bumpy neck.

Molly wrapped the wet rag around her neck then stopped mid pace, her eyes wide and her smile wider. "You guys, this looks amazing. The toboggan book shelves, the floors in warm honey with dark tones, the expanded view of the mountain," she said, before bursting into tears. Stone and Megan ushered her to the couch and sat on either side of her.

"Hey no tears, this is a good thing. Also, I talked to Walker and he'll have the electric squared away by this weekend."

"Megan, you are a lifesaver. I knew you could handle Walker."

Stone raised an eyebrow. Megan squinted an eye and shot him a look.

Rylee Ridolfi

"You and Stone make the best team ever. Thank you from the bottom of my heart."

"You're getting married, that is all you need to worry about," Megan said, squeezing her little sister tight.

The lodge door opened again and Sophie sprang in, "Aunt Molly," she said, rushing to the couch.

"Hey there princess. You look like you grew three inches since I saw you last."

"You're never around anymore."

"I'm sorry kiddo, wedding stuff."

"Where's Olivia?"

"Outside with her stupid fish."

****

Stone excused himself. He walked out the front door and found Olivia sitting by the lake. "Hey there little Red, what's up?" Looking closer he could see tears in her eyes.

"Oh no, you're leaking," he said.

She giggled. "I'm not leaking. I'm sad."

"Why would my favorite kid be sad?"

"Tommy Biglo said I can't be in the Thanksgiving pageant because Pilgrims don't wear glasses and that people who wear glasses are losers."

"He did, did he? Well that goes to show what Tommy Biglo knows. Was he there for the Pilgrims' first meal? I don't think so. I happen to think that some of the coolest people in the world wear glasses."

"Really? Who?" the little girl said, her eyes drying up.

"Let's start with the big guy himself, Santa Claus, and then there's Harry Potter, and of course Superman."

"Wow, you're right!"

"So, you tell Tommy Biglo, you need to have glasses to run with the big guys. And, I personally think you'll be the best Pilgrim ever."

"Will you come to the pageant, Stone?"

"There you are," said Megan. "What's going on out here?"

"Mommy can Stone come to the Thanksgiving pageant? I really want him to."

Megan could see Olivia's eyes were red and it wasn't the time to upset her. "If Stone wants to," she answered, giving him the look to nicely bow out.

"I'd love to," he said to her dismay. She rolled her eyes and instructed Olivia to get washed up before they headed to grandma's.

"Are you always this annoying?"

"It's a gift," he said before heading to his truck. "What time is this pageant and where?"

"Tomorrow night, seven o'clock, Meadows Elementary School, as if you really care."

"See you at seven."

The next night, Megan braided Sophie's long black hair into two braids and secured a headband around her forehead for her lead role as Indian princess in the pageant. Olivia put on her black pilgrim dress and bonnet, and waited for Sophie to finish. The three headed to the car.

"Daddy said save him a seat," said Sophie. "Make sure it's up close so you can see me greet the boat."

Megan knew what that meant; he wasn't coming. Something else would undoubtedly take precedence. She was used to making excuses for him. He would, without question, let the girls down.

Olivia stood next to the car, searching the lot. "Come on Olivia, get in the car. We don't want to be late."

"Where's Stone?" Olivia asked.

"Who cares, I'm the star! I need to get in there," Sophie said, arms crossed.

"Oh, honey maybe he had another job to do." Great now she had two men to make excuses for. Her blood boiled when she thought about Stone giving Olivia false hope. Why would he even agree to coming only to let her down? He's not her father, he has no obligation. Sophie repeated her one line over and over fifty times. Olivia remained quiet. Sophie had a small meltdown when she realized the other Indian princess feathers were taller. Megan turned to go address the costume crisis to find Stone standing behind her. He looked extraordinary, in a dark colored blazer with a white button-down shirt and khakis. His hair parted slightly on the left side and slicked back. He wore a pair of dark black glasses. Megan stopped in her tracks. He winked then moved toward Olivia.

"Come on mommy, I need those feathers now," demanded Sophie.

Megan and Sophie disappeared backstage. Olivia made her way to Stone.

"I didn't know you wear glasses," said Olivia looking up at Stone.

"That's because I wear contacts. Little glasses that rest on your eyes. Maybe that's what the pilgrims did."

"Maybe," she said.

"Where's this Tommy guy?"

"Over there standing with the cool kids."

"Wow, there's cool kids in pre-k, rough out there these days. Okay, let's go visit him."

She put her little hand in his then walked him over toward Tommy. She motioned him over.

"Tommy this is my friend, Stone."

"Hey Tommy, how's it going? I heard that you think people who wear glasses are losers. I wear glasses and I'm pretty sure I'm not a loser. Can I tell you a secret Tommy that not many people know?"

"Yeah what is it," said the little boy with big brown eyes and blond spiky hair.

"Some of the coolest people on earth wear glasses," he said as he opened his white shirt just enough to show a superman tee underneath.

"You're, you're Clark Kent?" the little boy stammered.

"Secret Tommy, remember. And Tommy just between us guys, not only are the girls who wear glasses cool, but they're pretty and smart. The whole package, man."

"Yeah," said the little boy smiling at Olivia.

A gruff voice announced over the loudspeaker that the children needed to report to their homeroom at this time."

Olivia put her little arms around his thighs and hugged him, "Thanks Stone."

"Go show them, little Pilgrim."

Megan had come out from backstage in time to witness the hug. She scanned the room for Chase and Bree, yet was not surprised that they were nowhere to be found. She texted Chase. His response, "Tell my loves I'm tied up, but I'm thinking of them." *Sure, he was,* she thought as she filed into row five, seat three. She waved Stone over. "I guess you can sit here, since I have two extra tickets. Big surprise, their dad isn't coming."

"Wow that's rough. Do they get upset?"

"Sophie makes excuses. Olivia doesn't say much. Chase never paid her half the attention he does Sophie."

"Stand up guy."

"Since when did you wear glasses?"

"Since tonight."

"Not that I'm complimenting you, but they look good. Hmmm, and that hug?" she asked, raising her eyebrows slightly.

"Now that's privileged info between me and my favorite pilgrim."

"Thank you for not letting her down."

"I'm a man of my word."

The curtains went up and Sophie entered front and center. The classes filed in one by one filling the stage with Pilgrims and Indians. Olivia stood next to Tommy and sang her little heart out. Sophie delivered the concluding line of the play. Everyone cheered. Megan's heart melted when Olivia gave Stone a tiny thumbs up.

Stone excused himself and left returning with two bouquets of flowers. Pink ones for Sophie and yellow ones for Olivia. Megan, overwhelmed by the gesture, felt a flood of tears roll down her cheeks.

"Hey, why the tears?" Stone said, placing his hand on her forearm.

Megan wiped away a tear and in a soft voice said, "Every year the other kids get flowers from their dads. Not my kids, of course. I brought them one year but Sophie said they weren't supposed to be from a girl, so I stopped. Chase would never even think to bring them flowers."

"Heads up, here comes Sophie."

"Are those for me?"

"They sure are. That was one great performance and that line in the end, you nailed it."

Her face beamed, she took the flowers and said, "Thanks," before trotting off with a group of friends. Stone made his way over to where Olivia's class stood. He bent down handing her the flowers and said, "Great job, Red."

Megan walked up behind them in time to hear his kind words.

Tommy walked up to Olivia and gave her a limp orange mum he took from the Mayflower. "Here, this is for you."

Olivia's eyes lit up; her smile so bright it rivaled the spotlight.

"Thanks Tommy," she said shyly.

Tommy's mom joined them and Tommy asked, "Can I get glasses? Olivia knows Clark Kent," as they walked away.

Megan moved the button on Stone's shirt just a bit to see the blue tee with the emblem right in the center of the chest. "Clark Kent, eh?"

He winked at Olivia. Olivia took hold of both of their hands and the three headed to get Sophie. Megan could feel her heart pounding. This would be the first time she had someone to share this with, and oddly enough, it was her carpenter. She didn't care about their differences, tonight, this felt right.

Stone leaned in over Olivia and whispered into Megan's ear, "Can I treat the girls to ice cream?"

"That would be lovely. How about Aunt Charlotte's?"

"You're on."

The four of them piled into Stone's truck, deciding to get Meg's car later. They headed to Aunt Charlotte's. The girls cheered when they saw the pink building. Inside, Aunt Charlotte greeted them.

Noticing the girl's costumes, Aunt Charlotte smiled and said, "Oh my do we have celebrities amongst us? Can I get you girls' autographs? Come on let's go to Aunt Charlotte's secret stash of goodies for extra special guests," the older woman insisted, ushering them away.

Megan and Stone sat down in a booth, and began searching the ice cream menu. "This is very kind of you, but not necessary," Megan said, giving him a tender smile.

"I'm enjoying myself and any excuse for ice cream is a good one," he winked. She found herself staring at him over the top of her menu, as he studied the menu. She had never seen him in anything other than work clothes. He still had a bit of scruff, enough to look like a bad boy, yet with his hair tamed and the suit jacket, he could almost pass for a sophisticated man. A hot sophisticated man, a delicious mix of good and bad. The type that spelled trouble. How could he be such a pain in her neck and a joy in her heart at the same time? The girls emerged from the back with little pink aprons, each holding a glass bowl. Charlotte told them they were hired for the day and allowed them to make all four sundaes. The girls returned with a waitress carrying the sundaes on a tray. Olivia slid in with Stone, and Sophie with Megan. The four ate their ice cream sundaes. Stone put a quarter in the jukebox and the girls took to the floor for some dancing. It wasn't long before Stone joined in. The three twisted to Chubby Checker's, "Let's Twist Again." Megan watched laughing until Stone grabbed her hand, ushering her onto the floor.

Around nine o'clock, Megan announced it was very late to be out on a school night. The girls kissed Aunt Charlotte and thanked her. Megan couldn't remember a time when she and the girls had laughed together like that. Stone drove the three back to Meadows Elementary. He opened Olivia's door to let her out and she threw her arms around his neck and kissed him on the cheek. Megan watched as she helped Sophie out of the belt.

"Thanks again Stone," she said as they walked to her van. Stone's smile told Megan how deeply that kiss touched him. His normal bravado melted away as he took her hand.

Megan thanked him again and headed back to the lodge. Sophie exhausted herself dancing and fell fast asleep minutes after Megan kissed her goodnight. Megan sat next to Olivia on her bed. Megan noted how tiny the little girl looked in a twin bed. She crawled in with her and snuggled Olivia close.

"Mommy I think Tommy likes me now," she said, reaching next to the bed and pulling the orange curled up mum from her backpack.

"Now?"

"Yeah he was mean to me at school. He said only losers wear glasses, and that I couldn't be in the play because pilgrims didn't wear glasses."

"Oh sweetheart, that wasn't very nice."

"Nope, but Stone told me special people wear glasses, like Harry Potter, Santa Claus and Superman. He told Tommy that, too. Now Tommy thinks I'm cool," Olivia said, with a bright smile.

Tears began to well up in Megan's eyes. "Well he should because you're a very special girl. Why didn't you tell me?"

"Stone gets me."

Megan laughed, "Oh he does, does he?"

"Yep, I like him mommy. Can we keep him?" she asked, with puppy dog eyes.

"Keep him? Honey he's not one of the pets you collect."

"I know, but I heard Aunt Molly say he was only here until Christmas, then he's taking a job in Europe. I don't know where that is, but it sounds far."

Europe, right after Christmas. Her heart pounded, a twinge of panic snuck in. What did it matter, he was just a handyman, she reminded herself, who lived in a shack and didn't get involved with his clients? She took a deep breath and said, "Get some sleep baby, it's late. I'm sure you can stay in contact with Stone wherever he goes."

"It's not the same," she said, her big green eyes welling up.

"I know baby, but things will work out. I promise."

Megan had no idea what she even meant by that. What was he doing to her? The ringing of her phone snapped her out of her internal conflict. "Molly, what's up?"

"Meggie, I know you have done so much, but would you be able to do one more favor for me?"

"Sure, what do you need?"

"If Alexander brings over the cake selections to the lodge tomorrow night, could you taste them? He's really pushing me. You know what I like, and to be honest, I barely have time to breathe let alone eat cake. Just pick a good one. We have the shower, and I'm completely overwhelmed. I haven't even had a chance to do a final check of Christmas Village's opening night ceremony."

"Okay Molls, I got this. The girls are going to moms for a Thanksgiving decorating night. Mom has all kinds of crafts and believe it or not, she is going to let them display them next to her fine china."

"No way. You know they are calling for snow tomorrow?"

Rylee Ridolfi

"Yes, I heard it might be a Nor'easter, with six to eight inches possible. Snow before Thanksgiving is crazy, but like hitting the lottery for Christmas Village."

"The girls will love it. Pack their boots. I love you. Thank you, thank you."

"Night Molls."

Chapter Fifteen

T he next day, Alexander delivered seven boxes of cake for Megan to try. She hid them from the girls. She didn't want to send them on a sugar high to her mother's. Maxie and Tony went to New York for the weekend, and Molly and Hunter headed to New Jersey for her bridal shower. Tonight, the house would be empty. She wanted badly to ask the girls to stay, but she knew how much they loved going to her parents' house. She would be alone in a big hollow lodge which was meant to house some sixty or so people. Sophie and Olivia came out with their little rolling luggage. The three sat on the couch and waited for Silvia to come. She had texted she would be about forty-five minutes late, and that Edward saw Chase and Bree at the Country Club last night. When the door to the lodge opened, they screamed, "Grandma!" It wasn't Silvia, but Chase in the entryway.

"Hey my princesses. How would you two like to spend the weekend with me and Bree?"

"Yes, yes!" screamed Sophie jumping up and down. Olivia remained quiet.

"You can't just march in here and demand them for the weekend. You have never had them as much as one overnight since you left," Megan said, her face flushed. She needed to remain calm, but this was too much.

"Megan, when Bree and I get married, we plan on petitioning the courts for joint custody, a fifty, fifty spilt."

"Joint custody, does Bree even know what that means?"

"I have every right. I'm their father. I'll be married and have a two-person support system in a single-family home. You live in a lodge, alone."

She could feel the breath stifling low in her lungs. She knew she was about to lose it. She couldn't, not in front of the girls."

"Mommy please," begged Sophie, grabbing her suitcase and rolling over to Chase.

"Look at that, they're already packed. Olivia what do you say?"

"They're packed because they have plans with my parents."

Olivia looked toward her mother. Megan knew Olivia's answer as she clutched Suppy close to her. Innocent Olivia was scared, and she had every right to be. She didn't really know Chase. He left when she was only two years old. She was also very good at reading her mother, and she knew Megan didn't want this.

"Well I don't see Silvia. I'm sure she won't mind. I saw Edward last night. We had a great chat. Now Megs, you don't want to make an ugly scene, do you?" Chase said, scooping Sophie up in his arms.

Yes, that's exactly what she wanted to do, scream at him, remind him he missed the show, remind him he constantly let them down, remind him he left and took all three of their hearts with him, but she knew he was their father and they deserved to see him.

Megan took Olivia in her arms; she gave her a reassuring hug. "It'll be okay sweetie. You and Suppy will have fun. You call me anytime if you need me." Olivia hugged Megan tightly and said, "Water my flowers for me."

"You have a boyfriend you forgot to tell me about?" said Chase.

"Stone got them for us. He came to our play last night."

Chase's face turned scarlet as his eyes narrowed. *Good job Olivia*, thought Megan, *stick it to the bastard*.

"Why don't you two go get in the car? Daddy will be there in a minute."

The two girls hugged Megan and did as they were told.

Megan wasted no time reminding him he doesn't always get to call the shots. "How dare you ambush me like that in front of the girls."

"Megan, get over yourself. You think you're their only parent."

"Maybe because you haven't been a parent to them since you left. You abandoning them pretty much assured me that I was correct in that assumption. Now you show up all 'family man,' wanting to be in their lives. And where were you last night? Oh, that's right, drinking at the Country Club, instead of supporting your daughters in their play."

"More importantly, what was that low life doing at my daughters' play? Are you so pathetic, you have to resort to paying hired help to attend functions with you?"

"It was his choice. He has every right to be there. He cares for them."

"Keep him away, Megan. I'm warning you." Standing within an inch of her face, his eyes burrowing into her soul, he said, "I'll bring them back Sunday at noon." Then he slammed the door in her face and her babies were gone.

Within twenty seconds of the door slam, tears poured from her eyes. She hated him. He bullied her, he lied to the girls, he never made good on his word. He left a path of destruction in his wake, yet for some reason Sophie believed he was the best thing on this earth. Olivia, wiser than her years, saw through his glitz and glamour and his empty promises. Megan paced for a half an hour after texting Silvia not to come. Her mother wanted Megan to come spend the night at their place, but Megan couldn't face her right now. Right now, she would eat cake, a lot of cake. She opened each box, set the six-inch cakes on plates, placed a fork on each plate then stabbed her fork into a five-layer Spice cake blanketed in cream cheese frosting. Next the Bavarian chocolate fantasy, then the white chocolate with raspberry. Megan allowed the decadent flavors to settle on her tongue. They were rich, carb loaded treats that she avoided, until today when they became the thing that sustained her. She continued to shovel heaping mounds of sugary concoctions in at an alarming rate. She moved on to the coconut cake with lime, then the pink champagne with a rum filled layer followed by the red velvet, and lastly carrot. Her senses tingled with each savory bite. This is what pleasure feels like when you're a single cat lady. After she shoveled the last bite she could possibly fit in her mouth, she laid her head on the table and sobbed at the image of her plump body covered in cats one day. The door opened. Behind it stood Stone, eyeing her as if she was perhaps suffering from a psychotic break.

"Is this a meltdown over a broken promise to living a carb free life?"

"No, he, he came. He took them."

"Who came? Took who?"

"Chase, he took my babies," she moaned then dropped her head back into the cake plates.

"Took them where?"

"He, they, court. It's going to snow," she said incoherently.

"Alright, let's first step away from the cake plates."

He stood her up and wiped globs of different color frostings from her hair. "Now let's calmly go over to the sofa and you can start from the beginning."

Megan told him everything through her sobs. She finished, saying, "I'm going to lose them. They're all I have. I don't even like cats."

"Hey, no one is losing anyone. You are a great mother, Megan. You have stood by their side during the toughest time in their young lives. You are a team, a strong team. It's going to be okay. I promise you that, we'll figure this out, and unlike Chase, I don't make promises I don't intend on keeping. I'm not sure why liking cats matters at this point, but one thing at a time." He pulled her in close and let her soak his shirt with tears.

"Do you know what you need?" he asked, wiping her tears.

"Alcohol, a hitman, more cake?"

"No, I had something a bit more fun in mind."

Holding her stomach, she sighed, "Sadly, I can't fit in pumpkin pie?"

"No, no I think you have had enough of the white stuff. I fear you may be riding a sugar high for a few days by the looks of that table. Get your coat."

"I'm a mess."

"Depends on who you're asking, I'm quite attracted to cream cheese icing," he said holding her coat out for her.

She smiled, wiped her face and slipped her coat arm in the jacket. "Where are we going?"

"You'll see."

"Stone, why did you come back to the lodge at seven on a Friday night?"

"It doesn't matter. I'm good." He led her to the door and a brutal blast of brisk air greeted them. They drove for about twenty minutes as swirls of snowflakes which began as big fluffy white mists now turned into icy pellets. He turned into a bar called Bobby Joe's Country Pub. The sounds of Florida Georgia Line filled the parking lot.

"Oh no, no your plan is to numb my brain with horrific country music played at decibels so loud my wallowing will be drowned out. I'm having the worst day of my life and you think bringing me to a country dive bar is going to help?" She paused and thought no chance of seeing anyone she knows here, "On second thought, numb sounds good. They serve alcohol, right?"

"Yes, they do. And I don't *think* it's going to help; I know it is."

"You're pretty confident."

"You got something better to do?"

"Ugh," she sighed, hopping out of the truck, winching as the bitter ice danced off her cheeks. They rushed toward the big wooden doors.

Inside the bar, guitars hung from the wall. Vintage posters of Patsy Cline, Dolly Parton, Johnny Cash, and Willie Nelson lined the walls. Strands of gold garland swung mercilessly from the heavy wood beams. Twinkling lights lit rustic stick trees surrounding the dance floor. Couples wearing cowboy hats and boots, all danced in three lines to the song. The music felt upbeat, the people non-judgmental, all having a good time. The atmosphere was exactly what she needed.

"What can I get you to drink?"

"Something strong if you think you're going to find me on that dance floor."

Stone winked, "Only a matter of time," he said as he headed to the bar. He returned with two of Bobby Joe's specials. She didn't ask, she took hold of the large vessel and slurped it down. After two cocktails, she was ready to take the dance floor. "I've never done this before."

"It's line dancing, just follow along." Lady Antebellum singing their version of Holly Jolly Christmas rang out as a jolly group of dancers took the floor. The group started with four steps to the front, stomp, then four steps back, stomp. Next, grapevine left then shake it, grapevine right then shake it. She awkwardly followed Stone until the turn to the left heel dig, which landed Megan right into his arms. The two, semi-entwined, laughed as they landed their footing, then jumped right back in. Before she knew it, she was shaking it with the best of them. Three songs later, a bit winded, the lights dimmed and Brett Eldredge's *Wanna Be That Song* came on. The slow song brought couples to the floor. The two said nothing, but found each other's bodies moving closer. He placed his arm around her low back and pulled her in close. The music swooned in the background as the two moved slowly, their bodies melting seamlessly into each other. Their eyes locked as he sang the words softly to her. His voice so deep, and smooth like honey, allowed her to get lost in the song. They stood still; eyes still locked. In that moment, Chase melted away; her anger subsided. If only for that brief moment, she was thankful to have this feeling. When the song ended, the lights brightened and they called out a two-step.

"I think I may be out for that one. Another drink?" she said.

"Maybe you should slow down," he said as the sounds of Christmas in Dixie filled the room. They headed back to their table.

"I don't want to slow down. I want to keep drinking." Two drinks later the DJ stopped the music and announced, Will the owner of a black Ford F-150, license plate 456KGP, please report to the DJ booth."

"Wait, that's me," he said, jumping to his feet. She stood, feeling a bit wobbly, then followed behind.

A woman shaking and visibly upset waited for him. "Are you the owner of the truck?" she said, sniffling.

"Yes."

"I'm so sorry. I didn't see it when I was backing up. I hit it, then in my panic I thought I put it in drive and I floored it and it hit again. It's sort of up against the building," she sobbed, her two hands motioning an accordion like gesture to describe his truck. Before Stone could speak, she went on, "My husband was here. I caught him with his secretary in the car. I, I..." she belted out before an all-out meltdown began.

"You what? How do you not see a truck? It's a truck!" Stone said.

"Stop. She's in shock, her husband just humiliated her. You can't yell at her," said Megan, putting her arm around the woman. "It's okay."

"I'm going out to see the damage," Stone said, grabbing his jacket.

"It's bad, really bad," cried the woman. "And it's snowing, really snowing," she said. Megan and the woman followed behind.

He marched straight to the door and barreled through. His eyes bulged with anguish when he saw the mangled truck sandwiched between the building and her car. The red lights of a police car appeared in the lot a few minutes later. The officer took a report. Stone looked at the woman shaking in Megan's arms. He saw the pain in Megan's eyes as her own heart break wounds opened again. He told the cop, "We'll settle this between us. Thanks for coming. Any chance of us getting a taxi out here?"

"Good luck. Have you seen the weather? The snow is barreling down and a thick sheet of ice is underneath, probably why she slid into you in the first place. Every tow truck and taxi for miles is unavailable. Your car isn't going anywhere tonight. You'll have to find somewhere to wait out the storm. I do have a buddy, Chuck who owns the cabins at the foot of the hill. I can put in a call to see if he has one," said the officer.

Megan said, "I'll call Molly. No, she's out of town."

"How about Maxie?" Stone asked.

"Out of town, too."

"What's the problem? Chuck owes me. You seem like a nice couple."

"Oh no, we aren't a couple," Megan said.

"No, we're not," said Stone.

"Do you two have a better idea?" asked the officer.

"No, please, make the call. We appreciate it," said Stone.

"What about Kathy?" Megan asked.

"Who the heck is Kathy?" Stone said.

The one-woman demolition crew honked her nose into a tissue and said, "That would be me, my sister is picking me up. We'd give you a ride, but Nel only has a Volkswagen bug and her three huskies ride in the back."

"Of course, they do," said Stone.

Butting in, the officer said, "I'd like to say it's your lucky day, but we kind of know that wouldn't be entirely accurate. But the good news is you're in. Chuck has one cabin left. Hop in and we'll give you two a ride to the cabin."

Kathy and Stone exchanged insurance information, then Megan gave Kathy her number. Stone grabbed a duffel of clothes from the truck and the two piled into the cop car.

Not a half a mile down the road, they turned left onto a dark road. At the bottom of the mountain sat five cabins; well-lit, picturesque little cabins. The fresh fallen snow frosted the tops of the roofs, with candles burning in each of the windows. Each cabin was lit with multicolored Christmas lights. The officer parked and went into the check in. He returned with a key.

"You ought to be able to get a ride tomorrow. Your truck is being towed to Harry's on Wessel Drive."

"Thanks, you've been a big help," said Stone, taking the key. He and Megan headed down the small snow-covered trail to the cabin. "It's so beautiful," Megan said, spinning once and losing her balance, she fell right onto the wet slushy pavement.

The two laughed until tears spilled from their eyes. He picked her up in his arms and carried her the rest of the way.

Inside the cabin, a double queen-sized bed with a comfy Sherpa throw sat against a wall of logs, a sofa with the frame made from thick pine with faded red and gray pillows faced the fireplace, and a worn pine table and two fluffy plaid chairs faced the sofa. A mini fridge, sink and microwave all lined the far wall by a small pine table with a bowl of red and green ornaments in the center. A small fresh pine tree stood right by the fire, dressed modestly in white lights and silver tinsel, with the bathroom just behind the dining area. It was clean and cozy, but freezing.

"Hey you're shaking," said Stone. "Why don't you take off those wet clothes and shower. I have some dry clothes in the duffel. Not Gucci, but warm. I'll make a fire. I noticed some wood on the porch."

"Sounds good," she said. stumbling to the shower. After peeling off wet clothes, she shivered before she stepped into the shower. The hot water melted away some of the chill along with the tension of the night. *This isn't good, cabin, shower, one bed, snow.* Her mind raced with a concoction of panic and desire.

Megan stepped out of the shower and wrapped a large white towel around her. She peeked her head out the door to see if he had returned with the clothes. He had left them on a shelf right outside the bathroom door. She spotted him over by the fireplace working the logs with a poker. He deliberately didn't look in her direction. Grateful, she reached out and grabbed the clothes, then quickly shut the door behind her. Opening the bathroom door once again, she stepped out in his flannel and her over-the-knee socks. "I'm afraid the sweats aren't going to work," she said.

"I kind of figured they might be a tad big. There is a blanket on the sofa if you're cold. This thing should be kicking in a few."

She made her way to the sofa in front of the fire and wrapped a blanket around herself. He turned to her but remained on the floor. "Megan I'm sorry about all this. It's my fault you're trapped out here in the mountains."

"No, I should thank you for keeping me from who knows what. If I had stayed in that big empty lodge all by myself, I would surely have eaten my way into a coma or gone mad. They write movies about that sort of thing."

"Well the ride to crazy town is short, since you've been well on your way since we met," he said.

She threw a throw pillow at his head. "Hey we're cheering me up, here."

With a playful smile he titled his head and said, "So, say it, country music's not so bad."

"I'll have to kill you if you repeat this, but I think I actually enjoyed the line dancing."

"Ha, I knew it! Sometimes you just need to mix it up. Try something different."

"I'm not buying boots anytime soon, but it was fun."

"Just wait and see. Those boots will be on your feet in no time."

"Never." She checked her phone, no service. "I can't stop thinking of little Olivia's face when she walked out the door. And Sophie, she is enamored by Bree. She's young and beautiful. like a shiny new toy."

"First off, Olivia is wise beyond her years, but she'll be just fine. I've seen Bree, she looks like the offspring of Dolly Parton and Shaquille O'Neal."

Megan belly laughed at the thought of her ridiculous looks. He was right, she was all smoke and mirrors, not a real thing about her other than her genuine dislike for children.

"I know it's not her idea to have the girls."

Rylee Ridolfi

"Of course it's not. And I bet a weekend with them might just cut that custody battle short."

"That's my dream. I don't mind them seeing their father, but he continually disappoints them. I can't stand the thought of him promising them weekends and breaking their little hearts, time and again."

He moved over closer to her, his blue eyes twinkling in the fire's glow, "They'll be fine for tonight. Now how can we get your mind off this?" he said fiddling with his phone. "Darn thing can't get any service." He stood up, "Hold on, would you look at that," he said as he made his way to the kitchen counter and retrieved an old cassette player. He brought it over to the couch. Inside an old cassette of Christmas music sat inside the dusty box. He tucked the cassette into the cassette player and the sounds of Dolly and Kenny's Christmas lit up the log cabin.

"How about a little Christmas game to get us in the mood?"

Her heart speeds up at the words 'get us in the mood'. Her eyes wide, she was certain she hadn't breathed in two minutes.

"Mind out of the gutter McKenna, the Christmas mood," he said, flashing those pearly white teeth and a smile that could steal the sun. "This is exactly what we need. Hey, and before we start, how about we give this sad little tree a bit of love." He grabbed the balls on the table and brought them over to the tree.

Megan felt her own cheeks rounding as she let out a laugh. "That may be a tall order."

"Chicken."

Christmas Under Construction

She jumped up and pulled a red ball from the bowl and hung it on the weak branch. He followed with the rest of the balls, until the little tree was filled.

"Now look at that, we can actually work together," she said playfully.

"Ok now. have you ever played 'name that'?"

"Name that what?" Megan asked.

"Could be a Christmas song, a character, a movie or a tradition."

"Oh, and you know Christmas trivia?"

"What's the matter McKenna, scared that this old softy might just shut you down?" he said with a devilish grin. The type of grin that got girls in trouble, the type of grin that taunted your inner bad girl. She wanted to say no, but found her competitive nature answer with, "What are we playing for?"

"I don't suppose strip trivia is an option?"

Again, she threw a pillow at him, "How about the winner buys lunch tomorrow?"

"Boring," he said. "Okay first category, name that movie. Because I'm a gentleman, I'll let you go first."

She sat Indian style in front of the fireplace and thought for a second before saying, "Movie where Santa is cancelling Christmas?"

"A Year Without a Santa Claus, bam!" Stone said. plopping directly next to her. "Too easy. My turn. Movie where singing saves Christmas."

Megan tapped her hands to her knees, "I know this, um," she struggled, "Elf."

Rylee Ridolfi

"Lucky. Alright name that 'tune'. I'll play the first few notes of this old cassette and you have to name it." He hit the play and the first few notes rang out. Megan jumped up and in a high-pitched voice yelped, "Hark the Herald Angels Sing."

After a small victory dance, Megan took the small box and pushed the forward button three times then hit play. The song, soft and sweet, filled the room. Stone's eyes squinted as he titled his head to the left, "What the heck is this?"

Megan hit the off button. "That's it, all you get, now name it."

"I have no clue."

"Are you kidding me? Only one of the best Christmas songs ever. Dolly Parton's Hard Candy Christmas," Megan said, hitting the play button and standing up to sway to the music.

He stood next to her, "I didn't peg you as a Dolly girl."

"Seriously, who's not a Dolly girl? I mean I realize she falls in the country lane, but her songs have such passion. This song is so powerful, she's saying through her pain she'll be alright." Her eyes focused on the paltry tree as she fought back tears.

He took her hand and sat her in front of the fireplace. "My mom had a saying, 'You can't worry yourself a positive result.' Translation: worrying never fixes things. So, for tonight at least, just watch that peaceful snow falling and trust that things will work out as they should."

"She sounds like a wise woman."

"She was," his voice trailed off.

"Oh my gosh, I'm sorry, I forgot Charlotte told me she passed."

"It's the biggest regret of my life."

"What is?"

"I put a relationship and work before going to see her."

"To see her?"

"I thought I could do it all. I wanted to please a woman, so I worked myself into complete exhaustion. My mom became ill, I got the call she was declining. My flight was scheduled the next day to come see her one last time. Working almost ninety hours a week, I hadn't slept or really eaten anything for I'm not sure how long. I was on scaffolding about twenty-five feet in the air..." A silent pause filled the room. "I lost my balance and fell to the concrete."

"You're lucky to be alive."

"I am. I didn't even know I was alive until about a week later when I woke up in Aspen Hospital. I had a concussion and was kept in a medical coma. I broke about seven ribs, fractured my left wrist and spilt my head open. It took me a bit to remember things, but when I did, I asked for my phone. Some fifty calls that week from my dad. The last one said she passed and that her last word was 'Stone.' I called him, but it was too late, the funeral was over. Didn't matter much because I couldn't travel, and spent the next two weeks in the hospital."

"And your girlfriend, did she feel awful?"

"No, when I called to tell her what had happened, she told me she met a guy who had the world at his fingertips. She left me a pleasant voicemail saying she hopes I heal.

Rylee Ridolfi

Then I sat alone in my hospital room filled with guilt and regret for having lost sight of my priorities."

"That's unfathomable." She could see the tears in his eyes. What she didn't know was if the tears were for the loss of his mother, the damaged relationship with his father, or the woman who had left him at his most vulnerable time.

Megan moved closer on the furry bear rug in front of the fireplace and put her hand on his shoulder. He turned to her and tears long fought rolled down his face. She found her arms pulling him in toward her. Stone held on tight allowing the comfort of Megan's soft embrace to soothe him. They sat quietly, then he turned to her. Their eyes met. His soulful blue eyes, tear-filled and pained, met hers.

"I've never told anyone that story. And I've never let myself cry before, because I deserve this pain."

She rested her soft hand on his rugged cheek. "No one deserves this pain. You couldn't have known you wouldn't make that flight. Some things are out of our control. Your mother knew deep in her heart you would have been there if you could. Mothers have instincts when it comes to their kids."

"I loved her so much. She was my rock. No matter how much my father and I disagreed, she never took sides. She just hugged me and let me know how much she loved me." His eyes wet again forced him to look away.

"Hey don't. Tears are our way of letting out the pain," she pulled him back toward her.

This time their eyes met, slowly allowing their lips to follow. This kiss felt different than the others they had shared, deeper and more intense. It had been a while since she felt the warm strong hands of a man on her skin. Unlike a kiss with Chase, Stone was present, passionate. Stone looked at her, really looked at her. His smile, genuine, made her feel beautiful, appreciated, and treasured. Neither one was prepared for the kiss, nor the emotions long pent up inside that would surface, tempting their explosive chemistry much like the storm raging outside.

The storm outside picked up in intensity, with fury sending branches and icicles smacking the windows. The wind howled at the old cabin walls, but inside the warmth of their bodies entwined made them forget about the cold, their pain or that they agreed to keep things professional. Megan laid down next to him and they allowed themselves to surrender to the kiss, the warmth, the passion. The smoldering fire lured them to sleep wrapped in each other's arms until the bright sun broke through the cabin window nearly blinding them.

She smiled, eyes still closed, reveling in the warmth of his body and the safety of his hug. "Last night was amazing," she said dreamily, not quite with it just yet.

"I second that," he said, smiling at her. Megan's eyes opened, his toned muscular leg resting across hers as she heard a gasping sound escape from her lungs. "Woah where'd you go?" he asked her in response to her face that went from ecstasy to complete panic.

The color drained from her face. "What did we just do? I mean you, me," she said, popping up and wrapping her body in his flannel. "I mean we are two adults. And adults do this kind of thing, right?"

"Yes, I believe it is fairly typical practice among the adult population."

"I mean, it didn't mean anything. It was snowing, it only made sense, right?"

"Right? I guess."

"You guess. What does that mean?" She paced frantically back and forth on the worn wooden floors. "I mean we certainly don't have feelings for each other. That would be weird. You're not my type at all. I could never in a million years be with a blue-collar man, who lives in a shack."

"You do know I can hear you, right?"

"Of course, this is like the movies. It snows, people kiss, right? They kiss passionately and snuggle, right because it snows?"

"I'm not exactly sure that snow and kissing are directly related, but okay if it makes you feel better."

"I've only dated Chase since high school, so this is my first snow with a guy, if you know what I mean."

"I think I do."

"Well it can never snow again. We're good on that, right? This never happened."

"If that's how you want it," he said, his face now looking largely confused and a bit hurt. Studying her expression, he tried to figure out what had just happened. He knew the closeness they shared was more than either had intended that night, but he didn't regret it. He had feelings for her despite the crazy bipolar affection she showed toward him. He wondered if he would ever be enough for a girl like Megan. He wasn't enough for Claire, despite his million-dollar jobs. It didn't matter, in a month he would leave Connecticut and get back to his real life, one where he had ten crews under him, traveling to exotic places, taking on architectural challenges and delivering masterpieces. He would be swimming in the kind of wealth that women like Claire and Megan required. Although money to him meant nothing, designing and building, creating masterpieces was all he cared about now. Money cost him his parents. He had learned the hard way that people are the only thing that have any real value in this life. He would never again make that mistake.

"It is. I'll get dressed in the bathroom and you call Chuck. See if the car is done."

"Okay Megan, but for the record, it was more than snow for me."

"Never happened," she said scampering into the bathroom. Holding her breath, she gazed in the mirror. What had she done? Soon she'd be on her way home and she could begin the daunting task of erasing this from her mind.

Chuck came through as promised in a four-wheel drive truck around noon. He drove them first to check on the car, then to a small tavern to wait for a rental. Brunch was as silent as an Olympic tennis match. The silence interrupted only by the ringing of Stone's cell phone.

He swiped the phone then calmly answered, "Hello.' She watched his face change. "Claire, hi. How are you? No, I didn't. Thank you, I had no idea. When is it being shot?" he said before whispering to Megan, "I have to take this," and disappearing.

Claire, Megan thought as she fought an unexpected pang of jealousy. *Was she the woman who had hurt him? If so, why would he still talk to her? Why did she even care why he was talking to her? The fact that she just had shared a passionate night with a man who she would never in a lifetime be with might have had something to do with her rollercoaster emotions.* She watched as he walked side to side in the lobby of the tavern. Megan hated the emotions that pulled at her heart as she watched his broad smile swallow his face. *This is utterly ridiculous* she told herself. After all, she had just made it perfectly clear that she wanted nothing to do with him. He returned a few minutes later, uplifted, renewed, different.

"Is everything okay?" she found the words just tumbling out of her mouth.

"Better than okay," he said, waving the waiter over for the check. Suddenly in a hurry to end this awkward lunch, he paid and they scurried off to pick up the rental. They headed back to the lodge. The snow-covered slopes, now blanketed in a fluffy layer of snow gave life to the mountains. He hummed along with the Blake Shelton tune, almost oblivious to her presence. Maybe he was honoring her wish to pretend it didn't happen. Maybe he was relieved to not have to address it. Either way, Megan had never been happier to see the lodge. They pulled up to find a delivery truck with lumber, counters and cabinets. Several extra workers were waiting to give Stone a hand installing the kitchen.

"Okay then, back to work boss," he said with a twang of sarcasm coupled with a dash of anger.

Stone went to work logging in the items. Megan went straight to her suite. Stone took Sunday off and the girls returned early. Bree looked haggard, not to mention annoyed. Sophie sang the praises of daddy's new house and Olivia went straight to the lake to check her fish. Chase clearly had taken on more than he bargained for and was all too quick to say the next few weekends were booked because of wedding things. Megan was grateful due to Thanksgiving being right around the corner. She would have the girls to herself.

Chapter Sixteen

Stone worked feverishly on the downstairs renovation, while Megan picked up pieces to accent the décor. Molly called for a meeting between the three, Megan tried to wiggle out of it, but to no avail.

Molly gathered Stone and Megan to the living area of the lodge. Her freckled face beaming with joy as her eyes canvassed the renovated lodge. "Thanks, guys, for meeting with me. I don't have words to describe how perfect this feels. You are truly capturing the warm, cozy, welcoming vibe while keeping it modern and fresh. You two are doing a remarkable job." She turned her eyes to the old kitchen. "I can hardly believe this old kitchen is now the home of Toasty Mugs."

Megan and Stone had converted the small kitchen just left of the check in desk into a coffee shop and bakery that would serve lattes, hot cocoa, assorted coffees and teas, and a wide variety of donuts, pies, cookies and bagels. The cabinets in a warm chestnut and the counters in a cream, brown and black Corian with walls painted in a warm Kahlua welcomed guests after a long day on the mountain or at the village.

"I can't believe how far you two have come since the beginning, not even looking at each other, now you're working in sync, like two minds became one. You two are a dream design team."

"Two minds become one, never heard of that one. Now two bodies becoming one yep," said Maxie as she entered the room.

"What are you talking about?" snapped Megan. "We are not one. Clearly!"

"Okay, geez, pipe down," said Maxie. "What's going on here?"

"Nothing, just telling these two how perfect they are together," said Molly.

"I agree," said Edward as he came in from the hallway. "Come to think of it, what are you doing for Thanksgiving, Stone? We'd love to have you join us at the house. Listen here, we won't take no for an answer after all you have done to make this renovation happen."

"Dad, I'm sure he has plans," said Megan, shooting Stone a death stare.

"No as a matter of fact, not a one. I'd love to join you, Edward. Thank you."

"Great, Molly will give you directions. Swing by say, around noon."

This was a disaster. She couldn't tell her sisters, her mother or father that she had shared a snow moment with *him* of all people. She felt like she might burst. She knew what she needed to do. She would bare her soul at her appointment on Wednesday. Every two weeks she escaped for much needed therapy. She would admit what she had done. It would be like a confession of sorts. After all, Judy never judged, just silently listened. Wednesday came around quicker than she expected. She drove downtown and waited patiently for her appointment. Judy, with her silky, dark hair, called Megan back. Megan took a seat across from her and wasted no time getting right down to what was bothering her.

Judy was perfect at her job. Her face wore an almost frozen expression; nonjudgmental. Her face said nothing at all, but that was fine with Megan. She could tell her anything with very little reaction. It was so freeing, just telling one person in the world what really was going on in her head. No judgements, no words, just an ear to unload on for an hour every other week.

"Okay, well a lot has happened since I saw you two weeks ago. I mean not a lot, you know the carpenter, the attractive sexy one I can't stand? I slept with him. Well, not actually slept with him. I mean technically I slept wrapped in his arms in nothing but his shirt. And we kissed, we kissed a lot. I mean not just any kiss, a *snow* kiss. You know, the kind that makes you tingle from head to toe, kiss. I have no idea why this happened. I mean it's completely out of character for me. He's completely wrong for me and now things are, well, awkward and if that's not bad enough, my dad invited him for Thanksgiving dinner tomorrow."

Judy pulled her mask down, put down her nail file and said, "You did what? Megan, you slept with the contractor?"

"Wait, you speak English? I've been getting my nails done by you for four years and you've never spoken a word. After all the stuff I've told you, you choose *now* to speak words? And to set the record straight, yes, we slept, not *slept together like slept together, more like just slept together.*"

"Chase seems like a jerk, and I was thinking one of you may kill the other, but this I didn't see coming," said Judy, shaking her head then picking up the red color polish and swiping a splash of color on each nail.

"Who could've seen this coming? He's a rugged, low budget builder. That's not my type. He gets in my head, drives me crazy with his analyzing me, making me laugh, playing with my girls, listening to me whine, oh no Judy, I like him, don't I? No, don't answer that. I can make this go away."

"No, you can't, you crazy girl. You got it good, or is it bad? I never understand you people's lingo. All I know is that you haven't stopped talking about him since the day he walked into your lodge a few months ago. You friend, are falling for the builder."

Megan dropped her head on the table. "This is awful."

"Was the kiss awful?" Judy said, placing Megan's hands under the dryer.

"It was mind blowing. I mean I was married for years, but I can tell you it was never like that. It was sweet, soft and strong all at the same time. I've made such a mess of my life," Megan said as she dropped her head on the table.

"It will be a mess if you get polish in your hair."

For the next fifteen minutes, Judy listened while Megan ranted about her situation. By the end, she felt marginally better. She had decided that he had no power over her. She could do this. They would be finished with the lodge in approximately a month and then she would never have to see him again. Megan made her way to the counter to pay. She reached gingerly into her purse to get out her money when she saw her phone blinking. She had turned it on silent for her therapy.

"Thank you, Judy. I just have all these stirrings in me and it's not because Stone's hot, funny, strong, and an amazing kisser but..." she stopped abruptly when she heard his voice.

"Megan," said a male voice from behind her.

"Hot builder twelve o'clock. I'm not sure what the clock has to do with it, but American expression," said Judy.

"He's behind me, right?"

"Yep," said Judy with a nod.

Not daring to turn around she blurted out, "Stone, hot, sexy, Stone?" She couldn't believe her mouth betrayed her like that. "I swear I've developed some type of sexual running of the mouth when he's around," she said, lowering her voice.

"Megan, I still can hear you. I'm less than a foot behind you," he said.

"Of course, you can. Did you need something?" she said as she turned around.

"Molly said you might be here. Chartreuse called, and the table came in. The shop is only a block down from the salon, so I was wondering if you would go have a look. If you don't like it, we don't buy it. What do you say?"

"Say yes," Judy said, pushing her toward him.

"Okay fine, but I'm certain I am not going to like some old snow table."

The two walked toward the door and the nail techs exploded in cheers. They strolled downtown noting that all the windows had changed from mums and scarecrows, to pine trees and Santa's. Ahead, they saw Chelsea's decorated in a sea of white and gold furs and glittering trees, a breathtaking display as usual.

"That's so beautiful. I would like to incorporate some of the whites into the rustic theme of Christmas in the main room," she said, forgetting for a moment the awkwardness between them.

"I'm sure they have a ton of things inside you could choose from."

Inside Chartreuse greeted them like old friends. "Loves, so good to see you again. How's the lodge coming?"

They both started speaking at the same time then sharply stopped. "You go," Megan said.

"The floor is all yours," said Stone. The tension razor sharp.

"Wait a minute, uh huh. Chartreuse knows what's going on here. A little snuppy puppy went down. You took my advice and test drove the merchandise. A little road test to clear the air. Very nice."

"No, no nothing like that. We never, we'd never. The thought of him kissing me, ugh," babbled Megan.

"Wrong," Chartreuse said, snappishly clasping his fingers down on his thumb quickly. "You can lie to yourselves but not me. Have you forgotten I have a keen sense of sextuition? You know, I can sense when two people have tested the undeniable chemistry waters. No worries, I'll keep your secret. Now we have the table and a few custom pillows and blankets for you, Miss Megan."

Megan felt a flush in her cheeks. Consumed by the thought that her family may also have some sort of sextuition, panic washed over her with the thought of facing them tomorrow. The two followed him over to the table. Megan wanted to hate it, but she couldn't believe how perfect it was. Two vintage snowshoes, a bit weathered, acted as the surface of the table that was anchored with vintage birch logs.

"Yes?" asked Chartreuse.

"That is pretty cool, I must admit," said Megan. "Yes."

"Next we have oversized white fur blankets. My personal fav pillow is the vintage Volkswagen with a wreath on the front while toting a snow-covered Christmas tree on the roof, love. Then of course, the buffalo check and the multitude of pillows with sayings." He held up the *Merry and Bright*, two cable knit pillows in cream, a giant red and white hooked pillow that read *Let it Snow*, several reindeer pillows, and a few white furry ones. They were exactly what Megan had envisioned. The two six-foot white birch tree lamps they had ordered were just right for either side of the sofa. Molly would be so proud. The last thing they would see was the massive chandelier Megan had picked to center the entry of the lodge. A hand-forged, five-tiered candle chandelier with bronze antlers. The light weighed nearly a hundred pounds and stood five feet in diameter. The remarkable light would surely be the focal point of the room.

Overwhelmed with joy, she felt a rush of emotion take over her. She felt a tear welling up in her eye.

"Hey, what's wrong?" asked Stone, placing his strong hand on her arm. "No tears, this is exactly what the guests are going to adore. You've done an extraordinary job at taking an outdated lodge and making it something people will line up to see."

She turned to him. It was the first time she had looked at him, really looked at him since that night. His eyes were soft, yet reassuring. His smile offered support and accolades. He meant it, just like he said, he was a man of his words. She wanted to lean in and kiss him, feel his lips on hers, feel the strength of his arms securing her body to his. They moved closer, silence, then closer. Their lips mere inches from each other's when she remembered Claire, the woman who called and had made his whole demeanor glow. She pulled back abruptly.

"Oh God, we were having a moment there. What happened?" said Chartreuse, standing but a foot away, also with a tear in his eye.

"Nothing," Megan answered quickly.

"Fine, for the record you two are impossible. Now darlings, I have one more thing I need to show you. It just came in, and well, of course I thought of our lodge."

"Really, what is it?" asked Megan.

"Come, come this way," he said, leading them to the inventory room. "This was just logged in this morning. I put a red tag on it to hold, in case you two complicated lovebirds in denial wanted first dibs."

They opened the double swinging doors that lead to the showroom design center and there it sat, a dining room table made of recycled barnwood, designed for the Ralph

Lauren collection. The table offered seating for twenty. It would complete the look of Toasty Mugs. Upscale, warm, rustic elegance. Megan knew she had to have this but feared even asking the cost out loud. Her face a mix of childlike enthusiasm and adult financial panic led Chartreuse to say.

"It is a bit pricey, but you can apply for a line of credit. It may not be a bad idea given that you have several other projects to complete in the lodge."

Megan thought about it then agreed. She decided Molly had entrusted her with this project and she would not let her down. After signing the paperwork, she was shocked to hear she was denied. Panic took hold of her. "Wait, denied? Why?"

"I'm unsure, but if you want, I'll hold it for you and you can check out what's going on."

"Thank you. Once I figure this out, I'll be back," she said. They loaded Stone's new truck with their newly acquired goods. "How about a coffee?" he asked.

"Yes, my treat," she insisted. They walked across the street to a Starbucks and Megan ordered two Caramel Lattes with extra whipped cream. The cashier rolled her eyes, "Yeah, so your card was denied."

"My card was denied? That can't be right."

"Ok, and I haven't heard that before. You going to pay some other way or what?"

"Yes of course; here, try this one."

"Denied," said the girl clearly annoyed at this point.

"There must be something wrong with your machine," Megan said, her face now boiling red.

"I got this," said Stone. "You get the next one," he said, handing the girl his debit card.

Megan walked over to a table in a fog. "I don't understand. I have enough money in my account to pay for a latte. I have been painfully frugal since Chase left. He hasn't paid me in a while."

"You look a bit pale. Let's get out of here. Can you make it to the car?"

She said nothing but responded to his hand when he helped her up. They headed to the car. The ride home was awkward as Stone tried to make small talk. They pulled into the lodge and she saw Giovanni, a retired chef from Anthony's restaurant. He had become a grandfatherly type to the girls. He often helped out if the girls arrived home from school before Maxie.

Stone opened the door of the truck and ushered her out. "Okay perk up, the girls will be inside."

Megan entered the lodge to find Gloria covered in flour, Giovanni with cookie batter smudged across his forehead and Sophie and Olivia screaming at the top of their lungs. The poor little man with the kindest face looked close to a nervous breakdown.

"What's going on here?" yelled Megan.

"Ms. Sophie was helping me cook, then she got a call and well, threw our chocolate chip cookie dough against the wall before engaging in a colossal meltdown."

"Sophie, this is unacceptable. Apologize to Giovanni right now."

"Hadley Hollins got the new Pretty in Pink doll that came out today. I asked you for that last week. I wanted to be the first to have it and you didn't get it."

The color drained from Megan's face remembering the expensive doll cost sixty-five dollars, something she wouldn't have given a second thought to a few years ago, but now this would be the first of many things she would have to deny her daughters.

"Sophie, first that is no reason to act out, second you can't just get everything you want. You need to go to your room and take a time out, young lady."

"Why not? I want it, and besides, I'm not the one who should get a timeout," she said, pointing her flour covered finger at Olivia who stood quietly next to Giovanni.

"Olivia, what is she talking about?"

"I'll tell you," said Sophie, both hands on her hips. "She cut up all her socks. Yep, now she doesn't have any. Now who's in trouble?"

Again, Megan's legs felt a bit weary as she tried to process this information. Then, like a volcano, she erupted, probably not much different than the meltdown Sophie displayed moments earlier.

"Olivia Grace Barrington, is that true?" Megan asked, glaring at the little girl.

Olivia wiped a puff of flour from her freckled cheek. Her tiny chest started to heave up and down as she struggled to speak.

Before the little girl melting down in her own quiet tearful way had a chance to speak, Megan continued. "Why would you do such a thing? No, don't even try to explain. I don't want to know. What do you think you are wearing to school tomorrow? Money doesn't grow on trees. You are ungrateful and your actions were reckless. Go to the couch and start your timeout. Now!"

Sophie stomped off toward her bedroom, Giovanni, who at this point looked a bit frightened of both Sophie and Megan, headed to the closet for a broom. Olivia sobbed her way to the sofa. Megan broke down in tears.

Stone took her by the hand and led her into the café section. "Hey, look at me. It's going to be okay. I promise. Now take a breath."

"I didn't mean to yell at Olivia. It's just I don't know what to do, it's so out of character for her" she said, realizing her rage had little to do with the girls, but rather her own issues.

Stone put his hands on her shoulders, "Okay, how about you go see Sophie and I'll talk to Olivia. Let Sophie explain her actions and I'll try and see if I can get to the bottom of the sock massacre."

"It's not her fault. I have spoiled Sophie in the beginning when Chase left. She is just like me; she likes the finer things. I thought it would make the pain a little less. And my poor sweet Olivia, she never asks for anything. And most of all, she never acts out. I can't for the life of me figure out why she would behave so poorly."

"There must be a reason. She seems to talk to me. Let me try," Stone said. His compassion and calm demeanor made her believe him. Megan headed down the hall and Stone made his way to the sofa.

****

Stone looked at the tiny redhead with big green tearful eyes. She clutched a plastic bag tightly to her chest.

"Hey there little Red, tough day? Mom had a tough day too. Did you really cut up all your socks?"

She nodded then pulled the bag tighter.

"Is that them? Maybe I can help. There must be a reason you cut those socks up."

She opened the bag and pulled out one of the butchered socks, each about two inches wide. "They're fish sweaters. I promised my fish in the lake I would bring them in before it got cold. Then it snowed and I couldn't get to them. It might snow again tonight." She sniffled and then sobbed, "The fish are cold, but mommy said no, my fish can't come in," she wiped a tear that rolled down her freckled cheek. "So, I made them all sweaters. I just wanted to protect them."

Stone had seen a lot in his life, good and bad, but in that moment, he felt his heart thump with emotion in the innocent words of this little girl. He struggled to find words to say to the little one who just took a beating from her mother's bad day. She didn't fight back like Sophie; rather she took her punishment like a trooper as to not add any more on her mother. He held the miniature sock sweater in his hand. He gazed into her tearful eyes and said, "It's okay, Red."

"I can't let them die, they're my only friends," she said. Then she threw her tiny arms around his neck and buried her head in his shoulder.

Awkwardly, he put his hands around her and pulled her a little tighter. "Now enough tears, Red. Can I let you in on a secret?"

She pulled back and shook her head, her fogged glasses sliding down her face.

"The fish in the lake don't need to come inside. They adapt to their environment. That means they will find a way to stay warm. They swim upstream in the winter, but they'll be back in the spring. You don't have to worry about them, but it was very sweet that you cared enough to make them sweaters. I don't think mommy will be upset with you when she understands why you cut up your socks."

"I'm sorry, I didn't mean to make Mommy so mad."

"I promise you; she'll understand. One more thing Little Red, what about me? I thought we were friends?"

She smiled. "Yep you are my best friend," she said before kissing his cheek.

His heart melted with the tiny kiss from the sweetest kid he ever met. "Hey, why don't you go check on Giovanni. I'll talk to mommy."

"Okay," she said, "What about my fish sweaters?"

"I'll hold onto them. There might just be a market for them, you never know, you could be onto something."

She ran off toward the kitchen.

Megan returned a few minutes later looking exhausted. "Sophie isn't breaking, she's still angry at me for not buying her the doll. She hates me because I can't give her that doll. I'm ruining her life."

"First of all, she doesn't hate you, and second I can say with great certainty that no child's life has ever been ruined because they weren't the first to get a new doll."

"What about Olivia's rebellious act?" she asked, hands on her hips.

He reached in the bag and pulled out several cut sock pieces. "There's actually a very good reason for the sock massacre."

"Really? What could that possibly be?"

"Fish sweaters."

"Excuse me?" she said, holding the miniscule sweater in her hands.

"Yep, apparently she was told she couldn't bring the fish inside if it got cold."

Megan held the frayed sock to her heart, "I told her they couldn't come in and she was so worried they would freeze."

"Yeah, so... that's the beginning of fish sweaters," he said, putting one on the end of his finger.

Megan broke down in a puddle of tears. "Oh my gosh, I put her in time out for trying to save her friends. I truly am the worst mother ever. How did I turn into this monster?"

He put his arms around her and held her close. "I beg to differ. You must be a pretty incredible mom to turn out a little person with such a caring heart."

She pulled her eyes up toward his, "She really has a wonderful heart, doesn't she?"

"Yes, like her mother," he said as their faces moved closer. She found her lips leaning into his. His strength allowed her to melt and be taken care of, and if only for a moment, she didn't need to be the adult. His hands moved to her shoulders to comfort her. The two jumped and pulled back, when they heard Giovanni's hearty laugh filling the room.

Megan jumped off the couch, "Giovanni, I'm sorry about earlier. I had a difficult day and well, lately the girls are in some sort of a battle most of the time."

"No problem, I have five daughters myself. Some days a blessing, some days a curse. I understand your plight. Tony needs my help at the restaurant for dinner."

"Thank you so much for watching the girls."

Stone shook his hand and said, "Five girls, I'm pretty sure there's a place in heaven for you, sir."

"You seem to have a certain skill for making a very sad little girl smile yourself," Giovanni said to Stone, winking at Megan before leaving.

Stone suggested they order a pizza so Megan could try and restore peace between the girls. Stone ordered a pizza and a two-liter bottle of Coke. The four ate and laughed at Stone's silly jokes. Megan smiled at how easy it was for Stone to converse with the girls. Chase never really talked to them as people, rather like short employees. He gave instructions and expected certain outcomes, but rarely concerned himself with their feelings. That was Megan's job. For never having kids, Stone had a wonderfully warm way about him. Suddenly she found herself feeling hasty in having dismissed him so quickly after seeing him take the call from Claire.

"How about a board game?" he asked.

"Yes, yes!" the girls cheered. Megan's phone rang. "Excuse me, it's my hairdresser," she said.

Stone ushered the two girls into the great room and set up the game.

"Hey Claudia, what's up? Did I miss an appointment?"

"No, you'll never believe who is in my house right now?"

"I'll bite, who?" Megan asked.

"Remember my brother's roommate from college, Johnny Rocco, you know 'the Johnny Rocco', third string backup quarterback for the Eagles for the last two years. He just retired a multimillionaire."

"Wow, that's nice."

"Nice? Focus girl. Hot, handsome, multimillionaire, single Johnny Rocco."

Megan laughed out loud. "Oh, I get it, a setup. It's sad that my hairdresser has joined the fix-her-up brocade."

"I got you, girlfriend. So tonight, we're all going out to Bailey's on Main. The night before Thanksgiving everyone hits the clubs. Come join us. He's perfect for you."

Megan looked over at Stone wearing a Santa hat, leading the girls in a rousing rendition of Jingle Bells, Gloria's tail wagging, wearing red pom-poms around her ears, and the girls beaming with joy. A smile crept across her face. "No, I'm good actually, but thanks for thinking of me."

"Megan, are you thinking clearly? This is the man of your dreams."

"I appreciate your effort really, but not tonight."

"If you change your mind, you know where we'll be."

She hung up and headed into the room. "Hey, you're missing all the fun," he said.

"Stone is a walrus," said Sophie laughing.

"Okay one more game then it's bath and bed."

Megan settled the girls and tucked them into bed. Stone waited for her on the sofa in front of a roaring fire. "Thank you for today. You were wonderful with Olivia. You made an otherwise awful day better for all of us. I don't know what I would have done without you."

"No worries. I had a great day too. I don't know what's going on with Chase and your accounts, but maybe you can talk to him."

"Believe me, I'm going to talk to him. I've left ten messages. He emptied my accounts."

"How does he have access?"

"I guess I never actually changed the status of the accounts to remove him, but I'm going to get to the bottom of this."

"Okay, enough about the bad day." Stone paused, then placed his hand over hers. His eyes focused on hers. "Megan, I don't know what happened that morning after it snowed," he winked, "but this isn't about snow for me.

I think you're an amazing woman and I enjoy spending time with you. I hope you feel the same way."

"I'm sorry, I think I may have overreacted to the whole snow thing. I've just never done that and it sort of freaked me out."

"So, we can start over?" he said, leaning in for a kiss.

"I did hear it may snow tonight," she said, smiling before melting into his arms. They kissed passionately. Then the lodge door opened and Maxie and Molly strolled in. Deep in conversation, they hadn't noticed the two on the sofa, until in their haste to get up, they rolled off the sofa slamming into the snowshoe coffee table.

"Megan?" Molly said. The two popped up, hair standing on end, clothes ruffled.

"Yes, hello," Megan said, welding her hair down with her hand while pressing her shirt with her other hand.

"Well hello to you, too," said Maxie with one eyebrow raised.

Stone nodded, "Ladies."

Megan shot Maxie a glance, "I didn't think you were sleeping here tonight."

"Apparently not," Maxie said snickering.

"I wanted to have a meeting with you before the tree lighting on Friday night," said Molly awkwardly, her face reddened.

"Well, I'll get out of your way," said Stone.

"No, actually I was going to call you to join us. The lodge has turned out far better than I ever imagined. I can't thank you enough." Molly's eyes met the coffee table.

"What is that? It's utterly perfect. How, how did you two work through all that bickering and meet on such a perfect vibe?"

"We found common ground and it sort of took on a life of its own."

"Sure did," said Maxie, winking.

Molly jumped in to keep Maxie from tormenting the two. "Friday night is our big night up at Christmas Village. The lights are working, thanks to Walker, the employees are trained, Mr. and Mrs. Claus are ready to ride in on their sleigh and light the tree. Tony is cooking up a storm and Hunter well, bless his soul, he's doing just about everything else."

"You'll be there, right Stone?" asked Maxie.

"I hadn't thought much about it, but yes, I wouldn't miss it."

"Hey Megan, I didn't see your car out there," said Maxie.

"Oh, my goodness I left it uptown."

"I'll take you back," said Stone.

"Will one of you stay here with the girls?"

"Sure, we have a few last-minute things to go over before tomorrow," said Maxie.

"See you tomorrow Stone," said Molly.

"Thanks, girls. I'll be back," said Megan grabbing her coat.

"No hurry. You two take your time. Maybe finish up whatever we interrupted," said Maxie, raising her eyebrows.

Megan opened her eyes wide giving Maxie the 'stop speaking' look. Stone helped her put her coat on and the two headed out to the truck. They headed back to town as light snowflakes began to fall. "Do you think it's fate talking to us?" Stone said, smiling at her.

"I'm just not sure there is an 'us.' I mean, you're almost done at the lodge, then what?"

"Whatever we want. Megan, I'd like to give this a chance. No pressure, just enjoy each other and see where it goes."

"I'd like that," she said. He turned onto Main street. The parking spots were at a premium with all the bars filled with people returning home for the holidays.

"You can just drop me by my car, really it's fine. Thanksgiving Eve is always crazy around here."

"Nonsense, I'm in no hurry. We'll find a spot. They circled the block and watched a couple walk to a van two spots away from Megan's. They waited for the spot. He parked, opened the door and pulled her out giving her a gentle kiss. They walked hand in hand to her car as tiny wet flakes kissed their cheeks. He opened the door for her. She shivered. "You better get in there before you freeze."

She slipped the key into the engine and turned it once, nothing. "Not, now," she said. She tried two more times.

"How about you wait in my truck? It's warm, I'll have a look." She kissed him then headed to his truck. He took care of her, she liked that. She opened the truck door and slipped into the cab's warmth. The keys still in the truck kept the heat pumping. She settled in and smiled when she heard Blake Shelton belting out, *I'll be Home for Christmas*. She watched out the window as he opened the hood of her van and tinkered. She heard a phone beep once, then again two more times. She looked over to see the phone adhered to the dashboard. She attempted to pull it off to bring it to him then noticed the text. Megan didn't intend to read it but her eyes found themselves fixed.

Doc: Hey there I hear congratulations are in order. This is big, man. When Claire told us the news, we could hardly believe it. Who would have thought in a million years? This is a game changer. I hope you got it all out of your system because your life is about to change, man. Tux is on order. You're one lucky guy. Italy is waiting for your new life.

Megan sat frozen for a minute. She remembered Olivia saying she heard he was leaving for Europe after Christmas. He was getting married to Claire and Megan was just something he needed to get out of his system. Her blood ran cold. She marched over toward her car. She was about to blast him when she heard a familiar voice calling her from across the parking lot.

"Megs, you came," said Claudia. Megan looked up to see Claudia, her brother and the famous Johnny Rocco in the flesh.

"I, well my," she started then remembered the text. "Yes, I did."

"Perfect, Johnny this is her, the beauty I told you about, the infamous Megan Mckenna."

Stone lifted his head and slammed it hard on the hood. "Ouch," he said, rubbing his head and peeking out from the hood.

"Hello Megan," said Johnny, eyeing her from head to toe before leaning in for a kiss.

Awkward, thought Megan, but she went with it.

"Megan?" said Stone.

"Who is this?" said Claudia.

"My contractor," said Megan, still in Johnny's arms.

"Hi there handsome, I'm Claudia and if you're free, tonight just might be your lucky night."

"Am I Megan, free?"

"You're not married, so go for it. Get it out of your system."

Stone's eyes, a blend of confusion and pain fixed on Megan.

"Come on baby, let's check this scene out," said Johnny, sliding his hand around Megan's waist.

Megan looked at Stone and said, "Don't worry about the car. It's not your concern. I'll get a ride from Claudia. Goodnight."

Stone slammed the hood and said, "Claudia, I think I would very much like to join you."

Megan shot him a look. She was onto him. It ended today, he was no different than the rest of them, maybe just a little smoother. They entered the club from the back entrance. Thanks to Johnny they avoided the massive line of near frozen party goers. Inside, the room stifling hot, was filled with barely legal party goers and a smattering of couples, singles and regulars. The locals swamped Johnny for autographs, while Megan and Claudia grabbed a booth reserved for Johnny. Claudia's brother disappeared into the crowd. Stone slid in the booth directly across from Megan. Their eyes met in a visual tug of war.

"So, Megan, how's it that this gorgeous man is not on your arm?" said Claudia, sliding in next to Stone.

"We're simply working together on the lodge. He's not my type. He's all yours."

Stone never took his eyes off her despite her insulting words.

Johnny made his way to the table and slid in next to Megan. A waitress nearly sprinted to the table. Placing his hand on Megan's thigh, Johnny said, "Top shelf baby, bring us whatever they want," all the while eyeing up the waitress.

"How about a dance, Maggie?" Johnny asked.

"It's Megan, but yes I would like that," she said. "Claudia, you up for a dance?" said Stone, staring at Megan.

"Heck yeah," she said, slipping out of the booth.

The bass pounded. The floor was jam-packed with sweaty kids whose bodies gyrated in moves straight from the set of Dirty Dancing. The lights were changing colors rapidly, keeping rhythm with the beat of the hip-hop music. Johnny pulled her close. Stone put his hand on Claudia's waist then he positioned himself back to back with Megan.

"So, what's your game? Guy with more money?" he said, over his shoulder in her ear.

She spun around, he followed suit. Shoulder to shoulder their eyes locked like deer in headlights. "You should know about games. You're the master," then she twirled away. Stone twirled Claudia, let her go, and caught Megan in his arms. He pulled her close with the force of a boomerang. "I told you, I don't play games so here's your chance to tell me what's going on."

Megan attempted to pull back to no avail. "I have nothing to say to you."

He leaned in and said, "Then we're done here."

"Yes, we are done."

He walked away, leaving her standing at the center of the dance floor. Her head spun trying to figure out how long he could keep up this charade. She watched as he spoke for a second to Claudia then headed for the exit. Johnny, working the crowd, danced with three girls on the small stage set up for the club's dancers. Megan watched as he winked her way, waving her to join them. She had enough, she made her point clear to Stone, and with any luck he would choose to abandon the rest of the project and leave early for Europe. She politely thanked Claudia and explained she had an early day and needed to head out.

Pushing her way through the crowd, she felt the air in her lungs being sucked out as anxiety set in. She pushed harder until the door opened and she felt the cold wind sting her sweaty cheeks. Inhaling deeply, she felt a surge of bitter air fill her lungs. What was she doing? She had allowed herself to fall for another guy who would toss her aside when the thing he really wanted was available. Walking the slushy sidewalks, she watched couples cuddling, kissing, laughing. She increased her stride as she felt tears spilling down her near frozen cheeks. Unaware that she had begun a slow trot, she spotted the van and ran full force unlocking it and burrowing inside. She slammed the door and permitted the tears to fall uncontrollably. She had fallen for him, more so than she allowed herself to admit before this moment. It wasn't just snow for her either. He was different from all those internet guys. He made her laugh, she felt safe in his arms, she had allowed him into her life, her kids' lives. She jammed the key into the ignition only to be reminded the van was dead. Her fists banged the dashboard, cursing like a sailor, she let out every emotion she had pent up in the last two years. It felt good, like an empowered, psychotic manic episode. When her body finally gave way to exhaustion, she picked up her phone and called a cab.

In ten minutes, she was loading herself into the back of a Mazda CRV. She quietly gave the driver directions to the lodge and curled into the worn seat. The driver pulled into the lodge. "The place looks great. Any idea when they're planning on opening for the public?" the driver asked.

"Thanks, we are shooting for a grand opening the first weekend in December," she said, fumbling for her wallet.

The driver wished her a Happy Thanksgiving before taking off. Thanksgiving, she had forgotten all about the holiday tomorrow. The girls would be up early, and there would be a herd of McKenna's with an arsenal of questions just waiting for Megan. Gently, she slipped her key into the door and quietly opened it. With any luck, Maxie would be fast asleep with the girls. Megan couldn't handle explaining anything, at least not tonight. She hung her coat on the coat rack Stone had built out of deer antlers. Puddles streamed down her flushed cheeks.

Rylee Ridolfi

She plopped down on the leather sofa and pulled the furry blanket over her and lay down. She gazed at the glass wall and watched the tiny snowflakes dance and swirl off the roof. Her eyes closed as she slowly drifted off to sleep.

Chapter Seventeen

E arly the next morning Megan woke to a tiny hand on her shoulder. Megan pried one eye open and heard Sophie yelling, "Mommy, wake up. It's turkey day."

"Sophie, you're shouting," Megan said, struggling to open her puffy eyelids.

"Mommy, grandma said we can go over early and help set the table," said Olivia.

"She did? That's unlike her."

"Can we go?" the girls sang in unison.

"Sure, let me get myself together then I'll drive us over."

"You don't have to, daddy is coming. He said he will drop us after breakfast. He said he called you," said Sophie.

"No, he didn't. I don't know anything about this," Megan said, sitting up reaching for her phone. Five missed calls. She must not have heard it in the club. A voice message verified what the girls had said. Before she could object, the door opened and Chase and Bree barreled in. Bree with two large bags in her arms.

"Bree," Sophie said, in a high-pitched squeal. "Are they for us?"

"Yes, they are," said Bree, handing out the bags wrapped in striped foiled paper. Sophie stuffed her little hand into the bag and screamed, "It's the new Pretty in Pink doll. I love you Bree. You're the best. I can't wait until you're my other mommy."

Megan, too upset to speak, stared at the scene unfolding in front of her. Chase had left her and the girls. He had taken every last dime from her, and now he took the only thing she had left; her title, *Mommy*.

"Go get dressed ladies. I think we need some pancakes and whipped cream at the diner," said Chase. The two girls ran off but not before Olivia made eye contact with Megan. Megan saw her sweet empathic eyes, letting Megan know she loved her.

Megan clenched her fists and marched toward Chase, "We need to talk. Now."

"I left you messages, but you didn't answer."

"It's not about that. I spoke with Mr. Portner from the bank."

"Bree baby, why don't you check on the girls to make sure they put on something stylish, it's your specialty." The bimbo bought his smooth-talking ways and sashayed her way down the hall.

When she was well out of earshot Chase softened his tone, attempting to use his handsome charm, he placed his hand on hers. He still smelled the same, her heart thumped. Her blood boiled.

"Meg, let me explain, sweetheart. I did it for us."

She stiffened her stance, "There is no us."

"Listen, I had the opportunity to make a pretty big investment and buy into the business. I'm going to be partner. It was a bit of a risk, but this is good for all of us. We are sitting on a gold mine, and it's about to pay off," his blue eyes staring into hers the way they had so many times before when he filled her head with promises. Promises that were supposed to be her future.

"How dare you touch my money?" she said, pulling away.

"I know it was wrong not to talk to you first, but have I ever let you down?"

"Really, did you just ask me that?" He had taken the most sacred thing they had, a marriage, and destroyed it. He shattered every hope and dream they made, yet he still, in his narcissistic way, felt he hadn't let her down.

He moved in close again and pulled her chin toward him. She remembered his touch. There was a time when she too, believed his every word.

"Megan, I'd never put you or the girls' livelihood in jeopardy. If this goes through, you and the girls will have everything you want."

"Sophie wanted a doll that I couldn't give her, yet you could. And how do you know what I want?"

"That was all Bree. She knew how bad Sophie wanted it so she got one for both girls." Again, he moved in closer, "I know you Meggie, you want the finer things in life. That's who we are. I still know you. I know that right now you're…"

He stopped short when the girls rushed out dressed in the outfits Molly had bought them for Thanksgiving.

Sophie clutching her doll in one hand and Bree's hand in the other. Olivia dragged the doll by its foot, clutching Suppy in the other hand close to her heart.

Chase leaned in and whispered, "We'll continue this after the holiday."

"Girls, remember grandma is counting on you to help her with the table. Now give me a kiss."

Sophie freed herself just long enough to give Megan a half-hearted kiss then headed straight back to Bree. Chase gathered up their coats and ushered them to the door. Olivia ran over to Megan and whispered in her ear, "Sophie didn't mean to hurt you. She loves you and you're the best mommy in the world." She put her tiny arms around Megan's neck, offering reassurance when she needed it most.

"My sweet Olivia, thank you so much honey. I'm sorry I yelled at you for your socks. Your heart was in the right place. You go and have fun."

"Can I cut this sweater off Ms. Pretty in Pink and make more fish sweaters? It snowed again last night."

Megan smiled, "Yes sweetie, we'll figure out something with your fish, I promise."

The group walked out, leaving Megan alone in the lodge. Certain that she didn't have any more tears left, she let herself melt to the floor. Silently, she sat there and wondered how she had let her world get so out of control. Chase's words stung. He did know her, but there was so much more to her than her love of money. He just never bothered to see her, the real her. Her phone rang once. Mustering up the strength, she made it to the couch. "Hello."

"Hi Meg. Is Stone there yet?" said Molly.

"Stone? Why would he be here on Thanksgiving?"

"I asked him to have a look at the back door. Maxie said the wind was howling through that drafty door last night. What a gusty night, huh? Don't know if we need a new one or weather stripping. When are you coming over?" Molly said.

"Now," Megan said, needing to be long gone before Stone arrived. Megan rushed down the hall past Maxie's room, where she heard the sounds of Christmas tunes blaring. Avoiding Maxie, at least for the morning, seemed like a plan. She showered, blew out her hair, and dressed in record time. A rust colored turtleneck and cream jeans with a pair of luggage colored boots and she was out the door with time to spare. The fresh fallen snow had disappeared, as November snow does, giving way to a relatively warm, sunny Thanksgiving Day. Once outside, she realized she had left her car on Main Street. Perfect, now she would need to talk to Maxie. She marched back inside and knocked on Maxie's door.

"Hey there wild woman, how was last night?"

"Rather not talk about it. My car is dead up on Main. Is there any way I can borrow yours?"

Maxie eyed Megan up and knew her well enough to leave it alone. She walked over to the kitchen table and rummaged through a pile of papers, then pulled out the keys. She tossed them to Megan. "Sure, if you stop at Tony's to pick up the pies. Tony is picking me up and he already has a car full of food. Then he won't need to make two trips."

"No problem, got to go. See you at mom's," Megan said, not waiting for a rebuttal. Hurrying to Maxie's car, she dove in and peeled out. She had avoided him, at least for now. After last night, she was fairly certain he wouldn't be showing his face at her parents' house.

She headed to Bennie's for a latte. She sat inside, gazing out the window, watching as families rushed to get last minute things for the big dinner. Before heading to Tony's, she walked along Main, then headed toward her van. The lot had emptied with the exception of her van and one other run down truck. She noticed something on her windshield. She snatched the crumpled paper from her windshield, "A ticket, really?" No one would be open to tow her today. She opened the door and grabbed a white tee from the back seat and hung it from the window. She made her way back to Maxie's car and headed straight to Tony's.

Inside, the smell of roasted pumpkin, caramel apple and pie crust enveloped the air. Giovanni and Tony waited with a large carton filled with fresh pies. The two men loaded them into her car.

Inhaling deeply, she thanked them, then gave Tony a quick kiss on the cheek. "Thanks Tony. See you at mom's," she said before heading out. She made her way to her parents' house and pulled in the back, drew in a deep breath, then she calmly told herself, *this is family, Stone was her business, none of their business. They won't harass me too much*, then she shrugged her shoulders at how preposterous that sounded, even in her head.

Inside, Olivia and Sophie ran to greet her, "Mommy, you're here. We helped set the table," said Olivia. Molly and Hunter stood in the center of the kitchen covered in flour after an epic fail at recreating Grandma Bunny's biscuits. Hunter met her at the door and helped her with the carton of pies.

"Meg is that you?" called Silvia from the dining room. "Maxie and I are putting the finishing touches on the table. Megan felt her tension begin to melt in the familiar chaos. She smiled, put the pies down on the counter, and took both girls' hands as they led her to the dining room.

"Meggie," said Maxie.

"Megan," said a familiar voice. There he stood, right in the center of the dining room, reveling in the reaction that clearly had overtaken her face.

"Stone," she said, her voice frosty.

"We made pilgrim people name tags with Aunt Molly. And look mommy, we put you right next to Stone," said Olivia smiling widely.

"Maxie, we forgot the cornucopia," said Silvia. The two headed off to the front hall table, awkwardly trying not to be too obvious that they were leaving her alone with the beast.

"What are you doing here?" Megan whispered through her teeth.

"I was invited," he said smugly.

"Well I'm uninviting you," she said, both hands on her hips.

"Doesn't work that way."

Molly ran through the dining room door in a huff breaking the icy tension. "There you are, just the two people I need to talk to. I'm freaking out. Melvin, you know, Santa, anyway he broke his leg last night. His wife Katie, Mrs. Claus, said he'll be in the hospital until mid-week. They are sending over a replacement from the agency but not until Saturday. So that means opening night, the tree lighting ceremony will have an empty sleigh and no one to light the tree," she said, barely breathing between words.

"Slow down, Moll. We'll figure this out," Megan said, placing a hand on her arm. Knowing her sister all too well, Megan realized this might be the final straw that broke Molly's weakening shell.

"I was hoping you would say that. I have a huge favor to ask. I need you two to step in as Mr. and Mrs. Claus. Please, everyone else is doing five other jobs. It would save my life."

"Moll, I know this is a setback, but I'm sure we can find someone else who…" Megan started before Stone jumped in.

"We'll do it."

"What?" said Megan.

"Oh my gosh, thank you two so much," Molly said jumping into Megan's arms. "I owe you two, big. Hunter, they said yes! You guys are the best," she shouted to the kitchen as she ran off.

"What are you doing?" Megan said, hands planted firmly on her hips.

"Helping a girl out. Molly needs us, I figured we could help. Do you have a problem with us helping?"

Megan squeezed her brows hard. "You need to leave, think up some reason and just go," Megan said, pacing.

"Like?" said Stone, clearly enjoying watching her squirm.

"Your great Uncle Bill is stuck at the airport. You suddenly got a horrific case of the stomach flu. I don't care, just come up with one now."

"Just the two I was looking for," said Edward as he barreled through from the living room. "Charades are set up in the living room. This year we'll have three teams. Let's see how you two do as a team. Tony just got here. Where's Molly and Hunter?"

Stone followed the crowd to the living room.

"This can't be happening," Megan said under her breath.

"Okay rules; when the timer goes on, you have sixty seconds to figure out your partner's word or words. Molly, Hunter, you're first," said Edward.

Hunter pulled a card and smiled. The timer rang. He pointed to his head. "Head," shouted Molly. He ran his hand under his chin, then dropped his head downward. "Headless," she said. He nodded then rode an imaginary horse.

"Headless horseman," yelled Molly, jumping into his arms. "One-point team Hunt," said Edward.

"Megan you and Stone are next."

Stone chose a card. Edward rang the bell. Stone put up two fingers. "Two words," Megan said. He nodded. He pointed to his watch. "Two-timer," she said. He shook his head no. "Two faced," she said. Again, he shook his head. The bell rang. "It was a time machine," said Stone, shaking his head.

The group went around merrily shouting out correct answers until it was their turn again. She waited for the bell and drew a card. She played an air guitar. Stone chirped out, "Player." She squinted her eyes and shook her head. Next, she strummed imaginary drums. "Madwoman," he said, right before the bell rang. "Rock band!" she snapped.

Maxie and Tony gave each other an awkward stare. Molly scratched the hives on her arms.

Megan's cheeks reddened as her Irish temper neared explosion. The chiming of the dinner bell interrupted her rage.

"Dinner," called Silvia. Molly, Hunter, Maxie, and Tony headed inside. Edward collected the girls and followed, leaving the two alone briefly.

"I want you to leave," Megan demanded.

"Okay if that's what you want, or is it? Do you even know what you want?" Stone said.

"Me? You should talk. Maybe you should consider that your actions have consequences."

"What actions?" he asked.

Silvia was not the type of woman who excused tardiness, shouted out the door, "Are you two going to make me call you twice?"

Megan huffed, turned her back to him and marched inside. The family already seated, engaged in banter fell silent when the two entered. Olivia pointed to the two chairs where a Megan pilgrim girl sat directly next to a Stone pilgrim boy.

"Right, you two set the table. Perfect," said Megan, reaching for the chair.

Megan unfolded the neatly wrapped napkin and placed it on her lap.

Breaking the tension Molly piped up, "Everything looks delicious mom."

"You mean Tony," said Silvia. "Thank you for preparing this feast for us," Silvia said, raising her glass, "To the chef, Tony, it's nice to have you finally join us. Honestly, the hours you keep, I don't know how you two stay together."

Maxie shot Tony a look.

"Yes, thank you Tony for cooking all day on your day off from the restaurant," said Edward, toasting Tony with a raised glass. Everyone raised a glass. Edward continued, "Speaking of thanks, I would like to take a minute for each of us to say what we are thankful for. I'm thankful for this wonderful family that sits before me."

Next Silvia said. "I'm thankful that my three girls are working on the Christmas Village and Mistletoe Lodge together."

Molly looked at Hunter and said, "I'm thankful for these amazing people, each and every one of you, for helping me to make my dream a reality."

Hunter looked back at Molly and said, "I'm thankful in that less than a month, I can call you my wife." A sea of 'awe's' filled the room.

Maxie said, "I'm thankful for a rare evening with my man."

"I'm thankful that this year has made my restaurant number one in the state." The group cheered and clapped for Tony.

Sophie stood up and clinked her glass with her spoon. "I'm thankful that Bree got me my Pretty in Pink doll and all her accessories." Megan drew in a deep breath and bit her bottom lip.

"Olivia, do you want to say something?" asked Megan, knowing the shy girl rarely spoke in front of a crowd.

"Sure, she does. Come on Livie, you must be thankful for something sweetheart," said Edward.

Tucking a spiral red curl which had escaped a lopsided ponytail behind her ear, Olivia pushed her glasses up then turned to Stone. She quietly said, "I'm thankful for my best friend, Stone."

Megan quickly tried to intercept a tear which escaped her eye. How had this man who came into her life by accident, taken the time to make her baby feel blessed enough to view him as her best friend?

Stone stared across the table at the little freckle faced girl and smiled warmly. "I'm thankful for the opportunity to get to know a fabulous kid like you Red, and your sister Sophie and this whole amazing family. It has been a pleasure to work with you and be a part of this amazing endeavor."

"Megan, dear you're up," said Edward.

"I'm grateful for you guys standing with me through this last year. I couldn't have done it without you," she said, sniffling.

Edward grabbed his fork and nipped the tears in the bud, "Now, I think we can all agree we're thankful, so let's dig in."

"Stone we all have to say we are grateful that you came on board to complete the lodge. You and Megan did an incredible job," Molly said.

"I'll miss the lodge and all of you when it's finished."

"Are you going to Europe? That's far, away right?" Olivia said with a little crackle in her voice.

Megan turned to him with a fork full of turkey and said, "That's a great question. When are you leaving exactly?"

"I'm not entirely sure I'm going anywhere. I guess it depends if I have a reason to stay around."

Megan slammed her fork to the table. "Oh please, you know exactly where you're going," she said, her tone now tense and accusatory.

The crowd fell silent until Stone's phone rang. He pulled it out, looked down at the phone then excused himself. "I'm so sorry, I'll need to take this."

Stone pulled back his chair and made his way to the living room.

All eyes now fixed on Megan awaiting an explanation.

"Is there something we should know Megan," Silvia said, calmly swirling her cranberry sauce around her plate.

Rylee Ridolfi

"No, mother there is not," Megan said just as the house phone rang. Megan pushed her chair back, dropped her napkin in her lap and said, "I'll get it."

Any excuse to escape the prying eyes. Megan picked up the phone to hear Nana Bunny's sunny voice on the other end. "Megan darling, how is my sweet granddaughter doing?"

"Bunny, you have the best timing in the world. I wish you were here."

"You sound knackered dear. Who's the Muppet that has sapped the life from your voice?"

"Bunny, I've made a mess of everything. I swore I wouldn't fall for someone and I did. Now I don't have a clue what happened between us."

"Oscar Wilde," Bunny snapped back into the phone.

"Who?"

"Oscar said, 'The very essence of romance is uncertainty.' The mess is the very heart of the journey. The most beautiful love stories are the damn convoluted ones. Give in to the uncertainty, it will lead you either in or out. Only two choices."

"This is why I need you here."

"Darling, I'm always there with you; remember your compass. You wear it to remind you that family is never far. Besides, I've met a dapper fellow and we are traveling from Ireland to Austria for some skiing."

"A new fellow? Every time we talk there's a new one. Maybe you're onto something. I love you Bunny."

Edward entered the room and said, "Is that my crazy mother?"

"Sure is," Megan said, handing the phone to Edward.

Megan returned to the dining room to find the group talking about the wedding and the rapidly approaching Christmas Village opening.

"Mommy, can we go watch TV?" asked Sophie.

"Yes, please take your plates to the sink first."

Megan felt the eyes of eight McKenna's peering into her soul.

"Okay Meggie, spill. What is up with you two?" asked Maxie.

"I don't know what you mean," Megan said as she gathered her and Stone's plates.

"You most certainly do," said Silvia. "Something has you two jumping out of your skin at the thought of being seated next to each other."

Stone appeared at the doorway of the dining room. "Allow me to help with that," he said, grazing Megan's hand as he took the plates. She pulled back so quickly she dropped two forks and a knife onto the china. The peering McKenna eyes switched back and forth between the two like a swinging pendulum.

"Stone, how about we check out the game on TV? You like football?" said Hunter.

"I sure do. Sounds good, be there in a few," he said, taking the plates as he followed Megan into the kitchen.

Slamming the plates onto the counter, Megan turned to him and asked, "What are you doing? You have overstayed your welcome. Now go."

"Is this still because we spent the night in each other's arms then you flaked? I thought we got passed that last night until you flaked yet again."

"Shh, keep your voice down. Yes and no, and I didn't flake."

"You definitely flaked."

"You're utterly impossible."

"It's a close one, Stone. Come join us," shouted Hunter from the family room.

"When you want to talk, you know where to find me," he said, walking out the door toward the cheering group of guys.

"That's the problem, I don't want to find you in my living room," she said, stomping her foot.

Molly and Maxie passed Stone in the doorway and gave him the once over. Maxie slid up next to Megan and smiled. "Okay now dish, it's just us girls. Mom is with the little ones. The guys are deep into football mania. What is going on with you two? The tension is so hot I'm melting."

"He's just so, I mean, I can't with him…"

"Just spit it out. You kissed, we saw you," said Molly.

Megan put the soiled plate on the counter and slumped down into the kitchen chair. "We well we…"

"Just say it, you kissed the man?" Maxie barked.

"Well Chase was threatening to take the girls, I ate seven wedding cakes, I was crying, then Stone said 'you need something' and I thought it was pie, but it wasn't. We country line danced, then a crazy woman hit his car, there were no Ubers and we had to stay in a cabin. Then it snowed, and well you know what that means," she said, barely able to catch her breath.

Molly and Maxie stared cluelessly at the nonsensical tirade. Molly said, "The air temperature was below 32 degrees?"

"No, you know, 'snow,'" she said air quoting. The two looked at her dumbfounded. "Come on everyone knows snow leads to kissing and then we well, you know," she said rolling her arms.

"Man, I wish I was first born, Silvia really put an interesting spin on the birds and bees," Maxie said. "Wait, back up the train, you, Megan McKenna went country line dancing?"

"Really that's the alarming thing here?" Megan said hands waving in the air.

"Well this is a good thing, right?" Molly said sweetly.

"Well it was good, great in fact, better than I ever experienced in my whole life. I mean he was sweet and gentle and we talked about personal things. He stared into my eyes and held me tightly. We kissed and cuddled and snuggled the whole night."

"Oh, Meggie that's great," Molly said, clapping her hands wildly while bouncing back and forth.

"No, it's not great. He's an arrogant jerk who lies and is only here sowing his wild oats every snowstorm he gets."

Molly turned her eyebrows down and shook her head back and forth, "No, boo, not great," she said, trying to stay with the script.

"And what's worse is Judy says I'm falling for him. And she might be right."

"Hold up, Judy? Judy your manicurist? You told Judy your nail tech before us?" Maxie said, both hands out with palms up.

"Well yes, in my defense I didn't think she spoke English."

"True. I've never heard or understood a word she says," said Molly.

"You're missing the point. He used me. The first time I get back on the wagon, I'm an oat."

"Scratch that, I'm glad I wasn't first born, back on the wagon, really? What exactly is an oat?" Maxie said.

"It doesn't matter what they call it. I'm such a fool."

"Wait one minute here. I'm not buying that. If he chose Miami or maybe Vegas to sow his oats, maybe, but no one comes to Connecticut seeking oats. Second, have you seen the way he looks at you girl? He's into you," Maxie said, softening her tone.

"You think?" Megan said, wide eyed.

"Yes, Megan, and the way he takes care of you and the girls doesn't seem like a man who's sowing oats," said Molly.

"That's true, but the next day, the day after, I got, well a little skittish so I wanted to get home. It was awkward and we were both a bit quiet, then he got a call from a woman named Claire. His old girlfriend called and he perked up."

Both girls looked at her silently waiting for her to continue.

"What?" Megan said.

"That's it?" asked Maxie.

"No there's more, in his car I saw a text."

"You read his texts?" Molly whispered, her eyes widening as she began wringing her hands.

"Not on purpose."

"Of course, she did. What did it say?" Maxie asked.

"It was his friend. He said Claire told him the news and he couldn't believe it. Stone's whole life was about to change. He mentioned a tux and that he hoped he got it all out of his system while he was here."

"Okay, let's break this down. You like him. He likes you. You had an incredibly passionate night during a snowstorm and because you're trying to piece together a bunch of nothing, you hate him?" said Maxie.

"Pretty much," Megan said, realizing how dumb that sounded.

"Do you know for a fact this Claire is still in his life?" asked Molly.

"Not a hundred percent, or even ten percent actually."

"Okay then you need to talk to him. Now," said Maxie.

"Now? I can't," said Megan.

Maxie, pointing to Stone standing in the doorway said, "Yep, now. Okay well, let's go Molly and do that thing."

"That thing?" Molly said.

Maxie took a hold of Molly's, arm pulling her, "Yes, you remember," Maxie said, squeezing a bit tighter. Then the two disappeared.

Stone came into the kitchen, his eyebrows pinched, without his normal vibrancy.

"Um Stone, I just wanted to ask you something," Megan said, tripping over her own words.

"Yeah, sure," he said before his phone buzzed. "Excuse me," he said reading a text.

"Busy night for you, huh?"

"Uh yeah, I have to go Megan. Thank your parents again for me."

"Oh okay, yes, will do."

He tossed his phone in his pocket and slipped his jacket on. Just before he reached the door he turned to Megan. "Hey, did you want to ask me something?"

"Just wanted to know if you wanted some pumpkin pie."

"No, I'm good, thanks though. And Megan, I hope I didn't ruin your holiday. Goodnight."

Then he disappeared into the blackish gray night. He was here right next to her all night, then she practically threw him out the door. Now when she wanted to talk to him, he was gone. Were her sisters right, was she letting her imagination get the best of her? Just because Chase was a liar, doesn't mean all men are, but why did he need to leave suddenly after the phone rang? Her thoughts were interrupted by Olivia running into the kitchen calling for Stone.

"Hey sweetie what's up? Stone had to go."

Olivia's big green eyes furrowed. "I made him a turkey," she said, showing Megan a turkey made by tracing her tiny hand. The small paper turkey had red hair and wore a pair of glasses. "It's me."

"I'm sure he'd just love that sweetie. How about we save it and give it to him next time we see him again?"

"Tomorrow night, right? Aunt Molly said you and Stone are going to be Santa and Mrs. Claus."

Megan found a renewed sense of hope with the little girl's reminder that they would be together tomorrow night. "Yes, that's right."

Molly and Maxie returned to the kitchen as Olivia skipped out. "How'd that go? Wait, where is he?"

"He's gone."

"What did he say?" asked Maxie with both hands on her hips.

"Nothing, I didn't really get a chance to ask him. He got a text and suddenly had to leave in a hurry."

"Well Mrs. Claus, tomorrow night you will have plenty of time with Mr. Claus. Maybe after the tree lighting you two can straighten this whole thing out," said Molly, giving her a gentle hug.

Chapter Eighteen

Friday started with a bang, literally, with the boiler exploding at the Village's main source. Workers were called for the emergency at six A.M. Maxie, Molly, Megan, Hunter, Tony, and Silvia and Edward reported for duty bright and early.

Tonight, would be a busy night with the opening night of Santa's Village. Santa and Mrs. Claus would arrive on horse drawn sleigh kicking off the season. Some six thousand guests were due to visit; however, a busted boiler certainly dampened the mood. Megan called Stone first thing in the morning to ask for help. An excuse to call him maybe, but the thought of hearing his voice made it worth it. The phone rang once, then twice, then after the third ring it went directly to voicemail. She convinced herself he may still have been sleeping and left a somewhat frantic distress voicemail. Three plumbers and a whole lot of cleanup eventually returned the winter wonderland back to normal by three in the afternoon, yet still no call from Stone.

Megan tried to busy herself with Molly's checklists. She worked with tech support to correct a glitch in the Naughty and Nice list. Parents could send a text to an app and have their child's name appear on the nice list. Appearing on the wrong list could have disastrous effects. Next, she visited Santa's workshop, where children were encouraged to write their lists and deliver them to Santa directly. A life-sized present anchored the courtyard where children could bring a wrapped toy to donate to those in need. Next to Santa's shop, was the Gingerbread House, a bake shop which invited kids to decorate cookies. Two doors down, the Candy Cane shop offered stocking decorating. Molly executed her dream down to the last detail. Tonight, a computer-generated image would light the sky with a hologram of Santa in his sleigh along with his reindeer flying over the forty-foot tree in the center of the village. Then the vintage sleigh carrying Santa and Mrs. Claus. Santa would arrive for the tree lighting ceremony. The giant tree covered in millions of twinkling colorful lights would set the stage for Christmas caroling. With any luck, the snow machine would be able to sprinkle fluffy snowflakes over the crowd. Yes, everything on the checklist was perfect except that it was five thirty and no one had heard from Stone. Megan knew the news of no Santa would send an already neurotic Molly over the edge. She decided instead to find Maxie.

"Max, I don't want to alarm anyone, but Stone is MIA."

"WHAT?" Maxie said at the top of her lungs.

Megan grabbed Maxie's arm and pulled her behind the Candy Cane Shop. She clasped her hand over Maxie's lips. "Did you miss the part about not alarming anyone? I tried to reach him earlier this morning. I left a message that we were in crisis, but he never returned any of my calls. Do you think I blew it? What if I ruined Molly's big day?" Megan said, as a rush of tears started to build up in her eyes.

"Hey none of that. Listen, he is a solid guy. I think we can trust his word. He told Molly he'd be here; we need to believe that."

"But what if he doesn't because I panicked and pushed him away? All those poor kids with no Santa." Megan's feet traced the same five steps forward then back.

"Listen if worse comes to worse, we throw Tony, the skinniest Santa ever, into the costume. You just worry about your role and no sad faces. Molly is literally three seconds away from a meltdown."

"Right, the girls are with Giovanni. Mom and dad are handling the front of house operations. You and Tony have the restaurants covered and I'll be the best Mrs. Claus possible."

A tall thin man dressed all in black appeared, "Which one of you is Mrs. Claus?"

Megan raised half an arm.

"I'm Michael from hair and makeup. Let's get moving, this is going to take some work."

"Show time, Mrs. Claus. Hair and makeup are waiting for you," Maxie said kissing her and giving her a hug for reassurance.

Megan headed toward the small building that housed the costumes, elves, reindeer, the Claus suits and plenty of candy cane dancer outfits. Inside, the place bustled with reindeers adjusting antlers, elves getting ears attached and no shortage of glitter on the red and white striped candy cane dancers.

"Aw Mrs. Claus, right this way," said Angela, the makeup artist who Michael assigned to Megan. "Where's your hubby?"

"Hubby" was something she no longer had, but her fake Santa was also seemingly gone. "I'm actually not sure. I hope he'll be here soon."

"We need to fatten you up and age you, oh let's say fifty years."

"Great," said Megan, not really embracing the thought of makeup doing the exact opposite of its design. Angela wasted no time in spraying Megan's dark hair a frosty white, then teased, sprayed, and tucked it into a loose messy bun. Next, she started the arduous task of plastering wrinkles on Megan's silky-smooth skin. She even managed to make Megan's large doe eyes shrink and appear to sink into her wrinkled face. Last, a pair of round wire rimmed glasses and a striped bonnet. After stuffing some pillows around her hips Megan groaned at the loss of her waist. The upside was never having to worry about too many bonbons, she sighed then looked at the finished product and shivered. Growing old was scarier than being attacked by a group of wild boar. Molly would owe her big time, after all she was the town's Ms. Winter Princess transformed into an ancient puffy sack of red velvet.

"Megan, how's it going?" Maxie asked before retreating with a gasp. "WOW, that's some really good makeup."

"Thank you for that. And why again is it that you can't do this?"

"Food patrol, sorry. Now they are calling for you, something to do with the sleigh."

"He's not here yet," Megan said, her eyes saddening beneath the wire rimmed glasses.

"Maxie!" a shout from the candy shop penetrated the air as Molly's near breakdown peaked.

"Got to go."

Megan took a deep breath and made her way to the sleigh. It'll be fine. Santa is busy this time of year, making toys or maybe a bad case of food poisoning. No, no he had to be here. Molly's sanity depended on it. She fumbled through the thick material of her wool skirt and felt her phone beneath her gloved hands. Time to call in backup. She bobbled the phone then felt it slip out of her hand.

"Looking for this?" said a voice from above her.

She looked up and at first didn't recognize the man under the full white beard, wire rimmed glasses, sporting a plump belly beneath his Santa suit.

"Stone is that you? How did you get here? I didn't think you were coming. You ran out so fast last night and…"

"Santa, Mrs. Claus, time to go. Here, step carefully into the sleigh. Remember Santa says a few words, then we count to three and poof the tree lights. Any questions?" asked Jimmy the production coordinator.

Stone held out his hand to Megan and helped her into the sleigh. "We got this. We're a pretty good team," he said. Inside the sleigh he asked, "Why would you think I wasn't coming? I know how much this means to your sister. I gave my word. Sorry I had to leave so quickly, a personal issue to deal with."

"Truth is I wanted to talk to you last night about something."

"Okay how about when we get finished here, we grab a bite to eat?"

"I'd like that."

He slid over a bit closer and put his arm around her. "You're pretty hot Mrs. Claus, you know that?"

"You're not so bad yourself, Mr. Claus." The sleigh moved slowly toward the tree. In the distance, they watched as the hologram of Santa's sleigh shot over the tree. The sound of thrilled children and parents alike resonated in the air. A wave of excitement filled Megan as she realized how much joy they would bring to this crowd. The sleigh bells began ringing before the sleigh could be seen, sending the crowd into a high-pitched roar with anticipation. As they rounded the corner, the first face she saw was Molly's, who as usual, had tears running down her pale cheeks at the sight.

Stone stepped right into his role with a deep, "Ho, Ho, Ho!" The crowd cheered. When the sleigh stopped in front of the massive tree, Stone stepped out and helped Megan. "Welcome boys and girls. Has everyone been good this year?"

Yes, and a few other words mumbled inaudible through the crowd. "Do you know what tonight is?" he asked.

"Tree lighting," yelled the crowd.

"Tonight, we start the countdown until Christmas Eve night, when we share love and joy with our families. Then, when you go to bed, I'll be visiting each and every one of you. So, let's begin on the count of three."

The crowd chanted, "One, two, three," then, on cue the lights illuminated the dark November sky. The sounds of oohs and ahhs filled the air as the families watched the twinkling lights dance around the massive tree. Then perfectly timed, the snow machines whirled, sending tiny flurries falling from the sky. The culmination of Molly's dream was even more magical than any of them could have imagined.

The choir started quietly with, *It's Beginning to Look a Lot Like Christmas*, then the crowd joined in. Stone took Megan's hand and sang along. After the sing-a-long, Stone suggested they enjoy some cookies, visit the naughty and nice list to see which one they were on, and check out his and Mrs. Claus's house on Candy Cane lane. They climbed back into the sleigh. It was the first time she realized the air temperature had dropped as the winds had picked up. They waved as the sleigh headed back toward the barn. The sleigh pulled into the large barn. Megan couldn't exactly explain why she had an irresistible urge to kiss him, beard and all. As he started to lift one heavy black boot off the edge of the sleigh, Megan pulled him back. He turned back toward her. She leaned in and kissed him.

Stone pulled back to yank down his beard and asked, "Regan is that you under that makeup?"

Megan ignored him and went in for a second steamy kiss.

Strangely enough, the kiss felt molten hot as he leaned his body weight in closer. Her breath quickened; her heart thumped beneath the multiple layers of Mrs. Claus's cape. She had been lying to herself, she wanted him every bit as much as he wanted her. Ever since the night in the cabin, she had been afraid to allow those feelings to surface again. She knew releasing the tight reins on her heart meant opening the door to the possibility of a flood of pain, but he was worth it. Maxie and Molly were right, he was one of the good ones. She had been so hurt by Chase. How silly to think her mind had built a whole scenario about some relationship with Claire. The sound of *The Christmas Song* filled the air. The brisk air whistled through the barn walls, yet she couldn't remember a more romantic kiss in her life, until she heard a voice.

"Stone Reynolds, what are you doing in that ridiculous costume?" said a voice, shrill and demanding.

Stone jumped up in response to the voice like a fourteen-year-old kid caught in the back seat of his parents Chevy. He tossed Megan aside and turned to face the woman.

"Claire?" he said, clearly surprised by her visit.

Claire, said Megan in her mind. Claire, the very woman that she feared. The very reason she had decided to steer clear from Stone Reynolds. *That Claire.*

Stone climbed down from the sleigh. "What are you doing here?"

"Well it was not my intent, but clearly I'm here to save you from yourself. Take that monstrosity of a get-up off and let's get out of here."

"This, Claire, is a Santa suit, and I'm not going anywhere."

"Don't tell me this pathetic town has somehow gotten under your skin." She paused then turned her attention to

Megan. "Please don't tell me that frumpy blob you had the unfortunate luck to be tangled up with is the reason."

It was the first time Megan had summoned the courage to look past Stone to see the woman behind the name. In her mind, Claire was some short, dumpy, average looking woman, yet her eyes told her a different story. Ice blond hair cut chic and angled to her jaw, large blue eyes that were framed by thick, perfect Elizabeth Taylor eyebrows, and lips swollen from injections anchored her tiny face. She was stunning, from her white fur vest to her white fur boots and everything in between. Megan had never before been referred to as a frumpy blob, but she found her hand patting her gray wiry mess of hair that sat tightly under her bonnet and could only imagine what she looked like; a disheveled, flushed version of Mrs. Claus.

"Claire, that's enough."

Claire fixed her eyes on Megan and said, "Can we please talk without Mrs. Big Ears over there eavesdropping?"

Stone turned to Megan, "Megan, this is Claire. If you'll excuse me for a moment, I need to talk with her."

Awkward had risen to new levels. Megan smoothed her rumpled skirt and tried to climb out of the sleigh with some modicum of decency. "Excuse me," she said as she slid past Claire. Unable to even look at Stone, she rushed out of the barn. The air had dropped a few more degrees and the snow machines were whirling tiny droplets of snow everywhere. What was she thinking convincing herself that Claire meant nothing to him? She saw the tears in his eyes when he spoke of her. She walked first then found her feet running as fast as they could take her away from the scene. She huffed as she pushed her feet harder on the lightly snow-covered village cobblestones. Her side cramped up and her heel slipped out from under her on the slick ground. Seconds before she hit the cold wet pavement, she felt his arms wrap beneath her.

Stone spun her around and pulled her in. She could feel his eyes studying her tear strewn face. "Why do you keep running from me?"

"Really, I know all about you and Claire," she said pushing off his chest, her own breath still labored.

"Right, because I told you about her."

"No, I know you're engaged, alright. Now stop playing games with me. I hope you got it all out of your system."

"Engaged, are you nuts? What's out of my system?"

Megan tugged her soggy skirt up and turned to walk away. She had heard enough lies from men in one lifetime. She felt his hands grip hard on her waist, swirling her around.

"No, you don't, you don't get to leave this time. We aren't finished," he said, his blue eyes sternly fixed on her.

She struggled beneath the strength of his grip, rendering her efforts useless.

Stone, pulling her closer, looked hard into her eyes. "First, I'm not engaged to Claire or anyone else for that matter. Second, the only thing in my system is you, Megan McKenna. And try as I have, I can't shake you. And believe me, I've tried."

"But I," she paused. "Well after the snowy night at the Inn," her voice trailed off to a pause. "Claire called and you just perked up. Suddenly you were on cloud nine and whatever happened between us the night before seemed a thing of the past."

"Yes, Claire called giving me some pretty exciting news about my work. It had nothing to do with her and me. And if I recall, the next morning I was about to tell you how I felt and you shut me down hard. You wanted nothing more than to get as far away from me as quickly as you could."

Megan remembered the panic that had immediately set in with the rising of the sun. Never had she intended to fall into his arms, or her heart to melt in his embrace that snowy morning.

"True, but what about the texts?" she blurted out, instantly regretting it.

"What texts?"

"Okay, not my finest moment, but on Thanksgiving Eve when you were looking at my car, your phone beeped. I honestly went to grab it to bring to you, but somehow the name Claire just popped out at me and well, I read it. The man said he spoke with Claire and he couldn't believe it. Your whole life was about to change and something about a tux. Then he said he hoped you got it all out of your system. I realized I was just part of your oat sowing game."

"First, that was in response to my work. I am being honored for work in my field. Second, I don't wear tuxedos. And third, I'm supposed to be here resting. That's what I'm getting the need to work twenty-four hours a day out of my system. Why didn't you just ask me instead of rushing to all these wild accusations?"

"Maybe because I was scared of your answer," she said, her eyes avoiding his while biting her lower lip.

His hands loosened from his grip and found their way to her face. He lifted her face toward his. "Are you really that blind that you can't see I'm crazy for you?"

Her eyes met his for the first time. "You are?"

"Yes, for the love of me, I don't know how I let this happen, but Megan McKenna, you are under my skin and worked your way into my heart."

She grabbed his neck and kissed him hard. He lifted her up. She swung her legs around his waist. They laughed then kissed again, until they heard the slushing of horse hooves pulling the sleigh rounding the corner with a frantic Molly in tow.

"I found you two. Just wanted to thank you again. So far, the response has been wonderful. The guests love it and everyone is asking about the lodge. I couldn't have done it without you. Off to check on Gingerbread making. And hey you two, get a room."

Before the two could utter a word, Molly disappeared faster than a shooting star. Megan grinned at the suggestion of a room.

"Well Mr. Claus, what do you think about her suggestion?"

Stone rubbed the stubble on his square jaw and then shook his head. "Nope, Mrs. Claus I'd like the chance to formally court you, date you, or whatever they call it these days."

She snuggled in and said, "I'd like that."

"Tomorrow night, seven sound doable?"

"I think I can make that happen."

"Dress semi-formal, I have a great place in mind for our first date."

"Our first date," she said with a smile.

Chapter Nineteen

The next twenty-four hours seemed to drag waiting to have an actual date with Stone. Megan stood in front of her full-length mirror, tugging at her knee length white full tulle skirt, tousling her hair, checking every angle. Judging by the pile of clothes on her bed, she figured she had to be on her tenth outfit. Her stomach twitched a little with nervous energy, good energy, she had decided. For the first time in a very long time, she was excited to go on a date. Tonight, would be special, just the two of them going out in public, as a couple. The thought of it made her lips stretch upward.

"Mommy, Stone's here," Sophie hollered down the hallway.

She smoothed her black turtleneck, cropped to the waist of the skirt giving him thoughts of a hint of skin. Her ankle wrapped Christian Louboutin black stilettos were the icing on the cake. She grabbed her wrap and clutch and headed down the hall.

"Wow mommy, you look beautiful," said Olivia.

"I second that," said Stone.

"Stone, this is for you. I made it on Thanksgiving night. It's me as a turkey," said Olivia, handing him the turkey cut from colored paper.

Rylee Ridolfi

Stone got down on one knee and studied the red-haired turkey with thick glasses. He held it to his chest, "Thank you. It is a stunning replica of you. I'll treasure it always, Red."

Megan searched the lodge's main area and asked, "Wait, where's grandma?"

"She called and said for you to call her right away," said Sophie.

"What? Sophie why didn't you tell me?"

Sophie casually walked over and handed her the phone. Megan dialed frantically. "Mom," she yelled into the phone. "Is everything alright?"

"Megan, I called an hour ago so you could see if you could get a sitter. Dad twisted his ankle climbing the ladder while putting up lights. We're at the ER."

"Oh my gosh, is he alright? Should we come down there?"

"He's fine, besides his bruised ego. Doc Southerton is here with us. He gave it to him pretty good. They wrapped it and we'll be heading home after we fill out this darn paperwork."

"Are you sure you don't need anything?"

"No, I just feel badly that we offered to watch the girls and then this happened."

"No, don't even think about that, just get him home safely."

Megan hung up the phone, and by the look of his face, Stone had already figured out that a mishap would prevent the evening he had planned. "Is everything alright?"

"Yes and no. My dad fell. He's okay, but they won't be watching the girls after all. I'm sorry, it appears we don't have a sitter."

He took both her hands and pulled her in a bit closer. "Nothing to be sorry about."

"But you planned a lovely evening," she said, noticing how vibrant his blue eyes looked in his crisp blue button down.

"Lucky for you, I'm great at improvising. I may need some help from my two favorite girls though," he said, motioning the girls to come over.

Sophie and Olivia ran to the kitchen area. He looked at Sophie and said, "Madam, I would like to reserve a table for four. Can you help me with that?"

Sophie smiled widely, "Uh huh."

"And the lovely Miss Olivia, can you direct me to some candles and perhaps some table settings?"

Olivia took his hand in hers and led him to the plates. She then headed over to the drawer by the check-in desk and pulled out two long white candles. "Mommy says these are for special occasions."

"Mommy is right and tonight is going to be just that," he said, searching his phone for takeout.

"Stone, what are you doing?" Megan asked as the girls swirled around the table with excitement.

"Giving you a perfect night, with a few minor adjustments. Gloria, you can be the hostess."

Megan was able to order the large pine table for the lodge with an expense card Molly set up. It was the perfect piece to anchor the large dining area for guests. The girls set the table with white snowflake placemats. Sophie gathered four plates, while Olivia grabbed the silverware. "Do we have wine glasses, Ms. McKenna?"

"Yes, I believe we do," she said, making her way around the counter.

"Wait Sophie, can you direct me to the music?"

"This way," she said, playing along all giddy.

He turned on the music, adjusting it to the country channel to find Kenny Chesney singing Christmas in Dixie. The doorbell rang about fifteen minutes later and a teenager with a skull cap and headset on handed him a bag of Joey's famous Burgers. "Order for Stone. Four burgers, two sweet potato fries, two curly cheese fries, a salad and a bottle of Coke, right?"

"Yes sir, thank you," Stone said, slipping him a hefty tip for the speedy service.

"Gloria, table for four please." The little pug wiggled behind Megan as she walked over to the table. Stone held the chair for each one of them then placed the bag of burgers and fries along with the salad in the center of the table. "Matches?"

"On the counter by the fridge," Megan said.

He returned and lit the candles. A single tear welled up in her eye. This was perfect, maybe even more perfect than Cristoforo's. The people she loved most, sharing an intimate candlelit dinner. Grabbing a plate, he dished out a burger, a handful of fries and bowl of salad for each one of them.

After eating, Sophie stared at Stone with a very pensive look, "Is this what grownups do on a date?"

Stone turned to her and with one raised eyebrow said, "Well, if you want to know the truth, it's not all we do," he paused.

Megan gathered all the air in her lungs turning a pale shade of blue from holding her breath, wondering where he was going with his answer.

"We dance."

"Really?" asked Sophie.

"Really," said Stone, heading to the stereo system built into the wall. He turned up KTU, home of Country music, and stretched one arm out toward Sophie.

"Ok this song is Luke Bryan's, *Shake It*. You remember this one, right Megan? Just follow along. Get on the dance floor Sophie and Red. If I recall, there are four people on this date," signaling to Megan and Olivia.

He formed a line then started instruction, "Truth be told, I don't know one dance from another, but let's go with it. First two steps forward, two heel taps, then two steps back, two toe taps behind you. Let's try that." The four counted it out then followed the next instruction, "Now sidestep right, hip to the left, hip the right now shimmy. Now let's put it together."

The four counted, giggled, had a few collisions, then started from the top. Before long the four of them danced in sync and when the song ended, they erupted in cheers. "We did it!" said Olivia, clapping her hands.

"We sure did," said Stone, winking at Megan.

"Okay ladies, I think it's time to get your pjs on," said Megan, hoping to salvage some part of this date.

"Can we watch Frosty out here on the big screen TV with you and Stone like a real family?" asked Olivia, whose glasses sat cockeyed after all that dancing.

Megan looked down at the little one and smiled, and wondered if the date could wait another half hour. Those words, *like a real family*, made Megan think about how the divorce had affected poor little Olivia. Megan searched deep in her memory and couldn't actually even remember a time when Chase was home long enough to participate in a family activity. She looked at Stone almost scared to ask, worried that Olivia's comment may have frightened him off.

"I'm not sure if that is such a great idea. I think it's grownup time," said Megan.

"Mom's right, grownups need popcorn with a movie. Are you guys alright with that?" he said, giving Megan a wink with those baby blues. The little ones jumped up and down singing, "Yes."

"Pajamas first," Megan said, pointing to the hallway. The two girls scampered down the hall toward their room, leaving Megan with just a few minutes alone with Stone. She had so many things she wanted to say to him; an apology, a thank you, a possible rain date, but all she could do was grab him and kiss him, an instinct that continually surprised her.

"Not that I'm complaining, but what was that for?"

"For being you. You were so amazing with my situation tonight and with my girls."

"They're a part of you, Megan. You're a package deal. Three for the price of one. I should thank *you* for sharing them with me."

"I'm beginning to think Regan is onto something," she winked.

Ronnie Millsap's, *Wouldn't Have Missed it for the World*, began playing on the radio. Stone placed his hand on the small of her back and swayed with her in his arms. They danced in front of the fireplace, in a moment she wished would never end.

The next song, Brett Eldredge's, *Wanna Be that Song,* came on next. She smiled remembering it was their dance at the country dance club. "You know Mrs. Claus, if we had a song, I believe this would be it," he said, singing the verse to her. Megan felt her knees weakening beneath her, her stomach felt like there was a bundle of butterflies fluttering in tandem. A giddiness took over her at the thought of them having a song.

"Look Stone, these are our new Christmas pjs," said Sophie, barely noticing the dance.

"What, and you don't have any for me?"

They giggled. "You're too big," said Olivia, her cheeks rounding from her widened grin.

"We'll have to see about that," said Stone with a wink. "Now where's the popcorn?"

Megan left for the kitchen and returned with two large bowls of buttery popcorn. The four snuggled up on the large leather sofas. Megan slipped the movie in the DVD player. The seventy-inch TV Stone had ordered for the room equipped with surround sound made a perfect place to light the fire and watch the show.

"Mommy, are we still getting a tree tomorrow for the lodge?" asked Sophie.

"Yes, we are, but they are calling for snow, so we'll see."

"Can Stone help us?" asked Olivia, sitting in between Megan and Stone.

"Can you? The whole bunch is coming over tomorrow to decorate. Molly and Hunter, Maxie, Tony and hopefully my parents." asked Megan.

"I think I can fit that into my day. What time are we thinking?"

"The gang is coming at four o'clock?"

"How about Aunt Charlotte's for lunch, then we decorate?"

The girls jumping up and down on the couch cheered, "Aunt Charlotte's!"

Megan smiled, "Perfect."

Before long, the credits were rolling and the two small sleeping girls snuggled warmly in blankets stretched across Megan and Stone. Gloria snored in front of the fireplace.

Megan leaned over Olivia and said, "I'm sorry about the whole Claire thing."

"All that matters is that you trust me, Megan. I won't hurt you. I'm not Chase. Give me a chance to prove that to you."

She leaned closer and kissed him. The door of the lodge swung open and Maxie blew in. "This is cozy. You're a bit overdressed for Frosty, but who am I to judge."

"It's a long story. Dad fell and went to the ER. He's fine but our sitters bailed, so we improvised."

"Is dad okay?"

"Yes, just a minor sprain."

"Well it looks like you made the best of it. I'm sorry I didn't answer my phone all night. Tony had a party of fifty at the restaurant. We were slammed. Wish I could've helped. Why don't you two go get a drink or a room now? I'll stay with the girls."

"Thank you, but I think we're good. It actually was a perfect night," Megan said, smiling at Stone. "I really should get these two to bed."

Stone slid out from Olivia and moved toward Sophie. "I've got her," he said, gently picking her up.

Megan removed Olivia's glasses and carried her to bed. Stone tucked Sophie in bed and headed to Olivia's room to help. He noticed a picture hanging above her bed. He looked a bit closer and recognized Olivia sketched in her yellow wading boots with red curly hair and glasses holding a tall man's hand. The man had on a red, blue and green plaid shirt with a light-colored beard. The caption read, "Me and my best friend saving the fishes." He turned toward Megan with a crack in his voice and asked, "Is that me?"

She smiled, "Yes, it is. She believes you are going to save her fish from the cold."

He pushed the curls back from her forehead and gave her a kiss. "She's right about that."

"Really, oh great fish saver, how do you plan on doing that?"

"I have a few tricks up my sleeve. I won't let her down."

"I believe that. Stone Reynolds, you're a good man."

"I've been telling you that, but some people can be hard headed."

She tossed a pillow at him. "Walk me to the door," he said, grabbing her hand.

They walked out to the lodge main room. "I had a great time tonight and your stunning outfit did not go unnoticed. Someday I'm going to get you into some cowboy boots, Ms. McKenna."

"Never gonna happen. How about the day I get you into a tux?"

"Never gonna happen." He pulled her close, she felt his warmth, his strength, his passion. He lowered his face to hers. Their lips met, sweet, warm wanting. She craved his kiss, more now than the first time. Now there was emotion attached to her desire. She hadn't felt this way in forever. He pulled back a bit and smiled. "Okay, I'm going to leave now, before I can't."

"I promise we'll have our night alone."

"I'm holding you to it."

Chapter Twenty

A cool crisp December morning found Aunt Charlotte's packed. The four sat at a table next to a tree decorated from top to bottom in pink. "Can we do our tree pink?" asked Sophie.

"Sophie, we talked about this, I'm not sure what we have left from the old house. I do know that the lodge tree has to be a rustic theme. Speaking of which, Molly asked if we could pick up the tree for the main lodge. She's got a fitting for her gown and Hunter is dealing with dueling elves at the village. I've already taken care of the ornaments. I bought antlers, plaid gloves, wooly ice skates, pine cones, you name it, and of course a ton of lights."

"With this crew, I'm certain we can pick the perfect tree," said Stone.

Aunt Charlotte arrived with large plates with three pancakes stacked in a row creating snowmen. She gave each girl bowls with chocolate chips for eyes or buttons and a can of whip cream for hats and scarves.

After breakfast, the four set out to find the perfect tree. The lot sat just blocks from the diner, so they chose to bundle up and walk. The winds had picked up and a damp chill promised snow would soon be there. The lot was right out of a Dickens story, with hundreds of lit trees, some dressed in white lights while others twinkled with shimmers of color. Carolers stood at the gates dressed in old fashioned dresses, hats and scarves. Olivia and Sophie ran through the gates, each setting out in a different direction.

"Go, I've got Olivia," said Stone as he headed after her floppy red curls. Megan trailed Sophie. The group met up at a tree just north of the biggest felt snowman they'd ever seen. "He must be a hundred feet tall," said Sophie.

"Maybe more like six feet, but I'm told snowmen are pretty important guys," said Stone.

"What do you mean?" asked Sophie.

"A friend of mine told me they are very dependable. They come back as promised every year. A girl can count on a guy like that," he said, winking at Megan.

Megan smiled.

"Can we buy him?" Sophie said, hands praying.

"I think we are going to hold off on that, besides, how would we fit our tree in the truck with a giant snowman?" Megan said.

"Right we need our tree," said Sophie.

Olivia stood staring up at a tree that seemed to reach the sky. "This is our tree. Can we get this one?"

"Hmm, let's see it's a Fraser Fir, which means it has one-inch needles and sturdy branches for heavy ornaments. I think it's perfect," said Stone, smelling the needles.

"Me too," said Olivia, reaching out to hold Stone's hand.

"Ladies, do you agree with us?"

"It's awfully tall, don't you think?" said Megan.

"I'd say it's about ten feet. The lodge has twenty-foot ceilings in the main area. I think it would speak volumes for the Christmas spirit your family has."

"Okay, Sophie what do you think?"

"Yes, yes."

"We're going to need a lot more ornaments than I bought," said Megan.

"Alright next stop, the Christmas Depot on Main," he said, waving the attendant over. He reached into his pocket to pull out his wallet. "What are you doing?" Megan asked.

"I got this. It's my contribution to the lodge. Can you wrap it up and I'll pull the truck around?"

The attendant's eyes rose to the top of the tree. "This could take a bit. Why don't you give us about an hour? We're really busy."

"No problem, we'll grab some hot cocoas and head over to the Christmas Depot."

Sophie let out one of her high-pitched squeals. "A snowflake. I just felt a snowflake on my cheek."

Megan smiled at her and squealed right along with her. "It's snowing."

Stone winked at Megan. "I have grown to be quite a fan of snow as of late."

The tiny willowy flakes quickly changed to a heavier larger flake. The winds howled and the air seemed to drop ten degrees in a few minutes.

"You girls okay to walk in this weather?" Stone asked.

"Yes," the girls sang in tandem.

"I think a snowy walk rounds out the perfect tree picking day," Megan said, reaching out for his hand. The girls danced around as the snow rapidly blanketed the walkways. Megan wondered how spending time with him and the girls felt more like a family than the all the years she and Chase had spent together. Stone stopped and bought four hot cocoas. As a distraction from the cold, Stone suggested they sing carols, starting with *Jingle Bells*. In no time they reached the Christmas Depot. They headed into the massive shop, every inch twinkling with Christmas cheer. Stone said, "Alright ladies, we need a plan. First, we get lights, then garland, and last, the ornaments."

The girls jumped up and down.

Megan snuck up behind Stone and whispered, "You're amazing, did you know that?"

"Back at you, Mrs. Claus."

Sophie giggled and pointed up, "Look mommy, it's a kissy toe."

Megan looked up and smiled, "You mean mistletoe."

Stone turned her toward him, "I think she got it right, are you going to kiss me or not?"

"Kiss, kiss," cheered the girls.

Stone pulled her in and dipped her back giving her a sweet kiss.

"Yay," the girls cheered.

Sophie and Olivia filled the cart to the brim. The girls spotted a tray of cookies being handed out by an elf. "Can we go mommy?" asked Olivia.

"Sure, stay together," Megan said. Sophie and Olivia held hands and ran off toward the elf. "Molly gave me the Lodge credit card. I know she wants it to look exceptional."

They headed to the register. As she passed the stunning elegant trees, Megan remembered the trees she had with Chase. Chase would give her a credit card with no limit. Megan would spare no expense. Their elaborate decorations set the stage for the work party Chase would host every year. Megan missed that life, not Chase, but the finer things in life. She and the girls were adjusting to life at the lodge; however, Megan was her mother's child, she longed for the life Chase had provided them. Last year they lived with Megan's parents, so this would be their first Christmas alone. Chase still held their grand tree and ornaments from their home hostage in storage. She thought maybe they'd pick them up and do their tree tonight. Interrupted by tugging on her jacket, she looked down to find Sophie, lips extended twirling the mistletoe around.

"Mommy can we buy a kissy toe?" asked Sophie.

"I think we can," Megan said, smiling at Stone who was now wearing antlers along with Olivia.

"I think the tree should be ready by now," Stone said.

His phone rang. "Okay great. I'll be there soon. Do you have everything we need?" Stone looked at Olivia. "It's kind of important that I get it in today with the storm and all," he said, sort of vaguely to the person on the other end of the phone."

"Is everything okay?" Megan asked, her insecurities fighting to surface.

"Better than okay. I have a delivery coming to the lodge. Final steps will be in place by tonight, but I'm going to need a bit of time there before you bring the girls home."

"I don't remember ordering any more deliveries for the lodge," Megan said.

"That's because you didn't. Promise, you'll see it tonight."

"Okay, girls how about we stop and check on grandpa's ankle."

"Yes, we can tell them all about the tree," said Olivia.

By the time they got to the truck, the storm had slowed enough for Stone to clean off the car. Stone opened the door and the winds swirled around, whipping squalls of snow in their faces. The massive tree strapped on the roof, covered the truck hanging well over the edge of the bed.

Stone drove carefully to Silvia's house. They pulled into the driveway and the girls asked if they could go in and surprise grandpa. Megan sent them in and turned to Stone. "Do you need help with the tree?

"No, a few guys are still at the lodge; they can help me get it in. Then I have to get to work."

"What are you up to?"

"Something that this storm has forced me to rush, but I got this."

"Okay we'll give you some time. Text me when we can come back. We'll get a ride. My parents are heading over to decorate anyway. Go finish whatever secret mission you're on."

"You know it's tough to leave you while it's snowing," he said, still holding her. He pulled her closer and gave her a kiss.

The door opened and the girls yelled to Megan, "Can we make cookies with grandpa?"

"I better go, but in the future don't kiss me like that if you plan on leaving," she said as she opened the car door.

After three dozen sugar cookies, two dozen chocolate chips and a room full of flour, sugar and sprinkles, Megan got the text. "Okay girls let's head back. Grandpa needs to rest. Dad are you up to this?"

Silvia patted Edwards shoulder and said, "Your father could use an extra day and Molly said she has some type of emergency. Let me get my coat." The girls gave Edward kisses and put on their coats, hats and gloves. The snow had stopped, leaving behind glistening branches and frosted windows. Megan filled the ride with tales of the day and hadn't realized how much she was talking about Stone, or how happy the thought of him made her until Silvia interrupted.

"I saw Chase last night."

"At the hospital?" Megan asked.

"Yes, he was meeting with a client; One of the prominent docs who may just land him the biggest deal of his life. He's about to be one of the youngest guys to make partner at his firm."

"He lies, mom."

"Not about everything Megan. Do you miss him? The life you had?"

"Absolutely not."

"The girls said you don't let them buy anything anymore."

"They don't need all that stuff."

"Megan do you know who you are talking to? I'm your mother, more importantly, you're my daughter. I know you, and we're cut from the same mold. Do you remember the party you held the year Molly and Hunter got engaged? Oh my, that balsam fir looked so real, I could have sworn you cut it down five minutes before, and all those crystal ornaments from Austria. What about your Lenox ornaments, such opulence?"

"Chase has it all in storage. I'm going to see if I can pick it up today. It'll be the same mother, you'll see."

"How for heaven's sake will it be the same in a tiny apartment in the lodge? It's really no way for the girls to live. This Stone fellow, he is you know, more Thriftmart than Bergdorf's. He's fun, in a Maxie bad boy kind of way. Get it out of your system dear, and then realign your priorities. Molly is our Little House on the Prairie girl, not you. Don't kid yourself Megan, it may feel good for now, but I promise you, one day you'll find yourself miserable, longing for the life you once adored."

"Enough mother," Megan said.

They pulled into the lodge and saw a glass installation truck out front along with Stone's truck.

"Hmm, I wonder what that's for?" Megan said, eyeing the truck.

Silvia put the car in park and turned off the engine. "That fellow is here again? Honestly did anyone really check his credentials? I mean for some run of the mill handyman; he's inserted himself in a little too deep on this project. You said yourself, he lives in a shack, has no real job to speak of. He probably took one look at you and thought 'pay dirt, I found a meal ticket.'"

"That's enough! He is an extremely talented professional. Anyone who has him on their project is lucky. Not everything is about money. Money means everything to you."

"To *us* Megan," Silvia said, in her condescending voice that reminded Megan that men like Stone were beneath her mother, and dating him would most definitely be a monumental disappointment. Megan gathered the girls and headed into the lodge. As far as she was concerned, the conversation was over. She knew on the inside, she had changed. She wasn't the same materialistic person she used to be, and it looked good on her.

Silvia dropped the three at the door and the girls swung open the door to find Molly and Hunter admiring the massive tree that stood in front of the glass wall flanked by the snowy landscape beyond it. The luggage colored leather sofas sat across from each other with red, navy and green plaid blankets strew over the back of them. The vintage snowshoe coffee table sat in the middle with a lantern, three carved wood trees and a few sprigs of pine.

"This tree is perfect Megan. I mean the whole room. It's all just magical. Tomorrow night I'd like to have a meeting about the finishing details of the lodge. I saw the room plaques you ordered, and they're just amazing."

Megan had named all ten suites with engraved name plaques. The honeymoon suite was named the Mr. and Mrs. Claus Suite. There was the Gingerbread Suite, the Winter Wonderland Suite, the Woodland Suite, the Sugar Plum Fairy Suite, the Mistletoe and Holly Suite, the Birch and Winterberry Suite, the Rustic Lodge Suite, the White Christmas Suite, and the Cabin Suite. Each suite decorated accordingly. For the first time in her life, Megan genuinely felt proud of her work. She looked over at the toboggan book shelves, now filled with all the Christmas classics; books and DVD's, board games and wonderful trinkets she had found in town. There were vintage frosted trees, pine cones in bowls, and birch logs by the fire. Everything was perfect.

"Hunter and I are going over to the Village. Sorry guys, the decorating has to wait until tomorrow, sort of a candy cane emergency. I already let Maxie know. Mom said dad could use the extra day to rest," Molly said, hugging Megan.

Megan said goodbye as they headed out of the lodge.

"Mommy, can we still decorate our tree tonight?" asked Sophie.

"Yes, let me call daddy and see if he can drop the tree off." Just as she spoke his name, he entered the lodge front doors.

"It's really picking up out there. Going to be a bad storm tonight. I think the lake has frozen solid," Chase said, walking in the lodge as if he owned it.

Megan ushered him toward the coffee bar and said, "Please be more sensitive about the lake, Olivia is worried about the fish. I was just about to call you. I was wondering if I could pick up my tree and ornaments that you stored for me last Christmas while we were at my parents."

Her phone rang and she recognized the number. "I have to take this; it's about the dinnerware I ordered for the main dining room. Keep an eye on the girls for a minute."

"The lake can't be frozen, not yet. The fish didn't get a chance to swim away yet," said a frantic Olivia.

"What are you talking about Olivia? Fish aren't your problem," he said. dismissing her.

"Daddy watch my Sugar Plum Fairy dance," said Sophie, twisting and stumbling about the kitchen.

Megan returned five minutes later. "Chase about the tree, can I get it?"

"Megs, Bree cleaned out the storage unit when we bought the house. She pretty much dumped everything. But not to worry, I'll get you a new one."

"I don't want a new one. What happened to all my ornaments, the ones I collected for the kids each year? She began to cry when she looked at Sophie's face. "Oh, sweetie come here. It's okay we'll get new ones. Wait where's Olivia?" she asked, canvassing the room for her.

"Megan what's wrong?" asked Stone as he walked in the room noticing the panic on Megan's face.

"Olivia, she's gone. Oh my gosh Chase, her hat and coat are gone. I left you for one minute."

"I know where she is," said Stone, grabbing his coat and heading out the door.

"Oh, thank goodness, Mr. Wilderness is here to save the day," said Chase, yelling at Megan as she ran out the door.

She followed Stone to the lake where a tiny snow-covered figure stood about one foot onto the icy patch of water. Stone called to Olivia, "Olivia, sweetie the lake isn't completely frozen. It's dangerous. Give me your hand."

"But the fish, I can't see any. They need to be rescued. I made more sweaters from my Pretty in Pink doll," she said right before the ice began to shift beneath her. A loud crack signaled they didn't have much time to get her to safety.

Olivia screamed, "Mommy I'm scared."

"Take Stone's hand baby."

"Trust me, Red, I'll never let anything happen to you," Stone said, extending his hand. She reached out just as the ice gave way. He pulled her to him and held her tight.

"Olivia, never ever go out here alone again in a storm," Megan shouted, shaking and crying.

"I'm sorry mommy."

Stone wiped her tears and held her tight. "Red, I was coming to tell you the fish are okay."

"How do you know?" she whimpered.

"I'll show you as soon as we get you warmed up," he said, collecting her in his arms and carrying her inside.

"Olivia, what is wrong with you? You scared us half to death," Chase yelled.

"Thank you for choosing this moment to yell at her after you lost her in the first place," said Megan.

"Sorry, unlike Paul Bunyan, I don't know her odd secret hiding spots."

"The problem is you know nothing about her at all. Now I think it's time you leave," Megan said. wrapping Olivia in blankets by the fireplace.

"I came here to tell you something Megan. We're not done," he said, kissing Sophie on the cheek and shaking his head at Olivia, then slamming the door behind him.

"Now who's ready to see my surprise?" Stone asked, realizing the girls had sensed the tension between their parents based on the look on their faces.

"Me," said Sophie. Olivia raised her tiny arm from inside a cream-colored argyle blanket.

Stone scooped up Olivia in the blanket. Sophie and Megan followed hand in hand. "Where are we going?" Megan said as they headed to the back steps that led to the basement level.

"Do you remember Molly saying she would like to make this large room into a game room?"

"Close your eyes ladies," he said as he opened the double doors. Behind them was a finished game room with pool tables, air hockey tables, and vending machines with prizes. Off to the side, a princess castle in pink stood five feet high, complete with a table and play food. However, the thing that had little Olivia's eyes brimming with tears was a five-foot by seven-foot wall-length aquarium filled with huge colorful fish.

"You did it Stone, you saved my fish!" Olivia said, dropping the blanket and rushing to the wall. She pressed her tiny face to the glass and stretched her arms onto the glass with a wide hug. Her smile melted all her fears.

"Not that I didn't think the whole sweater thing wasn't a great idea, but did you ever try putting a sweater on a fish? Nightmare, trust me."

Megan stood silently, her eyes scanning the room. "You did all this?"

"Heck no, I can't take credit for all this. The fish tank, yes that was all me, but when I told Molly about some thoughts I had, she and Maxie jumped into action. I simply said something about a little lady who goes by princess having an area, and shades of pink and doll furniture filled the room."

"How did I not know any of this was going on?"

"You've been a little preoccupied lately."

Megan turned her gaze toward the girls, now both faces pressed against the tank glass. Olivia described all the different types of fish. "Look at them, they're actually getting along and it's because of you."

"I can't remember a better Christmas than this one," Stone said, pulling her close.

Olivia jumped up and down and asked, "We still need to decorate a tree in our house."

Megan's face quickly changed from joy to anger, then a mix of sadness and despair when she saw the soured look on Sophie's face.

"We can't. Mommy said daddy gave our tree and all our ornaments away. We aren't having Christmas this year," said Sophie, stomping her foot.

"I didn't say that, I ..." Megan stammered. "I can't afford a new tree, so maybe we don't have a tree this year. I have lights. We can hang them in the apartment."

Stone, with his endless optimism announced, "Nonsense, Molly and I found a tree when we were cleaning out this area. We stuck it in the boiler room. It was left here with the lodge. Let's check it out."

The girls jumped up and down. "What's it look like?" asked a pensive Megan.

"I don't know, it's in a box," said Stone, leading the pack. They headed down the hall and opened the boiler room door. Off to the left, under a window sat a large box with a half-worn label. Megan pushed back the remaining label and saw the image of a woman in cat eye glasses with a Doris day haircut under the heading of Bergman's Tree Shop.

"This is from the fifties, are you serious right now? It's probably dry rotted."

"Nonsense Megan. Where's your sense of adventure? Let's take it up and check it out."

"Come on, mommy," said Olivia.

"Fine," Megan said, seeing the excitement in the girl's eyes.

A few minutes later, in the living room of Megan's small apartment, Stone opened the box and pulled out a large pole with holes in it.

"Oh no it's broken," said Sophie, clasping her hands across her mouth.

Stone laughed, "Not broken, just not together yet." He pulled out a fist full of branches.

"It looks like it's been scalped," said Megan, noticing missing needles on several areas of the branch.

"Have you people never built a Christmas tree?" he said, continuing to pull out the branches.

"I always had a real one as a kid, and the one exquisite one Chase tossed simply snapped together in one move and plugged in."

"What fun is that?" said Stone with a hearty laugh. "Now girls, the tips are color coated. Can you make piles, yellow ones here, red ones here, black here, orange here, and lastly green ones here?"

Megan felt a pit in her stomach. The mangled branches with bare spots, the spattering of blue green paper like needles covering her floor, and the sad pole that would hold those pathetic sticks made her feel anxious. Silvia's words taunted her, the opulence of her old tree. She wanted this paltry thing out of her living room now. "Stone, can I please speak to you in the kitchen?"

"Sure thing," he said, following her into the kitchen.

"I want this atrocious piece of trash out of my house now. Stop encouraging them to embrace a pauper's Christmas. We may not have money for a proper tree right now, but that doesn't mean we need to act like some pathetic trash tree pickers."

"Really, I had one of these when I was young. Does that make me some pathetic lowlife?"

"Look I'm sorry you were underprivileged growing up, but your customs don't have to be mine. My girls deserve a real Christmas for people with class, like they're accustomed to."

Stone's expression changed from confusion to anger, "If you could get your nose out of the clouds for one minute, you'd see what's right in front of you," he said, pointing to the girls sorting as a team, laughing and singing. "I feel sorry for people like you, so caught up in pretenses that you don't even know the meaning of Christmas. If you did, you'd see it right there. Christmas is people sharing laughter and making memories. It's love and tradition, not a fancy tree. You tell the girls we're done. I'll put the tree back in the box and be out of your way," he said, storming to the living room.

"Wait Stone," she called out to him.

"Stone we did it. Can we build it now? Please?" asked Sophie, jumping up and down clapping her hands. Stone looked at Megan, then began to speak, "Hey guys I…"

Before he could finish Megan belted out, "Yes, let's do this."

"Alright I think I'm heading out girls. You let me know how great it turns out okay?"

"Please don't go," cried Olivia, rushing to grab his hand. She looked up at him with a spray of fake needles swinging from her curls.

"No please stay, Stone. I want to make traditions, maybe I just need someone to help me learn how," Megan said with water-filled eyes.

"Don't go Stone. We can't do it without you," said Sophie.

His eyes met Megan's. She could see the pain she had caused. She had opened up wounds that Claire's money hungry habits had left him. She didn't know what was happening to her. She felt trapped between two worlds, lost. She was her mother's daughter, living a charmed life had made her inexcusably insensitive to any other lifestyle. Her stomach twisted as she realized she was unsure of how to move on and make new traditions and let go of the world she cherished.

Stone looked down at the little girl who clung to his leg. He would stay for the kids. "Okay, but if we're doing this, we are doing it right. Sophie, we need Christmas music. Olivia, how about you grab the lights mommy has on the kitchen table."

They gleefully scampered off to complete their task. "I'll stay for them, then I'm going. We're different people Megan, and I happen to be comfortable with who I am and have no intention of apologizing for where I came from."

"I'm so sorry, Stone. I didn't mean it. I don't know what's wrong with me. Please stay and let me try and explain when we're done."

The sounds of the Jackson Five singing *I saw Mommy Kissing Santa Claus,* filled the room. The girls returned ready for duty.

"Step one, and the most important step in tree building is fluffing."

The little ones looked at him confused, "Fluffing?" said Sophie.

"Oh yes. Watch and learn." He grabbed a branch and began separating the branches on the stick in different directions. The three watched in awe as they witnessed a paltry stick turn into a full branch. The girls clapped. He tucked the first one in the bottom, black row.

"It's like magic," said Olivia.

"It really is," said Megan, smiling.

The four sang along while fluffing and stuffing branches into color coded spots on the pole, until they reached the final one, the top of the tree. Who wants to do it?"

"Mommy, you do it," shouted Olivia.

"Me? Okay," she said, reaching up but not quite able to reach the top. Stone picked her up from the waist and she stuck it into the top of the pole.

"Yayyyy," screamed the girls.

"Now the lights, but we don't plug them in until it's all done. Part of the magic," he said.

"I have an extra box of lights in my closet," said Megan, rushing off to grab them. After stringing the final row of lights Megan quietly said, "We have nothing to put on it. All our ornaments are gone."

"Impossible, you have plenty of ornaments. When I was young, we used to find things that mattered to us to use on the tree."

"Like what?" asked Sophie.

"Okay Sophie, do you have any boas? They'd make a perfect garland," he said.

"Oh yes, I have tons of them."

"Alright you and mom go to your room and Olivia and I'll go to her room. Collect some of your favorite things you would like to see on the tree. Meet back in five minutes. Ready, set, go."

Giggling, the girls ran to their rooms. Megan and Stone right behind them.

In five minutes, Stone called time and they all ran back with arms full of goodies.

"I have garland boas in pink, white and gold. We found three pairs of ballet slippers and beanie baby princesses, ballerinas and one tiara," said Sophie, proudly displaying her treasures.

"Perfect! Olivia, show them what we have," said Stone.

"I have pine cones I collected from the lake and painted gold. I have my beanie collection of fish, and a whole bunch of pretty shells I found."

"Wow, that's wonderful sweetheart. What are we waiting for?" said Megan, who actually found herself enjoying the hunt. They started with the boas and added pine cones and ballerinas next. Then filled in with shells and beanie babies.

"I have an idea. Sophie grab your tiara," said Stone. He looked over to find it sitting on top of Gloria who snored loudly through her short snout. Megan shook her head at the sight. Sophie ran over and took it off the dog's head. He picked her up then pointed to the top of the tree.

"It's perfect," Sophie said, placing it on top.

"Are we ready to light her up?" Stone asked.

"Yes!" all three cheered.

"On the count of three, one, two, three," Stone said before plugging the tree in. Megan gasped. It sparkled with twinkling lights and glitter. She couldn't remember a more perfect tree. How could she have been so wrong? She looked at the tree that embodied the very hearts of her girls. This humble homemade tree filled with love defined the spirit of Christmas. It had taken a stranger and thirty-five Christmases to realize what truly mattered.

"It's my favorite tree ever. Thank you, Stone," said Olivia jumping into his arms. She wrapped her little arms around his neck and kissed his cheek. "You're the best."

"He really is, isn't he?" said Megan.

After hot cocoa and one Christmas book, Olivia's little eyes closed behind her large glasses. Megan announced it was time for the girls to head to bed. "Please Stone, could you wait one minute," Megan asked Stone as she followed the girls to bed.

"Can Stone tuck us in too?" asked Olivia.

"Can you, Stone?" asked Sophie.

He looked at Megan. "Please, it would be nice," she said.

He followed them, first to Sophie's room. He pulled her covers up and kissed her forehead. "Can you come to my Nutcracker performance?" Sophie asked.

"I think I can do that."

Sophie jumped up and pressed her lips to his cheek. A bit surprised, he smiled widely. Next, they went to Olivia's room. She was nearly asleep, so he tucked her in her yellow adventure blanket with navy arrows. He kissed her forehead.

She whispered, "I love you Stone," before drifting off.

Stone pinched his eyes together hard, then pressed his hand across them.

Megan watched this strong man wipe a tear from his eye. She felt a lump in her throat. She had no idea where to begin with an apology, but she couldn't let him leave with things the way they were.

The two went back to the living room. Stone slipped on his coat and collected the large box the tree came in. "I'll drop this back to the boiler room before I go."

"I lived on Holly Lane when I was young," she said.

He turned and looked at her confused. "Holly Lane by Aunt Charlotte's?"

She nodded. "Can you take your coat off? I think I owe you an explanation."

He did and followed her to the sofa.

"While it's true I never had one of those trees, I didn't have all the glitz and glamour growing up that I let on. We had a very modest home, a very modest life, until my dad got a huge promotion that took us to the other side of town. My mother was in her glory, she came from money and she was finally in her element. My sisters mourned the loss of our life as we knew it, but I sort of fell right into the country club lifestyle. By the time I met Chase, that was the life I had already decided I wanted. I guess until tonight, I really forgot what it felt like to take away all the trappings of the season and just enjoy the people I love, and I have you to thank for that. I said awful things to you. I don't know why, but sometimes I just feel like maybe

I'm scared I'm losing myself. I know that makes no sense, but it's all I have."

"Megan, look at me, you are more than a status. If you could see what I see in you, you might not see it as losing yourself as much as finding your real self. Your girls just want to have Christmas with you, it's not about big fancy trees, it's about time spent as a family."

"Time is something Chase never gave them, or me for that matter. We never did the tree together, as matter of fact, I started using the design team my mother used because Chase felt my decorating the tree may be inadequate for his parties. Looking back, it was all very generic and impersonal, then I looked at this tree and I saw the world through my girls' eyes, and I feel blessed to share their world. I wouldn't have known this without you, Stone. This feeling is real, genuine and wonderful. I think I'm falling in love with you." The words sort of tumbled right out of her mouth. Her face flushed.

"It's about time," he said, pulling her in for a kiss. "Stop trying so hard to make life perfect and you'll find it already is."

She pushed him back on the couch and kissed him. "Stay the night."

"Temptress, you're killing me. I would, but I really have to get home and finish up some things on the house. I've been spending a lot of time on the lodge, and fell a bit behind on my house project."

She kissed him again. "You're not playing fair." He laid back on top of her kissing her softly, stroking her hair, gazing into her pleading eyes.

Shaking his head, he said, "Megan McKenna, you just may be responsible for my name making the naughty list, because right now I just want to forget all my responsibilities and stay with you all night."

"Lucky for you, I have some pull with the big guy."

He kissed her again, then pulled back. "You're my weakness woman. I don't like being weak. Now can we make a date, a proper date tomorrow after tree decorating with the family?"

"I'll see if the girls can stay with my parents, but until then."

He pulled her off the couch into his arms. She wrapped her legs around his waist and they paused under the mistletoe. "Glad that kid insisted on the kissy toe," said Stone.

"Me too."

She watched him walk out the door, down the hall and disappear into the main lodge. She felt insanely happy, reborn like she had finally begun the journey toward finding who Megan McKenna really was, without Chase or all the trappings that came with that lifestyle. The little things in life seemed more joyful. She spun over to the couch and plopped down, admiring the twinkling tree. The fluffing was remarkably effective in transforming that old, dried out tree into a lovely little full tree. Ten minutes later, a knock on the door brought her to her feet. She scurried to the door, flung it open and said, "You changed your mind?"

"What?" said Chase standing in the doorway.

"I thought you were someone else. What are you doing here?"

"I felt bad about the whole tree thing so…" Before he could finish, Megan's phone rang. "Excuse me for a minute," she said, rushing into the kitchen. Molly frantically explained Chase was on his way up.

"Thanks, but you're a little late, he's here." She hung up and headed back to the living room. There he stood in the middle of the living room with the most amazing artificial tree plugged in right next to the little one. The seven-foot tree full and lit with dozens of tiny twinkling lights made the fully decorated tree look even more pathetic. He had already begun dismantling the ornaments.

"What is this heinous thing?" he said as he removed beanies.

"What are you doing? Leave that tree alone."

"You can't be serious. No daughters of mine are going to live in squalor. Megan Barrington, where have you gone? It's that low budget carpenter getting into your head."

"What I do in my house is my business. And if anyone is living in squalor, it's because you took my money. It's McKenna, if you remember, I changed it back."

"That's why I'm here, besides the tree." He cupped his hands on her shoulders, "I have the most amazing news ever. You remember the money I borrowed?"

"Stole."

"I got it back, times three. We, Megan, are now among the richest families in Connecticut. And the best news of all, I made partner. Do you know what this means for us?"

"There is no us. The real question is how did Ms. Snooty Pants take the news? I'm sure she's gloating right about now."

"I, I haven't told her yet." Chase rubbed his forehead and paced back and forth a few times. "I mean, as soon as Walt told me, the first person I thought of was you. This means something, Megs. Maybe it's a sign."

"Trust me, it's not."

He moved closer, "Look at me Megs. Tell me you don't feel it."

"Feel what exactly?"

"Just take the tree and let me sort this out. I'll be back," he said before pulling her into his chest and kissing her hard on the lips. He vanished as quickly as he appeared. She ran her fingers across her lips. She remembered the familiar smell of his cologne, Dior, he'd worn it for years. She remembered his touch. It had been forever since they touched in a romantic way. The skin on his face smooth and velvety, unlike Stone's rough five o'clock shadow. The feel of his cashmere coat, soft, warm, and expensive. She wanted to hate the kiss, but she didn't. She shouldn't care that he came to her first, but she did. A silent victory over the woman who had stolen him. And that tree, how she wanted to toss it out and embrace her newfound, smoky mountain Christmas simplicity, but her eyes couldn't help but beam when they caught the glimmering lights as they reflected off the massive tree. She paced, she willed herself to reset her thinking, then she knew what she had to do. It was time to call for backup. She banged on the letters on her phone as she sent out a frantic SOS to Maxie and Molly. "*Need emergent lobotomy, bring wine.*"

Not five minutes later the troops arrived with two bottles of Chardonnay and worried expressions on their face.

"What's going on?" asked Maxie.

"Chase," answered Molly, looking at the tree.

"I need an intervention. Don't hold back, not that you ever do Maxie, but give it to me. Yell at me. Make me snap out of it."

"Okay I think I might have missed a text or two," said Maxie, pouring three glasses of wine. "How about you slow down and start at the beginning."

"Stone is so amazing, he showed me the game room with the aquarium. How do I thank you guys?"

"Not really us Megan, he came up with the idea, brought it to us and then we just jumped in for color and princess back up."

"Right, so we agree he's amazing. Then the girls asked to decorate the tree, but Chase the jerk threw it out along with all our decorations. Stone, trying to be kind, said you had found a tree in the boiler room."

"Right in a big box," said Molly.

"The girls wanted to try and he was all, 'let's make the most of it.'"

Molly looked at the tree. "It's quite possibly the sweetest tree I've ever seen."

"Yes, and we decorated it, but not before I attacked him, reminding him that we aren't poor losers, which for the record we are, or were. He told me he had one of these pathetic, build-a-tree monstrosities and I basically said awful things."

Molly swallowed a huge gulp and scrunched up her face.

"Exactly, then I saw the girls faces when they were building it, so excited, and I realized what a snob I was being."

"Yep," said Maxie, taking a sip.

"Not helpful. I begged him to stay and then he suggested we find things we loved for ornaments. I've honestly never seen the girls happier."

"Okay, so why are we removing your brain?" asked Maxie, now on her second glass. "Sorry, sometimes Megan stories make me drink."

"Then we kissed. It was hot and sexy and I wanted him to stay. It's his fault for not staying. He said he had work to do on that stupid shack of his. He left, then as Molly knows, Chase appeared all 'we're rich again,'" Megan said, slugging a gulp and pacing. "He was all 'I made partner, here's a stunning tree, oh and I came to you before Bree, that must mean something.' I was like 'oh it doesn't,' then he kissed me."

Molly's eyes grew wide then she let out a little gasp.

Maxie slammed her drink down. "Did you whack him?"

"Not exactly, it all came rushing back, his touch, his smell, our life. No, no, no, I hate this man. What's happening to me?"

Maxie took a drink and stood up, staring dead into Megan's eyes. "Alright settle down. While a lobotomy would certainly be easier, we're going to break this down right now. Here goes. So, you like the finer things in life. You became accustomed to the big house, fancy car, country club lifestyle, it doesn't make you an awful person. It's a learning curve. Slowly you will begin to see that a guy like Stone is the real deal, you'll see that all that icing with no cake, is missing the foundation. In time, you'll begin to appreciate the smaller things, so stop beating yourself up. Next, the excitement about him coming here first and even the kiss confusion, simple explanation. Molly here, and I have been dumped, cheated on, passed over."

Molly shook her head, "All true."

"But you," Maxie continued, breaking only for another slurp of wine. "You have always been the 'it girl'. You had an unbreakable self-esteem until Chase left you for someone else. When he walked out that door, he took a piece of you with him. Tonight, he gave you some of that back. It has very little to do with him and everything to do with the 'oh yeah he wants me over her' moment that you're reveling in."

Megan jumped up from her chair, hugged Maxie and said, "Maxie you're a genius. You're exactly right, it's not that I want him, it's that he wants me."

"If only I had another bottle of wine, I could solve global warming," Maxie said, plopping down quite satisfied with herself.

Molly, less enthusiastic said, "Just be careful. Exes are a slippery slope. I don't trust him."

"I got this. I'm not falling for his nonsense," promised Megan.

"My work here is done. See you girls for tree decorating tomorrow night," said Maxie.

Molly hugged Megan and followed Maxie out. Megan looked at the sad little tree one more time, sighed then reminded herself it's a learning curve.

Chapter Twenty-One

The next day, Olivia spent most of the day visiting her fish, Sophie practiced her Nutcracker dance, and Megan put the finishing touches on the guest rooms. The lodge was nearly perfect. Each room infused with a unique personality, all filled with warmth and charm. The main floor was now complete and welcomed guests with simple rustic yet chic ski lodge hospitality.

Megan took a long proud glance at the work she had poured her heart into. Opening day would be here in a few days, and for the first time in her life, she felt an overwhelming sense of accomplishment.

One by one, the McKenna's poured in. Before long, the whole McKenna clan had convened around the large tree that sat in the lodge's main living room area. Molly brought Santa hats for all and Hunter had the Christmas tunes sailing through the lodge.

"Where's Tony?" asked Molly.

"As if that is even a question. With the holidays coming he's at work about nineteen hours a day," said Maxie.

Megan shot her a worried glance.

"Don't worry Megan, he isn't Chase," said Maxie.

"Speaking of Chase, I heard he got the big partnership," Silvia said, taking the opportunity to pitch Chase to Megan.

"When did you hear that?" asked Megan.

"He called us this morning dear, to share the good news."

"Why mother do you still talk to him?" Said Megan, raising her voice.

"Stone, great you're here," said Molly loudly as Stone entered the lodge.

Silvia had tabled the Chase discussion for now. Megan knew how manipulative Chase could be and didn't like him worming his way back in one bit. "Hey you, I haven't heard from you all day. I didn't even know if you were coming," said Megan wrapping her arms around his neck.

"Of course, sorry, I'm in the home stretch on the house. It's pretty exciting. I can't wait to show it to you."

Learning curve, Megan reminded herself. She tried to appear interested in the house, as images of the dilapidated tiny house flashed across her mind. She couldn't imagine what he could possibly do to improve that shack other than demolition. And a bigger question, why would he dump money into such a horrible little rundown dwelling? *Focus,* she reminded herself.

Edward piped in, "What are you working on Stone?"

Silvia shot Edward a 'how dare you engage with the enemy' stare, however Edward, propped up on the sofa with his crutches, paid her no mind. Stone sat down and the two chatted while the girls busied themselves with lights, cranberry garland, and tons of woodland ornaments. A few hours later, the tree dazzled in front of a snowy backdrop of the slopes. The fireplace was adorned with pinecones and greenery, and white lights and candles filled the massive stone wall with warmth. The main lodge doors welcomed guests with two large fresh pine wreaths aglow in tiny white lights. Stone's addition of the open great room showcased the second-floor rooms. They wrapped the stairway railings in fresh greenery and lights. After the last decoration, they lit the tree. Molly's reaction, a flood of water works, reinforced that Megan had achieved Molly's dream.

"I honestly couldn't have even envisioned how truly magical you two would make this old lodge look and feel. It's cozy, inviting, and filled with holiday charm. It is everything I dreamed and so much more."

The group clapped for the design team. "When we started, we had very different visions, however we seemed to find a way to blend them into something really wonderful," Megan said, leaning her head on his shoulder.

"I'll say you two are blending into something wonderful," Maxie said, clapping.

"No argument from me," said Stone, pulling Megan in close.

Molly was beaming and clapped her hands in tiny quick taps. Then she said, "We have a few days until our first guests arrive. I'm ecstatic to say Stone has finished the main dining room. We'll serve continental breakfast, bagels, eggs, make-your-own waffles with fresh fruit, cereal, and beverages of coffee, tea, and apple and orange juice. The dining hall will then reopen at four, serving a small dinner menu of wings, fries, burgers, soup of the day, and fresh salad bar. Late night menu will be a hot cocoa bar, along with cookies, pies and donuts provided by Tony's restaurant. We have Pete, Charlie, Burt, and Tiny who are our four security/maintenance guys, and Marge will fill in at the front desk. We'll have one of them on duty twenty-four hours a day. I have a staff of three maids and one groundskeeper. Megan will handle much of the guest services, and Hunter and I'll fill in when we aren't at the village. Ribbon cutting ceremony starts promptly at seven, and we'll be serving hot cocoa and gingerbread cookies. Megan, did I forget anything?"

"Maybe just to breathe. Congratulations Molly; you have finally made your dream a reality," said Megan, grabbing her baby sister and squeezing her tight.

Megan led everyone on a tour of the guest rooms to see the finished product. After they met back in the main lodge, Silvia stood up and said, "I think Edward has been out long enough. I need to get him home."

"I'm going to get these two sleepy girls to bed," said Megan.

"How about I do that? Tony's not home. The designers need to do a little celebrating."

"Is that okay girls?" said Megan, holding them both tightly.

"Yay, Aunt Maxie," they cheered.

"I'm the fun one," Maxie reminded them.

"That's what worries me," said Megan winking.

When the lodge emptied, Stone and Megan melted into the couch. "We really are a great team, aren't we?" Megan said.

"Seriously, if we had only listened to Chartreuse, the Love Guru, in the first place, we wouldn't have lost so much time," he said, pulling her closer.

"Well there's nothing stopping us now is there?" she said, crawling onto his lap. "How about we go to your place?" she asked, almost shocked at her own suggestion. Maxie was right; she could learn to love the smaller things if Stone was by her side.

"You don't have to ask me twice," Stone said. Kissing and laughing, they made their way to the door, stumbling over furniture on every step. She reached for her coat on the hook and Stone reached for the front door knob. About to twist it, he felt the knob turn beneath his grasp. The door pushed open and Chase stood in the entrance way.

"We're leaving," said Stone.

Megan found her footing. "What are you doing here?"

"I came to finish what we started last night. You don't share a kiss like that then leave it unfinished," he said his eyes on Stone.

"Chase you need to go," she said, panic now straining her voice.

"Do you two have something you need to work out?" said Stone, his eyes on Megan.

"We share two daughters, we have our financial lives entwined, and a history of two decades. So yes, Stone, Megan and I have some things to work out," said Chase, gloating in the reaction he had managed to get out of Stone.

Stone slipped his arms in his parka and said, "Megan, call me when you figure things out." Before Megan could utter a word, he disappeared into the cold night.

"What was that?" she said, her Irish temper boiling.

Chase leaned in to pull her close. She pushed back hard with both hands. "Stop."

"Megan, I need to explain last night. Everything happened so fast. I just came here without giving a second thought to Bree. You are the one I wanted to share this with because Megan, you are my soulmate. We have been together since we were kids. I screwed up, but it doesn't mean we can't fix it."

"Are you kidding? You cheated on me. You left me and the girls without a second thought. You're marrying her. Now all of a sudden we're soulmates?"

"I told Bree last night I don't want to marry her. I realized life with her could never be what we had. I know none of this makes sense, but give me a chance to change your mind."

"What did we have? Lies, empty promises, disappointments?"

"I'm different, Megan."

"I have to go. You have to go. Just go, now," Megan said, realizing his words were penetrating her heart.

He brushed her face with his hand. His face within inches of hers. "I'll go so you can let this sink in. Trust me, it's as surprising to me as it is to you."

She opened the door and pushed him out. Slamming it behind her, she pressed the weight of her body against it and steadied her shaking legs. She had waited forever to hear those words. Every night for a year, she prayed he would come back to her, then the engagement announcement shattered any hope of that. It took every fiber in her to accept the rejection, the pain, the loss. How dare he just expect her to fall into his arms! Her eyes caught the oversized chandelier made of antlers hanging in the foyer, "Oh my gosh, Stone," she said, grabbing her purse and running out the door. She frantically jammed the keys into the ignition and turned the engine, yet again to no avail. "No, no, not now," she pleaded. She reached into her phone and dialed his number.

"Hello," he said into the phone, his voice strained.

"Stone, please, let me explain. I'm in my car trying to get to you but my car is dead. Come back."

"It's late. We'll talk tomorrow."

"Nothing happened with Chase, I swear. He stopped by to give me a tree. He grabbed me and kissed me. He caught me off guard, it meant nothing."

"Why didn't you tell me?"

"I'm sorry, he just storms in and turns everything upside down."

"It's okay Megan, just watch him. I don't trust him."

Chapter Twenty-Two

The grand opening night had finally arrived. The whole McKenna clan in tow were present and filled with excitement for the chance to show off the stunning lodge. Mayor Hopewell greeted the crowd and handed the large scissors to Molly.

"Thank you, Mayor. The Mistletoe Lodge is the final piece in our Christmas Village project. I'm beyond thrilled to share it with the town and our guests. Our hope is that when you stay with us, you arrive as strangers who are just friends we haven't met yet, then leave as family. Now, I can't possibly cut this ribbon without mentioning two people whom this whole project would not have been possible without their combined talents. My sister, the designer, Megan McKenna, and the contractor/architect, Stone Reynolds."

The crowd applauded, "Now Megan, if you'll do the honors and cut this ribbon before I burst with excitement to let everyone come inside."

Megan took the scissors and moved close to Stone. She grabbed his hand and placed it on the scissor with hers. They snipped the ribbon to the pleasure of the audience. The press snapped dozens of photos before following them into the lodge. The guests, along with friends and locals, could hardly believe the warmth and beauty that welcomed them beyond those massive doors. With hot cocoa flowing and gingerbread being enjoyed by all, Molly and Hunter took the first group on a tour. Megan and Stone the next. Maxie took the last group. Guests were allowed to check in one day early for no added cost.

As promised, the lodge's main room greeted guests with the scent of pine, holly berry, and cinnamon sticks. The crackling fireplace roared with amber flames, inviting guests to grab a book and snuggle on the worn leather sofas, or nestle on ottomans on the white fur rug. The glass wall highlighted the snow-capped slopes. The sound of Bing Crosby crooning Christmas songs filled the air. Even the harshest of critics couldn't find a detail left unattended. Megan and Stone had truly worked magic on the old lodge. Together they created Mistletoe Lodge, the destination lodging Molly had dreamed about. Guests who had stayed in the lodge in the past marveled at how the two managed to keep true to its natural beauty while effortlessly marrying contemporary elements of luxe with rustic comfort.

After endless interviews with the press, Megan and Stone took the girls to their suite. Megan tucked them in bed and then strutted out to the living room with the look of a proud peacock. She let her weary body fall comfortably next to Stone on the sofa. She smiled glancing over at the little tree with boas and starfish.

"We did it."

"I never doubted your talent for one minute. You're good at this, Megan."

With genuine sincerity, she looked at him. He had blown her away with his talent. Never could she imagine the magnitude of his skill. "You are the one that surprised

Rylee Ridolfi

me. Who knew a small-town contractor could pull a job like this off?"

"Not all surprises are bad," he said. "So, about the tree in the hallway outside your room? Does it come with a story?"

"Chase delivered it right after you left. I honestly didn't know what to do with it," she said, knowing her statement to be only half true. Try as she may, the glowing beauty somehow tugged at her sense of entitlement.

"Megan, he wants you back, I can feel it. I know he's getting married, but it's a guy thing. I can tell."

"About that, he's well, not actually getting married anymore. Please trust me Stone, he won't come between us."

"He already has Megan."

"He made partner. Remember the investment that he lost with all of my money? Apparently, he has recovered it and tripled it. I called the bank and none of the supposed money has surfaced back into my account. I'm not sure if it's all a lie, but I don't care about the money. I care about you and me."

"Megan, I want you to know I'll always put you and your needs first. You have two young girls that depend on you. I love you, but I won't complicate things for my own benefit. If you want to repair your family, I won't make you feel guilty."

"He can't touch what we have, Stone. I love you, now kiss me before my lips just take matters into their own hands."

Words no longer mattered, all that mattered was the touch of his skin, the warmth of his body, and the deep emotional safety she felt in his arms. His hands found the curve of her back. He pulled her close. Her phone rang. She ignored it, longing for his kiss. The ringing continued. "I better," she said, struggling to force herself to break free.

"Hello," she panted into the phone.

"Megan, there's a guest who works with staging model homes, hotels etc. He wants to talk to you. Isn't that amazing?" Molly said into the phone in a near piercing tone. "Give me five minutes and I'll come over and sit with the girls while you talk. Go Megan."

Megan turned to Stone almost afraid to allow her excitement to show. "I heard. Now what are you doing standing here? I'll stay with the girls until Molly gets here. Go Megan, you deserve this. I actually should go, I have work to do on the house."

"Are you sure?"

"Get out of here," he said.

Miles Trent, a formidable realtor, sat by the hot cocoa bar waiting for Megan. As soon as she laid eyes on him, she recognized him from every major billboard in town. Her mouth felt dry and her hands were clammy.

"Mr. Trent," she said, extending a slightly damp hand.

"Megan, call me Miles. I'm impressed with what you've done here. I showed the property a few times before your family purchased it. Many folks couldn't see the potential of this old lodge, but you did. Have you thought about branching out and taking on some new projects? Do you have a resume or portfolio?"

"I," she paused, completely ready to sell herself short with the correct answer 'I have neither,' but caught herself. She stopped for a minute and thought about the trust Molly put in her to tackle this project. She had drawn on the skills she honed from her personal life. "I have a portfolio, of sorts, of the complete transition I tackled in my own home on Dillon Ave. Also, as a member of the country club, I have handled all the decor for every major charity event for the last five years. I can get you photos of each project."

"Impressive. I'm sensing a bit of event planning skills untapped as well. Here's my card. Get me those photos, and we'll talk."

"Thank you," she managed to choke out with her tongue now feeling like a furry cotton ball. He excused himself. She did a little dance with hands in the air while twirling around. She rushed back to her suite to tell Molly. Megan McKenna finally found her purpose. She was more than just mommy, sister, friend, and other non-paying titles. It may have taken her thirty-five years to figure it out, but for the first time she had confidence in something other than her outward appearance.

Chapter Twenty-Three

With a new spring in her step, Megan continued her duties at the lodge while preparing an expansive portfolio of social events she had chaired. The prospect of event planning became a goal. She even looked into some design classes at the local college. As the lodge merrily swelled on the weekends with happy guests, she and Stone had little time together between his project and Molly's upcoming wedding.

With one week left until Christmas and six days until the wedding, the McKenna clan was in full-on panic mode. Molly, Maxie, Megan, Silvia, and Olivia were meeting for a final fitting at the Bridal salon. Hunter was on Sophie duty. To further complicate the day, today was dress rehearsal for the Nutcracker performance.

"You sure you got this Hunter?" asked Molly.

"Of course, you ladies head out, do your thing. Ms. Sophie and I'll hang out for about an hour then head over to the rehearsal. We'll reconvene here after. How'd I do?"

"This is why I'm marrying this guy," said Molly, kissing him.

"You, Hunter, are one in a million," said Megan. She kissed Sophie and made sure she had her ballerina bag packed. "Are you all set, sugar plum fairy?"

"I think. I'm still worried about that first group of steps," she said, hanging onto Megan's sweater.

"Nonsense, you're going to be amazing."

Silvia and Maxie pulled up and honked the horn. "That's us," Molly said.

****

Hunter and Sophie sat on the couch watching TV. Sophie anxiously fidgeted with worry about the show. Stone opened the lodge door and called out, "Hey, there are two of my favorite people. What's happening here, a party?"

"Just hanging out while we wait to go to the Nutcracker rehearsal," said Hunter.

"You, my friend, just earned extra special honeymoon night points with this favor," said Stone, laughing heartily.

"You know, man?" said Stone, "What I've learned this week before your wedding is that survival means saying yes or no, whatever makes her happy and preserves your life."

"Alright then, good luck Sophie, and to you as well Hunter. I have to make a few quick adjustments to the shelves to make sure they're bolted in tightly, and I'll be out of your way." After about ten minutes, Stone packed up his tools and announced, "My work is done."

Hunter's phone rang. "Yeah? When? Is he okay? Ambulance? Crap, hold on, I'm on my way," Hunter said, pushing his hair off his reddened face beading up with perspiration.

"Man, are you okay?" asked Stone.

"Ernie, our lead elf, tripped on a skate in Santa's workshop. They think it's a broken wrist. I have to go.

Wait Sophie's the Sugar Plum Fairy," he said, rubbing his temples before gazing over at the small ballerina with both hands on her hips.

"I got this," said Stone. "Where's the hall? What time do we need to be there?"

"Are you sure, man? Molly's so stressed about the lodge, Christmas Village, and the wedding; this might just put her over the edge."

"Taking one for the team," Stone said, giving Hunter a wink.

"I love you man. I'll text you the address."

"Go save the elf. Sophie, we got this."

Stone looked at the address Hunter sent, then noticed the pensive look on the little ballerina's face. "What's up, Sugar Plum?"

"I can't remember the first part of my routine. It's very complicated. I don't want to mess up," she said, her eyes tearing up.

Stone was way out of his comfort zone on this but he wouldn't let her down. "Hey no worries. This is only a rehearsal. Everyone's a little nervous, that's why they have these, to get your jitters out," he said assuredly.

****

Several hours later Megan, Molly, and Maxie stormed through the front doors of the lodge as if they were running for their lives. Marge, the front desk clerk and longtime friend of the family jumped to her feet. "Where's the fire?"

"We can't reach Hunter. We've been calling him all day. Is everything alright? Where's Sophie?" Megan said, panting between words.

"Hold on now, that's a lot of questions. Sophie's in the main dining room's kitchen practicing. Hunter left for an emergency over at the ..." Marge said, unable to finish as the three darted toward the dining room. They swiftly moved past the tables and swung open the double doors to the kitchen to find Sophie in full ballerina gear and Stone with a pink tutu around his knee. They were moving to the sounds of Tchaikovsky's Nutcracker while repeating, "Lucy loves dogs, run Lucy run, please." Stunned, the three froze speechless.

"Oh, hey guys, you're just in time for Sophie's solo," said Stone.

"Where's Hunter?" asked Molly.

"He didn't get a hold of you? Ernie took a spill, but before you panic, he's going to be fine. Hunter took him to the ER. He didn't want you to worry."

"So, Sophie missed rehearsal?" Megan said, blood rushing from her face.

"Nope, Stone took me. He taught me a trick. I couldn't remember left, left, demi, turn, right, left, right, plie. Now we just say this; come on Stone, let's show them."

They moved together singing, Lucy loves dogs, run Lucy run please, perfectly in sync. The three women cheered.

"That's amazing Sophie," said Molly.

"And Stone, I'm not going to lie, that was pretty sweet. If this whole carpenter thing doesn't pan out, you might just have a place in the ballet," said Maxie giving him the thumbs up. "Sophie, I'm heading to grandmas. You want to come?" Maxie said, winking at Megan.

"Yes. Can I wear my tutu?"

"Sure, can sweetie. Give me a kiss. I'll get you guys after dinner," Megan said. Maxie, Molly, and Sophie disappeared into the dining room as Megan moved in close to Stone. "Nice tutu."

"Real men wear tutus," he said, pulling her in for a kiss.

"You really are the best. How can I thank you?"

"I have a few ideas in mind."

"When exactly are we getting that date?"

"I'm working on it, but how about for now we grab a bite to eat?"

"Sounds lovely." They headed out to the main lodge, said goodbye to Marge, and continued to exit to the parking lot. Stone tossed her a set of keys.

"What's this?"

"Spare keys to your car. Molly gave them to me. Start her up."

Megan looked at him then ran toward the van. She ripped open the door and threw the keys in. One turn and it purred like a kitten.

"Oh my gosh, how did you fix it?"

"Not me, a buddy of mine. He owed me a favor after I fixed his roof. It was an oxygen sensor. Your days of being stranded are over."

She wrapped her arms around his neck and pulled him close. "At this rate, my payback favor list should make for a pretty interesting date."

"There is a methodology to my kindness."

A voice penetrated Megan's ears like nails on a chalkboard. "Megan, I need to talk to you now," said Chase in an annoyed authoritative voice.

Stone moved back from Megan and squared off with him face to face. "Can I help you?"

"No, you can step away from my wife," he said, pushing Stone's shoulder.

Stone taller, more muscular, and definitely not one to back down, laughed. "Really? You're going to push me? Are we in eighth grade?" Stone said as he closed the gap between them, reminding Chase of his physical dominance. "I'll tell you what we are going to do. First, you're going to apologize nicely, then you're going to reword whatever you needed to say to Megan. Are we clear?"

Chase moved back a few steps and turned to Megan, who had stepped out of the car ready to intervene if a fight broke out.

"Megan, I need to talk to you about the girls and Christmas," he said, giving Stone a sideways glare.

"Not now you don't. I'm going out, so it'll have to wait."

"Call me tonight, Megan. I mean it. If not, my lawyer will be petitioning for me to get them from 7:00 p.m. Christmas Eve until 8:00 a.m. the day after Christmas. I've already spoken to him and since you had them

Thanksgiving, he assured me this is a done deal. If you want to compromise, I won't file the motion. Your choice. Megan, this is what shared custody looks like. Remember that before you rush to any decisions," he said, turning, then heading to his car.

Megan waited just long enough for him to close his door before breaking down. "No, not Christmas. He wouldn't take that away from me, would he?" she said, shaking with tears streaming down her face.

"Megan, look at me. There isn't time to get that to family court between now and Christmas. He's bullying you. Look at me. He has an agenda. He seems to think he always gets his way. That may be true in his business dealings, but you can't bully the courts."

"You're right, breathe," she instructed herself.

"You still need to eat, okay?" he said, holding her face in his hands.

"I'm sorry, I'm not that hungry anymore."

"I understand," Stone said, although his face told a different story. He dropped her at Silvia and Edwards.

Before getting out of the car, she reached in her purse and handed him a ticket. "You don't have to go, but in case you want to see your hard work pay off, the Nutcracker performance is tomorrow night at seven."

"It's going to be tough not to leap up on that stage with my new found talent, but I'll fight the urge and cheer our girl on."

Our girl, the words so simple, yet they ballooned in Megan's heart. He really had become a part of her world.

She loved the bond he had formed with Olivia, however today to see him with Sophie made her heart nearly burst.

"Alright then, tomorrow at seven. Remember, Lucy loves dogs, run Lucy run please. Got it?"

"Thank you, my knight in a shining tutu. Again, you saved the day."

Chapter Twenty-Four

The big night arrived. The Nutcracker stage shimmered with large toys and a row of seven-foot soldiers. Megan and the girls arrived in plenty of time. After putting the finishing touches on Sophie's hair, she and Olivia headed out to find their seats. They found three seats together, third row from the front. She ushered Olivia in and turned to see Stone coming in the door. Megan waved to him. Stone made his way into the aisle then stopped in his tracks.

"What's wrong?" Megan asked before turning to see who was behind her.

"Hey, there's my girls," said Chase.

Sophie ran out and hugged him. "Daddy you came."

Sophie looked at a bag that dangled from Stone's hand. Pink with nutcrackers in silver and a plume of silver tissue sticking out the top. "Is that for me?"

"Sure is, kid," said Stone, handing it to her. She reached into the bag and pulled out a Sugar Plum Fairy beanie doll.

"She's just like me. I love it. Thank you," she said, wrapping her arms around his waist.

Rylee Ridolfi

"Um, I too have a gift for you," said Chase, pausing, searching for something to say. "I got you... tickets to the Broadway show of the real Nutcracker."

"Mommy, did you hear daddy has tickets?" Miss Natalie called Sophie to join them backstage. She turned to Stone and said, "Lucy loves dogs, run Lucy run, please."

Stone gave her a high five. "You got it kid." She ran off toward the stage. Chase stared at Stone with daggers in his eyes.

"What is that, some low-class secret code?"

Megan said, "I'll move. Let's go find seats in the back."

"No, you stay here. I'll go to the back," said Stone.

"I feel awful. I don't want you to sit alone," Megan said.

"Alone? Who are you kidding? Look, my fellow dance moms are saving me a seat," he said, waving to a group of single moms he had met at yesterday's practice.

"Somehow you manage to make even the direst of situations plausible. Thank you for that."

"Don't thank me now, it's on your tab."

Stone took his seat among the women. The lights came up and the tiny dancers took the stage. Chase stared down at his phone the entire performance. Olivia stared back at Stone. Megan split her eyes between the stage and Stone until it was time for Sophie's big solo. She executed it perfectly, while mouthing the words quite visibly. Megan turned to Stone giving him a thumbs up. When the performance ended, Megan met Sophie and Ms. Natalie at the base of the stage.

"You were great, Sophie," Megan said before Sophie scooted off to Chase.

Natalie looked at Megan and said, "Girl, where the heck have you been hiding Mr. Hotness?"

"Oh, he's well, I," Megan stumbled on her words. "He's a good guy."

"I'll say. And Megan, you better keep him close, the piranhas were eyeing him up," Natalie said, pointing to the group of moms giggling like seventh grade love sick puppies surrounding him.

"Thanks for the advice." Megan gathered Sophie's bag, said hi to a few friends, then turned to look for Stone. He was nowhere in sight.

"Mommy, daddy's taking us out for ice cream like we did after the school play with Stone," said Sophie, spinning in place.

"Alright girls, a quick cone, but it's a school night. Get your coats," she said. After the girls had left, she peered at him. "What exactly do you think you are doing?"

"Megan, I want my family back. You know when I set my mind to something, I don't stop until I get it. I always win."

"We're not an account to be acquired. You don't just get to decide if and when you want us."

"Megan, I told you I want you. I want what we had when we were Chase and Megs. We were the 'it couple'. Everyone wanted to be us. We had the world in our hands."

"That was a long time ago, before the girls."

"Don't underestimate me, Megan. I'm working on a way to get us back and it's going to be even better than the first time. We can travel and see the world. The country club will be our second home, fancy dinners, shows, you name it. I'm going to give you the world on a silver platter."

"Speaking of shows, do you really have tickets to the Nutcracker or was that a lie?"

"Not yet, but I'll get them."

"Of course you don't, because lying is acceptable when it fits. You seriously think that you can get tickets? It has been sold out for months now. How can you do that to her? You could've bought her roses, chocolate, anything, but don't make a promise you can't keep."

"Like the worthless gift the lug bought her. Not for my daughter. She deserves nothing but the best."

"When are you going to see it's not about how much things cost, it's about being there for her. Remembering her." She paused to replay the words that just formed on her lips. It's not how much things cost. A smile spread across her face, "learning curve," she said quietly to herself.

She walked toward the girls, took their hands and headed for a night with the enemy. At Pickles and Pops, the ice cream parlor around the corner from the hall, the four sat in a red booth. Megan texted Stone a short note that she would call later. Her phone beeped back. She didn't recognize the number. The text read, *Hello Megan; I'm hosting a Valentine birthday party for my wife. The guest list consists of approximately a hundred people, mostly realtors. A great place to preview your work. The theme is Gatsby. I'll be in touch after the new year. Looking forward to working with you, Miles.*

She jumped up from her seat and dialed Stone. "I got my first real chance in design/event planning. Miles hired me to do his wife's birthday."

"It's just the beginning. Congrats; not only beautiful, but talented too. I'm a lucky guy."

"Megan, your ice cream is here," shouted Chase.

"Stone I'm sorry about us not being able to go out the other night. I really want to go on a real date with you, you know a movie, dancing, dinner, whatever, but every time, something happens."

"In time, Megan. We will, I promise."

"Can you come to brunch at my parents' tomorrow? My aunts, uncles, cousins, and the whole clan are arriving for the wedding."

"Text me the time."

Sophie talked nonstop, Chase ignored her and spoke only to Megan. Olivia fell asleep on her napkin. Megan drifted off thinking about Aunt Charlotte's after the play and how Stone interacted with the girls, how different she felt when it was the four of them. Chase was her past, Stone would be her future.

Chapter Twenty-Five

Friday, late afternoon found Silvia and Edward's home bustling with extended family members arriving for the wedding. A late brunch gave everyone time to settle in. With the wedding just a few days away, the McKenna sisters were working around the clock. All hands were on deck, except one. Stone had another commitment. Megan worried it had more to do with Chase's performance last night than actual work.

The girls loved having family around. Megan was grateful for the break from the girls. She sat on the living room floor working on wedding favors; tiny vintage cream-colored wreaths adorned with black bows.

Molly rushed in, phone to her ear. "Okay, I'll see if I can send someone to check it out."

"What's up?" Megan asked, knowing all too well the look on Molly's face.

"Marge said the swipe key to the Winter Wonderland suite isn't working. It's not occupied until Sunday, but if I need an electrician to look at it, I'll have to move those guests to another room," Molly said.

"No worries Molly, I'll check it out. You have enough on your plate. I planned on leaving soon anyway. It's actually almost six o'clock. The girls have a sleepover planned with their cousins, so I'm free. I'll give you a call when I figure out what's going on."

"You're the best," Molly said, hugging her big sister.

Megan said goodbye to her family and kissed the girls. She slid the key into the engine of her van and found herself pleasantly surprised by the purring of the engine. Stone made this happen. He took care of her and her girls. She missed him. She turned on the radio to kill the deafening silence usually filled with screaming kids. Stone set the station to country, filling the van with the crooning sounds of Taylor Swift singing Santa Baby. She couldn't help her lips from stretching into a wide smile. He knew the sounds of country music would make her think of him. What he didn't know was that lately, that's all she seemed to do.

The roads lightly covered by fresh fallen snow made her want him even more. The lodge, covered in sparkling snowflakes with a backdrop of snow-covered slopes, made her giggle with excitement of spending the winter with Stone. Inside she found Marge drinking a cup of tea and reading a murder mystery. A family sat by the fire playing board games and a couple reading books on the leather sofa. A smile spread across Megan's face watching the guests enjoy the lodge.

"Hi Megan, Molly told me you were going to check on that lock."

"Sure am. It's actually my favorite room."

"I didn't know," said Marge, offering Megan a cookie from the tray on the check in desk.

"It's the only room where I veered a little away from the real woodland feel of red and black. I went with steel grays and white fur. The room already hosts the best view, with a French door and that little balcony facing the Black Diamond slope. With the white pine paneling and the gas burning stove, it truly gives the luxe lodge feel."

"Well it's booked through the third week in February. I guess that luxe feel is pretty popular."

"That's so exciting," Megan said, taking the electronic card. "These silly keys can be tricky, but we'll get it squared away before the guests get here," she said. She made her way up the pine staircase lit with white lights and headed down the hallway to the Winter Wonderland suite. Megan slid the key into the lock. With one twist, the knob opened. "Hmm, strange, seems to be working fine to me," she said, pushing the door open to take a peek at her favorite room. She stopped and drew her breath in hard. "Oh my gosh," she said as she pushed the door open all the way. Her eyes panned the room with laser speed scanning side to side. The room greeted her with hundreds of tiny white lights and tons of white candles in forged steel lanterns. A table in front of the fireplace had been set with candles and fine china. A white fur rug laid in front of the doors facing the sparkling snow-covered sky trails. Stone, dressed in a white turtleneck sweater and gray khakis stood by the bedside. His beautiful face lit by the candlelight made her head spin a bit, her knees go weak.

"Megan McKenna, welcome to your date night. We've missed out on a few dates, so, I've incorporated several dates in one night."

"I, I don't know what to say," she said as a few tears slid down her face.

"You can start with it's about time we got our date. The girls are taken care of all night. Maxie and Molly know all about this, so as far as the world goes, you are invisible until tomorrow morning."

"Of course, they knew," she said, shaking her head.

Megan dropped her purse and ran toward the bed, scaling it as she leaped across it into his arms. Her arms around his neck, her legs around his waist, she kissed him passionately. Not removing her lips from his, she threw her scarf to the ground then ripped her coat off. She found herself breathing so hard, she feared she might lose consciousness, until she heard what sounded like a knock at the door.

"No, no, don't get it," she pleaded, struggling for air. Stone ignored her.

"You might want to get down for a second," he said, attempting to peel her from his waist.

"What are you doing? I'm invisible, remember."

He opened the door. "Thanks Marge," he said.

"Marge knew too?" she whispered.

He returned a minute later pushing a cart with two dishes loaded with decadent entrees. Chicken Florentine, asparagus with gruyere cheese, and twice baked potatoes brimming with cheese, bacon and chives. In the center, a bottle of champagne and two crystal glasses.

"A dinner date," she said, inhaling the fragrant feast.

"Tony is to thank for all this."

"Everyone knew?"

"Pretty much. Dating you is a ten-man job," he said, smiling as he rolled the cart over to the table. "Table for two," he said, pulling out the seat for her.

They feasted on the gourmet dinners while sipping the champagne. Savoring each bite as if it was her last, Megan said, "You've no idea what a pleasure it is to actually taste food instead of inhaling it."

"Do you know what a pleasure it is to sit across from you and watch your beautiful smile brighten up this room?"

"No, am I a pleasure?"

Stone pulled his chair out and smiled a devilish grin, "You, Ms. McKenna, are indeed a pleasure."

Scraping the last bits of gooey mozzarella cheese from her potato, she sat back and smiled. "I like where this is going."

"Not so fast. Your pleasure will have to wait until we have date number two. Madam," he said, extending his hand. He brought her to the closet and opened the door. Inside a pair of ice skates rested on the floor.

She reached in and pulled them out. "Let me guess, Maxie gave you these." He nodded. "I haven't skated in years."

"The shallow end of the pond is frozen and this is a perfect night for us to be under the stars. Come on, trust me on this," he said, handing her jacket to her. "I've a feeling I'm going to regret this," she said, leaning in and grabbing the skates in one hand and her jacket in the other.

They bundled up and made their way to the main lodge. Marge greeted them.

"Heading out?" she asked.

"Yes, for a night skate on the lake," said Stone, giving Megan a wink.

"Oh, wait right there," said Marge as she scurried off to the kitchen. She returned with a thermos and two mugs. "Nothing like some hot cocoa on a lovely winter's night."

"You're the best," said Stone.

"Thank you, Marge. Hot cocoa will undoubtedly be the highlight of this endeavor," said Megan, shaking her head.

Stone led her around back to the pond. Two logs were centered in a metal fire pit.

"I see you were confident, I'd say, yes."

"I can be very convincing," he said, striking a match and tossing it into the pit. The dry wood caught quickly bringing a warm orange glow to the ice. They sat on the log to slip on their skates. He kneeled down wrapping the laces behind her ankles and securing them tightly.

"Tight laces help the ankles steady themselves. Okay, baby steps. Follow me," said Stone, taking her hand. She awkwardly took one step then tried a series of tiny ones, until her left skate met the ice. In a semi-split, her right foot refused to join the left foot which slipped further onto the ice. Stone, doubled over with laughter asked, "What the heck is that?"

"I told you it's been a while. Molly will kill me if I'm in a cast for the wedding."

He took her hands, gently pulling her into him. He anchored her hips with his hands. A quick rush ran through Megan's body.

"Now bend a little and put your hands on your knees. Do you feel the stability of that position? That's your go-to if you feel unsteady," he said, removing his hands just inches from her hips, allowing her to balance. "Okay now one foot, then the next, in little strides. I'm behind you, I won't let you fall," he said, as she took a few tiny steps then began to glide.

"Hey look, it's coming back," she said, as she slowly made her way around the rink. He smiled with those delicious dimples dizzying her a bit. After a few laps, she began moving around a bit stiff, but with confidence.

"I can't believe it. I'm doing it. I thought I was too old for this."

"Too old, are you nuts?" he said, skating up behind her and wrapping his arms around her waist.

She stumbled to the left. "Hey no fair, you scared me," she shouted, turning around to face him. He leaned in and kissed her sweetly, then a bit more passionately.

"I think we're moving toward date three," she said, shivering a bit.

"You're cold. Let's sit by the fire," he said, guiding her off the lake to the logs by the dancing flames.

"This is nice," she smiled, removing a gloved hand to undo the lid of cocoa. She poured them each a mug then snuggled in next to him. Wrapped in each other's arms they watched the sky as twinkling stars dotted the black night. The lights lining the trails made the icy slopes glisten.

Stone turned to her, his face a bit more serious and asked, "What do you want, Megan McKenna?"

"That's a loaded question, but if you asked me at this moment, I'd settle for staying like this forever."

"I meant out of life."

"Well, to see my girls grow up happy, healthy and successful, I guess."

"No, I mean you, Megan. What do *you* want?"

She paused and sat quietly, gazing up at the night sky. "I don't know. I never really thought about what I want. I want genuine happiness with a man I can trust. I really want to succeed at this new business opportunity. I mean, I realize I have no formal training, but neither did Rachael Ray and look at her. I think I'm good at design and when I'm doing it, I feel alive, excited, accomplished. Wow, I can't believe I said that out loud. I hadn't even thought it out loud in my head."

"Megan you're allowed to be happy doing something for you. You're talented. I believe in you. I saw your work first hand. You're a bit like a mad scientist when the ideas are flowing, without the thick glasses and bushy eyebrows of course."

She gave him a push. He grabbed her and they fell backwards off the log. Landing squarely on top of him she felt her sides hurt from laughter. "Thank you for this," she said. "I've never had more fun on a date, and it's not a fancy restaurant or the country club. It's just us enjoying each other."

"About that, what do you say about enjoying each other upstairs?"

"I'd say yes," she said, as a wicked smile crossed her face.

They unlaced their skates, put on their shoes and rushed back to the lodge. They hurried their way up the steps. Barely able to keep their hands off each other, they removed hats, coats, scarves, as they kissed moving down the hallway. When they reached the door, he picked her up legs around him and slid the key into the lock. Giggling like teenagers, Stone stopped and smiled. His eyes locked with hers and said, "I love you, Megan McKenna."

Her heart nearly tore out of her parka, "I love you too."

"Now this seat is reserved for you," he said as he directed her to a furry rug lined with pillows facing the slopes. They gazed out onto the snow-covered mountains. Megan had never before felt so loved, cherished or complete.

Stone wrapped her in blankets and turned on the TV, popped, *White Christmas,* into the DVR and snuggled her tightly. Watching the movie, the world stood still, if only for that one night.

"Since we're finally on a roll with dates, how would you feel about being my plus one to the wedding tomorrow?" she said as she wrapped his strong arms around her and nestled her head on his chest.

Chapter Twenty-Six

A round two o'clock Christmas Eve, a bang followed by a loud booming sound shook the lodge. Molly, one-inch shy of a nervous breakdown, nearly fainted with the explosive sound.

"Molly relax, it's thunder snow. The real storm isn't set to hit until midnight. We're fine," said Megan, pouring her a cup of tea.

"Tea? What the heck is tea going to do for her? Does anyone know where the vodka is?" Maxie said, rushing into the hall to yell over the massive banister.

"Rain on your wedding day is good luck, but no one ever said anything about thunder snow on your wedding," Molly said, pacing the floor of the Mr. and Mrs. Claus suite.

"Look at me Molly, today is going to be perfect. You're marrying your best friend on your birthday, not to mention your favorite day of the year. How could anything possibly be wrong with that?" said Megan, offering a cheerful optimism to the mood.

Maxie, standing in the doorway, bit her bottom lip and said, "Well about that, Megan can I see you in the hall please?"

Megan kissed Molly's forehead, then suggested she start getting into her dress. Megan opened the door and stepped into the hallway. "What now?"

"Chase is downstairs."

"What, why?"

"Mom invited him. Says he's been a part of our family for twenty years and somehow that means he should be here."

"So has Ralph the Terminix guy, is he coming too?" Megan said, barely able to catch her breath.

"Alright now, before you go all fatal attraction on him, remember it's Molly's day and she's as fragile as a snowflake."

Megan, in her white satin robe encrusted with Bridesmaid in rhinestones, hair in large curlers and furry white slippers, marched down the stairs with the force of a pack of pregnant elephants. Chase waited at the bottom of the steps in a black suit with a crisp white Swiss dot shirt and pink bowtie. *Why is he so blazing hot? Fat, bald, snaggle toothed would just make everything so much easier*, she murmured to herself.

"Hello beautiful," he said suave and confident.

"Why are you here?"

"Molly's wedding, I did get the right day, yes?"

"I mean you don't belong here. I didn't invite you. I have a date."

"The plumber?"

"He's not a plumber. It doesn't matter, you have no place here."

"Megan why are you making this so difficult? How can I show you how serious I am if you keep pushing me away?"

"Chase, you don't know what you want. A few days ago, you were engaged to Bree, now you're in love with me? Think about how preposterous that sounds."

"I agree it sounds utterly mad. It sounds like a man who finally figured out the rest of his life and isn't going to waste one more minute without her."

"MEGAN," a scream similar to one of a woman in labor echoed from above.

"Stay, leave, I don't care. I have to go," she said, racing up the stairs two at a time.

Megan opened the door, took one look at Molly, her eyes widened. Maxie shook her head back and forth like a terrier in a cone of shame urging Megan not to show panic.

"Hey there Molly. How are we doing?" Megan said, trying to avert her eyes from the cluster of hives that had formed across her nose, swallowing her freckles.

"My zipper, it's broken. I can't, it won't..." Molly gasped.

"Alright breathe. The dress is on inside out, so let's first step out of it then try again," Megan said, shooting Maxie a look.

"What? I don't wear dresses."

Megan repositioned Molly into her gown, a full white tulle skirt with a high collared neckline in lace with long fitted bell sleeves. She zipped up the back. A tear fell from

Megan's eye. "My baby sister is getting married. Look at you, you're stunning."

"AWWWWW," Molly wailed as she gazed into the mirror and spotted the hives clustering on top of one another like teenagers at an outdoor concert. "Oh, it's a sign. Hives are a sign your body is fighting off something dangerous."

"I'm fairly certain there are no studies to back that," Megan said, grabbing her compact.

"Vodka, where's the vodka?" Maxie yelled out the door.

"Maxie, she isn't going to do shots," Megan said, shaking her head.

"It's not for her," Maxie said, opening the door to a knock. Stone stood on the other side of the door with three glasses and a bottle of caramel sea salt vodka. "We all okay up here? I was instructed by Edward to deliver this."

Maxie peeked out the door, snatched the vodka and glasses then said, "We are now. Megan, doors for you," she said, opening the bottle and taking a swig right from the bottle.

Megan marched over to the door, swung it open and shouted loudly, "GO Home."

"Okay," said Stone, squinting one eye.

"Oh no, no, not you. Sorry, kiss me now," she said, planting her lips on his then grabbing the bottle from Maxie and taking a swig, while noting how incredibly handsome he looked in navy pants, a navy button down and green and navy tie.

"Alright then, I didn't know Regan was coming to the party. I kind of dig the whole Sybil vibe, but I think I'm just going downstairs and see if I can help with anything. Seems, I don't know, safer."

"Yes, good idea. I love you," she said, before slamming the door in his face.

"Um Megan, can I see you a minute?" said Maxie while Molly panted out instructions for the flowers to the ushers on her cell.

Maxie pulled Megan into the bathroom. "We suck at this. I mean I know I do, but you're the girly one. Get it together woman. What's up with you and Chase? He's under your skin."

Megan sat on the toilet and buried her face into her hands and wailed.

"Oh no, I'm not good at tears. Here," said Maxie, handing Megan the bottle of vodka.

Megan took a swig and proceeded in a sing-songy voice trailing and cracking. "He wants us back. You know the family. He says he made a mistake with the bimbo. When he realized she wasn't the one he wanted to share his life with, it was an epiphany of sorts. He says he knows now I'm the only woman he could ever really love. Do you know what this means Maxie? It means me being able to give my girls their daddy back. Their family would be whole, not one of those broken ones with two mommies and two daddies, three half siblings, shared holidays along with alternating therapy days."

Maxie yanked the bottle back and drank a quick hit then placed her hands on Megan's shoulders. "Hey listen to what you're saying. That means saying goodbye to Stone, the man who is currently making you happier than I've ever seen you. I'm not saying it's ideal Megan, but plenty of families make it work. The kids are well-adjusted and happy because their parents are happy. And more importantly, Chase is a liar, a cheat, and a grand manipulator. How can you trust anything he says?"

"I know, I know. See why I'm so confused?"

Wave two of the labor pain screams rattled the bathroom mirror.

"We're up. Now listen to me, you don't need to make a decision today. Today you need to be Molly's big sister, bridesmaid and example of how to do this. Remember, I haven't been married and you know I'm not the gushy one. Step up, for heaven's sake."

Megan swished a cold splash of water on her face, inhaled deeply then turned to Maxie. "You're right, yes absolutely. I don't need to think about this today. Today is about Molly and Hunter."

Megan returned to Molly and dusted a fresh coat of pressed powder over Molly's red and white splotched nose. "See, all gone. The sun is slowly emerging for your special day," Megan said, directing Molly's eyes toward the large glass windows facing the slopes where the sun hazily peeked out from the ominous snow sky. "I saw the flowers downstairs, Molly, they are fabulous, your red roses with sprigs of pine look beyond amazing and the white roses with holly for us are magical. Everything is just as you dreamed it would be."

"Really?" said Molly, inhaling deeply then exhaling in an attempt to ratchet down her nerves.

"Really. Now let's finish up your makeup. You have a handsome groom waiting for you," Megan said.

Megan and Maxie slipped on their one shoulder green satin gowns. The gowns loosely followed the curve of their body with a large green bow on the one shoulder. Megan took her hair from the curlers and twirled it into a high loose ponytail teased at the roots. She swiped on her favorite red lip and then gathered her and Maxie's fur wraps.

Silvia and Edward knocked. "Are we ready?" Silvia asked.

Maxie opened the door to find Edward, Silvia, Sophie, and Olivia at the door. The four entered the room with all eyes on Molly. Edward cried with the first glance at his youngest daughter. Molly's wild red curls were tamed into loose romantic waves with the front pieces twisted back into a tangled loose knot anchored with a diamond encrusted barrette.

"You, Sweet Potato, are a vision of loveliness," said Edward.

"Thank you, daddy," said Molly, welling up.

Silvia wiped her tears and smiled. "Molly, you really look like that Christmas fairy you loved as a child."

"You look like a real princess Aunt Molly," said Olivia.

Molly smiled then said, "Wait." She nodded to Megan who opened the closet and pulled out the white fur hooded cape.

"Wow fur," said Sophie, with both hands on her face.

The two little ones wore green satin boat neck long sleeve bodysuits along with full length green tulle skirts. Sophie picked up her skirt to show Megan a pair of ballet slippers that had been dyed to match. Each girl wore a white fur muff.

Megan took both girls in her arms. "You two are the prettiest flower girls I've ever seen. I love you both with all my heart. You know that, right?"

The girls hugged her tight. "Of course, we do mommy," said Olivia.

Sophie smiled, and twirled around.

Edward summoned the group's attention with a loud clap. "Okay McKenna women, It's showtime."

The group piled into white limos and headed to the church at the foot of Mistletoe Mountain. The skies, just beginning to deepen, set the white lights ablaze on the forty-foot Christmas tree that stood at the base of the driveway.

Inside the church, an army of red and white poinsettias decorated the altar. Maxie entered first. Tony, seated in the second row smiled. Megan next, caught Stone's eye. He sat midway in the church; eyes fixated on her. He looked at her the way a man looks at a woman, as if she is the only woman in the world. She smiled. He winked. As she moved closer to the altar; she spotted Chase sitting with the family. Her thoughts changed to disgust, seeing how he worked his way back in. When she spotted Hunter looking like he may faint with nerves, she watched his best man Kyle rubbing his shoulder and quickly remembered it was Molly's day.

She turned to see Sophie and Olivia coming down the aisle together. Sophie as if she had just won the Miss America pageant, head high, removing one hand from the fur muff to wave to guests. Olivia stared mostly at her feet, looked up long enough to give Stone a smile.

Molly and Edward entered to *The Wedding March*. Molly's love story was everything Megan dreamed of since she was a little girl. Megan thought she had found that in Chase, but now looking back, she wondered if he was even capable of that kind of love. They were a team, a well-oiled machine that worked well together, her cheerleader to his football player, her devoted housewife with appropriate social status to his successful Connecticut country club big shot. A sort of scripted love story that came with the outside influences directing the lines rather than ones from the heart.

Molly and Hunter exchanged vows they had written, each with a deep personal message. Megan longed for that kind of connection. Glancing at Stone, her heart told her with him, it was possible. They were from different worlds. They didn't fit in the traditional sense of the word, but every fiber in her felt a connection to him. He made her laugh, anchored her, and gave her hope. As the priest announced you may now kiss the bride, the church erupted with cheers.

Hunter pulled a mistletoe from his pocket and held it over Molly's head. He took her in his arms and kissed her with both passion and relief. They had done it. Made it to the finish line. Together they would begin the life they so wished for. The two moved down the aisle, both grinning ear to ear. Next the little ones, then Maxie and Megan.

Stone smiled as she passed. Her heart thumped a little, wishing she could grab him and fall into his arms.

Molly and Hunter rode a horse drawn sleigh over to the reception. The rest of the party waited inside. The hall was lit with millions of tiny white lights, and they played their first song, *Unforgettable* by Nat King Cole. The next song, *The Christmas Song* began as the bridal party was invited to the floor. Maxie and Tony, Kyle and Jeffery made their way out. Megan motioned Stone to join her, then felt a hand on her waist. Chase pulled her close to his chest.

"May I?" he asked, nuzzling his face close to her ear. Stone stopped in his tracks.

"Chase, I told you, you're not my date."

He held her close with a slight bit of force. "Just give me this one song."

She looked at him, fully ready to lay into him then saw the face she had spent much of her life with. His smile familiar, his touch commanding, just like in high school where he reminded everyone, she was his. They had grown up together. Everything about them fit. She remembered the life they shared, a glamorous life. She felt ashamed to admit how much the life of luxury meant to her. He held her gaze and sang to her. For a minute she forgot that he had humiliated her, crushed her, and had thrown their commitment away. Right now, looking into his eyes, she saw the boy she fell in love with. She inhaled the cologne she always found so irresistible. She remembered losing her virginity to him. His voice singing in her ear brought back the night of their own wedding. The night they made their love permanent. He put his forehead against hers and said, "Megan McKenna, I want you to be Megan Barrington again. I want us back."

She pulled away and ran from the dance floor to the ladies' room. She cowered into a stall and shook uncontrollably, angry with herself for allowing his gravitational pull to suck her back in. She heard footsteps, then a knock on the stall.

"Megan are you in there?" said Stone.

"What are you doing in the Ladies bathroom?" Megan said from the stall.

"If you come out, I won't need to be in here. Oh, hey ladies. I'll just be a minute," he said to a few guests that came in then quickly rushed out.

"If you don't come out, I'm coming in," he said.

Slowly the stall door opened. "Hi there," he said.

"I'm sorry," she said, burying her face in her hands.

"Can we talk about this somewhere else?" he said, extending his hand.

She took his hand as he led her to the bathroom door. They walked back toward the hall. The traditional daddy daughter dance had just begun. Sophie and Chase danced front and center putting on a show for everyone to see daddy of the year. Olivia darted over toward them. She held out her tiny hand to Stone. "Want to dance?" she asked, pushing her glasses up her small button nose. He turned to Megan.

"Yes go," Megan said, smiling with joy at the fact that Olivia and Stone had forged such a special relationship. Maxie appeared next to Megan handing her a Texas

Twister in a goblet glass. "Thought you could use this," as she looked at the dance floor with Sophie and Chase dancing a few feet from Olivia and Stone.

"Maxie, what am I going to do?"

Silvia popped up on the other side. "Megan, Chase poured his heart out to your father and me last night. He made a mistake, yes, a monumental one, but he's human. He loves you and wants to repair your family. Do you know what a gift that is to give your girls?"

"Back off mother. She has to make this decision. It's not yours to make," said Maxie.

"What would you know about love? You and Tony never even see each other. What kind of love can you possibly have?"

Megan could see Silvia's words had hit a nerve. Maxie's face softened from her usual tough stance. "We aren't talking about me, mother. You need to stop meddling in our lives. We're grown women."

"Megan, you're not exactly acting like one. You're acting like a love sick teenager. Stop thinking Stone is the answer to all your problems. Look at the bigger picture. You established a life in the community. You're a beloved couple in the country club. You are mommy and daddy to two young girls. Think about it, Megan. Stone is handsome, like a shiny new toy. He's a passing fling. Chase is your future, your family's future. Someday you'll thank me for this when you understand the sacrifices mothers have to make."

When the song ended, Olivia skipped over to the three women. "Grandma, Aunt Molly wants you," said the innocent little girl caught in the tangled web Megan had weaved. Silvia and Olivia walked away hand in hand.

Maxie took both of Megan's trembling hands in hers. "You're a good mother, never doubt that. I know that family means everything to you Meggie, but this doesn't mean those two girls are losing their chance at family. You are their family."

They hadn't realized Stone had come behind them when the song ended. He turned to walk away when Megan spotted him. "Stone, wait.."

Maxie called the members of the wedding party to join the bride and groom for a toast. "I'm sorry I have to..." Megan started.

"Go, I understand. We'll talk after dinner," Stone said, kissing her cheek.

Kyle, Hunter's best man, went first.

"I was lucky enough to get to know these two when they first met. While it was rocky at first, they quickly fell into best friend status. These two could finish each other's sentences. They had each other's back. Each wanting only the best for each other. When Hunter first told me he was in love with Molly, I thought, of course you are. Molly's warm and beautiful, inside and out. The perfect match for Hunter. While it took a bit of nudging on my part to get this guy to tell her, he knew that the kind of love he felt for Molly was the kind you find once in a lifetime, if you're lucky. You see when they say marry someone like you, they're saying it because it's the formula that works. These two are cut from the same mold. They think alike, they act alike; heck I'm waiting for Hunt's hair to turn red."

The crowd laughed out loud.

He continued, "But let me tell you the thing that sold me is the fact that with Molly by his side, Hunter is a better man. When I look in the mirror, I see my faults and I pray I find my Molly to make me into the man I am supposed to be. These two have taught me things aren't always perfect, but love forgives, love withstands, and love shouldn't be entered into lightly. It's a commitment to be seen through faults, mistakes, and all. My dear friends, Molly and Hunter know this oath means forever, and I know they'll honor this vow. To Molly and Hunter, a shining example of love done right."

The guests raised their glasses, clinked them and cheered the bride and groom.

Megan, who was up next, had written a speech to honor the couple, but the words she just heard stung so deeply, she felt she was in no place to give any type of toast. Her mind raced with thoughts of mistakes, promises, and never giving up on a marriage. Her legs barely found the strength to bring her to her feet. She stood frozen, feeling every eyeball in the place judging her for her own failed marriage, her inability to honor that commitment when faced with the worst side of for better or worse. She felt like a hypocrite spouting off about love. Her trance shattered when Maxie pinched her thigh hard under the table, with a not so gentle reminder that it was about their baby sister.

"Um," Megan said, pausing for a sip of water. She glanced over at Molly beaming with love, awaiting the words of joy to tumble out of her mouth. Megan looked up to face the crowd. Chase sat next to Silvia with Sophie on his lap, Olivia next to him, the family she gave up on.

"I, I've never been one for public speaking. I believe I may have failed that class, but here goes," she stuttered. The crowd chuckled. "Tonight, I watched my baby sister say 'I do.' I watched as her face filled with delight while reading her vows. I watched her first sweet kiss as a wife, her first emotional dance with her new husband, and I witnessed love in its purest form. The love of a man and a woman still remains one of life's most complicated, fascinating mysteries. Two people come into one another's life as strangers. At first, they share a laugh, maybe a drink or dinner. Then they slowly begin to mesh into one entity. They grow together, teach each other, and eventually depend on each other to breathe. They realize that life isn't easy, love isn't easy, commitment isn't easy, but the alternative is life without that person. An alternative that never enters their realm of possibility. Love is forever. This vow isn't to be taken lightly, rather cherished like the gift that it is. Molly, Hunter, may you have an entire life of happiness by each other's sides." She raised her glass and said, "Here's to the beginning of your forever."

The crowd responded with applause shouting for the couple to kiss. Megan took the opportunity to escape the spotlight. She rushed to the doors that led out to the terrace. Her chest heavy, her breathing restricted. The frigid night air stung her face. Her thin satin dress did little to fight the chill, but she didn't care. She wanted to be numb. Goosebumps covered her exposed skin until she felt a jacket slip over her shoulders. Before she could turn around, Chase appeared in front of her.

"Megan, that speech was about us. Love isn't easy, commitment isn't easy, but the vow we took meant forever. We built a family together. We can fix this Megan. They deserve us to be adults and try. We can get counseling. You name it."

"Stop, just stop. You don't get to make me feel guilty. You did this to us," she said, stuffing his coat in his chest.

"Do you really want the girls to grow up and learn one day that you threw us away? I made a mistake, but you want to tear this family apart. Those girls deserve to spend every day with both of their parents. To feel whole and happy like they did when we were together. Do you really want to share holidays? Do you really want to drop them on Wednesdays and every other weekend? You'll miss out on thirty percent of their lives because of your wounded pride. Look at me Megs, we're the whole package. Together we can have it all. The big fancy house, trips to the islands, country club dinners. You name it. Say the word and it's yours," he said, before locking eyes with Stone who had been standing there long enough to hear the whole thing.

Megan turned to see Stone. "Stone I, I…"

Chase turned her back around to face him. "You need to choose one of us. I won't wait forever to put my family back together while you play with the hired help. Think hard Megs. Choose the one that can give you the life you really want. I'm your forever."

He let go of her and walked past Stone, feeling confident he had made his case. Stone moved closer to her.

"Megan I've been watching you all night. You're unsure. I can see it in your eyes. I won't pressure you. I love you, but I won't come between the family you've built. I'm not their father. I'm not their family. I'm just a guy who fell in love with their mother, and somehow fell in love with those two little girls along the way. I'm not a parent, so I can't say I know what you're going through, but I do know that it isn't as easy as loving you is for me. I'll understand and respect your decision, because Megan your happiness is what I want most of all. I want you to choose me, but I think I know what that decision is. I won't make you say it," he said, lightly kissing her on the cheek. He headed back into the dining room. She wanted to follow him. She wanted to call out to him, but she didn't move. Her heels felt as though they were frozen to the icy decking of the terrace, holding her motionless. Molly opened the doors and rushed out to her.

"Hey, I just saw Stone come in from out here. What in the world are you doing out here? You're freezing."

Megan threw her arms around Molly and held her tightly.

Remembering what Maxie had said, she closed her eyes and summoned all her strength, then said, "Just needed a breath of fresh air. Now come on, let's get in there before we miss the birthday slash wedding cake."

Molly grabbed her hand as they entered the ballroom. Molly spotted Aunt Tee on the dance floor. "Oh my gosh, look at her go, come on Megan," Molly said, before taking off to join the spry eighty-year-old. Megan scanned the room for Stone, her eyes panning left, then right. Unaware that Sophie and Olivia had stormed toward her, she heard their voices in tandem say, "Mommy, it's the Chicken Dance, come on."

Before Megan could resist, she felt two little hands pulling her to the center of the floor. Surrounded by a sea of people flapping their arms and stomping their feet, she stretched her neck to see if she could find Stone. When the song ended, she pushed her way through the lined formation of dancers. She headed to his table. His name card sat unaccompanied.

"Hey there sis. I can call you that now, right?" asked Hunter.

"Yes sure," she said looking toward the bar.

"Lose something?"

"Did you see Stone?"

"Yeah he left about ten minutes ago. I figured you knew. Is everything alright?"

She turned to see his worried expression in response to her panicked reaction. "No, it's good. I need a drink. How about you?"

"I'm good thanks. I think I'm going to join Aunt Tee for Cotton Eye Joe."

"Great, okay," she said, melting into his empty chair. Unsure if the words she used in her speech were actually about Chase. He had a way of confusing her. Stone on the other hand, knew her too well and wouldn't put the pressure on her. The weight of the world lay in her choice. She dropped her head onto the table and prayed the night would swallow her up.

Chapter Twenty-Seven

Megan, startled by a loud pounding on the door coupled with the piercing screams of the girls announcing it was Christmas day, opened her swollen eyes and sat up. She pulled herself to the edge of her bed, pulling on shearling slipper boots and a red house coat. She twirled her thick long mane into a knot that hung sadly off the side of her head. It reflected how she felt; sad, droopy and listless.

"Okay, okay, the Santa alarm worked, I'm up," she said, making her way down the hall to find the girls already in their pjs and slippers jumping up and down.

"Someone's at the door. Can I get it?" asked Olivia.

"Go on," said Megan. Olivia reached up and twisted the lock, unleashing it and pulled back on the handle. The little girl's eyes tumbled downward as she met the glance of Chase standing on the other side.

Megan was sure her own expression wasn't far off as she wondered why she thought it was Stone after the way she treated him last night. She didn't follow him. She didn't choose him, instead she let him walk out. Although she didn't officially choose Chase, her actions by all accounts suggested it. She still harbored deep rooted feelings of some commitment in the promise she made to provide her girls a home with both mommy and daddy, yet her heart told her differently. Choosing Stone would be a risk, something new, something she would need to put her whole faith in. She wasn't entirely sure she would ever give that type of faith back to a man, any man.

"There's my girls," Chase said, rushing in with an armful of presents. He dropped the gifts on the couch, made a beeline to Megan, and planted a kiss right squarely on her lips before her face could object. "I have the most wonderful presents for you, all of you. Here, sit. Sophie you first."

Megan watched as he hijacked her Christmas morning.

Sophie jumped up and down grabbing his hand while pulling him to the sofa. He handed her a large box, to her delight. She tore the paper off wasting not a second to pull back the lid. After fluffing some tissue paper, she looked inside the box, her face perplexed. Out of the box she pulled a set of knee pads, wristbands, a helmet and a polo mallet.

Her confusion turned to anger, after digging deeper in hopes of something pink. "Ballerina's don't wear knee pads!" she said, both arms crossed over her chest with one-foot tapping.

"I've signed you up for polo. It's an amazing game where you ride a horse while hitting a ball to your teammates. Of course, you'll need to learn to ride first."

Olivia's eyes perked up when she heard horse, Sophie's eyes furrowed into disgust.

With pinched eyebrows Sophie stomped, "I am not riding a smelly horse, not now, not ever."

Megan wanted to say don't be rude, say thank you, but the fact that he knew nothing about his own daughter made her blood boil. Olivia stood up and said, "Can I please open mine now?"

"Sure," he said, reaching over for a long tall thin box. The box was nearly as tall as Olivia herself. She pulled back the paper and opened the lid. First, she pulled out a bow nearly two feet long. She studied it before attempting to get the odd shaped instrument from the box. The weight of a wooden cello over three feet tall tipped the little freckle faced girl to the ground.

"A cello, really? What were you thinking?" Megan blurted out, unable to control her own words. She wanted to scream from the top of her lungs, *do you know anything about your children?*

"What? She has the whole glasses vibe; she looks like a band person. Olivia you'll love it, just give it a chance. Wait until you meet the other kids, they're just like you. Maybe you'll find a place to fit in," he said.

"Do you even hear the words that are coming from your mouth?" Megan said, clearly losing her temper at his insensitivity.

Completely unfazed by the obvious unhappiness that he had just unleashed, he continued, "Listen, I have the most wonderful surprise planned for this family. Hopefully today I can officially share it with you. You'll see it's the answer to our family being perfect again. But here, open this. I think you'll see how serious I am about getting my family back."

Sophie's face now softened at the mention of getting their family back. Olivia hunched on the couch, clutched Suppy close to her heart, unsure of what any of this meant.

Megan gave him a death stare. "Listen girls, we're a family no matter what." She opened a white envelope and pulled out four airline tickets to Switzerland. "Switzerland?" Megan said, completely taken aback.

"Our first family vacation. Do you know the origins of Christmas started there? It has one of the largest Christmas market places in the world. And chocolate and endless lights and the chance to show our girls Europe. Have you ever seen the Swiss Alps? A site to behold. This is our new beginning, Megan."

Megan flipped through the glossy pamphlet and couldn't disagree with what a fabulous opportunity it would be to share this experience with her girls. Chase was trying to be a family. They had never been on a family vacation before. Her phone rang, breaking the tension. On the other end, a very merry Molly yelled at the group to hurry down to the main living room in the lodge.

The McKenna sisters had reserved every room in the lodge for their aunts, uncles, cousins, and grandparents after the wedding so the family could do Christmas together. Tons of McKenna's descended into the living room filled with presents. A roaring fire blazed as light snow fell outside. The kids all dug in searching for their names and ripping into the gifts. Molly had Christmas carols playing, while Hunter worked at making as many gingerbread pancakes as he could.

After all the presents were opened, Megan sat in front of the crackling fire. She canvassed the room she and

Stone had made into a winter wonderland. Every detail of the room reminded her of him. She pressed her eyes hard to fight her tears. She noticed out of the corner of her eye, four gifts sitting on the ledge of the fireplace. She made her way over toward them. The first one she picked up read, *To Sophie,* the next read, *To Olivia,* one *To Megan*, and the last *To Gloria.* Each tag signed, Love *Stone.* He must have put them there yesterday before the wedding. Her heart sank. Her palms felt sweaty as she held them close to her heart.

"Girls, we forgot these four," she managed to choke out. The girls ran over to her and sat in front of the fireplace. "These are from Stone," she said, handing each girl a small box. The three opened them at the same time each pulling out an ornament from their box.

"I got a pink satin ballet slipper ornament," said Sophie, dangling them in front of Megan. "What did you get Olivia?"

"Look mommy, Stone got me an ornament that's a pair of yellow rubber boots just like mine," beamed Olivia, clutching them to her heart as if she had just received a piece of gold.

"Who is that one for?" asked Sophie.

"It's addressed to Gloria," said Megan, handing it to Sophie to open. Inside was a bulldog ornament with a tiara on its head. The girls giggled. "It's Gloria's."

"Stone even remembered our dog. These are our first ornaments to add to our new collection," said Olivia.

Megan opened the lid of the box and pulled out an ornament of red and brown cowboy boots. "Wait, there's a note," she said, pulling a piece of paper out of the box.

A keepsake to remember our first Christmas tree decorating together. PS: Megan you'll find your other gift out back by the pond, Love, Stone

Tears filled Megan's eyes. He knew those girls better than their own father. His gifts showed genuine thoughtfulness.

Chase, a few feet away, interrupted announcing, "Megan, I saved the best for last. Your big present is outside. Grab your coat. Come on you two, you are going to want to see this," Chase said to Maxie and Molly.

The three sisters grabbed their coats and headed out into the light wintry mix.

"Okay, I had Pierre put it around back so no one would see it this morning," he said as the three girls followed him around to the back of the lodge. There stood a white Mercedes Benz wrapped in a huge red bow. Megan stood motionless; her eyes glazed. A smile slowly crept across her face. She let out a squeal, clutched her arms across her chest then took off running. She ran right past the car as if she hadn't seen it. Beyond the car, as if guarding the lake, stood a snowman. Not just any snowman, but one that's black hat nearly grazed the two-story roof of the lodge. She ran as fast as her feet could carry her, then she threw her arms around the massive white beast. Giggling like a schoolgirl, she held on tight as frosty snow brushed against her cheek.

"Oh my gosh, isn't it amazing? It must be twenty feet tall. How did he do it, a crane maybe, or a crew? He has them, you know. He loves me. Don't you see it's a promise, he'll never leave me. It's him. I don't care about money. I'll shop in discount stores, cut coupons, and wear polyester. I don't care. I choose him. I have to go. My cars blocked in; can I have your keys, Maxie? Maxie, I choose him," she said, slightly exasperated from not taking a breath. She scurried past Chase toward Maxie.

"Wait, I got you a Mercedes. He made you a snowman and you choose him? You're not thinking clearly. Where are you going? Are you serious, you choose him?" Chase said, yelling after her.

"Seemingly, she is," said Maxie. "Wait up, I'll get you the keys. Go get him, girl!"

"You can't buy my love. It's not for sale," Megan said, skipping to the lodge.

The three girls hurried back into the cabin. Maxie grabbed her keys, Molly gathered together an argyle sweater hat with a pom-pom on top and a scarf. She wrapped them on Megan. Megan found Sophie and Olivia sitting with Edward who was deep in a brochure of instructions, putting together a farm and barbie house.

"Girls give me a kiss. I have to go somewhere; I won't be long. I love you and Merry Christmas." They kissed her, barely hearing her words as they returned to handing Edward miscellaneous parts.

Megan, Maxie, and Molly headed to the front door. "How do I look?" asked Megan.

"Umm, well," stammered Molly.

Maxie rubbed her hand under her chin then squinted, "If I'm being honest, like a cat lady. First, you're in your pajamas, your hair, well it's, none of that matters. He loves you for the amazing woman that you are. I'm not sure what took you so long to realize it, you thick headed girl. Don't wait another minute in telling him, he's the one."

"Right," she said, looking down at her shearling slippers and pajama bottoms with Christmas trees and Santa's. "No time to waste, I'm at the top of my learning curve."

Megan flew out the door with renewed enthusiasm, yelling, "I choose Stone." She jumped into Maxie's car and sailed down the driveway. She would rush into his arms and tell him he's the one. Her heart fluttered with pure joy. She wasn't quite sure if she had obeyed the speed limits, but found herself in Stone's driveway in record time. She pulled down the rearview mirror and checked herself. Sighing deeply, she gave her hair a quick tuck and took her cheek between her thumb and forefinger, giving it a pinch. Rushing up the driveway, she caught herself from slipping on the damp slick icy patches. Her eyebrows raised as she saw the old siding was replaced with a fresh white cedar shake siding, black shutters hung on newly replaced windows and the on red door, a simple pine wreath with a large red ribbon. She couldn't help but smile at the old fashioned, large colored bulb lights that strung the porch. Next to the door, a flexible flyer sled with three black lanterns, each with a candle inside. The tiny house looked remarkable. The old house, which barely stood on its perch, resembled something out of a magazine. Scampering up the steps, she balled her fist about to pound on the door, then paused momentarily.

This is it, she told herself. Releasing her breath, she went in with somewhat frantic pounding. Her eyes met the knob, slowly twisting to open the door. She burst into song, "I choose you. I love you. I want you," she said, shocked to find herself staring into the worn eyes of an elderly gentleman in plaid pants and a bow tie.

"Um, I'm sorry, I'm looking for the owner of this house," she said, feeling her cheeks flush.

"That would be me," said the man, adjusting his bowtie beaming with pride.

She leaned back looking up at the numbers that hung above the door. "This is 223 Lexington Lane, right?"

"Sure is."

"I don't understand, there must be some mistake, I'm looking for the owner that bought this house a few months ago." Suddenly, the familiar sound of pounding paws came barreling down the hall. It was Mack.

"You mean Stone. Allow me to introduce myself, my name is Colter Reynolds. You must be Megan. I'd know you by those big pretty eyes and dark hair, just like he described you. Come in out of the cold dear," he said, opening the door wider for her to enter.

She walked inside, awestruck with the design of the old house. With a newly renovated floor plan, walls were torn down, opening up a great room that connected with the redesigned modern kitchen. A white and gray stone fireplace ablaze with flames stood next to a tree. The renovation was straight out of an episode of HGTV. Every detail met with precision. The sad little home now brimmed with pride. She moved closer to the fireplace.

Her eyes teared up as she saw the beautiful art deco pieces from all over the world that adorned the ledge. In the center sat a gold frame, inside it, Olivia's picture of the turkey with glasses she had made for him. Megan picked up the picture and said, "He kept it," holding it to her chest.

"Kept it, that darn picture is his prized conversation piece. Ask anyone who's been by to see the renovations."

"Where is he?" Megan asked, her heart thumping with anticipation.

"I'm sorry dear, he's gone."

"Gone as in, 'to the market for cranberry sauce?'"

"I'm afraid not. His plane left for Milan this morning at eight."

"He took the job," she said, feeling the weight of her legs shifting unsteadily beneath her.

"Here, you should sit down. Can I get you some water, tea, juice?"

"Just water, please."

He returned, with a tall glass in hand with lemons painted on the side, filled to the brim with ice water. "Here drink this. I was hoping we would have met under different circumstances. Stone told me he planned to invite you to dessert tonight with Charlotte and me."

"He never mentioned you were living here," Megan said, sipping the water.

"Well he probably told you we were on the outs. He returned to heal from his injuries with one thing in mind. That boy wasn't leaving town until he mended things with me. He bought this house. I guess you know this is the home he grew up in."

Megan choked mid swallow. "He grew up here?" she asked, remembering the awful things she said about the home.

"It didn't look like this when he was a boy. It was a really nice home, filled with love. Anna Lynn and I just loved this old place. After Anna passed, I sort of, well," he paused, his eyes filled with water. "I guess you could say I checked out. The old place got away from me, all those years caring for my Anna. She was the love of my life. I lost the house. Stone bought it back from the realtor, made it look all fancy and picked me up at the nursing home. He wouldn't take no for an answer. Stubborn, that one. 'He pulled up and said, we're done fighting. I made a mistake putting money before family. I'll pay for the rest of my life for not saying bye to mom, but I'm not going to lose you, too.' When I walked inside, I realized I wasn't really mad at him. I was just mad my Anna was gone, and I took it out on him."

Megan now in full blown meltdown said, "Why didn't he tell me?"

"I'm not sure dear, but he did tell me about you. Your relationship was complicated, but trust me I've never seen my boy in love, until now. It was the kind of love my wife and I shared. Stone said he realized that real love is sacrifice. He only wanted what would make you happy. Leaving nearly ripped his heart from his chest, but he could never sleep at night thinking he was responsible for standing in the way of you putting your family back together."

"I made an awful mistake. I love him with everything in me. I just felt like I owed it to my girls to have both of their parents living in the same house with them day in and day out, and to be able to keep them in the lifestyle they had become accustomed to. But I realized what I really owe my girls is a mom that is truly happy and can show them an example of what real love looks like. I know now that money doesn't matter when it comes to real happiness," she sobbed.

"It took Stone a while to learn that lesson as well. You did what you thought was best for your children. That makes you selfless, and the true definition of a mother."

"I'm sorry I don't even know why I'm burdening you with all this?" she said, wiping her tears with her scarf.

"No burden. You're just as he described you," the old man said, handing her a box of tissues and laying a reassuring hand on her shoulder.

"But now he's gone and I have myself to blame," she said through a blurring flood of tears.

"Dear, if there's one thing I've learned in my many years on this earth is that life takes us in many different directions, but in the end, we always find our way back home. I thought Stone was really done with his old life, jet setting from one continent to another. All those pretentious people who kept him from what really matters, but this time he didn't leave with the same hunger, excitement. Rather he left because the alternative, staying, was too painful."

Megan stood up, wiped her eyes and went in for a big hug. "When I met him, I was convinced I could never be with a man like him, he is different than any man I've known. Then he just overwhelmed me with genuine kindness and sincerity. He's honest and empathetic, and his ability to naturally interact with my daughters was remarkable. He never had an agenda; he doesn't try to impress. He is comfortable in his own skin and I simply couldn't resist him no matter how hard I tried. Now I can't imagine being with any man but him. I've messed up everything. He probably hates me."

"That my dear, isn't a possibility. Don't you see he loved you so deeply he didn't care about his own happiness, only yours."

"Thank you so much for your kindness. I'm so glad you restored your relationship with Stone. He beat himself up every day for not being here. Now at least you two can move past this and be father and son again. Family and love really are all that matters."

Colter walked her to the door. "Thank you, Megan, for giving Stone back his passion, the ability to see what a client desires most, and his drive to stop at nothing until he achieves it. And for showing him what real love feels like."

"It was lovely meeting you. Please tell Charlotte Merry Christmas for me," she said, giving him a hug before she walked toward the door. Megan waved goodbye then headed to the car. Once inside, her body gave in to the pain and tears burst from her swollen eyes. Chase had crushed her once, now he came back for a second swipe at ruining any chance of happiness she could ever have. After sending an almost incoherent text to Maxie and Molly she drove back to the lodge. Her sisters waited on the front steps, taking her into their arms and allowing her to melt. "I have to pull it together for the girls."

"Not to worry, Hunter and Tony took them tubing since the mountain is closed. Come on in and tell us everything," said Molly.

Upon opening the door, she spotted Chase sitting by the fire with a beer. "Why is he still here?" she said, exhausted from the whole day.

"He's persistent, I'll give him that," said Maxie, "But Megan, there's something I think you should know. Tony overheard him talking to a man at the country club. He said, 'if a family was what he needed to secure the deal he'd deliver'. He knows the shareholders love you and mom and dad. Getting you back would guarantee him partner."

"So, this whole thing was just so he could make partner?" Megan said, standing up, shaking out her hands.

"Look out, I've seen that face before on Linda Blair right before her head spun," said Maxie.

Megan placed her phone down on the check-in desk, then full speed ran toward him. "How dare you lie to us! Make us think you loved us, just so you could make partner," she said before punching him square in the nose.

"Calm down, don't you see; this is a win for all of us. Think about it, you by my side, watching me climb the ladder of success. Megan, the perfect wife, hosting parties, the kind of woman the country club loves. You get all the perks of being Mrs. Barrington and I get the position." he said, pulling his hand away from his nose wiping a trickle of blood.

"This was never about getting our family back together. This was as usual, all about you. Get out of here, NOW."

"Megan, where did you learn to hit like that? You aren't thinking clearly, you're acting hormonal," he said, covering his nose.

"For the first time in a very long time, I'm thinking perfectly clearly. I don't love you Chase. I'm not sure I ever did. But what I am sure of is you're done ruining my life," she said.

"Really, ruining your life. Is this about hard hat?" he pulled a letter from his suit pocket. "I read his pathetic letter. Real men fight for the woman they love. They don't just roll over like a pansy."

Megan stepped closer, ripping the letter from his hands. "Where did you get this?"

"He left it by the pathetic presents on the fireplace."

"We're done Chase."

"You'll regret this when you realize you're nothing without me. For the record Megan, I made you."

She calmly put the letter in her pajama pocket, grabbed his coat and scarf and jammed them in his chest, sending him back a step. Molly bit her lip, Maxie put up both fists in a boxer stance, swinging left then right into the air.

"You're crazy, you know that?" he said, before marching to the door and slamming it behind him.

Maxie and Molly slowly approached her.

"Are you okay Megan?" Molly said, reaching a sympathetic hand onto her shoulder.

"Girl, you went all MMA on him. I'd say you finally got him out of your system," said Maxie.

"I have no idea where that came from, but it felt great. I'm done being manipulated by him. I'm in control of my own destiny and my destiny is Stone." She gasped turning ghostly white before letting out a tearful groan. "At least it was, until I ruined it." Tears she had been holding back with every fiber in her now rained down her forlorn face.

She pulled the letter from her pocket. She hugged her sisters, and asked if they could hold onto the girls a little longer when Hunter returned from the mountain. "I think I need to be alone to read this."

In the quiet solitude of her apartment, she opened the envelope and removed the letter.

Dear Megan,

I returned home for two reasons. First to heal my injuries, and second to repair the damage I had done to my relationship with my father; however unexpectedly, you happened. I never believed the kind of epic love found in the movies and in books, until I met you. The true power of love caught me off guard. I had closed off my heart, but you broke down my barriers. I realized that real love is being able to put the happiness of the other person before your own. You and the girls' happiness are all I want. I won't stand in your way or further complicate your feelings. You deserve to have the chance to put your family back together. I knew the chances of you choosing a guy like me were a longshot, but I don't regret one minute I spent getting to know you. I'll never forget you, or your amazing little girls. I meant what I said, I wish you only happiness. Be happy and tell the girls I had to go. Thank you for renovating my heart, Megan.

Stone

PS Promise me you will continue to follow your passion of design and event planning. You're very talented, McKenna.

He loved her, he loved her girls, and for the first time ever a man saw her value for something other than her looks. That night, Megan climbed into her bed vowing never to come out. She had made a choice by not choosing, and it cost her Stone.

Chapter Twenty-Eight

The next morning, Maxie and Molly took the girls to brunch. Later they entertained them until it was nearly time for the town's holiday party. Maxie knocked once, then opened the door to Megan's bedroom.

"Hey there, it's time for the party," Maxie said halfheartedly.

"I'm not going."

"Don't be silly. Are you going to lock yourself up here for the rest of your life?"

"Maybe, yes, that's the current plan," Megan said, pulling the pillow over her head.

"Hmm as well thought out of a plan as that is, unfortunately for you it isn't going to work. You have two sisters, two daughters and a mother who are expecting you to be there. You've worked so hard at making this lodge the success it is, and this party is celebrating us, the small businesses that keep this town alive and thriving. Now, put on your big girl panties and get dressed. We'll be waiting downstairs for you. And Megan, we aren't taking no for an answer."

They sent Maxie as the messenger knowing she would be the most convincing, not to mention scariest. Megan knew it would be a futile effort to try and ignore her demands. She reluctantly made her way to the closet and dropped her head, as if she were choosing an outfit for sentencing at dawn. After ten minutes of staring blankly at the mass of dresses that mocked her, she chose an off the shoulder nude lace long sleeve dress cinched at the waist with a brown leather belt. She wore a single braid pulled to one side dusting her right shoulder. She slowly made her way over to the shoe rack to choose a pair of stilettos. Megan thought about how important shoes are, how they told a lot about a person. She knew what her shoes needed to say; however, she was fairly certain she didn't own a 'you're an idiot for losing the best thing that could have happened to you' shoe. Remembering a pair she had purchased two days before Christmas, she drew a breath in so deeply her ribcage pressed hard against her belt "Who knew? I do own a pair of shoes that said it all." Opening up an orange box from the Rodeo Stop, she gazed at the brown cowboy boots she had bought to surprise Stone. The pointed toe leather beauties taunted her. Tonight, she would wear them as a reminder of the man she threw away.

Megan had always loved the town's annual holiday party. Unlike the country club events with pretentious people judging your every move, this one felt like family. Good, hard working people being acknowledged for their contribution to the community. It gave the little cluster of shops a small-town feeling of togetherness. Tonight however, small talk, laughter and friends felt much like a punishment. For her family, she would endure the torture, trying her best to put up a good front. The group piled into her van and headed over to this year's venue, a barn. Again, the universe had a cruel sense of humor.

Rylee Ridolfi

The Kessler's red barn lit with white lights and iced with snow made the perfect place to host the town's annual holiday party. Inside the newly renovated barn with weathered gray hardwood floors and white ship lapped walls housed seating for three hundred guests set to attend the evening's festivities. The crowd thickened quickly with many of the shop owners and restaurant folks who, until tonight, had little time to enjoy the holiday. A row of tables lined the left wall with tombola prizes to be raffled off. The proceeds of the prizes, along with the donations collected tonight, went to the town's decorations and annual holiday parade fund. The dance floor quickly filled up with kids and adults as the DJ played upbeat dance tunes.

Megan was not in the mood to dance, or eat or breathe for that matter. However, despite her unsuccessful pleas to stay home under her covers and eat bon bons, she would fake it for one night. She spotted the bar and decided if she had to be there at least she could disappear into a dark corner with wine, lots of wine. Barely two sips into her wine, Caroline Bisset appeared with newly botoxed lips and eyebrows so tight that blinking potentially threatened the removal of her hairline. Megan gulped looking to the skies, "Really?"

"Megan Hun, how are you? I'm so sorry to hear about you ending up alone again. But there is an upside to it," she said, smiling or not, Megan wasn't sure what that frozen expression actually meant.

Megan raised the glass to her lips and said, "This should be good."

"Well you know the Robinson's Shoe Repair shop suffered a fire. I know what you're thinking, who repairs shoes for heaven's sakes, just buy new ones, right?"

"Ironically I'm thinking many things, yet that wasn't one of them," Megan said, gulping another huge drink from her glass.

"Anyway, Mayor Trundal had this fabulous idea that we auction off a date with Johnny Rocco, you know the football player. Well naturally, he was generous enough to say yes. Two dollars a chance."

"Yes, fabulous. Okay, good talk," Megan said, attempting to walk away, dropping a twenty on the bar and taking the bottle with her.

"Silly Megan, I didn't get to the good part yet. You know Reese Calvin, the new 'it girl' for Revlon? Well of course you do, pretty little thing. She is in town for a photo shoot with Constance Preri. Here's the best part, she had agreed to be our female date night raffle gal. Can you imagine the money we could make on that? Well anyway, sadly she was called away to a shoot in London. So…"

Megan rolled her eyes. "Pity really."

Caroline drew her eyes to the ceiling.

The taut skin across Caroline's rigid expression distracted Megan momentarily. Remarkable, thought Megan, nothing moved, not even an eyelash, simply eyeballs rolling in their sockets.

"Okay, well for the life of me I'm not sure why your name came up to take her place. I mean the only thing I could figure is that you're one of the few single women in town. So, Mayor Trundal floated the idea and believe it or

Rylee Ridolfi

not, there actually were a few guys who said they would
be willing to put up a few bucks for a chance to go on a
date with you. Go figure, right," she laughed, or at least a
sound familiar to laughing eked out of her mouth. She
flung her hair off her overly shiny chipmunk cheeks. "So,
what do you say?"

"I'm still waiting for the good part."

"Oh, darling it's that you're single and most likely
won't have that easy of a time finding a date at your age.
Dear, we're helping a girl out. Don't look a gift horse in
the mouth."

"How did I miss that obvious benefit?" She noticed the
mayor heading in her direction.

"Oh good, Caroline has already approached you. What
do you say? After all, you were Ms. Winter Princess for
two years. I'm sure there are a ton of single guys that
missed out on the chance to date Ms. Winter Princess,"
said the mayor, hands folded in a praying position.

"I'd love to help, but I'm just not in the right frame of
mind."

The mayor turned his eyes over to the Robinson's, an
elderly couple who operated their shoe shop for nearly
thirty years. While not a thriving shop, it did manage to
keep itself afloat and Megan knew how much they loved
their work. The mayor drew in a deep sigh, his eyes
sinking into a lost puppy face. "We just thought if we
could give them some hope, but I understand if you can't
help."

Megan took a hearty gulp then huffed out, "Fine."

"You're the best, Megan McKenna," said the mayor.

"Yes, thank you Megan, for well, being the last woman standing. And Megan, what is up with those monstrosities on your feet?" asked Caroline, attempting to squint.

Megan walked away, not even the wine could allow her to tolerate Caroline's particular brand of abuse tonight. Again, she reminded herself that stretchy pants and bon bons really were a girl's best friend. Maxie headed to the table that Megan had slammed her head onto.

"Hey there sis. Doesn't the place look fabulous? How much wine have you had?" said Maxie.

Megan lifted her head just in time to see Walker, strolling by, giving her the point, "Hunting down the person with the tickets right now," he said, winking and making an odd clicking sound with his teeth.

"Why is the twelve-year-old electrician winking at you?" asked Maxie.

"You mean you haven't heard the new level of humiliation that my life will endure tonight?" said Megan, dropping her head back on the table.

"What did I miss?" said Molly joining them.

"Megan is wallowing and apparently taking it out on the table with her head," said Maxie.

"Your head is so low, I thought you disappeared," said Molly.

"If only the universe would be so kind as to swallow me whole," said Megan. She picked her head up long enough to explain the latest event in her otherwise miserable existence.

"How the heck did this happen?" asked Maxie.

"I honestly don't know. Just proof when you think you hit rock bottom, there's yet another level."

"Now it's not all that bad. The proceeds go to the sweet little Robinsons," said Molly, trying to offer a bright take on the dreadful situation.

Megan watched as families took the dance floor, laughing, dancing, and singing. She watched her own two girls swirling around with Hunter, giggling and enjoying the evening. Two hours later, she felt a tad bit lighter, mostly due to the amazing ability wine had to dull the painful truth of reality. In fact, she had all but forgotten the awful raffle, until Mayor Trundal took the stage, turning the sound of the microphone up and tapping it loudly three times.

"Can I have your attention, gang? It's been a wonderful night so far, right?" he asked, raising a hand for applause. "As you all know, tickets are being raffled off for one amazing date at the Lurane Cafe with our own Mr. Johnny Rocco." The crowd cheered loudly. A few women cackled then whistled. "Unfortunately, the lovely Ms. Calvin will not be attending tonight, however in her place, is our own beautiful, Megan McKenna." Again applause. The McKenna clan stomping loudly. "Now Caroline, if you could take it from here," the mayor said, handing off the microphone.

Then with dramatic pause, the music stopped and Caroline took the stage, waving as though the President of the United States had just arrived. "If I could have all eyes up here on me. It's that time you've all been waiting for; the date night raffle."

The crowd pushed up toward the stage cheering.

"First, could the one, the only, Johnny Rocco, join me on stage." He made his way up the three steps, both arms waving in the air to his adoring fans. Megan muttered, "Arrogant self-adoring third string quarterback."

He took the mic, but not before laying a kiss on Caroline's cheek. "Ladies, while it would be my pleasure to take each and every one of you out, it is my understanding that I have to choose just one name," he said, beating his hands on his heart, pointing out toward the swooning crowd of women. Again, the woman shrilled with anticipation.

Shaking a wooden box filled with orange raffle tickets, Caroline said, "Pick one name, Mr. Rocco. Who is the lucky lady?"

He shook the box up and dug deep. He pulled out a ticket and read it aloud, "The lucky lady I chose is Wendy Bellner." A piercing scream penetrated the crowd as a plump woman in a loud reindeer smock rushed the stage, leaving behind a row of carnage in an attempt to claim her date.

Caroline took the mic as the woman squeezed the football player tightly before walking off stage. "Alright that's one happy lady. Now Megan McKenna, if you'll join me on the stage. I know you're all thinking, why Megan right? Well short notice and all, she has agreed to try and generate a few bucks for the Robinson's. Bless her heart."

Megan would rather be abducted by aliens than join her, but what choice did she have? Slowly, she slunk through the crowd and climbed onto the stage.

"Alrighty Megan, here you go," said Caroline lifting the box. "Geez that seems pretty full, go figure. Now Megan, who is the man you choose?"

Megan froze hearing the words *Who is the man you choose?* That ship had sailed. The man she chose will never know. An awkward silence engulfed the room. Maxie cleared her throat loudly. Megan looked up at the crowd then back down at the box brimming with blue raffle tickets. Surprised by the sheer volume she shifted the tickets around then went in. She pulled a ticket then read the name. Her face twisted then turned a bit pale. The crowd silently waited and watched.

"Sorry that one's illegible," she said, reaching in for another name.

Maxie whispered to Molly, "Must be the twelve-year-old."

She dug into the box once again, looked at the next name then tossed it to the floor, then continued reaching and tossing one after another. Her fingers were pulling tickets quicker than a lottery drawing. The crowd now mumbling among themselves, a bit of chaos began to take hold. Completely unaware of the ensuing mob growing relentless, she continued as if Willy Wonka's golden ticket was somehow hiding in the bottom. Grabbing, shuffling, tossing, filling the floor beneath her with a growing pile of blue rumpled tickets.

Trying to quiet the crowd and regain some sort of assemblance, Caroline asked in a perturbed voice, "Megan, is there a problem? What is the name? You have to choose someone. Don't keep us in suspense, choose a guy already. The name on the ticket Megan what is it? Who do you choose?"

From the back of the room a voice yelled out. "I believe I can help you with that, McKenna. The name on the ticket is Stone Reynolds. I know this because you'll find it on every ticket. I bought every one of the two thousand tickets on the roll. You see this time McKenna, there is no way I was going to take a chance that you didn't choose me," said Stone, appearing from the darkness as a spotlight shone brightly on the back of the barn.

Caroline's mouth dropped open. Megan's eyes squinting to see with the bright spotlight shining in her eyes.

The crowd split, creating a walkway for him to emerge. He began again, "Megan, I almost lost you once. I won't test fate twice," he said, his voice growing stronger now.

As he came into the light, Megan's eyes welled up. There he stood in a black and white crisp slim fit tuxedo. His face clean shaven, his hair perfectly slicked back. His hands filled with a large bouquet of flowers, standing by his side, Mack his loyal Golden Retriever. Mack carried two smaller bouquets in his mouth.

He continued, "You see, I made a mistake. I thought I was doing the right thing by leaving, but as I sat in the International waiting area of US Airways, I ran into a very insightful man."

Chartreuse stepped into the light and waved a pink tuxedo arm.

"I'm not sure why, but I poured my heart out to him. I told him how crazy, impossible, funny, smart, caring and beautiful you are. I told him that you taught me that real love does exist. You showed me that I am capable of giving my whole self to someone, but that I had walked away for your happiness. At first Chartreuse cried, then he slapped me. He paused, then slapped me again. He asked what I was doing in the airport instead of here fighting for you. He reminded me that families aren't just about DNA, they're about love, commitment, and building memories and traditions. He made his way toward the girls. Sophie, Olivia," he said, waving them over to him. Mack trotted next to him, then nestled in between the two young girls. He handed Sophie a small slobbery bouquet of pink roses, Olivia an equally slobbery bouquet of yellow daisies and then held up the largest bouquet of red roses that Megan had ever seen in her life. He walked closer to the stage and laid the roses at Megan's feet. He stepped away from the stage, then got down on one knee. The crowd gasped.

"Yes, Megan Mckenna, your life is complicated, messy, and unpredictable, yet I can't think of any place I'd rather be than right there beside you through it all, from stomach bugs to fish sweaters, I'm in. All in. I promise if you give me a chance, I'll show you that we're already a family. We've already begun our own traditions," he paused, swallowed deeply then continued, "For example our tree decorating tradition, Friday night line dance parties with the girls, and Sunday brunches at Aunt Charlotte's. Not to mention Mack here is sorely in need of two big sisters and a furry buddy named Gloria."

Charlotte nodded approvingly, then stepped up to one side of Chartreuse and linked arms, Colter joined on the other side. With his family behind him, he pulled a small black box from his tuxedo jacket. He opened it revealing an antique two carat diamond on a marquee setting and said, "I guess the only thing left is to ask these three beautiful girls a very important question. Sophie, Olivia, Megan, will you marry me?"

Stone barely finished his sentence before Megan rushed to the edge of the stage. She shouted to the rafting's of the barn, "Yes, yes a thousand times yes. I choose you, Stone Reynolds. I choose you forever."

He stood up in time to catch her as she leapt from the stage into his arms in an epic Dirty Dancing trust dive. The crowd exploded in jubilation. He pulled her close. His lips met hers in a kiss that felt different this time. Yes, it smoldered with passion, but its tenderness and honesty, told Megan that she had found forever in those lips.

Mayor Trundal with tears rolling down his chubby cheeks tapped the microphone. "Congratulations, Megan and Stone!" The crowd roared again. "I can't think of a sweeter couple. I just want to say thank you to the women's Elderberry group for their donations for the tombola table. We raised nine hundred and thirty-six dollars on the fine gift baskets. And a special thanks to Johnny Rocco who brought in a whopping one hundred and fifty dollars in 'Win a Date Raffle' monies. And the largest 'Win a Date' ticket sales in the history of our Holiday party can be attributed to Megan McKenna, for her persistent bidder who donated four thousand dollars to the pot."

Cheers rocked the barn. "I'm pleased to announce the Robinsons will be reopening their shop this spring."

Rylee Ridolfi

Stone picked Megan up and twirled her around. "You are the hottest thing I've ever seen in cowboy boots."

"And you Stone Reynolds, clean up pretty nicely yourself, in a tux no less," she said.

The next thing they knew, a mob scene surrounded them, Molly, Maxie, Hunter, Tony, Silvia, Edward, Chartreuse, Charlotte, and Colter, all cheering, congratulating and wondering what took them so long. Megan showing the ring, Stone beaming.

Silvia made her way through the crowd, pulling her aside. "How can a mom argue with that swan dive?" she said, shaking her head laughing at the thought. "He really makes you happy, doesn't he?"

"Yes mom, a happiness I've never felt before. I'm not going to lie, I do love the finer things in life, but when I'm with him, none of that seems to matter. He makes me feel like the richest girl in the world, no money required."

Silvia hugged her, something that didn't happen often, but this time she held her tightly. "I'll thank God every night for the smile he put back on this face," she said, holding Megan's face in her hands.

Stone approached hesitantly, extending a hand to Silvia. She pushed his hand away and pulled him in for a hug. "Welcome to the family, Stone."

His smile brightened, "Thank you Silvia. I promise I will honor and love her forever."

"I know you will," she said.

Megan smiled ear to ear at the site of them embracing.

Silvia excused herself and Megan stepped in to fill his arms.

"I have a question. How did you know I'd be here tonight?" she asked Stone.

"That was all Chartreuse," he said, pulling Chartreuse over. "Megan wanted to know how I found her here."

"Easy, just a bit of detective work. I called Charlotte and asked if she knew where we could find you. She told us about the event tonight and that she would be attending, then we got creative. Charlotte has connections with her Elderberry group," said Chartreuse, waving to the group of some twenty blue haired ladies surrounding the dessert table. "The rest just fell into place, well except the purchase of a whole roll of raffle tickets. Again, my ladies came in, in a pinch. Without them it would have been darn near impossible for us to fill out two thousand tickets with our boy's name." Letting out a squeal, Chartreuse wrapped his arms around himself gloating and said "Oh how I love a happy ending."

"You, my friend, really are what you claim to be, an expert in romance as well as furniture, and I'm one lucky girl to have met you," said Megan, kissing Chartreuse on the cheek.

"Got to go, my ladies are beckoning me to get jiggy with it," he said, before heading off to join a group of Elderberry's on the dance floor.

From deep inside the crowd, Stone felt a tugging on his jacket. He looked down to see Olivia with her big green eyes looking up at him through her large glasses. He knelt down.

She shook her red curls and said, "Yes."

"Yes?" he asked.

"Yes, I'll marry you. I asked Santa if we could keep you forever. I asked mommy too, but she said you weren't like one of my stray animals we could just keep, but now we can. Her tiny arms wrapped around his neck. She placed a gentle kiss on his cheek. He scooped her up and spun her around. Megan's eyes met his as her heart melted at the sight. He and Olivia took the dance floor. Sophie and Megan joined them.

A country song came on as the crowd lined the floor. "Come on girls, let's show them what we got," said Stone. The four lined up and joined in laughing, dancing and making a new memory for their family. After the girls ran off with friends. Stone pulled Megan in close as the DJ tapped the microphone, "This one goes out to Megan." The first few notes of *Wanna Be That Song* played. "May I have this dance?" he asked.

She smiled and rushed to his arms. Looking into his eyes she said, "Stone Reynolds, I don't care about money or fancy things, well I do a little, but I've learned a life with those things, yet without you, is worthless. I realized money can't buy love."

"Funny you should mention that. There is something I've been meaning to tell you about money," he said, before feeling a tap on his shoulder.

"Stone Reynolds, are you *the* Stone Reynolds, the one from the cover of Architectural Digest? Wait let me get it right, it read '*The Rembrandt of the Architectural World.*' I told my wife it was you. Your work on the billion-dollar renovation in Dubai really set you apart from the rest. I guess that's what earned you the title '*Architect of the Year.*' It just so happens I'm in the market for the best, and apparently that's you. Jonathan Redmond," he said, extending his hand. "Here's my card. If you're staying in the area, I have a ground breaking project. I know you don't come cheap, but I assure you, I'll compensate you generously."

"Thank you, Mr. Redmond."

"Call me Jonathan," the man said, and patted Stone on the back.

"Well then Jonathan, I look forward to hearing more about this project. I'll be in touch."

Megan stood mouth agape. "What just happened? You said you were a small contractor. You said you had no money? You said you were poor."

"No, actually you said those things. I never said anything of the sort."

"Wait so you're a world-renowned architect?"

"So they say. That's what I was about to tell you. I'm not a handyman. I'm actually an architect who has designed some pretty amazing projects. The money is insane, but I've learned the hard way its people, not things, that make up life's greatest moments. I didn't tell you because I wanted you to love me for who I am, not my money," he smiled, before resuming the kiss.

"I do love you for you. But out of curiosity, how much money are we talking about?" she winked.

"Follow me," he said, taking her hand.

They walked to the entrance of the barn. Outside he directed her to the back of the barn toward the open fields.

There in the middle sat a helicopter with *Marry Me Megan McKenna,* painted on the side.

"What's that?"

"My personal helicopter. It's fueled to take us to the airport where my jet will fly us to Paris for the evening."

Her eyes swished back and forth between the aircraft, his tux, and his gorgeous face. "I'm glad you didn't tell me about the money, because discovering you for who you really are without all the trappings taught me how to love, truly love. A year ago, the idea of me falling in love with a flannel shirt wearing, country music lover would have made me laugh or possibly cringe. Then I met you, an impossible, strong willed, confident man who didn't need anything to win a girl's heart other than himself. I don't know how, but you made me love flannel, snowstorms, and I'll admit, country music. You taught me to believe in myself, in my ability to be a good mother, in my talent as a designer, and that I'm way stronger than I ever realized. I honestly didn't think I could be any happier than I was ten minutes ago when you asked me to spend the rest of my life with you, however this moment, you, Paris, a girl couldn't ask for more," she said, jumping into his arms.

"And don't worry, I cleared it with the troops."

Megan turned to see Sophie and Olivia running toward her, arms open. Olivia holding Mack by his leash. Maxie, Molly, and Silvia followed. The five of them embraced. Her troops, she thought as Megan looked at her two glorious meddling sisters, her two amazingly supportive young daughters, and one wonderfully impossible mother. Then she stared at the man standing before her, and while she still held to her conviction that dating when you're older with a bit more baggage, along with two young daughters and two interfering sisters was as easy as teaching a T-Rex to apply lipstick, she realized falling in love with the right man is as easy as breathing.

Megan and Stone had taken on a renovation project with full intention of restoring a lodge to its greatest potential, however what they hadn't realized was the real renovation was one that took place within their own hearts. Walls came down, trust was built, and the foundations of love were laid, paving the road to forever.

As the two headed toward the helicopter, she said, "Stone Reynolds, you are a man of your word. You came back to me. You're my snowman."

Megan felt the familiar sweet kiss of delicate snowflakes as a few flakes brushed across her cheek. As the tiny flakes fell softly from the December sky, a devilish grin spread across her cheeks, she whispered in his ear, "It's snowing."

He returned the smile, took her hand in his. Wearing his own sly smile, he replied, "Lucky for me."

Make your reservation for the next adventure at the Mistletoe Lodge...

Up next for the McKenna sisters is Maxie's story.

After a successful first season for both Christmas Village and Mistletoe Lodge the sisters are thrilled with their new endeavor. However, Maxie, who handles the finances, quickly realizes that three successful months will not sustain the business throughout the year. With Megan planning her posh wedding to Stone and Molly pregnant with twins, Maxie realizes she must fix this problem on her own. She just needs a little time and a plan. When an unexpected guest, Lieutenant Noah Townsend, shows up to Mistletoe Lodge, she realizes she has a much larger problem. Noah has a secret and plans of his own for the lodge. All she has to do is to uphold her maid of honor duties to Megan, keep Molly calm during her pregnancy, make a plan to increase revenue and get rid of the Lieutenant.

Rylee lives in New Jersey with her husband. She loves Christmas, ice cream and waffles, fabulous shoes, and her family, not necessarily in that order. When not writing, you can find her snuggled by the fireplace with a good book, spending time at the beach or enjoying her three children and one sweet grandson.

Visit her at www.ryleeromance.com . Or catch up with her on Instagram @ryleeromance.

Made in the USA
Columbia, SC
05 December 2020

26400042R00236